Forever Waiting

W9-BLR-152

Brunswick County Library
109 W. Moore Street
Southport NC 28461

WITHDRAWN

By DeVa Gantt

FOREVER WAITING
DECISION AND DESTINY
A SILENT OCEAN AWAY

Don't miss the next book by your favorite author.
Sign up now for AuthorTracker by visiting
www.AuthorTracker.com.

WITHDRAWN

HICKMANS

Forever Waiting

COLETTE'S APPEAL

De Va Gantt

AVON
An Imprint of HarperCollinsPublishers

Brunswick County Library
109 W. Moore Street
Southport NC 28461

This book is a work of fiction. The characters, incidents, and dialogue are drawn from the author's imagination and are not to be construed as real. Any resemblance to actual events or persons, living or dead, is entirely coincidental.

FOREVER WAITING. Copyright © 2009 by DeVa Gantt. All rights reserved. Printed in the United States of America. No part of this book may be used or reproduced in any manner whatsoever without written permission except in the case of brief quotations embodied in critical articles and reviews. For information address HarperCollins Publishers, 10 East 53rd Street, New York, NY 10022.

HarperCollins books may be purchased for educational, business, or sales promotional use. For information please write: Special Markets Department, HarperCollins Publishers, 10 East 53rd Street, New York, NY 10022.

FIRST AVON PAPERBACK EDITION PUBLISHED 2009.

Designed by Rhea Braunstein

Library of Congress Cataloging-in-Publication Data
Gantt, DeVa.
Forever waiting : Colette's appeal / DeVa Gantt.—1st ed.
p. cm.
ISBN 978-0-06-157826-7
1. Aristocracy (Social class)—Fiction. 2. Virginia—History—19th century—Fiction. 3. Domestic fiction. I. Title.
PS3607 A59F67 2009
813'.6—dc22

2009012885

09 10 11 12 13 WBC/RRD 10 9 8 7 6 5 4 3 2 1

Forever Waiting *is dedicated to*
the three important men in our *lives:*
Dad, Joe, and Dave,
who encouraged the pursuit of our dream

Our patient children,
who indulged us during writing time
and are now our most ardent promoters

And finally—our artistic inspiration—"the boys"
Wherever you are, you are here . . .

We'd also like to thank our agent, Sandy Cokeley,
for loving and believing in the work

Our editor, Lucia Macro,
for offering sage advice and giving the Colette Trilogy a second look

Our publicist, Joanne Minutillo,
for arranging many fabulous book-signing events

Esi, for keeping us on schedule, Adrienne for her selling savvy,
and the rest of the HarperCollins's staff
It's been a pleasure!

DIRECTORY OF CHARACTERS

ON CHARMANTES:

The Duvoisin Family:

Frederic Duvoisin—Patriarch and master of Charmantes; son of Jean Duvoisin II, founder of Les Charmantes (deceased); brother of Jean III (deceased)

Elizabeth Blackford Duvoisin—Frederic's first wife (deceased 1808)

John Duvoisin—Only son of Frederic and Elizabeth; heir to the Duvoisin fortune (born 1808)

Paul Duvoisin—Frederic's illegitimate son (born 1808)

Colette Duvoisin—Frederic's second wife (born 1810; deceased 1837)

Yvette and Jeannette Duvoisin—Twin daughters of Frederic and Colette (born 1828)

Pierre Duvoisin—Youngest son of Frederic and Colette (born 1834; deceased 1837)

Agatha Blackford Ward Duvoisin—Older sister of Frederic's late wife, Elizabeth; John's aunt; Frederic's third wife

People living in the Duvoisin Mansion:

Charmaine Ryan—Heroine of the story (born 1818 in Richmond, Virginia), governess to the Duvoisin children; only child of Marie and John Ryan

Rose Richards—Elderly nursemaid to Yvette, Jeannette & Pierre; formerly nanny to John & Paul; originally hired by Jean II to care for Frederic as a young boy

Professor Richards—Rose Richards's husband; formerly tutor to John & Paul; initially hired by Jean II as a tutor for Frederic (deceased)

George Richards—Rose and Professor Richards's grandson; close friend of John & Paul; production manager and overall supervisor of island operations (born 1809)

Duvoisin Servants:

Jane Faraday—Head housekeeper
Travis Thornfield—Butler and Frederic's personal valet
Gladys Thornfield—Travis's wife; Agatha's personal maid
Millie and Joseph Thornfield—Travis and Gladys's children
Felicia Flemmings—Housemaid
Anna Smith—Housemaid
Fatima Henderson—Cook
Grace Smith—Head-housekeeper on Espoir
Rachel—Scullery maid
Gerald—Head groom
Bud—Stablehand

Islanders:

Dr. Robert Blackford—Island physician; Agatha's twin brother; older brother to Frederic's first wife, Elizabeth; John's uncle
Dr. Adam Hastings—Island's new physician
Harold Browning—Charmantes' overseer
Caroline Browning—Harold's wife; sister of Loretta Harrington
Gwendolyn Browning—Harold and Caroline's only daughter
Stephen Westphal—Charmantes' financier; manager of the town bank
Anne Westphal London—Stephen's widowed daughter; resides in Richmond
Mercedes Wells—Anne London's personal lady's maid and attendant
Father Benito St. Giovanni—Island priest
Jake Watson—Harbor foreman
Buck Mathers—Dockworker
Madeline Thompson (Maddy)—Mercantile proprietress
Wade Remmen—Lumbermill operator
Rebecca Remmen—Wade's younger sister; friend of Gwendolyn Browning
Martin—Livery hostler and town farrier
Dulcie—Proprietress of the town tavern

In Richmond, Virginia:

Marie Ryan—Charmaine's mother, abandoned as a young child at the St. Jude Refuge; (deceased 1835)
John Ryan—Charmaine's fugitive father
Father Michael Andrews—Pastor of St. Jude's Church and Refuge
Sister Elizabeth—Nun and teacher at the St. Jude Refuge
Stuart Simons—John Duvoisin's production manager
Brian Duvoisin—freed slave; John Duvoisin's overseer
Nettie Duvoisin—Brian's wife; freed slave
Joshua Harrington—Charmaine's first employer
Loretta Harrington—Joshua's wife; sister of Caroline Browning
Edward Richecourt—Duvoisin lawyer
Helen Richecourt—Edward's wife
Geoffrey Elliot III—Duvoisin lawyer
Mary & Raymond Stanton—friends of Loretta and Joshua Harrington

In New York:

Lily Clayton—freed slave; John Duvoisin's former housekeeper at Freedom.
Rose Forrester—Lily's sister; freed slave; former housekeeper at Wisteria Hill.
Dr. Hastings—John's friend; uncle to Dr. Adam Hastings

Ships' Captains:

Jonah Wilkinson—Captain of the *Raven*
Philip Conklin—Captain of the *Tempest*
Will Jones—Captain of the *Heir*
Matt Williams—Captain of the *Destiny*

In Memory:

Adele Delacroix—Colette's mother (deceased)
Pierre Delacroix—Colette's brother (deceased)
Pascale—Colette's childhood girlfriend
Thomas Ward—Agatha's first husband

Chapter 1

Friday, October 20, 1837
Freedom . . . fifty-six miles west of Richmond, Virginia

BRIAN Duvoisin was black. Born on the Duvoisin plantation thirty-five years ago, he had been a slave for most of his life, that is, until the day John Duvoisin signed the document that freed him. Having no surname to place on the legal paper, John suggested he use Duvoisin. Brian agreed. Grinning, John shook his hand and called him "brother."

At first, Brian was wary of John's motives, but he remained on the plantation. He really had no choice. Where else in the South could a penniless, unskilled colored man go?

John emancipated many other men, women, and children that week, and his indignant neighbors swiftly dubbed the Duvoisin estate "Freedom." Within the month, John erected an elaborately carved sign above the plantation's main gates. Freedom it was.

John grew to respect Brian and, with each passing season, placed greater responsibility upon his shoulders. The field workers respected him as well. If John wanted the plantation to remain productive, especially when he was away, Brian was the man to have there.

Brian's wife was also free, for John had purchased Wisteria Hill, the adjacent estate where she lived, releasing those slaves as well. At first, Brian puzzled over his wife's emancipation; leaving Virginia was possible now. He'd gained some skills beyond the backbreaking field labor. He could travel north, take Nettie with him, earn a living, and keep a roof over their heads. Why he didn't go, he couldn't say, other than John relied on him.

Today, he was the only black overseer in the entire county. It did not sit well with John's neighbors, who opposed paid Negro help. But John never caved in to the pressure; rather, he seemed to revel in the controversy, holding firm to his decision. His staunch resolve garnered Brian's steadfast loyalty and trust. Now, four years later, the two men were close friends.

Stuart Simons was white. Though born and raised in the South, he was a Northern sympathizer, a posture embraced by his Quaker parents, who had instilled in him a deep sense of right and wrong. Because he rebuked a number of Southern viewpoints, finding employment had been difficult until he met John. Eventually, he became Freedom's production manager.

John knew Brian needed the protection of a white man, especially when he was abroad in Richmond or New York. Therefore, John situated Stuart on the plantation to discourage his neighbors from harassing the black overseer when he was away. It proved a wise move. The first time John had left Freedom on an extended trip, there had been an incident, one easily quelled when Stuart appeared to greet the men who just happened to stop by for a "visit."

Because Stuart had an easy manner, and because he also respected Brian, they became friends. Stuart quickly learned the workings of a tobacco plantation. He already knew the ins and outs of the shipping business, overseeing the loading and unloading of Duvoisin vessels in Richmond after the fall harvest. This year, John had relied heavily on both men, for he had been away the entire summer and fall. But the plantations rested in capable hands, so Freedom and Wisteria Hill's harvests were the least of John's worries.

Tonight, the two men sat at the kitchen table, discussing the year's production. Cotton prices were down fifty percent, and although cotton was not grown at Freedom, John wasn't going to like it. The brokers in New York were not buying. If the newspaper reports were correct, Congress had authorized the issue of ten million dollars in short-term government notes to stem the panic that was sweeping across the country.

It was thus John found them—deep in worried conversation.

Though John's comings and goings were always unpredictable, they looked up in surprise. He'd notified them some months ago that he had traveled to Charmantes. They knew him well, having spent many a night with him after an onerous day in the fields, drinking and talking into the wee hours of morning. For John to go home, something had to be wrong. One look at his face and they knew they were right.

"Good God, man," Stuart breathed, "you look awful."

John grunted and slumped into a chair.

"What's the matter?" Brian asked.

"Everything," John chuckled wryly, "as always."

Stuart leaned forward. "Did you see them?"

"Just my son," John said softly, tenderly. "Colette was dead before I reached Charmantes." Propping his elbows on the table, he drove his fingers through his tousled hair before whispering, "Pierre died a week ago."

"John," Stuart murmured, "I'm sorry."

"Me too, John, me too," Brian consoled. When the silence became uncomfortable, he asked, "What are you going to do now?"

"Try to forget . . ."

"Maybe this will help," Stuart offered, extending the paper with the rankling financial figures.

For the next few hours, they examined plantation documents, discussed the tobacco yield and production costs, shipping, the New York brokers, and the economy. John seemed unconcerned with the rumors of the dissolution of the conservative Bank of the United States and the failure of three banks in England. Stuart shook his head; the man obviously knew what he was doing.

When all topics had been exhausted, John stood up and stretched. "I've had enough for one night."

As Brian and Stuart rose, he broached another subject. "You'll be going into Richmond tomorrow?"

Stuart nodded. "I'll be leaving at the crack of dawn."

"Do me a favor, then, would you?"

"What's that, John?"

"Visit Sheriff Briggs and find out if a John Ryan was ever apprehended."

"John Ryan?" Stuart puzzled. "He used to work for you."

John's brow lifted in interest. "Really?"

"I believe he was being sought in connection with his wife's death."

"That's the one."

"I remember Briggs coming to the wharf and questioning the men. I don't think he was found. Why in heaven's name are you interested in him?"

"Locating him is important to a friend of mine and it's important to me."

"I'll see what I can find out. If the authorities aren't a help, I'll make a few inquiries of my own around town."

John nodded a thank you and turned to leave.

"How long are you planning to stay in Virginia?" Stuart asked.

"Aside from a trip north, you'll be seeing more of me from now on."

Both Brian and Stuart smiled, happy to be in the man's company again, but reading John's face, they knew the sentiment was not reciprocated.

The next afternoon, Stuart went directly to the sheriff's office. Briggs seemed annoyed, grumbling something about "white trash" and that wife beating wasn't a crime. Disgusted, Stuart realized he was getting nowhere fast. He might uncover something at the wharf. With the Duvoisin clout, the authorities might be persuaded to reopen the case. He was not disappointed. A few longshoremen had seen Ryan scrounging around for odd jobs, but his appearances were sporadic, and no one remembered exactly when they'd seen him last.

John was displeased. "Could you ask the men to keep an eye out for him?"

"Sure, John," Stuart agreed, "next time I'm in Richmond."

Saturday, October 21, 1837
Charmantes

Charmaine and the girls arrived in the dining room well before nine o'clock. Today was the first Saturday they would spend with their father. True to his word, Frederic was waiting for them. After breakfast, the threesome departed the manor, leaving Charmaine alone.

Yvette dragged her feet, her father's steps quick and sure by comparison.

"What is the matter, Yvette?" he asked as they arrived at the paddock.

"Nothing," she grumbled sullenly.

Frederic only smiled.

Gerald appeared with Spook and Angel, and Yvette perked up. "We're going riding?"

"That and other things."

Paul emerged from the barn with a meticulously groomed stallion.

"Papa," Jeannette breathed in alarm, "you're riding Champion today?"

"I intend to try, Jeannette."

Paul had his doubts, but he'd been unable to talk Frederic out of this folly and knew it would be futile to try again now. "I ran him hard yesterday," Paul said, "so he shouldn't be straining at the bit today."

"That's fine, Paul. I might need some help getting in the saddle, though."

Frederic swallowed his pride and endured the humiliation of mounting the horse he'd ridden countless times. He stumbled only once, his lame arm buckling under him as he pulled up and into the saddle, his chin hitting Champion's neck hard. His eyes shot to Paul, who swiftly averted his gaze, pretending he hadn't seen. The awkward moment passed as Frederic situated himself atop the steed. Paul secured the cane to the saddle, nodding in approbation. They were all set. Frederic breathed deeply. "Come, girls," he encouraged, "we've Duvoisin business to attend."

His smiling daughters were already on their ponies. Together, they trotted down the cobblestone drive and out the gates.

"Where are we headed, Papa?" Jeannette asked enthusiastically.

"The mill."

"The lumber mill?"

"I have a great deal of catching up to do," he answered, "and I'd like to start by meeting the newest men working for me. Wade Remmen is first on the list."

Jeannette was beaming. This was going to be a wonderful Saturday! As for Yvette, it would take more than a visit to the mill to please her; however, the ride was pleasant.

Paul watched them go, then headed toward the house. Charmaine was all his today. He found her in the gardens reading a book. A melancholy smile greeted him, causing his heart to hammer in his chest. He remembered the feel of her in his arms just one week ago, and he longed to hold her again, to comfort her. He sat next to her on the bench they had shared an eternity ago.

"So, Miss Ryan, what are we going to do today?"

She regarded him quizzically. "You're not working?"

"I said we'd spend time together."

Her smile turned sweet.

"A visit into town?" he suggested. "Or perhaps a walk along the beach?"

The mill was abuzz. Yvette and Jeannette's eyes widened as they approached, for they had never imagined the sweaty toil here. A score of men labored with teams of draft horses, pulling long, thick logs to a central building where they would be milled. A huge waterwheel rotated briskly at the far end of the structure, plunging into a deep ravine. Planks were emerging on the other side, where they were swiftly hoisted onto a buckboard for transport to town. The screech of saws, the shouts of men, and the whinny of horses punctuated the air.

"Yvette, Jeannette?"

They tore their eyes from the engrossing commotion and looked down to find their father had already dismounted.

"Are you coming?"

As Frederic and his daughters approached, one man looked up, then another, until all work was suspended. Jeannette searched for Wade, spotting him near the tree line, speaking to a young woman. Her smile vanished. "Now where is this Mr. Remmen?" her father asked, puzzled by her glum face.

"Over there," she pointed.

Frederic eyed the couple. The young woman was quite lovely, with straight black hair. She didn't belong at the mill, and apparently Wade Remmen was telling her so, his voice raised in agitation.

"I don't care if it *is* Saturday, nor that you're bored, I've work to do!"

Dismissing her, he turned back to the mill, immediately spotting Frederic and the girls. His momentary shock gave way to a frown. He strode toward them with a determined gait. "Mr. Duvoisin," he pronounced, extending a hand. "Yvette," he continued with a nod, "Jeannette. What can I do for you, sir?"

"My daughters and I are abroad for the day, and having heard a great deal about you, Mr. Remmen, I thought it was time we met." Frederic glanced over Wade's shoulder to the edge of the forest, but the woman was gone. "We didn't mean to interrupt—"

"No," Wade replied, "that was my sister. She wanted to spend the day with me, but Paul asked me to work. She's young, and I don't like her going into town on her own. So what does she do?" He threw up his hands in exasperation. "She walks here instead." He exhaled loudly, then shook it off. "Would you like to see the mill in operation?"

An hour later, they set off again, this time toward town and the warehouse, where they would reconcile invoices against lumber deliveries and finish up the day's business at the bank. Frederic had something he wanted to show Yvette.

Stephen Westphal was astounded when Frederic stepped up to his desk. He scrambled to his feet, sputtering, "Well—isn't this a surprise?"

"Yes, Stephen, the first of many."

"What can I do for you today, Frederic?"

"The mill account—I'm going to put Yvette in charge of it."

"Pardon?" the banker exclaimed loudly, his astonished query overpowering Yvette's similar response. "But she is a mere child—a female!"

"She is also a Duvoisin and my daughter," Frederic replied. "Like her mother, she has an acuity for figures. Now that Paul is preoccupied with Espoir, I'm going to make use of other resources." He draped his arm affectionately across her shoulders and drew her close. "I'm willing to *gamble* on Yvette's ciphering abilities and see if she is capable of handling the books. If her sister shows some interest, I'll find something for her to accomplish as well. Now, if you'd be so good as to provide a ledger of this month's transactions, I'll go over everything with her this evening."

They lunched at Dulcie's, a place Yvette thought never to see again, let alone in her father's company. The townsfolk stared openly at them, which made her feel important. *So this is what it means to be a Duvoisin.*

"Did you ever give that money to the poor?" she courageously asked.

"What money, Yvette?"

"You know what money."

"Actually, no."

When her father didn't elaborate, she dropped the subject. Still, their banter was easy, and she truly enjoyed being with him.

"Papa?" Yvette asked as they rode home. "Will I really be in charge?"

"Of the lumber mill books? Yes." She smiled exultantly. "But I warn you now, Yvette, it is not going to be easy."

"Don't worry, Papa," she assured, "I'm capable. I won't disappoint you."

Frederic chuckled, unable to remain serious. For the first time in years, his heart swelled with pride.

"What about you, Jeannette? Would you like to take charge of something?"

"Well, I'm not as good with figures as Yvette is, Papa, but I'll help if I can."

"Only if you want to, princess, only if you want to."

They arrived home by three o'clock. At the girls' insistence, Frederic allowed them to groom their ponies in the paddock. He retreated to the house.

They had just finished currying Spook and Angel when their stepmother swept past them without so much as a word of greeting. Yvette eyed her suspiciously as Gerald rushed over. They exchanged a few words and the stable-master nodded toward the carriage house, where a chaise stood ready. Agatha climbed in, flicked the reins, and steered the buggy through the manor gates.

"That's strange," Yvette murmured.

"What is?" her sister asked.

"Auntie going out for a buggy ride."

"Why is that strange?"

"When have you ever seen her riding out alone—without a driver?"

"Never?" Jeannette supplied thoughtfully.

"That's what I thought."

* * *

Agatha was in no rush to be on time for her customary three o'clock appointment. She was close to an hour late when the carriage rolled up in front of the tiny abode. She alighted from it and stepped up to the door, not bothering to knock. Her adversary sat at a small table near the hearth, pen in hand. He looked up, seemingly unaffected by her unannounced entrance. When he did not speak, she took charge. "This will be my last visit," she announced.

"Your last visit? Why? You haven't run out of resources, have you?"

Agatha looked around the room, noticing the bottle of expensive wine on the table, the well-stocked pantry, and the silk curtains adorning the windows. The man was living well at her expense. "My resources are of no concern to you. I'm through providing your finances."

He was surprised. "What are you saying, Mrs. Duvoisin?"

"I've informed my husband of the small matter over which you've been extorting money," she replied triumphantly. "He knows all the details and has been most forgiving. Your threats are inconsequential now."

A low, deliberate laugh erupted from his unctuous smile. "Mrs. Duvoisin," he started magnanimously, "I've grown quite accustomed to my stipend. It has helped offset my humble circumstance. Do you really think I would place it in jeopardy without insurance?"

Her eyes narrowed. She was not following him, so he hurried to explain. "I reflected for hours on your little lie, pondered your motives, puzzled over the role your brother played in it all. Robert's situation has dramatically improved as well: his new house, lavishly furnished. Has his medical practice really grown that much? Or was he rewarded for assisting you?"

Agatha's pulse throbbed, apprehensive yet irate over what was coming.

The man chuckled at her tight-lipped demeanor. "Yes, I've done some investigating, gleaned a bit of evidence that would be of great interest to your husband."

"I don't believe you!" she expostulated furiously. "You are bluffing."

"Ah, but do you really want to take that chance, Mrs. Duvoisin?"

She stood before him in stony silence.

"I thought not. So, since you arrived empty-handed today, shall I see you next week at the appointed time? Oh, and by the way, my silence has become more expensive. Let us make your visits weekly ones from now on. So, do come prepared. Good day, Mrs. Duvoisin."

After dinner, Yvette and Frederic disappeared into the study. Charmaine had been told all about their wondrous day. "Wondrous" was how they'd described it. Thanks to their father, their healing had commenced, and Charmaine was grateful. Her own heart was another matter.

An hour later, Yvette looked up at her father, who was reading over her shoulder. "This is not so difficult, Papa. I can cipher the rest tomorrow afternoon when lessons are over, and you can check my work in the evening."

"I have a better idea," Frederic said. "I think I can persuade Miss Ryan to substitute your arithmetic problems with this bookkeeping. After all, what is the purpose of education if not to benefit from its application?"

"You're absolutely right, Papa."

"I thought you'd agree," he chuckled. "Shall we finish tomorrow, then?"

"Yes, Papa, I'm quite tired." She rose, stretched, and placed a mild kiss on his cheek, but as she reached the hallway door, he called her name. "Yes, Papa?"

"You are quite a young lady—so very much like your mother."

"Mama?" she asked in astonishment. "But Jeannette is much more—"

He didn't allow her to finish. "No, Yvette, *you* are like your mother."

She rushed across the study and gave him a fierce hug. Then, embarrassed, she raced from the room. With a heavy heart, Frederic watched her go. Not so long ago, Colette had sat at this desk doing the very same job.

The warm days of October turned unusually cool and blustery, heralding the onset of the Caribbean winter. Charmaine marveled at Frederic's transformation. Most days, he ventured out with George to monitor work on the docks, at the mill, or in the sugarcane fields, master of his empire once again. When he was at the house, he was usually working in the study. He was hardier, his weak side growing stronger. Though he still favored a cane, his limp had also improved.

True to his word, he spent every Saturday with his daughters, and though it was a challenge at first, he managed quite well. In fact, Charmaine was impressed with the things he taught them, the engaging outings he embarked upon, all of which revolved around Duvoisin business. Although he and Jeannette had always been close, Yvette flourished under his guidance. Both girls looked forward to Saturday now, often speculating as to what the next excursion might be.

Charmaine remained uncomfortable in his presence, preferring to keep her distance. Though she tried to suppress them, she could not forget the revelations of that bleak October morning. Sadly, she could not regard Frederic with the same respect, despite his titanic effort to begin anew. She often contemplated the ugly word uttered only by John, though not denied by his father: *rape.* Had Frederic raped Colette or was it as *he* claimed—a seduction? Instinctively, Charmaine knew the latter had to be closer to the truth. She recalled Colette's remarks: *I was attracted to him from the moment we met . . . He's handsome still . . . I love him still . . .* No woman would use such words to describe a man who had raped her; there had to be more to the story. Nevertheless, pardoning Frederic of rape did not acquit him of stealing Colette from John.

The frenzied pace Paul had previously kept abated when Frederic reassumed control of Charmantes. Espoir's development was suddenly unimpeded, and he spent most weekdays there. But every Friday night, he ventured home. *She* commanded his Saturdays now. A stroll on the lawns, afternoon tea, even lunch at Dulcie's became a ritual. She was amazed he chose her companionship over his fledgling enterprise. Their discourse was direct, free of the previous games and guile, and they chatted and laughed together as never before. His attentiveness was comforting, a welcome distraction from the grief over Pierre, a piercing emptiness that often gripped her unexpectedly.

Agatha was not pleased. Charmaine often caught her disapproving glare. The woman continued to ingratiate herself with Paul, mindful of her future and the comfortable lifestyle to which she'd grown accustomed as Mrs. Duvoisin. Clearly, she hadn't forgotten her disdainful nephew's threats to cast her out, so she curried Paul's respect in an effort to secure her future in the manor. She certainly didn't want Charmaine around to interfere.

To Agatha's chagrin, Frederic postponed the christening of Espoir. She objected, but he would not be swayed, maintaining such a celebration was inappropriate so soon after Pierre's death. Paul agreed, and so the affair was set for early April, before Easter, when the weather warmed. Better accommodations could be arranged, and travel to the islands would be easier.

There had been no word from John. The twins missed him fiercely and were downtrodden when ships arrived from Richmond carrying no letters. But Charmaine understood; the wounds were still fresh, the happy memories too painful. She often reminisced about that winsome time, especially the two weeks before Pierre's death. They had been a family then, a loving family. She had lost more than Pierre in October; she had lost John as well. But even if he returned today, those carefree days could never be recaptured.

Pierre was gone forever. Far better to cherish her recollections than dwell upon what wasn't meant to be.

In mid-November, a young physician arrived in town. Recently graduated from medical school, he'd jumped at the prospect of opening up a practice where there would be little competition. Charmaine had unexpectedly encountered Caroline Browning one day, who lost no time in asking whether John had made the arrangements. It was rumored he distrusted his uncle's competency and was subsidizing the new doctor until a clientele of patients could be established. Charmaine didn't doubt the assertions, the traumatic hours before Pierre's death foremost in her mind, but she cut the conversation short when Caroline inquired about the accident, asking why Pierre had been left in John's care.

Saturday, November 25, 1837

Paul turned an admiring eye on Charmaine. She was seated confidently on the dappling mare, handling the steed competently, unaware of his regard from astride his own mount.

The Saturdays they spent together were the one silver lining in the cloud of disasters that had befallen his family over the past months. He wanted Charmaine more than ever. Those bleak days in October had served to make her more alluring: the quiet dignity with which she bore her grief, her warmth in comforting his sisters, her forbearance to move on. He longed to take her in his arms and teach her about the pleasures of the flesh, yet he did not press her. Although there was a candor between them now, her passion lay dormant. She was still grieving Pierre, he reasoned, desire would return in time.

"How is Espoir coming along?" she asked, glancing his way.

"It's nearly finished," he replied, pleased with her interest. "The light will be installed in the lighthouse next week. I intend to launch some limited shipping. It's impractical to delay until April. Some early runs will also allow the crews to become acquainted with navigating the port." Impulsively, he asked, "Would you like to see it?"

Her eyes left the road altogether, taking in his broadening smile, white teeth flashing against bronzed skin. He was serious! "Yes, I would!" she exclaimed.

"Why not next week? We can take the girls and spend a few days there."

He noted her fading enthusiasm, signaling her concern over an unchaperoned voyage. "I'll ask Rose to join us and give you all an extended tour."

Mentioning Rose did the trick; her face brightened again. "I think it's a wonderful idea!" she said.

For the first time in weeks, she was looking forward to something.

Monday, December 4, 1837

The twins welcomed their first excursion on a Duvoisin vessel, their alacrity unrestrained. With Paul in close attendance, they took turns at the helm, though he did the work. Most of the time they were at the bow, arms extended, flaxen hair and skirts dancing in the headwind. Occasionally, the ship cut into deep waves, hurling sea-spray over her sides, startling them into squeals of delight.

They arrived by late afternoon and headed straight to the new house. Aside from Frederic and Agatha, they were the first to take up temporary residence there. The house was magnificent, constructed with the highest quality materials. Paul noted that though the main floor was sparsely furnished, many of the bedchambers were fully appointed in anticipation of the guests who would be visiting in the spring. He showed them to their rooms; the twins would share one, but Charmaine and Rose had their own. He also brought them to the master chamber suite, which was larger than Charmaine's childhood home. She imagined the life of the mistress of this manor and, fleetingly, fancied herself in that role. But she quickly brushed those thoughts aside. Even as the governess to the Duvoisin children, she enjoyed comforts and privileges she could never have fathomed. Could she ever go back to her humble beginnings? Someday she might have to, so it was wise to stay anchored in reality.

Millie set up the kitchen, serving them a simple meal by late evening. Afterward, they retired to the drawing room, where Rose took up her knitting and Charmaine, Paul, and the twins played a game of cards, which, along with chess and checkers, they had brought for evening entertainment. Jeannette tired of the game and went to Rose, asking for a knitting lesson. With an extra pair of needles and spare yarn, Rose set up a basic stitch. Jeannette caught on quickly. After completing a few rows, she brought her handiwork to Charmaine.

"Very good!" she praised. "I think you have a knack for knitting."

Yvette boasted she could knit just as well, and when Paul said she didn't seem the domestic type, she pressed Jeannette to show her the stitches.

He regarded Rose. "Every night you take up that knitting, Nan. What do you do with your finished work? Nobody can use it here."

"I send it to family in the States, and they usually donate it to the poor."

Yvette tired of the tedious task much as Paul had predicted.

"What are you knitting, Jeannette?" he asked.

"I don't know. What *am* I knitting, Nana Rose?"

"Why, a scarf, of course."

"But, you don't need a scarf, Jeannette!" Yvette exclaimed.

"No, I don't," she replied, "but I can send it to Johnny for Christmas!"

"That's a wonderful idea," Rose said with a smile, "and I'll show you how to knit his initials into it when you near the end."

Jeannette happily agreed.

"Just make sure he knows I helped make it, too!" Yvette insisted.

"I'm sure he'll know exactly which two rows you knitted," Charmaine chuckled, eyeing Yvette's loose, uneven stitches.

Friday, December 8, 1837

The weather was fair, and the week on Espoir sped by quickly. In the mornings, Charmaine and the twins worked on lessons. After lunch, Paul joined them, and they ventured out on horseback to the sugarcane fields, some under preparation for planting, others growing tall. One afternoon they passed endless stretches being cleared of vegetation. The twins enjoyed riding along the trails that bordered the fields, traveling the entire circuit connecting one to the next.

On the last day of their excursion, the weather turned brisk. It had drizzled overnight, and cold air followed the rain. After dinner, they settled into the drawing room. Paul struck a fire in the hearth to chase away the chill, and the girls sat in front of it, Jeannette with her knitting and Yvette with a book. Before long, both had fallen asleep. Paul carried them to their room, where Charmaine tucked them in for the night. When she returned to the parlor, Rose stood and announced she, too, was retiring.

For the first time that week, Charmaine was alone with Paul, and she could feel herself growing tense—a strange mixture of excitement, anxiety, and reluctance. She remained on the sofa, watching him. He was banking the fire with fresh kindling, his masculinity silhouetted by the glowing embers. She admired the play of muscle in his thigh as he crouched low to press the logs deeper into the blaze. His handsome face was striking in the orange light. He rose and moved to the sideboard where he poured two glasses of wine.

Paul inhaled as he handed a glass to her. She was lovely tonight. He hadn't kissed her in months, and the urge to do so now was overpowering.

Charmaine blushed as he settled on the sofa next to her, his arm cast across the back of it. He was so close she could feel the heat of his body. "I don't drink," she said, gesturing with the glass.

"Try it, Charmaine. It's a vintage wine. It will help you relax."

"Very well," she said, taking a sip. It was smooth and warm going down.

"So, did you enjoy the trip here?" he asked.

"Very much. I'm impressed. I see what has kept you busy all these months."

"There is still much to do before Espoir will stand on its own merit."

"With all the care you've taken, it will be very successful."

"I hope so. Still, it has distracted me from other important things."

She looked at him quizzically. He was studying her intently. "You'll find time for those things," she said quickly, wishing to redirect the conversation.

"I'm trying to." His hand, warm and persuasive, caressed her cheek, found her chin, and coaxed her head back. With her face upturned, he leaned forward, his lips meeting hers. "You are lovely, Charmaine Ryan," he murmured against her mouth. "It has been so long since I've kissed you, I was afraid this week would pass without the opportunity."

His kiss deepened, and his arm slid off the sofa, closing around her shoulder. The minutes gathered, and his ardor grew, his hand stroking her hair, her shoulder, and coming to rest on her thigh. She felt feminine and desirable, yet as the sensual moment heightened, a visceral tide of resistance took hold. She pressed her hands against his chest and slowly drew back.

He looked down at her searchingly. "Are you all right?"

"Yes, yes," she replied, standing up and moving to the fireplace. This situation was very dangerous.

"Charmaine," he started, coming to stand behind her. "I know you have been very sad these past two months. I had hoped to comfort you."

She faced him. "And you have. You have been a great comfort, a good friend, and I appreciate your concern."

"Are you in better spirits now?" he asked, not relishing the title "good friend."

She smiled. "Some days I am. This week I have been."

The silence between them seemed endless.

"What do you want, Charmaine Ryan?"

"What do I want?" she queried, awed by the unexpected question.

"Yes, what do you want—for your future, for your life?"

Was this trite banter, or was he asking how she felt about him? Somewhere inside, she knew the answer to his question, but it was too sublime, too frightening—*too impossible*—to even ponder.

"Six months ago, I could have answered," she replied. "Now . . . I don't know." She paused, then turned the question over to him. "What do *you* want? And don't say me."

"And if I did say I want you?" he asked sincerely.

"I would say that I'm flattered."

"But?"

"What do you mean when you say you want me?"

"It means I want you at my side. It means I want to make love to you."

"Does it mean you want to marry me?" she inquired brashly.

His smile faded, and she was strangely relieved. "What does it matter, anyway?" she chuckled lightheartedly, waving away the frivolous query, intent upon soothing him. "It's not even in the realm of consideration, is it? After all, I'm just a governess, hardly a suitable spouse."

Marriage . . . Not exactly the subject he wanted to broach right now. *Marriage* . . . Why was it so frightening? Why did he hesitate? *You will rue the day you threw away happiness with both hands.* If it weren't Charmaine, who then? *Marriage* . . . For what was he waiting?

"I don't think of you as just the governess, Charmaine," he replied. "You are a fine woman: compassionate, intelligent, attractive. Social mores have never been important to me, and they certainly won't dictate whom I marry. Look at my parentage. In society's eyes, I am less worthy than you."

She was surprised and heartened by his words. "And?"

He didn't have to make a commitment this moment, and he wouldn't be lying if he told her he had considered marrying her. "And, to answer your question, I've never felt for any woman what I feel for you. So, yes, I would consider marrying you, have, in fact, contemplated it more times than you would imagine. But I'm a rogue, Charmaine. I don't want to hurt you, have you grow to hate me." He paused, still thoughtful. "Marriage, the vows, they are simple. But how can either of us be certain of our feelings years from now? Yes, I want you tonight, desire you greatly, and, yes, I love you. But I'm a man. I can't promise another woman will never turn my eye. That is what I fear most. A pledge to love, honor, and cherish for all eternity? I won't make such a vow lightly."

He pulled her into his arms and his lips snatched away her reply. Slowly, her hands encompassed his back, relishing the feel of his sturdy body, the warmth of his flesh under her palms. He coaxed her back to the settee, his caresses extending to her breasts and hips, awakening sensations that teased her insides. She relaxed into the cushions, he half-kneeling, half-prone above her, his kisses growing furious, his breathing heavy and unsteady. Then he was shifting his position, pressing her farther back. As he lowered himself, she could feel the weight of his body, something hard against her thigh, and an inkling of reluctance washed over her again. She pushed onto her elbows, coming up for air.

"Charmaine . . ." he murmured, his voice husky, "if you're worried about conceiving a child, you needn't be—"

She frowned, disconcerted. Curiously, that thought hadn't crossed her mind, but she quickly capitalized on it. "That is easy for you to say."

He leaned in close again. "There are ways—"

She turned her face aside, hands braced against his chest. "I can't," she whimpered, "I'm sorry, I can't."

Disappointed, he moved to the end of the sofa. She stood to bid him goodnight. "Don't leave," he said. "It's our last night here. I won't press you if you're not ready. Please, come and sit with me."

Again, she was gladdened by his words and returned to him. His arm closed around her, his hand stroking her hair, nudging her head onto his shoulder. They stayed there late into the night, talking and staring into the fire . . .

Christmas Eve, 1837

Charmaine and the girls spent the day decorating the house: weaving pine and holly sprigs, fastening fruit to them with string, and garnishing the balustrade, mantel, and French doors with the festive boughs.

After dinner, the family gathered in the drawing room. It was quite chilly, lending the day a true holiday air. Paul lit a fire in the hearth. Frederic invited the staff to join them, and so, the Thornfields, Jane Faraday, and Fatima settled in for eggnog and Christmas cookies. Felicia and Anna were spending the night in town with Felicia's parents. The girls sang to the Christmas carols that Charmaine played on the piano. When she tired, Paul took over at the keyboard and entertained his sisters, who were as surprised as Charmaine to hear him play.

The twins begged to open the packages that had arrived yesterday. They were from John, the first they had heard from him since October. Charmaine acquiesced; there would be more gifts tomorrow. They dove into the wrapping, revealing two finely tailored riding jackets in royal blue, complete with tan jodhpurs, velvet riding hats, boots, and crops.

Agatha began to object to Frederic's daughters wearing boys' clothing, but her protests over the breeches Charmaine had sewn for Yvette last September had gotten her nowhere, so she took a sip of her brandy instead.

The package also contained a book for Yvette and Jeannette: *The New-York Book of Poetry*. A note from John was inserted like a bookmark at the page where the poem *A Visit from St. Nicholas* appeared. They greedily read the brief letter aloud, then the poem, and the letter again . . .

Dear Yvette & Jeannette,

Perhaps St. Nick will fill your stockings this Christmas Eve—that is, if his eight tiny reindeer don't need snow, Auntie allows them to land on the roof, and Yvette is well behaved. The odds are not very good. If St. Nick does not visit, then I hope my gifts will do. Happy Christmas.

Love, John

Agatha gripped tight the arms of her wing chair, offended. John continued to ridicule her, even across the Atlantic. The girls, however, were thrilled, and the poem sent them scrambling to find stockings to fasten to the mantel.

Charmaine was heartened by their enthusiasm, amazed once again at how John could cast a whimsical spell on them, even from so far away. She looked to Frederic, who observed the tableau with intense interest. When he realized she studied him, he turned away, his gaze lifting to the painting that hung above the fireplace. *What is he thinking?* Her heart answered: *He never imagined it would be like this. He doesn't want it to be like this.*

There was also a small package for her.

"Open it, Mademoiselle," Jeannette said. "What do you think it can be?"

Charmaine glanced at Paul, who had moved to the fireplace, staring into the flickering flames. She untied the ribbon and pulled the wrapping aside. Inside was a simple ivory hairbrush. She smiled, running a finger lightly over the smooth handle. It was much finer than the one John had broken that first night last August.

"A most pleasant evening," Agatha declared. "It truly feels like Christmas: a warm room, a crackling fire, and the family together. So much like England this time of year. Everything Christmas should be."

Charmaine bristled at the callous remark. She glanced around the room: at Paul, with head bowed, George hiding behind a magazine, Frederic with his turbulent eyes, and Rose with her mournful face, even Fatima Henderson, lips pursed indignantly. She wondered where John was this evening. Instinctively, she knew he was alone.

Later, as she turned down the lamps in the nursery, Charmaine nearly cried when Jeannette innocently asked, "Do you think Saint Nick can bring Pierre and Mama back to us for Christmas?"

She looked with a heavy heart at Pierre's empty bed and remembered sleeping there with him, remembered John sleeping there. She would be glad when this Christmas was over. As she completed her nightly toilette, she thought of her mother . . . of Colette and Pierre . . . She lay down and wept. But tears were futile, so she prayed, prayed for her deceased loved ones and comfort for her grieving. But mostly, she prayed for the Duvoisins.

Christmas Day, 1837
Richmond

The crisp air frosted John's breath as he descended the steps of the St. Jude Refuge. He tightened Yvette and Jeannette's scarf around his neck, unhitched Phantom, and pulled up into the saddle. It was early, and although the Richmond streets were deserted, the refuge was busy. He had stopped in to see Father Michael Andrews before morning Mass and the ensuing bustle of the refuge's customary turkey dinner for the poor.

"Why don't you join us, John?" the priest had asked. "We can have dinner together after the soup kitchen has closed."

"No, no. You would have to hear my confession, and that could take all day," John had quipped hollowly. "You'd best direct your efforts where you'll have some success. There's no redemption for me."

In truth, John wanted to be alone this day. He couldn't think of anybody with whom he cared to be, save perhaps Charmaine. Pulling his woolen overcoat closed against the cold, he prodded Phantom into a brisk trot, setting him west on Wilderness Road toward Appomattox. He would ride to Freedom, a trip that would take most of the day. The road would be empty and the plantation house deserted, precisely what he wanted.

Michael had hoped John would spend Christmas day with him and had purposely set time aside yesterday to stop by his Richmond town house and extend the invitation. When the butler let him in, he found John at the piano. Michael knew from the steward that John had gone home to the family's islands late last summer. He surmised something grave had happened there. Michael had seen this distant mood before—the day they had met at the refuge four years earlier. Then, John had drowned himself in alcohol, seeking succor in drunken oblivion. This time, he was sober, and Michael thought it best not to probe. Yesterday, they had conversed briefly. As Michael pulled on his coat, he was encouraged when John agreed to stop by the refuge. But today, it was painfully apparent John was spurning his company, for he'd stayed all of ten minutes.

A disturbing disquietude welled up in Michael. *I was naïve to think I could make a difference in this pitiable world. Another year of useless ministering to those I serve—of meaningless existence for myself . . .*

He turned away and opened the leather purse John had handed to him at the door. Twenty banknotes were inside; the sum easily exceeded the soup kitchen's expenses for the day, not to mention the Christmas donations he expected to collect at Mass. "You *are* redeemed, John," he intoned with a shake of his head, his moment's antipathy assuaged. He entered the church to lay out his vestments for the Christmas Day celebration.

Saturday, January 6, 1838

Yvette insisted she and her sister wear their new riding habits. When they arrived at the breakfast table, she was beaming. Frederic's brow raised in amusement as she sashayed before him like never before in any feminine apparel. "What do you think, Papa?" she queried. "Do you like it?"

"No," he answered, "but I can see you do, and that is all that matters."

She pretended to pout, but her happiness quickly bubbled over.

Rose chuckled. "I'd say she looks like a Duvoisin ready to do business."

Frederic nodded as he considered his other daughter. "What of you, Jeannette? Do you like wearing boy's clothing?"

"It feels strange, Papa. I think I prefer a dress."

When they left for the day, Charmaine sighed. Paul was preoccupied as well, and she would be alone. She and Rose talked for a while, but when the older woman went upstairs complaining of her rheumatism, Charmaine stepped outdoors for a peaceful stroll.

She meandered about the grounds, finding herself at the family cemetery. It was no longer gnarled and ill kept. She surmised Frederic had ordered it manicured and maintained. A bench had been placed near the two newest graves, and she sank down on it, as she had often done over the past few months, lifting and hugging Pierre's soiled lamb. She closed her eyes to her gathering tears and jumped when Paul placed a comforting hand on her shoulder.

"I'm sorry," he said, "I didn't mean to startle you."

Unable to speak, she shook her head.

"Gerald said you were headed this way," he commented, allowing her a moment to compose herself, offering her his handkerchief.

She read compassion in his eyes as he sat down beside her. "I thought you were working today," she said.

"I was. But Father and the girls caught up with me and sent me home." He chuckled softly. "Yvette is a wonder. She's starting to impress even me."

Charmaine smiled. Yvette had indeed taken over the mill's books, and Charmaine had yet to find a mistake in her ciphering. Even Frederic was pleased; he checked her figures only once a week now.

"Do you come here often?" Paul asked.

"Occasionally," she whispered, her grief regrouping. "Oh Paul," she murmured, surrendering to it, "when my mother died, I didn't think the pain could be any worse. But I was wrong! I miss him every day. I think of him every morning. Sometimes I even forget and go into the nursery . . ."

"There now," he said, gathering her in his arms, cradling her head against his shoulder. "This is only natural. You loved Pierre like a son."

She sobbed until her body shuddered, and still Paul held her.

"I scolded the girls after Colette died!" she declared angrily. "Their mother had been dead for only a month, and I scolded them. And now, look at me! It has been three months and . . . How could I have done that to them?"

"Charmaine, you did what was best. You brought them out of despair and made them whole again. With time, the same will be true for you."

Charmaine nodded, deeply consoled.

Paul closed his eyes to agony. *Why did this happen to my family?*

He was nine years old again. The sun was setting, the harbor cast in long shadows. He watched anxiously with John and George on the quay as the last casks were rolled off the ship. The crew was loitering nearby, waiting for their mates to finish up. Then, they all fell in together, a boisterous, smelly, backslapping procession making its way to Dulcie's. Frederic had taken the captain into the warehouse office to reconcile invoices. The brigantine was theirs!

Paul scrambled up the gangplank with his brothers. Tonight John, George, and he were pirates. They battled the crew with pistols and swords, vanquished them and commandeered the vessel. They made the captain walk the plank and crept into the bowels of the ship, plundering the coffers of gold and jewels nestled in the hold. Down below, they could barely see, but they could hear their father calling for them. The fantasy was over.

Paul swallowed hard and pulled Charmaine closer. Little boys didn't die on Charmantes. This was, after all, paradise. But then he remembered: three little boys had lost their lives on this paradise island, over fifty years ago, during a pirate raid. His father had been little more than two, with an elder brother and sister, ages fourteen and twelve, and three brothers in between, ranging in age from five to nine. The boys slumbered peacefully in their beds as a fire was ignited over their heads, destroying in one short, horrific hour, the first house ever constructed on Charmantes.

Charmantes had enjoyed twenty years of peace, guaranteed by the deal Jean Duvoisin had struck with the pirates who roamed the waters of the West Indies. He allowed them safe haven in the hidden coves of his three islands as long as they did not set foot on the beaches. The quietude nurtured a fallacious sense of security; Charmantes should have been wary of the carnage wreaked upon neighboring islands, careful about boasting of its own prosperity.

According to Frederic, the renegades waited until his father traveled abroad, landing on the western shore in the middle of the night and penetrating the island's limited fortifications in less than an hour. They spent the remainder of that bleak night pillaging and destroying. Frederic's mother was only able to carry her youngest son to safety, perishing when she re-entered the inferno. By the following afternoon, only ashes remained.

When Jean returned, he proclaimed the ground hallowed. Embittered, he turned from his life on the seas and became a farmer. He built the mansion in which they now lived, complete with back staircases: escape routes should they ever be threatened again. He settled in with his three remaining children, hired Rose to help raise Frederic, and nursed a broken heart for the rest of his days.

Today, there was little threat of a pirate attack. With Great Britain's sovereign claim to the Bahamas, the British navy patrolling her waters, and Frederic's allegiance to the crown, complete with tithing and the upholding of British law, Charmantes enjoyed military protection that had not existed fifty years earlier, when Caribbean raids were commonplace. And yet today, the sorrowful past lived on. *Little boys did die on Charmantes.*

With a deep sigh, Paul leaned his cheek atop Charmaine's head.

Her arms encircled his waist, and he drew strength from her vulnerability. Taking solace from each other, they rose and walked back to the house.

New York

John looked out the bedroom window of his row house and stared, unseeing, at the street below. It was busy, even for late Saturday night. The noise of the city had awoken him. But then, he hadn't been sleeping very well these days. He breathed deeply and sighed. The woman in his bed stirred. He regarded her for a moment, but when she didn't awaken, he turned back to the window.

He thought of Colette. He thought of Charmaine. Strange, last night, Charmaine had been the centerpiece of his fantasies. *Charmaine* . . . How he'd love to hold her, cry with her, laugh with her again.

Saturday, January 13, 1838
Charmantes

Charmaine had plans to meet Paul in town. The sun was quite bright for January and because she would be riding Dapple, the name Jeannette had dubbed her gray mare, she turned back to the house to fetch her bonnet.

From her room, she could hear the twins conversing with their father in the nursery. Apparently, they were remaining at the house today. The door stood slightly ajar, and Charmaine listened, appreciating the easy banter between them.

"Papa, do you think Pierre is really in heaven with Mama, now?"

A moment's silence, then, "Yes, Yvette, I'm certain he's with your mother."

Charmaine could hear sorrow in Frederic's voice. He changed the subject. "I was late today because I was involved with some of the planning for Paul's celebration. We're to meet with Mr. Westphal tonight."

"I don't think this celebration is ever going to arrive," Jeannette lamented.

"April isn't far off. It will be a splendid affair—the first one on Charmantes in many, many years." Frederic sounded enthusiastic, and Charmaine realized he, too, was looking forward to the event. "There will be a great ball, elegant ladies and gentlemen, and musicians."

"Will we go to the ball?"

"Of course, and you shall wear beautiful dresses, which have already been ordered."

"Where will all the fine ladies and gentlemen come from?"

"Georgia, the Carolinas, Virginia, Maryland, and even New York. Some Caribbean farmers have also been invited."

"Will Johnny come?" The inevitable question came from Yvette, and the room fell into another awkward silence.

"No, Yvette, I'm afraid not," Frederic murmured.

"You won't allow him to come, will you?"

"He can come if he likes," her father answered in earnest.

Unconvinced, she added, "It wasn't his fault, Papa. He loved Pierre."

"I know he did, Yvette, but there is more to it than Pierre."

"But you're better now!" she said. "Why do you still hate him?"

"I don't hate him. He is my son."

"So why won't he come?"

"Because he is very angry with me."

"But why?" Jeannette asked searchingly.

"I made many mistakes with John and did things that hurt him terribly."

"What things?"

"Things you are too young to understand," he replied, "things that are difficult for me to explain to you."

"Then why don't you apologize?" Yvette offered. "That's what Mademoiselle Charmaine tells us to do when we've made a mistake."

"It is not that easy . . ." Frederic faltered.

"Yes, it is!" Jeannette chimed in. "I have an idea, Papa. You can write him a letter and tell him you're sorry. We can help you write it, can't we, Yvette?"

"Yes! We'll make it the best apology ever! And you can invite him to come to Paul's celebration, too!"

"Come, Papa, let's find some paper! *Please?*"

"Perhaps you are right, my dear daughters," Frederic mused. "Very well, let us see what kind of a letter we can write."

With tears in her eyes, Charmaine left her room, thanking the heavens above and praying John would receive the invitation with an open heart.

Later that afternoon, Frederic's letter sat atop others on the table in the foyer. Agatha noticed her husband's scrawl as she swept by, and she scrutinized the address. She was not pleased he was writing to his errant son.

Bending closer to the mirror, Paul fumbled with his cravat. The sun was fast setting, the pier glass cast in shadow. Travis should have arrived long ago to light the lamps. He'd do it himself, but the tinderbox was nowhere to be found, so he swore at his reflection and ripped the atrocious knot apart again. A man shouldn't have to suffer the nonsense of proper attire after a full day's labor. He had spent most of the afternoon in the cane fields, his intervention urgently needed when a press broke down and half a tract of produce was in jeopardy of being lost. That catastrophe had forced him to abandon his outing with Charmaine, but both problems had been easier to deal with than his tie. Irritated, he leaned into the mirror again.

Travis eventually arrived.

"Where have you been?" Paul gruffly inquired.

"With Mr. Westphal."

"Damn! Is the man never late?"

"No, I'm afraid not, sir."

The butler was about to say more, but thought better of it, stepping up to the ill-humored Paul with arms extended. "Allow me, sir," he offered, smiling when Paul's arms dropped to his sides. "What you need, Master Paul," he mused as he worked at the cravat, "is a wife to see to tasks such as this."

Paul snorted. "Travis, if I take a wife, it will not be to dress me."

The man blushed. He would never get used to the ribald remarks of Frederic's sons. To Travis, they would always be the lads he chased after to keep out of such trouble. "There," the steward sighed, "that should do it, sir."

"Thank you," Paul praised, patting the knot, satisfied with his reflection.

"I think you should know, sir, the mistress is with Mr. Westphal."

Paul shrugged. "Better if she talks with him first. Then he'll be free to speak with my father and me without interruption."

"Yes, sir."

"Where is my father, anyway?"

"He arrived back quite late with the girls, sir. I'm to see to him next."

Paul grunted. He suddenly thought of Colette, and how little his father had relied on Travis that first year they were married. *A wife . . .*

He left his dressing room and, with head down, walked straight into Charmaine. Catching her in his arms, he set her from him with a stern frown. He apologized curtly and descended the stairs quickly, leaving her puzzled.

Much to his relief, dinner was relaxed. All his hard work was coming together. Following the meal, he spent over two hours in the study with his father, Agatha, and Stephen discussing the arrangements for the monumental spring event. The invitation list had been finalized, guest transportation and accommodations planned, and the week's expenses estimated.

The clock struck eleven, and Agatha noted Stephen and Frederic shared her exhaustion. The financier's tie had long been loosed, dinner jacket doffed, waistcoat unbuttoned, and now, in the dim library light, he stole a yawn as Paul leaned forward to scribble some last particulars. Her husband had closed his eyes more than once in the armchair where he now reclined.

"Paul," Agatha interjected, gaining the man's regard, "perhaps you should continue this tomorrow—" she looked to the banker "—I fear our guest is growing weary."

"Tomorrow would be fine," Stephen concurred wholeheartedly.

Paul had lost track of the time. It *was* late. "Forgive me, Stephen," he apologized, setting down his quill. "I've forgotten this is not as exhilarating for you." He stood and went to the door. "I'll see to it that your carriage is brought to the portico. Would you like an escort home?"

"That's unnecessary. I doubt I shall encounter any highwaymen."

Everyone but Frederic laughed. "I'll say goodnight, then," Frederic said.

Agatha was pleased when Paul and her husband departed. She grabbed the banker's jacket and helped him slip it on. Gathering his belongings, she walked him into the foyer. "Stephen, you mentioned contacting Mr. Richecourt."

He nodded.

"When you do, could I trouble you with a favor? You've done one of this kind for me before."

"Miss Ryan again?" Stephen queried with cautious interest.

"No, she is insignificant. This concerns John. He's been spending a great deal of time in New York. He said as much months ago, before Pierre's tragic accident. Perhaps you could bring your influence to bear on Mr. Richecourt to find out exactly what his transactions are in the North. I'm concerned over these bank accounts he's been closing out, and I'm afraid my husband has been more trusting than wise."

Westphal nodded in disdain. "I've thought the same thing myself, but wouldn't presume to say so to Frederic. John is—"

"You needn't expound," Agatha interrupted, patting his hand in understanding. "Rest assured you will be compensated for your efforts."

"I'll see what I can find out, Agatha. Goodnight."

Agatha's smile turned radiant. "Goodnight, Stephen."

He stepped out onto the portico to await his carriage.

Saturday, January 20, 1838

Yvette had a plan. She was going to discover where her stepmother went every Saturday afternoon and why she went alone. Naturally, there were obstacles to surmount: she'd have to get around her father, and she'd have to pick a day when Charmaine was off with Paul. Today was that day. Frederic was planning to take them to the harbor. So, when Charmaine set off for town after breakfast, Yvette complained of a stomachache and asked to stay home in bed. Frederic acquiesced, leaving her in Rose's care. She went straight to her room, pulled on her nightdress, and lay on her bed with her knees pulled up to her chest. She heard Frederic and Jeannette leave in the carriage. When Nana Rose came in to check on her, she pretended she was asleep. She was starving by lunchtime, but she dared not show up in the dining room. Nana checked in on her again around two o'clock, bringing some toast, tea, and a fresh pitcher of water, soothing her when she pushed the tray away, moaning her stomach still hurt. She closed her eyes and pretended to doze again. She heard Rose step softly from the room, pleased with herself. She still had the knack, completely fooling the woman. Rose would not return for another two hours. Perfect! She could be out and back without anyone ever knowing she was gone.

She jumped up, pulled on her breeches, and shoved her hair into Joseph's cap, which she'd lifted yesterday. She could pass for a boy from a distance. She tiptoed from her room, dashed down the staircase behind her father's suite of rooms, and darted furtively out of the house toward the stables. It was a blustery afternoon. Thankfully, all the stable hands were off to town, except Gerald, who was napping in the tack room. She saddled up Spook and led him out of the stable, noting the chaise awaiting her stepmother, the horse already harnessed and tied to the fence. Pulling up and into her saddle, she set her pony into a trot, passing quickly through the main gates. When she found a spot alongside the road with heavy underbrush, she dismounted, led Spook into the concealing thicket, and waited.

Fifteen minutes later, she heard the rhythmic beat of hooves and the squeak of a buggy coming up the road. It passed her hiding spot, and she saw Agatha plying the whip to the horse's back. When it rounded a bend up the road, she scrambled from the thicket and jumped back onto Spook, in pursuit until she caught sight of the chaise again. She followed at a safe distance. About a mile farther, it turned onto the thickly wooded road that led to Father Benito's cabin. Yvette was surprised. *Why is Auntie visiting Father Benito?*

Yvette held Spook back as Agatha alighted and entered the priest's abode, carrying a leather pouch. Yvette tied Spook to a tree behind a copse a good distance away and approached the cabin surreptitiously. There was a window on one side, a pile of wooden crates and scattered refuse below it. She climbed the crates and peered in. The window was closed, the voices inside muffled. The curtains were also drawn, but she could see the priest's kitchen and living area through the slit. Agatha and Benito were engaged in a heated dispute, Agatha's rigid posture betraying her anger. Yvette held her breath, straining to hear. Benito took the pouch from Agatha and opened it. Jewels sparkled.

Suddenly, the pile of crates teetered, caving under and spilling Yvette onto the ground. She clambered to her feet and ran to the outhouse, taking cover behind it. She prayed Benito wouldn't think to look there. She stole a peek around the corner and saw the priest walking around the cabin, stopping at the toppled crates. Agatha was behind him. He looked around, casting his gaze up to the road. He eyed the woman suspiciously.

"It must have been the wind," Agatha theorized. He considered her again, then retreated, slamming the cabin door behind him. Agatha left.

Certain the priest was peering out his window, Yvette crept deeper into the woods, picking her way through brambles and underbrush and arcing around to Spook. Once she'd led him safely to the road, she kicked him into a gallop, frowning when she realized she didn't have her riding crop. It couldn't be helped; she'd dropped it along the way and would have to complain about misplacing it the next time she went out to ride. All told, she'd been gone just over an hour and was back in bed when Rose came in to check on her again, exclaiming the nap had helped. She felt much better now and was hungry for dinner.

Sunday, January 28, 1838

Paul snapped the portfolio shut. He and his father had spent two hours poring over Charmantes paperwork, and he was of a mind to pass the rest of the day in a leisurely manner. He'd arrived home late last night and, because he'd been on Espoir for the better part of the week, had promised Charmaine and his sisters at Mass this morning that he'd spend the afternoon with them. Time was getting on.

"There is one thing more," Frederic said as he stood to leave.

Paul eyed him thoughtfully. His father seemed anxious. "Yes?"

Frederic hesitated. "I've invited John home for your celebration."

"*What?* In God's name, why?"

"Jeannette and Yvette requested it."

Paul ran a hand through his hair. "He won't come," he said.

Frederic was disheartened. "You are likely right, though I hope he does."

"For the girls' sake," Paul supplied.

"And mine. I'd like to make amends, even at this late date."

"It wasn't your fault. None of this was your fault."

"It *was* my fault," Frederic refuted. "He loved her, Paul, more deeply than I wanted to believe."

Paul scoffed at the idea, but Frederic's earnestness gave him pause.

"Pierre's death put everything into perspective," Frederic continued, "everything. It was easier, safer, to discount John's feelings. But in so doing, I made this place a living hell for everyone—including you. You were forced to choose sides, which undermined the camaraderie you once shared with John. I should never have stolen Colette from him."

"And Colette had no say in the matter?" Paul threw back at him.

Frederic's eyes hardened, but he didn't respond.

Exasperated, Paul exhaled loudly. "I don't understand. He's had months to stew over this tragedy. That's all it was—a terrible tragedy. And now you unleash Pandora's box? If he decides to come home, it won't be to make amends."

"We shall see. All I ask is we try to move forward—as a family."

With his initial anger spent, Paul accepted his father's plaintive plea and was moved to remorse. "Very well, Father. I'll welcome him home. I just hope John accepts the invitation for what it is."

Wednesday, February 9, 1838

Agatha had been holding interviews in the study for two days now. Since early Monday morning, a steady stream of villagers had made their pilgrimage to the manor in the hopes of securing one of the fifteen positions that would be available here and on Espoir during the weeklong festivities in April. An inside glimpse of the Duvoisin mansion was as much a motivation to make the nine-mile trek as the employment opportunity, for even those whose names did not make it into the mistress's little book smiled as they left.

Yvette and Jeannette stole away from the nursery many times during those two days, observing the strangers in the foyer or those walking up the drive. They conjured games, wagering over which ones would be selected.

Travis escorted one after the other from entrance hall, to drawing room, to library. The few that gained Agatha's approval were ushered into the ballroom, where they met with Jane Faraday or Fatima Henderson. The rest were released and walked to the portico, where they lingered before heading back to town.

At the close of the day, Agatha shut her ledger and leaned back in her chair.

"Finished?"

Frederic drew her away from her preoccupation. She nodded contentedly.

"I have three cooks and six maids assigned to Espoir. Fatima has chosen an additional two for our kitchen. On the morning of the ball, those from Espoir shall be transported here to assist. Jane will spend the next month training the housekeepers, including the four I've hired for us. All ten should perform splendidly; they know five permanent positions are available on Espoir. In addition, Anne London has graciously arranged a retinue of waiters and table staff to depart her country estate and arrive here a week before the banquet."

"Agatha, you've assumed the role of mistress with the authority it demands," Frederic praised. "Paul's debut will be remembered for years to come."

Her heart soared with his admiration. "Thank you, Frederic," she murmured tearfully. "With all the money you've spent, how could I not lend it my best effort? I've done this as much for you as I have for Paul. I'm so pleased to see you up and about again, as strong as ever."

She stood and went to him, running her hands down his arms, brushing a stray lock of hair back into place. "I love you, Frederic."

He caught hold of her wrist and brought her fingers to his lips. "I thank you for all you've done."

Sunday, February 25, 1838

George Richards was smitten.

He'd accompanied Paul to the harbor because the *Destiny* was due in port. Stephen Westphal's daughter, Anne London, was expected to be aboard. Since Paul planned to escort her back to the house, George would take charge of unloading the vessel. The ship arrived, and the mooring went very smoothly.

Anne was above deck, anxiously waiting for the gangplank to be lowered. Paul, George, and Stephen climbed the ramp to greet her. George took an immediate disliking to her. She was pretentious and cloying, and she wore too much rouge. In a matter of seconds, she gave her father a dismissive kiss on the cheek and turned her smothering attention upon Paul. Irked, George jumped at the opportunity to get her luggage from her cabin.

It took a moment for his eyes to adjust to the light as he stepped inside. Then he saw her: a young woman gathering up parcels. She had long auburn hair, hazel eyes, olive skin, and high cheekbones. She was exotic and took his breath away.

"Good day," he greeted, "I'm here to collect Mrs. London's things."

She nodded and blushed, lowering her eyes to the floor before scurrying through the doorway.

He hastily grabbed a few bags and rushed out in pursuit. It was bright and warm above deck. The young woman was not far ahead of him. As she reached the gangplank, she stumbled and grasped for the railing, the parcels spilling out of her arms. George dropped his baggage and hurried to help her.

"Are you all right?" he asked, taking her elbow until she regained her balance. He picked up the packages, their eyes locking as he straightened up.

"Thank you," she replied with another blush.

"You're welcome," he smiled. "Here, take my arm."

She slid a delicate hand into the crook of his elbow, and he walked her down the ramp to Paul and Anne.

"You're going to need another carriage," he commented.

"I'll hire one from the livery," Paul replied, "if you'd get the other trunks."

George agreed, but by the time he'd returned, the first carriage was rolling away, Anne, Paul, and the lovely young lady inside. *Who is she?*

* * *

A ruckus resounded in the hallway. Charmaine stepped out of the nursery with the twins close behind. Travis and Joseph had deposited a mountain of leather traveling cases outside John's bedchamber door, then disappeared down the steps. Charmaine looked at the twins, who returned her regard with quizzical shrugs. Yvette dashed back into the nursery and out onto the balcony.

"Come and see, Mademoiselle!"

Jeannette and Charmaine followed. Two carriages had pulled up to the portico, and two women were on the lawn, one of them conversing with Paul and Stephen Westphal. She was elegantly garbed in a pale yellow dress, cut low to reveal the swell of her ample bosom. A wide-brimmed hat was cocked to the side of her head, and she held a parasol. She had strawberry-blond hair that was swept up and pinned neatly under her hat. Her face was heart-shaped, with expressive brown eyes and a finely arched brow. Her cheeks were rosy, and she had a curvaceous body. She was quite attractive, though she did not come close to the delicate, graceful beauty of Colette Duvoisin. Anne London, Charmaine surmised. The woman's eyes were locked on Paul, her head tilted back and a smile tugging at her lips.

Her companion was younger, perhaps Charmaine's age, and dressed in plain clothes. She was tall and slender, her long hair tied back with a ribbon and falling to her hips. She was busy unloading hatboxes from the second carriage, which was piled high with luggage. The top box wobbled, then fell altogether, spilling a frilled bonnet onto the lawn.

"Really, Mercedes," Anne London exclaimed with a click of the tongue, "do be more careful! I haven't even worn that hat yet, and already you've managed to soil it!" Mercedes scrambled to pick up the expensive item, blushing in embarrassment as both Stephen and Paul turned to see. "Why don't you follow the butler and bring the boxes up to my room?"

"Who is it, Mademoiselle?"

"Mrs. London," Charmaine replied, gaining Yvette's grimace.

"Good thing Johnny isn't here!"

Charmaine chuckled.

Again, they heard the commotion in the hallway. Travis had opened John's dressing room door and was carrying two trunks into the chamber. Charmaine was instantly annoyed. "Mr. Thornfield," she called when he reappeared empty-handed, "what are you doing?"

"Delivering Mrs. London's things to her room, Miss. Why do you ask?"

"You have the wrong room," she replied.

"Master Paul told me to bring them here, Miss Ryan."

"Take them to another room," she insisted. "Two doors down will be fine."

"I beg your pardon?"

Paul and Anne arrived. "Is something the matter?" Paul interrupted.

"Miss Ryan seems to think I'm placing the baggage in the wrong room."

Paul turned quizzical eyes on Charmaine, and Anne's gaze followed.

Charmaine watched her nose wrinkle disdainfully and knew what she was thinking: *So this is the governess, Miss Ryan, the daughter of a murderer—worse than common*. Charmaine tore her eyes away and looked pointedly at Paul.

"May I speak with you privately, Paul?" she pressed, pleased when Anne appeared aghast at hearing her use his given name. "It will only take a moment."

Paul seemed oblivious to the silent exchange. With a courteous smile, he excused himself and followed Charmaine into the nursery.

"Those are John's quarters," she said when he had closed the door behind him. "Mrs. London can stay in another room."

"What difference does it make?" Paul asked, entirely befuddled.

"Those chambers belong to John and shouldn't be disturbed. He was pushed out when I took his room. Now it's happening again. It's not right."

"But he's not here, Charmaine. I don't think he would care—"

"*I* care," she replied, unmindful of his annoyance. "And what if he should come home for your celebration?"

"That is unlikely," Paul replied, taken aback by her disappointed expression. "Very well," he replied, rubbing the back of his neck.

He returned to Anne and directed Travis to move her bags to the next suite. "The children are early risers, Anne," he explained urbanely. "You'll have peace and quiet if we place a little distance between your quarters and theirs."

"How kind of you," she smiled artificially, glancing Charmaine's way.

"Would you like to join us for lunch?" Charmaine asked from the door.

The young woman turned from her task of hanging dresses in the armoire. "I have to unpack all these gowns first," she told Charmaine and the twins.

"It's getting late," Charmaine remarked. "You must be hungry. Can't you finish this after lunch?"

"I had better do it now. Mrs. London will be furi—upset if they're wrinkled."

"Well, then, let us help, so you can have lunch, too. Come, girls."

Charmaine stepped into the chamber, followed closely by the twins, and proceeded to take one beautiful garment after another out of the traveling cases.

"I'm Charmaine Ryan, Yvette and Jeannette's governess," she offered, extending a hand to the lady's maid. "Welcome to the Duvoisin manor."

"I'm Mercedes Wells. It is nice to meet you." For the first time, the young woman smiled. Charmaine knew she had made a friend.

Thursday, March 1, 1838

George admired Mercedes from the armchair where he sat, as he'd done for the past three nights after dinner. Paul had invited Anne London's personal maid to join them. Though George was pleased to enjoy her company, if only from afar, the words he'd exchanged with Paul earlier at the mill still rankled him.

"Not this one, Paul—you're not going to have this one."

Paul threw him a puzzled look. "What are you talking about?"

"You know goddamn well what I'm talking about—encouraging Miss Wells to join the family after dinner."

Paul remained bewildered. "She and Charmaine have struck up a friendship. Don't tell me you're annoyed I've invited her to . . ." Suddenly, Paul was laughing. "Oh, now I understand. You're jealous."

George's face reddened. "Just leave her alone."

"She's not beautiful, George," Paul teased, "comely, but not beautiful."

"The hell she's not!"

Paul chuckled again. "If she were beautiful, my friend, do you think she'd be Anne London's attendant? I assure you, Anne would never place a delectable dish so near her own plate. She's far too vain."

George remained tight-lipped, simmering.

"I'm not interested in Miss Wells, George. I leave her to you."

Mercedes Wells *was* beautiful—in George's eyes, the most beautiful woman in the room. Abruptly, he stood and walked over to her chair.

She looked up in surprise.

"Miss Wells," he heard himself say, "will you take a stroll with me in the gardens?" He was elated when she murmured, "Yes."

In the days that followed, Charmaine saw very little of Paul. He was busy with preparations for the celebration, and when he was free, Anne London rarely left his side. She now commanded his Saturdays.

Anne and Agatha got along famously. When Paul wasn't around, they spent much of their time together. Agatha was engrossed in planning every detail of the affair, from receiving invitation responses to selecting flower arrangements, preparing menus, organizing table settings, hiring musicians, establishing lodgings and other accommodations. Anne advised Agatha on all these matters, and they spent many an hour locked away in Agatha's boudoir.

Charmaine and Mercedes's friendship continued to grow. Mercedes was a sensible, down-to-earth woman, with a keen perception of people and their motives. Because she was Anne London's lady's assistant, she was at the widow's beck and call for anything and everything. Up and out of bed well before dawn, she laid out Anne's clothes and placed her breakfast order before she awoke. When Anne did rise, Mercedes didn't know a moment's peace until long after lunch, shuttling food trays to and from the widow's chambers and helping with her morning toilette and coiffure, a laborious process that took hours. Afterward, she ran errands: posting Anne's letters, acquiring incidentals from the mercantile, bringing her drinks, or fetching her books from the library. Anne was condescending and abusive, constantly threatening to dismiss her for the most minor infraction or mishap.

Mercedes despised Anne London, but she was paid well, and she needed her job. Like Charmaine, her mother had died a few years earlier, after a prolonged illness. Mercedes's father was a stable-master on a Virginia estate, and she had an elder brother, also a stable-master, who had a wife and children. Her father was rarely around, and Mercedes felt it was time she set out on her own in the world. Because she'd grown up around horses, she was an experienced rider.

When Yvette told Frederic this, he gave the young woman free rein to ride Colette's mare, Chastity, since the horse was in dire need of regular workouts. So in the afternoons when Anne went off with

Agatha, Charmaine, Mercedes and the twins went riding to all corners of the island, having a fabulous time.

Whenever he could, George returned to the manor for lunch, and after work, he avoided Dulcie's, preferring to go straight home. Occasionally, he'd get lucky and Mercedes would go for a walk with him after dinner. He despised the way Anne London treated her. Much as he wanted to defend her, he didn't dare, certain Anne would dismiss her on the spot.

Some weeks before Paul's gala, George asked Mercedes to be his partner at the banquet and ball. She accepted eagerly, but the very next day, she told him Anne had forbidden her to attend.

"This isn't a servant's affair," Anne had remonstrated sarcastically. "It's a business engagement and a society soirée, reserved for gentry with social status. It will be very embarrassing for Mr. Duvoisin and for me if you show your face there. I will not allow it."

Friday, March 9, 1838

Anne had been on the island less than two weeks, and already Paul had had enough of her. Out of deference to her father, and because she knew a good many influential men from Virginia, he escorted her around Charmantes, as every polite host should. He was glad when she went off with Agatha to gossip and plan. Guests would begin arriving in just over a fortnight.

Today, he was with his father, handling routine business that had been neglected with the imminent unveiling of the new island and fleet of ships.

Frederic rubbed his brow. "I hope there's enough capital to cover this," he mused. "We may have to liquidate other assets."

"I thought the same thing," Paul agreed. "I'll talk to Stephen about it later."

"You'll be seeing him again?" Frederic asked with surprise.

Paul sighed. "With Anne here, Agatha has invited him to sup with us."

Frederic leaned back in his chair and considered his son for a moment. "And this 'relationship' with Anne London," he proceeded cautiously. "Are you interested in this woman?"

Paul shook his head. "There is no relationship, Father, but it is in my interest to be hospitable while she's here. Anne knows many people, has many connections through her deceased husband."

"I see," Frederic breathed. "And what of Charmaine Ryan?"

Paul was confounded. "Charmaine?"

"You've spent a good deal of time with her over the past five months. I have eyes you know. I can see how you look at her."

Paul was embarrassed. He'd never had a heart-to-heart talk with his father about a woman before. When he didn't speak, Frederic continued. "You could do worse than Charmaine, you know."

"What are you saying, Father?" Paul asked, stupefied.

"You could do worse than Charmaine," he reiterated. "You don't need to marry for money. Why not choose a woman who will make you happy? I could be mistaken, but I think you'd be far happier with Charmaine than with Mrs. London."

Paul smiled broadly. "There is no comparison."

"I thought not," Frederic nodded, turning back to the documents before him, happy he'd found the right moment to speak his mind.

Paul was heartened that Frederic cared—was concerned that money might influence his choice in a spouse.

He suddenly thought of the banquet and ball. As yet, he had no partner. Inspired, he coveted Charmaine in that role. *She should be very pleased if I ask her. How many other governesses have received such an invitation?*

His mind raced ahead to that night. Charmaine was in his arms, and they were dancing the first waltz. She was smiling sweetly up at him, blushing, as she had that first year, before John had come home and interfered. The evening would be magical, and anything could happen.

Charmaine Duvoisin—yes—he liked the sound of it.

Sunday, March 11, 1838

Like every evening since Anne London had arrived, Charmaine ushered the girls from the dinner table straight to their rooms. "I don't want to go up there yet," Yvette complained, but Charmaine had given her a reprimanding scowl.

An hour later, Paul said goodnight and went to the nursery. He found Charmaine reading to his sisters, who groaned when he asked to speak to her privately. "Why don't you go down to the drawing room for a few minutes?" he queried. "Fatima has set out some delicious sweets."

Charmaine gave her consent, sighing as they left. "You'll send them back up to me?" she asked, certain she'd struggle to extricate them from the parlor later on.

"There is something important I want to ask you," he said instead.

Disconcerted by his stern face, she was sure she'd done something wrong.

"Has anyone asked to accompany you to the dinner and ball?"

Charmaine looked down at her hands. "No," she whispered. She thought of Mercedes, and her throat constricted. *He's about to forbid me to attend, too.*

"Well, then," he inhaled. "*I* would like to be your escort."

Astonished, her head snapped up before she could conceal her tears, but they told Paul he had made her very happy. He smiled devilishly, and she felt like throwing herself into his arms.

"I gather that is a 'yes'?" he asked.

"Yes!" she cried with disarming exuberance.

He pulled her to him and savored the kiss she was willing to give. His embrace tightened, and his kiss grew passionate. Abruptly, he tore away, unsettled by the spell she had cast upon him, his breathing ragged, his eyes smoldering with desire. "I had better say goodnight, Mademoiselle," he said lustily, "lest I take you to my room."

Her blush thrilled him, his desires fanned by the realization his words still affected her. "I will send the girls up to you," he murmured.

Charmaine waltzed around the nursery when he was gone. The ball! Paul's partner! It didn't seem possible! She needed a gown! Tomorrow, she would have to ride into town. She would invite Mercedes to come along. Yes, Mercedes could help her pick out the very best one!

On his way back to the drawing room, Paul wondered why he had been content to wait so long to make love to Charmaine Ryan. She was the only woman he had ever waited for, and yet, if he desired her, if he loved her as he was beginning to believe he did, why was he content to wait? Sometimes, he was able to put her from his mind completely, but other times, her stubbornness not to submit vexed him to distraction. Didn't she realize if she pleased him in bed, he'd do the gentlemanly thing and marry her? Perhaps he'd just grown comfortable knowing she would always be here waiting for him. Sooner or later, desire would prevail, and they would consum mate their love. Sooner or later, she would scorn her empty bed and fall into his. Sooner or later she would want to become a woman, his woman. Perhaps she'd succumb sooner than later—on the night of the ball.

Chapter 2

Sunday, March 18, 1838
Richmond, Virginia

FATHER Michael Andrews had heard talk of Paul Duvoisin's gala celebration every Sunday now for the past month. Greeting his congregation after Mass, it was a favorite topic of conversation among the clutches of chatting parishioners gathered outside St. Jude's. Anticipation was building for the weeklong event.

Michael had last seen John two months ago. He was headed for New York and hadn't mentioned anything about his brother's debut. Michael wondered if he planned to attend. Though he knew John wouldn't have dreamed of going home to Charmantes last year this time, John's unexpected trip last summer made *this* visit a possibility. Something urged Michael to find out, so after dinner, he went to John's town house. The butler answered and told him John had returned from New York, but had gone directly to the family plantation for the planting season. He wasn't due back in Richmond until mid-April. Perplexed, Michael climbed back into his buggy and flicked the reins. He was only a short distance down the street when intuition compelled him to turn back. The steward opened the door again and gave Michael directions to the plantation. He would set out first thing in the morning. Mondays were quiet at the refuge, so he could afford to be away.

Monday, March 19, 1838

Michael arrived at Freedom around four o'clock in the afternoon. Only the house staff was at the quaint plantation house. John had left with his overseer at dawn and might not return from the tobacco fields until dusk. A manservant let Michael in, and he settled into the parlor with tea, biscuits, and a book. Michael tried to read, but his thoughts meandered.

He'd been worried about John for months now, seeing through his jovial front, disturbed by the despair in his eyes, like the John he'd met four and a half years before. Michael wondered again about the man's trip home—the single place on earth John had vowed never to return. *Give him time. You gave him time before and he talked . . .*

Michael shuddered with the memory of that "talk." It was the spring of 1834, and they had known each other for six months. John had received news from Charmantes, upsetting news. With Marie Ryan's insistence, Michael had finally driven to John's Richmond town house and heard the man's confession that fine spring day . . .

John was angry Michael was there. "Did Marie send you?" he bit out, half-drunk. "That's the last time I tell a woman anything."

"She didn't *tell* me anything, John," Michael refuted, "she's worried."

John scoffed at the answer, but Michael was not easily dismissed. "John . . . when are you going to tell *me* what happened? Perhaps I can help."

Gulping down a mouthful of whiskey, John eyed the priest derisively. "I don't need you to hear my confession, *Father*."

"Not a confession, John. Just a heart-to-heart between friends."

Taking another long draw off the glass, John gazed out the window.

"You're not the only one who has done things of which he's not proud, John," Michael offered when the accumulating minutes became uncomfortable.

"Oh really?" John sneered dubiously. "And what could you have possibly done, Michael? A little nip and tuck in the sacristy with the consecrated wine?"

Michael welcomed the sarcasm with a smile. "I'll confess if you confess."

John's brow raised in interest. "You've got a deal, Father."

Michael froze. He hadn't thought John would take the bait.

"Well?" John nudged, eyes intent, relishing his distress. "I'm waiting . . ."

Michael cleared his throat. "When I was much younger . . ."

"Yes?" John prodded again, leaning back against the liquor cabinet, crossing his legs and folding his arms over his chest.

"I broke my sacred vows of celibacy—with a woman, whom I loved . . ."

Silence. "That's it?" John asked disappointedly. "That's all?"

"That's all?"

John chuckled and shook his head. "At least it was with a woman. That will be nine Hail Marys, three Our Fathers, and one Act of Contrition."

With downcast eyes, Michael smiled, but he wasn't going to release John from his end of the bargain. "Your turn, John."

John leveled a piercing gaze on him, his reticence gone. "I took my father's wife to my bed and fathered a baby with her. When I bragged to him about our affair, we nearly came to blows, causing a seizure that's left him an invalid. I fled Charmantes, leaving her to contend with his wrath alone. I hated him so much, I prayed, in your holy sanctuary, for him to die so I could be with her and my child . . ." Swallowing his pain, John laughed wickedly. "Tell me, Father, does it get any worse than that?"

Michael saw through the evil. "You love this woman, don't you?"

"More than my own life," John freely admitted, turning away as if to barricade his grief. "My son was born three weeks ago . . . Pierre," he whispered hoarsely, "his name is Pierre." After an interminable silence, he looked over his shoulder. "Tell me, Michael, if I suffer a lifetime never knowing the boy, will I be forgiven?"

"You've been forgiven already, John."

"No, Michael," John denied fervently, irately. "To be forgiven, one must feel remorse. I'm not sorry; Colette belonged to me!"

Michael learned the whole story that night, leaving John close to dawn. John had vowed never to return to Charmantes, allowing Colette to live the life she had chosen. He would punish himself by never beholding his little boy. And the world would know Pierre Duvoisin as his younger brother. It was Colette's choice, and now it would be his.

But, John *had* returned to Charmantes. Why?

It was nearly dinnertime when Michael heard the yapping of dogs. He looked out the window. John, dirty and sweaty, was walking up to the house with another man, presumably his overseer. Two large hounds bounded around them.

"What the hell are you doing here?" John asked, once they'd walked through the door, his crooked smile broadening, hand extended. "No, let me guess . . . Pope Gregory found out the truth about you, and you need a job."

"The truth about me?" the priest asked warily, taking his hand.

"Admit it, Father, you've been using your priestly powers to turn bread and wine into steak and ale. So where's dinner?"

Michael laughed along with John's overseer, sending his eyes heavenward. They went into the kitchen for drinks, and John introduced Michael to Brian. John grew serious and asked, "What brings you all the way out here?"

Michael looked at Brian, who took the cue he wanted to speak to John privately, stepping out the back door and heading toward a row of cabins in the distance. The cook, who'd been running furiously between cookhouse and kitchen, disappeared as well. Michael and John sat down at the table, cold glasses of water in hand.

"Parishioners have been mentioning your brother, Paul, lately," the priest began. "There's talk of a big celebration for the launch of his shipping concern."

John shrugged. "He's been developing another of the family's islands for over a year now. My father gave it to him. He'll run his own shipping line from it. So?"

"I don't mean to meddle, but a few of my congregants say they'll be leaving shortly for the affair. Aren't you going?"

John leaned back in the chair. "I wasn't planning on it."

"Why not? Wouldn't your brother appreciate your support?"

John scratched his head. "Have you forgotten my vow, Michael?"

"John," the priest breathed, "I know you traveled there this past fall."

John was surprised, but Michael continued. "Your butler told me."

John bowed his head to the unwelcome memories and his heart began to race.

"Are you going to tell me what happened? Why did you go back? You said you'd never go back."

John massaged his brow, and the room fell disturbingly quiet as he searched for words. "Colette wrote to me. My friend, George . . . he delivered the letter. He had trouble finding me. I was in New York, and it took him weeks to track me down. By the time I got home, Colette was dead." John's throat tightened, and he could say no more.

He still loves her, Michael realized sadly. *After all these years, he still loves her.* "And the boy?" Michael braved to ask.

"I killed him, too," John pronounced somberly, his voice cracking. "I killed him, too." When he regained his composure, he told Michael the whole story.

"It's over now," Michael comforted. "It's time to move on."

"I know that," John agreed, "and I am."

"Then why not go back?" Michael prodded. "You are invited, yes?"

"In effect."

"In effect? What does that mean?"

"My father invited me, which is as good as Paul inviting me."

"Your father?" Michael asked in surprise. "So why aren't you going?"

John's grim silence was his reply.

"Are you angry with your brother?"

"No. I hope his business succeeds beyond his wildest dreams."

"It's your father. That's the issue," Michael pressed. "You still hate him."

John clenched his jaw. "I'm not going back because every time I do, there's a disaster. It's best for everyone concerned if I stay away."

"But your father has invited you. That means he's forgiven you."

"That means," John sneered, "he wants all his guests to believe we are one big, *happy*, wealthy family—for my brother's sake."

"No, John. It means he's forgiven you. I know it. I think you know it, too. He's never invited you home before, has he?"

"No, he hasn't."

"John," Michael implored, "if you ever want to get on with your life, you have to face this. Do it now, while your father wants it, while he's willing to forgive you. You may never have this chance again."

"I don't want his forgiveness," John confessed acidly. "And he certainly won't get mine."

Astounded by the ferocious declaration, the depth of John's prolonged bitterness, Michael shook his head sadly. "Perhaps there is more to it than you understand, John. Is it possible your father loved this woman, too?"

John snorted, repulsed by the idea. "He married my aunt not three months after Colette died, Michael. So you tell me—is that love?"

Michael inhaled sharply. The sordid story only grew worse. Even so, he rejected the obvious answer. "Perhaps you can't forgive your father now, but you should accept *his* forgiveness," he reasoned. "Go back for your brother's sake—and your sisters'. I'll warrant they will be thrilled to see you."

John pondered Michael's words. He thought about his last visit to the island and how dramatically his life had improved. Though Colette's death had cut deeply when he'd first arrived, it changed nothing really. He had long resigned himself to life without her. And lately, even the pain of Pierre's death was subsiding. Because he didn't discount the existence of God, entertaining the belief Pierre was with his mother in the afterlife consoled him. He was beginning to step away from the past. Charmaine had been right; now he *could* think of Pierre dumping sand on his head and chuckle about it, rather than fight back tears. He knew Yvette and Jeannette would be overjoyed to see him, and then there was Charmaine. In fact, seeing her motivated him to go back more than anything else. He might even be lucky and find she wasn't married to Paul yet.

"Where has this anger gotten you and your family anyway, John?" Michael asked. "Isn't it time to let it go? It appears your father wants to bury it, so why not you? The future might be brighter than you believe possible."

Suddenly, John was disgusted with the entire matter. Michael made it sound so simple. Why go through that again? "I'll think about it," he lied.

The priest decided it was best not to pressure him and walked to the vestibule.

John followed, dismayed and disgruntled, certain he had prodded Michael into a hasty departure. "You're not leaving now," he objected. "The sun will soon be setting."

"I have a lamp in the carriage," Michael replied, pulling on his coat, "I also passed an inn along the way. If need be, I can stop there. In either case, I must get back."

"Would a bit more money help?" John asked, certain his friend was working himself into the grave.

"You've been far too generous already, and it's better if I keep busy."

"Busy with work or with killing yourself?"

Michael's brow lifted. "Is it that obvious?"

"I'm surprised Marie hasn't insisted on a bit of leisure," John said with a twinkle in his eye, perplexed when the priest's face went white. "Michael?"

"Marie is dead," Michael pronounced. "I thought you knew, John. I thought everyone knew. It's been over two years now."

"Dead?" John murmured, nonplussed. During his brief visits to the refuge, he hadn't thought to ask for her, taking it for granted she was alive and well. Two years and he hadn't seen her! He was immediately angry with himself. Was he so absorbed in his own misery he overlooked his friends? Marie had been a savior, a sympathetic confidante who had helped him through the worst times of his life—the months following Pierre's conception and birth. "Dead," he reiterated as the truth set in. "But how?"

"It was terrible—" Michael struggled to explain.

John shook his head, for he knew the priest, this good man, this equally good friend, had loved Marie. "Michael, I'm sorry, so sorry."

"She was a very special woman, John."

"Yes, Michael, she was."

Words exhausted, they pondered the finality of death. The bleak mood was broken when John strode into the small library and rummaged through his desk drawers. He found what he was looking for and walked back to the hallway, studying the envelope in his hands.

"Funny," he said, "Marie gave this to me years ago, and—" he looked up at Michael "—she asked me to give it to you should anything happen to her." He gingerly extended the missive to the priest.

Michael accepted the letter, cradling it as if it were a precious gift.

"Aren't you going to open it?"

Michael broke the seal, removed the single paper, and began to read. His hands were trembling by the time he'd finished. He looked up at John, tears in his eyes. "I have a daughter," he whispered. "Dear God . . . a daughter."

Burying his face in his hands, he slumped into the nearby armchair. Now he knew why Marie had deserted him twenty years ago. He believed it was because of that one intimate encounter. For nearly six years, he'd worried over what had become of her and chastised himself for having shamed her. When she did return one bitterly cold day, she had a young girl with her—her daughter. She was married, she was happy, she told him. She and her husband had started a family. Marie kept him at arm's length, so Michael believed her story. They never talked about what had happened between them, but he wondered if she thought about it as often as he did.

Suddenly, he was furious: furious with himself—the priesthood—God. He should have turned his back on the ministry when he knew he loved Marie. She would still be alive if he had walked away!

"Are you all right?" John asked, shaken by the man's expression.

"I'm not certain where she is," Michael said, his anger gone, enervation seeping in.

"Perhaps Marie placed her with a good family. She's likely surrounded by brothers and sisters."

Michael looked up at him quizzically. "No, John. She's a young woman now—nineteen or twenty."

John was surprised once again.

"I knew Marie for many years," Michael explained. "She was orphaned and raised at St. Jude's. I was young when I was assigned there, and she was beautiful, inside and out. It's no excuse for what I did, but I did love her. I still love her."

"I know that. So why berate yourself? You loved her, and she you."

"That 'love' forced her into a loveless marriage."

"Marriage?" John puzzled. "She never mentioned a husband to me."

"She rarely spoke of her life outside the refuge," Michael whispered. "Apparently, she chose it to spare me the shame of fornication. According to this, she didn't want me to leave the priesthood, something she feared I'd contemplate if I had known about the baby. So she sacrificed herself instead."

Laying the letter in his lap, Michael pressed his hands together in prayer and brought his fingers to his lips, tapping them in deep thought. "Now, what am I to do, John? Do I track down my daughter? Do I tell her I'm her father? I know she despised the man she thought was her father."

"How would you know that?"

"She grew up at the refuge, attended Sister Elizabeth's school. I heard many of her confessions."

"Find her first," John suggested, "and make certain she's all right. You can decide about telling her the truth later."

"You're right," the priest nodded, reconciled. "Marie would want that."

Barking dogs and a rap on the door drew them away from Michael's problem. Annoyed by the interruption, John opened it to five men staring up at him from the lawn below, their horses tethered to the hitching post at the edge of the drive.

"Good evening, Mr. Duvoisin," said a sixth man who'd parted from the pack and stood on the porch, seemingly oblivious to the snarling hounds. "We'd like a moment of your time."

"Concerning?" John queried.

"Two runaway slaves. We have reason to believe they are in the area and traveling at night."

John listened, expressionless. When he didn't respond, another man stepped forward with a newspaper clipping, which he shoved into John's hand. John glanced down at it. "A strong buck and his woman—spotted about thirty miles south of here the night before last. Take a good look at that paper, Mr. Duvoisin, and tell me if you've seen any nigger fittin' that description."

A reward of one hundred fifty dollars was offered for the fugitive. The article gave the date of his escape, the state from which he'd fled, his owner's name, and a description. The bounty increased the farther from home the slave was captured.

John shrugged, passing the paper to Michael. "They all look alike to me."

The men grunted in agreement, the remark putting them at ease. The ringleader remained staunch. "We understand you've freed all your slaves, Mr. Duvoisin, that they work for you here. There'd be a high price to pay if your niggers were harboring someone else's property. Best we speak with them."

"The men and women on this plantation know better, Mr. . . . ?" and John waited patiently for the name.

"Reynolds," the man supplied.

"Mr. Reynolds," John acknowledged. "They'd lose their position here. Unlike the Yankees, I don't fault the South for using slave labor. After all, my family's wealth has been built on it. Freeing my slaves was a business decision, nothing more. I find they work harder because they're paid; I don't need a whip, and I don't have to hire expensive bounty hunters like you to track them down. They don't run."

The men eyed him suspiciously, but could not refute what he said.

"All the same, we'd like to see their quarters," the first man replied.

"As you wish," John relented.

He descended the porch and led them to the humble Negro quarters behind the plantation house, passing Stuart's abode first. Stuart stepped out and nodded to them. "My production manager," John explained.

As they approached, the children swiftly abandoned their games. John singled out one cabin and rapped on the door. Brian opened almost immediately, evidence he'd been watching from the window.

"Brian," John began, "these gentlemen are looking for two runaway slaves from North Carolina. They were spotted south of here two nights ago. Is that right, gentlemen?" They nodded. "Have you or anyone else seen them?"

"No, sir."

"Unfortunately, I cannot take your word for it," John said. "I'm sure these gentlemen will not rest until they have searched your home."

The men mumbled in agreement.

"Yes, sir," Brian answered. Stepping aside, he allowed two of them in.

The others paired off and searched each cabin. They came up empty-handed, and Reynolds turned to John. "We're sorry to have troubled you, Mr. Duvoisin."

John smiled. "No trouble at all. I'll keep an eye out for your runaways."

They trudged back to the main house and mounted up. John climbed the front steps, rubbing the back of his neck. When they were out of sight, Michael came out onto the porch. "They're gone?" he queried anxiously.

"They're gone," John affirmed.

Michael still clutched the news clipping in his fist.

"May I have that?" John asked. "I keep them," he explained, "every one of them, as a reminder of what I'm doing and why."

Michael handed the paper over. John glanced at it and said, "Let us see if they made it to Freedom last night."

Michael chuckled, and together, they retraced John's steps to the cabins.

Stuart came out onto the porch again, smiling in relief.

"So, they *are* here?" John asked.

"Yes, John, since dawn, but I didn't know you were up at the house."

"No harm done," John replied. "Today continues to be their lucky day. Since there are only two of them, and Father Michael will be setting out for Richmond in the morning, he can transport them to the refuge in his buggy."

Michael nodded; it looked as if he'd be spending the night.

They slid a heavy, crude hutch off two movable floorboards,

and the couple emerged from the crawlspace beneath Stuart's cabin. Nettie gave them dinner, then prepared a bed for them, and at the crack of dawn the next morning, they were on their way. The pregnant woman sat beside Michael and did not look out of place; the advertisement had not described her and she could pass for his housekeeper. Her husband, however, was tucked uncomfortably behind the carriage seat, concealed under a blanket. Still, it was better than walking.

John wished them well and pressed some money into the woman's hands.

"Thank you, sir," she whispered, grabbing hold of his arm and cradling it to her heart. "God bless you and your family."

"And you, ma'am," he rejoined. He shook Michael's hand and said, "I'll stop by when I'm back in Richmond."

The priest flicked the reins, setting the buggy in motion.

Saturday, March 24, 1837
Charmantes

Charmaine and Mercedes stepped out of Maddy Thompson's cottage, in no hurry to return to the manor. Charmaine sighed contentedly. Two weeks ago, she had worried about what she would wear. She was determined to turn every eye at the banquet and ball, but the dresses on display in the mercantile were far from elegant. Certainly, the other maids and matrons would be wearing gowns purchased abroad, in Paris and in London. Paul had said as much when he insisted he purchase her entire ensemble. Thankfully, he and Maddy had come up with a solution. Fashionable gowns were advertised in the magazines on the mercantile counter. Charmaine would choose amongst the finest fabrics in stock, and Maddy, who had been a seamstress for a couturier in Charleston, would do the rest. So, for the past two Saturdays, Charmaine had stood like a statue on a pedestal in Maddy's parlor as the gown took shape. One final fitting and it would be ready, and Mercedes would take care of any minor adjustments at the house.

They crossed the busy street and headed toward the livery. A large sign hung in Dulcie's window: ATTENTION SAILORS: NO VACANCIES, and in small letters: LODGING AVAILABLE AT THE WAREHOUSE. The most influential guests would be staying in the mansions on Charmantes and Espoir, and Frederic was paying Dulcie well to accommodate the others. Earlier in the week, the saloon had been whitewashed, and the shutters repainted. Today, the second-story windows were thrown wide, and six women were in the side yard bleaching the bed linens. The whole town was busy preparing for this unprecedented event.

When Charmaine and Mercedes turned their mounts onto the main road toward the manor, Charmaine couldn't contain her excitement. "Thank you, Mercedes, thank you so very much. I wish you could be there, too."

Mercedes discounted the sympathetic remark. "Don't fret about me. You'll enjoy it for the two of us. And on Paul's arm, no less! I can't believe it. I really thought he'd ask Anne. She had her eyes fastened on his brother last year. She'd kill for that spot, you know."

Charmaine smiled, the pleasantness of the day expanding.

"Why *did* he ask you?" Mercedes queried, making the most of Charmaine's elation, yet hoping she wouldn't think her impertinent.

"Paul and I have grown very close, especially over the past five months."

"Close?"

"He's a friend, Mercedes, a very good friend."

"A friend?" Mercedes mused doubtfully. "Charmaine, do you realize how many girls would give an arm and a leg to be in your shoes? How jealous they will be? And you're telling me you're just 'good friends'? Aren't you attracted to him? Why, if he squired me, I'd have a fit of the vapors, or blush scarlet at the very least!"

Charmaine laughed in spite of herself, recalling those early heart-thundering days when all she did was blush. Nowadays, she kept her composure around Paul without a worry, and she wondered what had changed.

"Well?" Mercedes asked, leaning forward.

"Well, what?"

"Well—are you in love with him? Is he *interested* in you?"

"Interested," Charmaine mumbled. *You should be interested to know Paul has but one interest in you . . .* Why had she thought of that? "Yes." Charmaine smiled. "He is interested in me."

"Then what are you waiting for?"

"What do you mean, what am I waiting for?"

"Go after him! Don't let him get away! Don't allow Anne to sink her claws in! You'll never have an opportunity like this knocking at your door again."

Saturday, March 31, 1838

The ball was fast approaching, only a week away. Travis had been stationed in town days ago, receiving ships as they made port and establishing the prestigious visitors at their assigned lodgings. Many had already arrived. Tomorrow afternoon there would be a reception at Dulcie's to commence the weeklong conference.

This morning, the breakfast table buzzed with happy conversation, filled to capacity with guests. Everybody was talking except Frederic, who remained distant, his eyes solemn. Charmaine wondered if he was as downtrodden as she. *Is he thinking of John? Did he remember today would have been Pierre and Colette's birthdays? That Pierre would have turned four? That the anniversary of Colette's death was only a week away?* Charmaine sighed with a heavy heart.

As if reading her thoughts, Frederic spoke directly to her. "Miss Ryan, you seem unusually pensive today. Is something wrong?"

"You have been uncommonly quiet this morning, too," she replied, "for the very same reasons, I believe."

All eyes were instantly on them, the clamorous table falling silent.

"What reasons?" Agatha queried, eyeing Charmaine suspiciously.

Frederic smiled sadly and answered laconically. "Miss Ryan is very astute." Then, "I'm afraid I shall be busy all day, Miss Ryan, and need you to mind the twins. Perhaps a ride with my daughters will lift your spirits."

"Yes, sir," she whispered dismally, certain nothing could do that.

Yvette and Jeannette lit up with Frederic's suggestion and quickly ran off to the kitchen to invite Mercedes. As Anne opened her mouth to object, Frederic intervened. "Mrs. London, I assume you will be assisting my wife today?" With her slight nod, he said, "Then why not allow Miss Wells to accompany my daughters? Agatha's itinerary should only require the services of the house staff."

Not wishing to appear cruel, Anne smiled unhappily. She would have a private word with Mercedes later.

Heading toward the paddock, Jeannette noticed a cloud of dust kicked up on the dirt road beyond the entry gates. "A rider!" she exclaimed.

Yvette stopped dead in her tracks, eyes riveted to the road.

"What is it, Yvette?" Jeannette queried, turning to her sister.

"It's Phantom!" she screamed, dashing across the lawns, "and Johnny!"

Jeannette broke into a run behind her, arriving at the gates as Phantom cantered through them. "Johnny!" they squealed, grabbing at him before he could dismount. He jumped off the stallion and hugged them with a jubilant laugh. "This is wonderful! You must see Mademoiselle Charmaine! And Papa, too!"

A stable-hand hurried over and took charge of Phantom. John slung his knapsack over his shoulder and walked up the lawns, the girls on either side of him. Jeannette's arm was clasped tightly around his waist, and Yvette beamed up at him as if he were a mirage that might disappear if she dared to look away.

"So, what have I missed while I was gone?" he asked, squeezing Jeannette's shoulder.

"Papa spends Saturdays with us," she gushed, "and we have ball dresses!"

"I'm the bookkeeper for the mill!" Yvette interjected.

"We went to Espoir, and Mademoiselle Charmaine can ride Dapple now!"

John was gladdened by their enthusiasm. Their joyous reception always made him feel welcome here, that this *was* his home. He pulled them closer, wondering where Charmaine was.

Charmaine stepped out of the house, adjusting her bonnet as she went. Her heart caught in her throat. There was John, walking toward her! Her eyes feasted on him: the cap cocked to the back of his head, his wavy brown hair falling on his brow, his self-assured gait. In that rush of joy, the urge to fly down the steps and throw her arms around him was overwhelming, and she had all she could do to hold to her spot. He looked up as he arrived with the twins at the foot of the portico, and their eyes met.

He drank in the sight of her: the plain, well-worn riding dress, her shaking fingers belatedly tying the strings to her bonnet under her chin, and her large brown eyes betraying her excitement to see him. Instantly, he was indescribably pleased he had come back, and he inhaled slowly, relishing the ineffable elation expanding in his breast. He *had* missed her, more than he'd realized. Jeannette scurried into the house, eager to tell her father the good news. He hardly noticed.

"You look well, Mademoiselle," he said in that crisp voice, long denied.

Blood thundered in her ears, and her heart pounded in her chest. His regard was warm as he and Yvette climbed the steps. A crooked smile broke across his lips, bathing her in another wave of happiness. "I am," she breathed, tilting her head back to study his face. "How are you?"

"I'm fine—just fine."

"You've come home for the celebration?" she commented more than asked.

"Yes," he replied, "my father invited me. Apparently, he'd like to mend some fences." She nodded, and his eyes went to Mercedes, who had stepped out of the house with her. "Good morning, Miss Mercedes."

Mercedes murmured a quick greeting and looked at the ground.

Charmaine suffered a pang of jealousy before remembering Mercedes had made John's acquaintance through Anne London. She was delighted when he chuckled and turned back to her.

"Will you be staying long?" she asked, hopeful the answer was yes.

"That depends," he replied, sizing up her attire. "I see you are on your way out."

Charmaine was about to respond when the front door opened and Frederic joined them. His eyes glinted, and his smile widened.

"John," he started, "welcome home."

John fought a sure and congealing repugnance, the impulse to retreat.

"Come inside," Frederic motioned. "There is cool lemonade in the study."

John hesitated, then forced himself forward. The twins tagged along, but Frederic stopped them. "Girls, go for your ride with Miss Ryan and Miss Wells. You will have time with your brother when you return."

"Come, girls," Charmaine commanded, "the ponies are waiting, and if we dally any longer, it will be too hot to go."

They reluctantly capitulated, turning away from their beloved brother. But Charmaine's eyes followed the men into the house. There was Agatha, standing in the foyer, her hate-filled regard reserved for John. Then, the door closed.

Mercedes stepped nearer Charmaine. "You're in love with him," she murmured close to her ear.

Charmaine spun round, shocked. "Don't be silly!"

Mercedes chuckled knowingly. "No wonder Paul is just a 'good friend.'"

* * *

Paul greeted John with a handshake, amazed he had returned. John clasped an arm around his shoulder. "So, Paul, this is your big week. Are you ready?"

"Never more in my life," he replied, surprised by John's affable manner.

Anne descended the staircase and turned her head aside in blatant disdain when she saw John. That suited him fine.

Everyone stepped into the study, rejoining Stephen Westphal, whose anxious eyes darted from John to Frederic, a folder clasped tightly to his chest. Frederic resumed his seat behind the desk, while Paul and John took the chairs across from it. Agatha walked over to the French doors, and Anne perched on the settee. Felicia scurried in with lemonade and poured everyone a glass.

"I gather you came on Paul's ship," Frederic said. "How was the crossing?"

"The sea was calm, the wind strong. We made the voyage in no time. A fine packet, Paul. Those makeshift apartments were very cozy. When your guests got a glimpse of Dulcie's, they ran back to the captain to make reservations for the week!" Agatha frowned, but John's deviltry only intensified. "Yes, a fine vessel, perfect once the leaks are repaired, but there are always flaws on a virgin voyage."

Paul's eyes darkened apprehensively. "Leaks? There shouldn't be any—"

"Not to worry, Paulie," John chuckled. "Everything was fine."

The jest registered, and Paul laughed, too. "What is the latest news from the States, John?"

"That depends where you are in the States."

"Why not start in New York?" Agatha interjected, her gaze steely upon him.

He eyed her suspiciously. "What would you like to know, Auntie?"

"It's not what I'd like to know," she returned smugly, her voice sweet, "it is more a matter of what your father would like to know."

Befuddled, Frederic's attention shifted from his son to Agatha.

"Stephen," she continued, "why don't you tell John what you've learned about his dealings in New York?"

Westphal inhaled. Agatha was supposed to divulge the information he'd garnered. But Frederic's eyes were leveled on him, a hardened regard Stephen knew all too well. There'd be no release until Frederic's curiosity had been satisfied. Stephen glanced at John, who wore the same expression, and he shifted uncomfortably, not wanting to get on either man's bad side. "Perhaps we can discuss this at some other time . . ." he sputtered.

"No, we'll discuss it right now," Frederic pronounced, his confusion growing. He thought to shoo Anne out of the room, but what was the point? She could extract the story from her father or even Agatha, if she didn't know it already.

Westphal cleared his throat. "My banking contacts have mentioned things . . ."

"Go on," Frederic pressed in irritation.

"They've written John has been investing heavily in canals and railroads in the North, using Duvoisin monies withdrawn from the Bank of Virginia."

Paul glared at John in astonishment. Westphal hesitated to say more.

"And?" Frederic urged.

The man cleared his throat again. "I also have it on good authority John is an abolitionist. He has ties to the Underground Railroad—provides them with financial support."

"Underground Railroad?" Frederic queried, the term unfamiliar.

"The name hasn't made its way into print yet, but it's an association many Southerners whisper about."

"What exactly is it?"

"A group of Southern and Northern abolitionists who aid and abet runaway slaves. It is rumored John is one of them—that he uses Duvoisin vessels to transport slaves from Richmond to New York."

"Is this true?" Frederic asked, his eyes shooting to John. Memories of his early days with Colette took hold. She was in this room, with them right now. He could feel her at his side.

"Have you taken to spying on me now, Father?" John asked, his voice mildly amused, though his face was stern. "Is this why you invited me back? I'm not here five minutes and already I'm under interrogation. Why the inquisition?"

"Is it true about the Virginia bank accounts?"

"Yes, it's true. Did your brilliant Mr. Westphal tell you there was a bank panic last year? That hundreds of farmers lost everything when the U.S. bank was dissolved? But not you, Father. Why? Because of the Northern securities I purchased in your name *before* the panic. Your banker, Mr. Westphal, hasn't noticed you're already the richer for it. No, he's been too busy discrediting me to see past the nose on his face!"

"Since when are we in the canal and railroad business?" Frederic demanded.

"I thought I was in charge on the mainland, Father," John jeered. "Shipping is shipping. What does it matter if it's ships or canals or trains? Whenever I've found a sound investment, I've purchased it—with my own money, as well."

"Why not make these investments in the South, where we have our roots?"

"The South as it stands will not last," John replied. "I'll be long gone from Virginia when it comes tumbling down. If it were up to me, I'd transfer all your assets north."

"And what of this 'Underground Railroad'?"

"I support it," John replied simply, "with my money."

Frederic sighed in exasperation. Ten years ago he'd waged this battle with Colette. John had embraced her convictions, while he had suavely sidestepped them.

"And you've used Duvoisin vessels to smuggle runaways?" he pursued.

"Occasionally."

Frederic's anger began to percolate. "If this gets out, it will be devastating to my holdings and trade in Virginia. Harboring runaways is against the law! Imagine what the authorities will do if they find you've been pirating them!"

Agatha gloated. At last, they were getting somewhere.

"You are right," John declared, satisfied when Frederic's expression turned to one of bewilderment. "So, I have a solution. I'm resigning as manager of your Virginia estates, and I demand you remove my name from your will."

"John—" Paul sputtered "—you can't do that!"

"Oh yes, I can."

Anguished, Frederic murmured, "Now you use my wealth to thwart me?"

"I've learned well from you, Father," John answered flatly.

"I won't do this," he rejoined.

Agatha stepped forward. "Why not, Frederic?" she demanded, afraid John might rescind his request. She indicated Paul. "Surely you can place it in more worthy—competent—hands?"

"Silence, woman!" Frederic thundered, before turning back to John. "Why—why are you doing this?" he beseeched, nonplussed.

"Because the price of your great fortune has been evil, misery, and tears," John replied in disgust. "I've had my fair share of it, and I don't want it anymore."

Frederic gaped at him, reluctance and dismay branded on his face. Agatha beamed ecstatically. Anne leaned forward, savoring the unfolding story.

"I can accept your resignation," Frederic said, "but I will not remove you from my will."

"If you leave my name on it," John sneered, "I swear, on the day you die, I will turn every parcel, every packet, every penny over to the Underground Railroad. Why not give it all to Paul? He deserves it far more than I do."

Paul shifted uncomfortably, looking from Frederic to John. "John—" he started again, but his brother waved him off, his eyes fixed on Frederic.

"John is right, Frederic," Agatha desperately chimed in. "You'd be wise to agree to this proposal immediately. It is the right thing to do. You have overlooked your worthy son for far too long."

"Agatha! I said—"

"For once we agree, Auntie," John concurred, cutting his father off. "What I don't understand is why you're such an advocate for my brother. He hates you as much as I do. One might think you were his mother."

Paul's eyes shot from Agatha's injured face to his astonished father, a spark struck, a thought ignited.

"Frederic, you have no choice!" Agatha pursued irately. "Would you really see the family fortune tossed to the dogs? Why do you hesitate?"

"Silence, woman!" Frederic bellowed a third time. He studied John sadly. The chasm between them was growing wider.

John watched Frederic, confused by the genuine regret on his face. Why had the man spent the better part of a lifetime setting him aside, pushing him away, scorning him, even undermining him, if he really cared?

"You leave me no choice," Frederic muttered, echoing a triumphant Agatha.

"Don't worry, Father," John offered sarcastically, "I do have one redeeming request of you."

"What is it?"

"Guardianship of my sisters when you die. They are all that matter to me."

Frederic's eyes welled with tears, but he quickly hid them behind the hand he brought to his brow. Once composed, he nodded his assent.

"I'm sure Edward Richecourt will be here this week," John continued. "Shall I make the arrangements for a meeting with him, or will you?"

"I will make the arrangements," Frederic rasped, his plaintive eyes going to a stunned Paul. With a nod, John pushed out of his seat and left.

Frederic turned on Westphal. "Why wasn't I given this information sooner?"

"I—I—" Westphal sputtered, red-faced. He didn't want to betray Agatha because she had paid him well for the information.

"Stephen," Paul jumped in, "we can finish up later—at your house."

"Very good," Westphal replied gratefully, hastily grabbing his portfolio and shoving the folder into it as he scurried from the room, Anne on his heels.

Frederic waited out their departure, his fury rising. "I warned you, Agatha," he snarled, "yet you deliberately interfere with John and me time and again!"

Her chin jabbed up, but she did not speak.

Paul stepped between them. "Is what John said true, Father?" he asked, eyeing them both, reading their expressions as they glared at one another.

"Is what true?" Frederic asked, bewildered again.

"About Agatha."

Frederic bowed his head, but Agatha smiled victoriously.

"You *are* my mother, aren't you?" Paul demanded, incredulous, yet enlightened.

"Tell him, Frederic," Agatha pressed. "Isn't it time your grown son know the truth about us?"

Frederic looked at Paul's harrowed face, a testimony to the total betrayal he now felt. "Paul, I need to explain. It's a complicated story."

"I'm sure it is," Paul snorted, holding up a hand to hold him silent, "especially with all the lies you built around it. But I don't want to hear it now! I have guests to greet and the reception tomorrow. I don't want my plans for the week spoiled by this odious admission. I've worked too hard!"

* * *

John entered his room and threw his knapsack on the bed. He'd walked into an ambush! With his head pounding, he considered returning to town and boarding the first ship to Richmond, but he couldn't disappoint his sisters, or Charmaine. He sat down and massaged his brow, breathing deeply to calm himself. The entire conversation came back to him now, and he wondered whether Westphal had taken his father by surprise. After all, Agatha had prompted Westphal's diatribe. Yes, she hated him, but John hadn't realized just how much until now. Though his taunting infuriated her, he doubted that alone motivated today's tactics. There had to be another reason. *But what?*

When Anne London dined with her father later that evening, he forbade her to repeat a word of what she'd learned that afternoon, threatening to reveal her best-kept secrets if she dared to jeopardize his position on Charmantes.

Sunday, April 1, 1838, 4 a.m.

Paul could not sleep, yesterday's incredible revelation magnifying in the darkness. He'd avoided his father for the remainder of the day and brushed aside two Caribbean farmers with whom he should have made time to speak. His mind was not on ships, steam propulsion or export commodities. The looming week was suddenly a heavy yoke, a burden to bear. He paced his bedchamber, grinding his left fist into the palm of his right hand, grappling with the truth he'd have to come to grips with and shake off, lest all his hard work go to waste. Agatha was his mother—the mother who was supposed to be dead. According to his father, she was dead! It wasn't possible! But it was logical.

How had it happened? What had brought them together? Had Agatha offered Frederic succor after the death of his beloved Elizabeth? Was that it? But it couldn't be. He was told he was older than John. Or was that another lie, too? Why did he even want to know?

You don't want to know, he tried to convince himself, *not yet anyway. Set it aside. Don't let it distract you.*

He needed air. With that thought, he left his rooms for the stable. He saddled up Alabaster and rode the stallion hard into town. Once there, he boarded the *Bastion,* the ship that had brought John to Charmantes. Standing on her empty decks, he cast his eyes beyond the thin peninsula, out to sea. A light rain was falling, and he breathed deeply of the salty air, letting the gentle drops wash away his turbulent thoughts. *You will forget. Until the week's end, you must forget!*

Frederic lay abed, listlessly contemplating the ceiling. *Paul knew . . . he finally knew.* Frederic had dreaded this day, dreaded it with a passion. He had lied to Paul all those years ago. When the bright five-year-old found out he and John did not share the same mother, telling Paul his mother had died as well seemed the simplest, least painful, solution. It also protected Agatha. She was married and living a respectable life; it became important to keep the secret for her sake. Though Paul had never asked about her again, Frederic wondered if he longed to know more. Evidently, he did. Frederic recalled the torment in his son's eyes, and he worried where his dishonesty would lead.

Then there was John. This afternoon's fiasco had been another setback, not the step forward for which Frederic had hoped. Though he'd always allowed John free rein on all mainland business matters, he'd been embarrassed to learn about the family's financial business through Westphal, so he'd lost his temper. Still, he'd endured far worse where John was concerned. The investments, though not traditional, were sound enough, reassuring Frederic the Duvoisin fortune was in capable hands. As for the abetting of runaway slaves, he had grave misgivings. Yet now, hours later, he knew John's crusade had nothing to do with retaliation or revenge. It was a cause in which John believed.

Frederic sighed deeply. Thanks to Agatha, both sons were angry with him. Somehow, he had to repair the damage. He would begin by speaking with John, alone. After that, he'd direct his attentions to Paul. For the first time, the son who had always honored him was more difficult to approach. He'd respect Paul's wishes and wait until the week was over.

When John had first returned to Virginia last October, fitful sleep and fragmented dreams tormented him, despite long days of strenuous work. Nearly every night, he had nightmares that transported him to remote places where he roamed aimlessly along unfamiliar streets and spiritless strangers passed him. They were all ugly. He would turn a corner onto a crowded thoroughfare littered with refuse, carts, and animals. In the midst of the throng, he could see Pierre, lost. The boy's face was streaked with dirt and tears, his clothes tattered and filthy, his eyes searching the faces around him. As John hastened to rescue him, the boy would move just beyond his reach until the pushing and shoving bodies swallowed him. Ultimately, his powerlessness would startle him awake.

By Christmas, the dreams were all but gone. Then, on the night of Michael's visit to Freedom, the harrowing dream recurred, and it plagued him relentlessly over the days that followed. But unlike before, when he dismally attributed the nightmare to his guilty conscience, this time he felt it meant something more. Inexplicably, it pointed to Charmantes, telling him he had rushed back to Virginia too quickly—that he would never put the past behind him until, for some unfathomable reason, he returned home. Stranger still, he slept peacefully every night once he decided to return. That is, until tonight . . .

Succumbing to fatigue, bizarre images beset him. Colette was coming to him again, the first time since last October. She sent the breeze as her scout, clearing the way into this room of clandestine encounters. The drapes billowed with a gust of wind, coaxing the French doors open. John turned on his side, determined to ignore her, but the air was already imbued with her scent, and her shadow fell upon the threshold. He didn't want her there, but she seemed to need him tonight. As she glided closer, he rose, transfixed by the blue eyes desperately beckoning him. As he lifted his hand to touch her, she grabbed it, pulling him across the room toward the French doors. But he planted his feet firmly and wrenched free. When she grabbed at his hand again, he cried out as if burned, and awoke.

He stared, unseeing, at the shadowed ceiling. Had he screamed? He threw a forearm over his eyes, feeling the sweat on his brow. The bedclothes were damp from perspiration. He sat up, his head spinning and stomach nauseous. Inhaling deeply, he rose and went to the bowl and pitcher on the nightstand. He splashed water in his face and on his chest and braced his hands on the edges of the table to steady the lurching room.

Charmaine could not sleep, and in the early hours of dawn, she abandoned her futile sheep counting and Hail Marys. Pulling on her robe, she left her bedchamber and went downstairs. Perhaps a book from the study and a warm glass of milk would do the trick.

The house was deathly quiet, but to her surprise, she found John seated at the desk in the study, his eyes closed and head tilted back against the leather cushions. The lamp was burning low.

"John?" she whispered. "John?" she called again, touching his arm lightly when he did not respond.

Startled, his eyes flew open. "Thank you, Miss Ryan," he muttered, "the first bit of sleep I've had all night, and you've come to spoil it."

"I'm sorry," she sputtered, stung.

He leaned forward and propped a throbbing head in his hand, closing his eyes once again. In the awkward silence, she turned to leave, but his voice stopped her. "Why are you up and about at this hour?"

"I couldn't sleep, either," she replied, facing him. "My mind kept turning, and I couldn't stop it. Hasn't that ever happened to you?"

He was smiling now. "Far too often I'm afraid, my Charm."

She relaxed with his use of her pet name.

"Why couldn't you sleep?" he asked.

"I'm nervous about the coming week and the social graces needed to see it through."

"You'll be fine," he reassured. "Are you attending the ball on Saturday?"

"Oh yes!" she exclaimed eagerly, her eyes lighting up. "Maddy Thompson has sewn the most exquisite gown! The fittings have taken hours and I've had to stand stock-still the entire time."

His smile grew in proportion to her enthusiasm, his chin propped on a fist, his eyes sparkling. "Will you accompany the twins, or do you have an escort?"

She hesitated. *Is he offering to take me? Why am I reluctant to tell him?* "Paul has asked me," she said, battling a pang of disappointment.

His eyes betrayed no reaction. "I must admit I'm surprised. I thought the fair Lady London would be his consort. She was glued to his side yesterday."

"But he has invited me," Charmaine replied defensively.

"You must be pleased."

"I am. We've gotten to know each other better over the past months."

John frowned slightly.

"Is there something wrong with that?" she probed.

"Nothing at all. Has he made any plans with you beyond this week?"

She knew what he was implying and did not answer.

"You realize, of course," he expounded, "that after this celebration is over, Paul will be living on Espoir. You will see much less of him."

The observation hit her head-on. She hadn't thought of it before, but it was true. "The future will take care of itself," she said. "I will have to wait and see."

"You've done a lot of 'waiting and seeing' with my brother."

When she appeared indignant, he harassed her further. "Do you still harbor hopes for him?"

"Should I not?" she asked directly. "What is your advice?"

John grew quiet, and she could tell he debated what to say. "I don't think my brother is ready to make a commitment to any woman," he replied. "He has yet to understand himself, and he won't be ready to marry until he does."

"What do you mean by that?" she asked, baffled by his last remark.

"It doesn't matter," he said. "To state it more simply, he has had plenty of time with you and hasn't proposed marriage yet. His romantic overtures could turn out to be a seduction and nothing more. That is my honest assessment of the matter, but you have heard it before."

"Your opinion could be wrong."

"It could be," he conceded, thinking his advice had once again fallen on deaf ears. The room fell silent. "So how long are you willing to 'wait and see,' Charmaine, before you grow tired of it?" he asked pointedly.

"He is not my only prospect," she objected, realizing how foolish she appeared.

"He's not?" John teased. "Who else has arrived on the scene? Have you been kissing someone behind my brother's back?"

"He's not the only man I've ever kissed!" she insisted heatedly, blushing when his brow rose in merriment, the discourse reminiscent of their early days.

"*Now* we have the confessions," he pursued devilishly. "Who else have you kissed, my Charm? You can tell me. Wade Remmen, perhaps?"

"I've kissed you!" she gushed, annoyed he'd forgotten the two occasions he'd taken her in his arms. Belatedly, she realized she'd put her foot squarely into her mouth.

He leaned back and chuckled. "Ah, but that doesn't count . . . Or does it?"

"Of course it does!" she expostulated. "I mean, no—it doesn't!"

His sagacious grin widened. "Then why did you mention it?" he asked.

But as her mouth flew open again, he waved off her retort and rushed on. "I think we had better drop this conversation, because you are growing annoyed with me, and I'd hate for the week to be spoiled so early on."

"What about you?" she rejoined, her chin lifted in miffed vexation.

"What about me?"

"Will you be escorting a lady to the ball?"

"I have no plans yet. Who knows? Perhaps they'll change."

She wondered what he meant, but didn't ask. She grew serious. "Will you be staying on after the ball?"

"I'll be returning to Virginia."

"Right away?"

"I might stay a few days longer—for the twins, but not many." He rose from the desk. "I'm going to retire. I'd like to get some sleep before everyone begins to stir. Goodnight, Charmaine."

After he'd left, she stood in the center of the study for a long time. She abandoned the idea of a book and sought her own room, determined to get dressed. She wouldn't be able to sleep now.

Three days' sailing and the unpleasant confrontation with his father caught up with John, and he fell into a deep sleep. He rose after lunch and found nearly everyone had left the house to attend the kick-off festivities in town. He was pleased; he needed the afternoon to himself. Memories of Pierre were strong, so after he ate, he saddled up Phantom and rode to the family cemetery to contemplate, pay his respects, and come to terms with the past. He meandered around the island for the rest of the day, visiting old haunts and letting go.

Right now, the night air was balmy, and the leaves rustled, riding the easterly breeze. Crickets chattered in the grass, and the moonlight cast long shadows on the lawns. Voices from the drawing room carried on the gentle wind. Since George and Mercedes had gone off for a walk, and Charmaine had disappeared with the twins, John shunned Agatha and Anne, his father, and Paul, for the peaceful haven of the portico.

Charmaine was headed for the drawing room when she heard Anne London's pretentious laugh. She walked straight to the main doors instead; she'd enjoy the refreshing breeze before she retired.

She was surprised to find John sitting on the top step of the portico, his elbows propped on his knees, his fingers entwined between them. He turned to see who was coming out of the house.

"I'm sorry," she apologized, turning back toward the doors, even though she wanted to sit down next to him. "I didn't know you were out here."

"You don't have to leave, Charmaine," he called after her, halting her step. "I was enjoying the peace and quiet. Come, sit with me."

She gladly joined him.

"We didn't see you all day," she commented, arranging her skirts.

"The journey caught up with me, and I slept late," he replied. "Why aren't you abed? You didn't sleep well last night, either."

"I'm not tired. I suppose I won't feel tired until the week is over."

John smiled at her ingenuous remark, his eyes coming to rest on her face.

"How did you fare with your father yesterday?" she asked, daring to broach the subject that had slipped her mind last night.

"It didn't go well," he replied. "Westphal had a long list of my latest transgressions. My father and I were at it again in all of five minutes. I don't understand why he invited me back."

"Your father didn't ask Westphal for that list," Charmaine replied, her anger swift and sure. "Agatha did."

"Really?" John asked, surprised she'd come to the same conclusion he had.

"She had Westphal get information on me, too," Charmaine

explained. "He's the one who found out about my father, and Agatha tried to use it to have me dismissed. Fortunately for me, it didn't make any difference to Colette or Paul."

She studied John for his reaction to Colette's name, but he remained impassive. "It was fortunate for the children, too," he said.

"Not if it had fallen to Agatha. She'll stop at nothing to get rid of anybody she doesn't like. I'd lay money down she instigated yesterday's confrontation sure as she plotted the one last October. Your father wasn't sending the twins to a boarding school, but she made the girls believe he was, knowing Yvette would run to tell you. I can't tolerate her. I don't know why your father married her."

"He married her to punish Colette."

Charmaine grew quiet, the silence catching his attention. "I don't think so," she replied softly, debating her next thoughts. She was treading on dangerous territory. "He loved her, John."

John scoffed at the assertion, impelling her to speak her mind. "I don't know if I'll ever understand the relationship your father and Colette shared, but I'm certain he loved her." She hesitated before adding, "And Colette told me she loved him."

"Of course she'd tell you that," John said derisively, "to keep up appearances."

"Perhaps," Charmaine replied, realizing John wasn't willing to entertain such an idea. There was no point in pressing it. "Still, your father didn't have a confrontation in mind when he invited you home. I know he is very sorry about what happened. He has changed since you left: coming out of his isolation, taking charge of business again, and spending time with the girls."

"It didn't appear as if he'd changed yesterday," John mused.

"Perhaps he was taken off guard." She sighed deeply. "He invited you back to make amends. I'm certain of it."

John mulled over her words; they echoed Michael's sentiments. "I trust what you say, my Charm," he ceded. "Still, he's off to a pretty bad start."

"I'm sure he is, but old habits die hard, so give him a chance."

She thought to lighten the mood and changed the subject. "What are your latest transgressions?"

"The list is long, my Charm," he chuckled. "I wouldn't want to bore you."

"Then tell me about Virginia. You never talk about it."

"I go back and forth between Richmond and the plantation."

"Do you like it there?"

"I hate it: the slave business, the classes, the games one must play to survive. But, a few people there depend on me, so I'm bound to it."

"What would you rather be doing?"

"Live in New York, play the piano, be a composer. But there isn't any money in it, and I like having money too much to do without it."

Charmaine laughed. "You don't realize how true your words are. You've never been poor, but I have. There's no going back!"

John laughed, too. When their mirth died down, she asked, "Why do you like New York so much?"

"It will be the center of the world before long—bigger than London, bigger than Paris. In New York, if you've got ambition, you've got a chance. The only thing to hold you back is yourself. In New York, you can start over."

"Is that why you go there—to start over?"

"Perhaps, but right now, I travel between two worlds."

"I'd love to see it," she stated with conviction, turning her regard to him.

"And I'd love to show it to you," he replied, his eyes captivating her.

She could not look away, thrilled by the plummeting lurch in her stomach, her quickening pulse, and her heart thudding in her breast. Slowly, almost imperceptibly, John leaned in to her.

The door opened behind them, and Paul stepped out of the house. "Here you are!" he exclaimed. "Jeannette had a bad dream and is calling for you."

Blushing, Charmaine quickly stood and, without a backward glance, rushed past him. Paul watched her go, then considered his brother. But John had turned back to the lawns, apparently disinterested in Charmaine's departure.

Monday, April 2, 1838

"No, John," Paul said, "they are not paddlewheels. The European engineers are manufacturing what they've termed a corkscrew propeller, which they claim will cut Atlantic crossing time by half."

"Well, if locomotives are possible, I suppose anything is," John rejoined.

"Do you realize what this could mean for Duvoisin shipping?"

Charmaine listened to their civil banter, amazed by it. The girls were playing outside, and she could keep an eye on them from the open French doors, so she meandered to the drawing room casement and paused in the archway.

Presently, Paul was asking John's opinion on the New York guests and how to persuade them to use his fleet for their exports. The Duvoisin barristers were due to arrive shortly, and he was waiting for them. When a carriage rolled up and two distinguished gentlemen stepped out, she assumed it was them.

One man was middle aged, of medium height, with liberal touches of gray in his hair and beard. The younger was short, but good-looking in a pretty sort of way: with blue eyes, long aristocratic nose, protruding chin, and oiled-down blond hair.

"Mr. Pitchfork," John exclaimed, extending a hand to the elder solicitor when George showed them into the drawing room, "you've arrived!"

The man's face twisted into a grimace, but his associate snickered. George laughed outright. "I'd appreciate the use of my proper name," the lawyer replied curtly, "Richecourt—Edward Richecourt. When will you realize you've worn out that witless name?"

"When you've worn out getting angry at it," John quipped.

George chuckled again, and Richecourt's assistant joined in.

Though the latter had never met John before, he'd heard talk of the man's acerbic wit. He was quite funny.

Scratching the back of his head, John turned mischievous eyes to the young lawyer. "Who's your friend here, Pitchie?"

"This is our most promising junior associate," Richecourt offered, ignoring John's gibe, "Geoffrey Elliot III."

"There are three of you?" John exclaimed, eyeing the younger man.

Geoffrey extended a hand to John, still chuckling in camaraderie. "My father was Geoffrey Elliot II."

"Ah, that explains it: if at first you don't succeed . . ." John shrugged. "Are you the one who consigned two shiploads of sugar here when my export broker took ill last January?" he continued, leveling his gaze on Elliot while ignoring Paul's deepening frown.

"Why, yes, I am!" Elliot replied proudly.

"And where do you suppose those boatloads of sugar came from, Geoff?"

Momentary confusion washed over Elliot's face as John shook his hand. "I'm pleased to make your acquaintance, Mr. Idiot," he declared merrily. "What else are you promising at, Junior?"

Elliot's face dropped in injured astonishment. "Why—I'm a lawyer. I'm a graduate of William and Mary—I've—I've—I've—"

"Yes—yes—yes?" John asked unimpressed, the devil in his eyes.

"Mr. Duvoisin!" Elliot rejoined angrily, his back stiffening. "I warn you now, I am not Mr. Richecourt! I'll not tolerate name-calling. Do so again, and I'll not hesitate to remonstrate you!"

"Mr. Idiot," John cut in, "I don't question your ability to remonstrate or reprobate. I'm concerned with your ability to contemplate and concentrate. And while you ruminate on that, this will make you fulminate: tell me, do you ejaculate when you mastur—"

"We get the idea, John," Paul cut in sharply, averting his face from Elliot as he crossed the room; he didn't dare look at George, who was howling hysterically. Instead, he turned to Richecourt. "Welcome to Charmantes," he greeted, once he could speak without laughing. "Sit down and make yourselves comfortable. I'll ring for refreshments. No doubt you're weary from the journey."

As they found seats, Paul turned to the bell-pull, casting murderous eyes upon John, who smiled sheepishly back at him. Elliot glared at John in utter disbelief, his face beet red, but he didn't dare open his mouth, lest he be cut down quickly.

John is in rare form today, Charmaine thought. She wondered why he called Mr. Richecourt "Mr. Pitchfork." There had to be a reason.

Richecourt summarized the business matters he would address in detail later on in the week, then eyed John, who lounged in an armchair, thumbing through a magazine, his booted legs propped on the low table. "John," he called, "Geoffrey has prepared some important documents at your broker's request."

"Really?"

"Yes," Geoffrey jumped in, composed and ready to begin anew, "and I will personally bring them back to Richmond. Mr. Bradley needs them posthaste if he is to finalize agreements before others step in to undercut your price." He placed his valise on the table and fished out a thick stack of papers, a quill, and a bottle of ink. "Here, I can show you where to sign."

"Leave them with me, Geffey," John replied, "I want to read them first."

"I assure you everything is in shipshape order, just as your broker specified." He dipped the pen and extended it to John. "Now, allow me—"

"No, Geffey, I'll read them first," John insisted, "lest I end up shipping ladies' undergarments to West Point instead of tobacco to Europe."

Elliot's face reddened again.

The twins came skipping across the porch, petitioning Charmaine to take them into town to fetch their dresses. When she agreed, she caught Geoffrey Elliot's interested gaze on her. "We'll have to take the carriage," she said.

Yvette nodded, then turned to her brother. "Johnny? Will you come, too?"

"Yes, I'll come," he agreed, happy to disengage himself from the pompous Geoffrey Elliot III. "Will you show me your dresses?" he asked. "Or will you hide them away until Saturday?"

"We'll show you!" Jeannette exclaimed. "They came all the way from Paris! Stepmother ordered them for us last fall, but we've grown since then, and Mrs. Thompson had to make quite a few adjustments. I can't wait to try mine on!"

"And what of Mademoiselle Charmaine? Will she model hers as well?"

Paul's eyes shot to Charmaine. He had yet to see the expensive finery.

"Why?" Yvette questioned.

"I want to see if it meets with my approval," John replied.

Paul's scowl darkened, and Charmaine's cheeks burned, knowing the twins waited for her to respond. When she didn't, John only chuckled. "I'll ask Gerald to ready the carriage," he offered, tossing the magazine onto the table.

"But, Mr. Duvoisin," Geoffrey objected, "what about your contracts?"

"Don't get your knickers twisted, Geffey," he called over his shoulder, already out the door, "or there won't be a Geoffrey Elliot IV."

Paul watched as Charmaine and the twins followed, disconcerted by the expression on Charmaine's face. She looked pleased. He'd seen that expression a few times already this week, and he didn't like it—he didn't like it at all.

John heard the twins' voices as he climbed the stairs, and he strode to the open bedroom doorway to say goodnight. He was surprised to find his father there, sitting on Jeannette's bed, telling them a story about a gentleman pirate, Frederic's father, Jean Duvoisin II.

Apparently, he was tucking them into bed. Perhaps this transformation Charmaine had talked about yesterday *was* real.

"Did he truly steal ships and plunder treasures?" Jeannette asked.

"He always claimed he did," Frederic chuckled. "But I think he exaggerated a bit for my sake. What he actually did was look the other way when pirate ships entered Charmantes' coves. They found safe haven here, and in return, they didn't attack my father's merchant ships."

Frederic looked up to find John standing in the doorway. They hadn't spoken since Saturday afternoon, and he didn't want the week to go on like this, cringing again with the memory of Saturday's dispute. If the mood remained strained, John would leave for Virginia as soon as Paul's gala ended.

"Come in, John," he encouraged with a smile. "I was telling Yvette and Jeannette about their grandfather."

"He was a pirate!" Yvette exclaimed as John hesitated and then stepped across the threshold, settling on the end of her bed.

"So I've been told," John replied mildly.

Frederic's eyes danced. "And your brother is following in his footsteps," he declared, looking pointedly at John and gaining all of their quizzical regards.

"He is?" Yvette queried.

"First of all, he's named after his grandfather. Jean means John."

"But Johnny is not a pirate, Papa," Jeannette reasoned.

"He *is*—of sorts."

Again, Frederic's gleaming gaze met John's raised brow.

"But Johnny wouldn't smuggle diamonds and gold," Yvette countered, certain her father was telling a tall tale. "He's already rich!"

"There are other things to smuggle besides treasure, Yvette," Frederic replied. "But let us save that story for another night. It is time to turn down the lamps."

Despite their protests, he leaned heavily on his cane and rose from the bed. He doused the light and kissed them goodnight. He and John stepped into the hallway together.

As John turned toward his own chambers, Frederic called to him. "John, we have guests arriving during the week, brokers from Boston and New York. I've been told you suggested they contact Paul."

"I did," John nodded.

"Since you know these gentlemen, would you be willing to entertain them at the celebration Saturday night? I understand tensions run high between Southerners and Northerners these days, and I want everyone to keep a level head. I thought I'd have them at their own table with you seated there."

"That's fine, Father," John said.

Frederic hadn't moved, and John knew he had more to say. Finally he spoke, his voice earnest. "I'm glad you came home, John. I wasn't spying on you, and I didn't ask Westphal to get that information. I was as astonished as you."

"My aunt has been very busy, then. I'm not surprised. She has always hated me. I deserve it now, but I didn't when I was a child."

Frederic nodded. He thought about asking John to reconsider his request to be taken off the will, but stopped short of broaching the topic. He knew John had made up his mind, so he turned toward the stairs instead. "Goodnight, John."

"Goodnight, Father."

Tuesday, April 3, 1838

John rose early, but not early enough. His sisters were not in the nursery. He turned from the doorway, but had a change of heart and stepped into the room.

Unlike last night, all was peaceful. He was alone, alone with his memories. He crossed to Pierre's empty bed and sat gingerly. He caressed the pillow, remembering the last time he sat here.

Charmaine was three steps into the children's bedroom before she realized John was there. Embarrassed, he stood and turned away, wiping at his face with his forearm. She wanted to cross the chamber and comfort him, but knew he wanted to bury his sorrow, not reopen the healing wound. *Most times it's easier to cry than to laugh.* Now she understood, truly understood.

"We are going for a stroll. Would you like to come along?" she offered.

"No," he rasped. "I'd rather be alone today."

Charmaine hesitated, then turned away, leaving him to his mourning.

Wednesday, April 4, 1838

Charmaine grabbed the doorknob and pushed into the study, coming up sharply as she found herself in the midst of a meeting between John, Edward Richecourt, Geoffrey Elliot, and another man she did not recognize. All three men shifted in their seats as she entered, conversation suspended, their eyes fixed on her. She, in turn, regarded John, who lounged in the large desk chair, his elbows propped casually on the armrests, one booted leg crossed over his knee, and Jeannette's cat in his lap. Fleetingly, she thought he was angry, perhaps at her, for barging in so unceremoniously.

"I—excuse me," she stammered and began to back out of the room, groping behind her for the doorknob.

John's voice cut across her apology. "Miss Ryan, where are my sisters?"

She was stunned by his formality, the annoyance on his face.

"They are with your father. I had some time to myself."

"You mean leisure time," he corrected tersely.

"Yes," she capitulated, still taken aback. *Is this meeting confidential?*

"Miss Ryan, you are not paid for leisure time. So, since you have nothing to do right now, I will find something."

Charmaine stood dumbfounded. Was he Agatha in disguise or was he showing off in front of the lawyers? Maybe he was out of his mind.

"Come, sit beside me." As he leaned over to drag a chair nearer the desk, the cat leapt out of his lap. "Here is a pen and paper. Take notes on our discussion."

He couldn't be serious! She didn't know whether to frown or laugh.

"Come now, Miss Ryan," he pressed, "time is marching on."

He *was* serious, but she was too stupefied to reply. As she settled into the chair and took up the pen, she began to simmer. He *was* showing off!

John introduced her to the stranger, one Carlton Blake. He was good-looking and tipped his head, smiling suavely at her. He was about the same age as John, and she surmised he already knew John from the States.

Edward Richecourt resumed the conversation, and Charmaine was transfixed with this talk of prices and exports, supply and demand, contracts and deals, and she found herself enjoying this eye into the Duvoisin's world. She tried her best to take notes, but her pen struggled to keep pace with the issues that bounced back and forth, and changed on a dime. She wondered why John needed her there, noticing he'd taken up a quill as well.

As Carlton Blake turned the conversation to Midwest shipping via the Erie Canal, Charmaine became aware of John's eyes upon her. She was wary of meeting his gaze, but the caramel orbs were warm now as he reached over nonchalantly, took her sheet of paper and looked over her notes, his chin poised upon thumb and forefinger. He tucked her paper under the one he'd been writing on and passed both sheets back to her. She looked down at his sloppy scrawl. *How long do you think it will take Geffey to ask me if I've signed his papers yet?* Her eyes flew from the paper to Geoffrey Elliot to John, whose face was expressionless as he listened to Mr. Blake. Charmaine read the next line. *I think Mr. Blake is enamored of you, my Charm. Perhaps I won't invest with him after all.* She smiled and looked at John. His eyes were trained on her, as if daring her to laugh first. Feeling a tickle bubbling forth, she looked down at the paper again. *Mr. Pitchfork has to relieve himself, but he'd rather sit there and hold it than ask to be excused.* Charmaine stole a sidelong glance at the man, who was squirming in his chair. She giggled, gaining the stoic stares of all three men, the room suddenly silent, save her laughter echoing off the walls. Highly embarrassed, she dropped her gaze to the paper, dramatizing great interest in it.

"Miss Ryan," John commented coolly, "is something amusing? Perhaps you'd like to share it with us?" He leaned cockily back in his chair.

"Only your handwriting," she responded smugly, lifting the paper as if she fully intended to hand it to Carlton Blake. "Perhaps your guests would like to see it. I think they'd agree."

"No," John countered, snatching it away. His eyes sparkled with admiration. "That won't be necessary. They've seen it before. May we proceed?"

"Certainly. Do excuse me."

She retrieved her paper and pretended at note taking, realizing now she'd been duped, John's stern demeanor bolstering the success of his prank. She looked at him again, but he'd turned his attention back to his associates. She eyed the paper in front of him, and noticed he'd written yet another line meant for her eyes only, the sheet tilted in her direction so she could read it. His last message held the promise of long-denied distraction: *If I can finish my business with these gentlemen today, I will take you and the girls on a riding excursion tomorrow.*

Thursday, April 5, 1838

When Jeannette spilled the beans at breakfast that they were going on a picnic, Geoffrey Elliot invited himself on the outing. Edward Richecourt followed suit with his wife, Helen. Anne insisted Paul had run himself ragged for the first half of the week and deserved a leisurely afternoon, then told Mercedes she'd require her services. And so it went, until the small party became a crowd.

They met at the paddock at eleven o'clock, where the grooms

were readying the horses. When Gerald emerged from the stable with Champion, Geoffrey stepped up to take the stallion's reins.

"I'm sorry," George intervened, "but that is Mercedes's mount today."

"Mr. Richards," Geoffrey objected, "do you think it advisable the young lady sit such a spirited animal? I am an experienced equestrian. Please, allow me to take charge of this one."

"She's an experienced rider, too," George replied, as Mercedes swung up into the saddle, "she'll be fine."

Geoffrey suspended his protestations when Gerald tied Phantom to the fence. John noticed his avid interest. "You'd best forget that idea, too, Geffey. Fang bites."

"Fang?" the lawyer queried. "Certainly, that's a queer appellation."

John snickered and glanced toward Yvette who was giggling softly. "Not so queer. I'll explain—later. That is, if you're fearless enough to look into Fang's mouth. Right now, Bud has found you a suitable mount: a nice docile gelding."

Geoffrey simmered, but didn't say a word as Bud led the horse, one usually reserved for the carriages, over to him. Though insulted, he took the reins.

Charmaine had just mounted Dapple when a fierce whinny drew her around. There was the old gelding, frantically circling in place, saddle askew, and a terrified Geoffrey hanging off his side. The lawyer gripped the horse's flank like a vise, one leg looped over the beast's back, the other tangled in the stirrup that had slipped under its belly. The horse continued to trumpet furiously, bucking to shake loose its clumsy burden, hind legs shooting out like pistons and jolting Geoffrey about like a kernel of popcorn in a hot kettle.

Paul guffawed at the pathetic spectacle, wiping away tears of mirth with his forearm. The twins and George were laughing, too, but not John. He stared in disbelief, uncharacteristically silent.

The beast pivoted once more, and George had seen enough.

Lunging forward, he grabbed the gelding's bridle, and the animal quickly settled, its anger evident only by its flattened ears.

Geoffrey hung on still, looking up at George helplessly.

"Let go," the latter ordered, but the red-faced solicitor just stared up at him from the horse's side. "Let go of the saddle and reins!"

Reluctantly, Geoffrey obeyed, dropping to the ground like a sack of potatoes. He kicked his foot free of the stirrup and stood, patting the dust from his trousers.

"I thought you were an experienced equestrian," George remarked dryly, pulling the saddle up and onto the gelding's back. "Or was that one of your maneuvers?"

John laughed loudly. "Good one, George!" he commended.

"That is not humorous!" Geoffrey protested testily, his humiliation gone. "Anyone can suffer a mishap. I assure you, I know what I am doing!"

"Then why didn't you tighten the girth strap?" George rejoined.

"That service should have been performed by the grooms."

"And it was. But any 'experienced' equestrian knows to check it again."

"Ah, leave him be, George," John interrupted, his merriment settling into a crooked grin. "He'll never admit he wanted to ride side-saddle."

An hour later, they were enjoying a scrumptious lunch on Charmantes' western beaches. Paul began complaining he was wasting the day away. "I should have used the time to take another group of guests on a tour of the island."

"How many times do they have to see Espoir to know you're well on your way to financial success?" John chided facetiously.

"Not Espoir. Charmantes. I should have shown them Charmantes."

"You're showing me," Anne London piped up. "Don't I count?"

Paul smiled blandly. "I was talking about the plantation," he responded, realizing he hadn't exploited his ten years' experience here.

John chuckled. "Don't show them the tobacco fields, or they will jump in the harbor and *swim* straight home! A tobacco farmer you're not. Those fields should have lain fallow for a while."

Paul only grunted.

When they finished eating, Yvette and Jeannette asked to go exploring. Only John and Charmaine seemed eager to join them, so they parted company, heading north to some caves John had discovered as a boy.

"This is more like it," he commented as they strolled down the beach. "That 'picnic' was about as bad as it could get. Then again, Auntie could have come along."

Yvette's brow gathered, as if she had just remembered something. "You know, Johnny, Auntie Agatha is up to something," she said.

John's curiosity was immediately piqued. "What do you mean, Yvette?"

"I've been keeping an eye on her."

"Keeping an eye on her?" Charmaine asked suspiciously. Since Pierre's death, the girl had abandoned her mischievous jaunts.

"Well . . ." Yvette faltered, reticent with Charmaine present. "It's only a suspicion. Sometimes Auntie acts very strange. That's all I meant."

They arrived at the caves, where the beaches turned craggy and cliffs jutted toward the sky. The tide was low, and John suggested they go inside. Charmaine decided to wait for them on the dry beach.

"So, Yvette," John pursued once they'd left her behind, "tell me about Auntie's strange behavior."

"You have to promise not to tell Mademoiselle Charmaine."

When he'd given his vow, she said, "Every Saturday at three o'clock, Auntie goes for a carriage ride. I thought it was strange because she always goes alone, without a driver. So one day, I pretended I was sick when Father took Jeannette into town. Then I followed her on Spook. She went to Father Benito's cabin. I peeked in the window. She gave him a pouch. I think there was jewelry inside."

John canted his head, eyeing her doubtfully. "What did she say to him?"

"The window was closed," she replied with the click of her tongue, annoyed she didn't have more information for him. "You believe me, don't you?"

John didn't know what to make of it. "Yvette, you're not to follow Agatha anywhere, understand? If she catches you, you'll be in trouble with Father."

"Yes," she brooded, disappointed with his reaction.

"Why do you call Mr. Richecourt, 'Mr. Pitchfork'?" Charmaine asked John as they walked back to the blanket.

John grinned. "My Charm, you're the first person who has asked me that."

"Well?" she pursued.

His smiled grew wicked. "Late one evening, I stopped by Mr. Richecourt's office and caught him in an unsavory act with a woman who was not his wife."

"And?" Charmaine pressed, though her cheeks were stained a deep crimson.

"And . . . when his face turned redder than yours, I pictured little horns growing out of his head, so I said to him, 'Mr. Richecourt, you little devil, you—from this day forward, I dub thee Pitchfork.' So there you have it. Lucky for him, you're the first person who's been intuitive enough to realize there's more to that name than meets the eye."

Charmaine giggled in spite of herself.

When they returned to the picnicking area, they found Paul and George arguing over who would tell John the news. "What news?" he asked, his eyes narrowing.

"Geoffrey rode off—on Phantom. After the gag you and the twins pulled on him with 'Fang,' I suppose he wanted to prove himself. He kept insisting your stallion was not too much horse for him to handle."

Cursing, John threw up his hands. "He's going to break his neck."

"Then you won't have to sign his papers," George offered.

"We had better find him before he breaks Phantom's neck," John added.

Edward Richecourt stepped forward. "May I make a suggestion?"

Paul, George, and John regarded him derisively. "Suggest away, Pitchie."

"Perhaps you're overreacting," he ventured with courteous concern, "Geoffrey will bring the beast back in good condition. He is an extremely gifted horseman."

"Geffey is an extremely gifted horse's ass," John rejoined.

"May I make another suggestion?" Richecourt offered with an infinite amount of patience. "We should establish a search party."

"That's a brilliant idea, Mr. Richecourt," John agreed.

"Thank you, John," Richecourt responded modestly, "I always knew a worthy compliment was not beyond your character."

"Neither is lying," John commented dryly. "Now, since a search party was your idea, I'm going to put you in charge of returning to the mansion and rustling up some stable-hands to go out on a search. Can you manage that?"

With his assent, John explained there was a shortcut back to the house. Richecourt was to proceed directly into the woods for about one hundred yards and make a left at the great cabbage palm tree. If he continued straight, he would arrive at the compound in about fifteen minutes time. Richecourt repeated the directions to the word and set off on his horse.

George and Paul looked at each other bemusedly.

"I never knew about that shortcut," George said, scratching the back of his head. "A great cabbage palm? Come to think of it, I don't see how those directions could possibly take him to the estate."

"They won't," John replied, low enough that Richecourt's wife couldn't hear, "but you know that old gelding—when he gets hungry, he'll wander back on his own, and we'll be spared Pitchie's brilliant suggestions for the remainder of the afternoon."

They found Geoffrey Elliot on the logging road a half-hour later. Phantom had jumped over a fallen tree at full gallop and had thrown Geoffrey some ten feet away. The horse lay whinnying in pain, abrasions on his chest, though by Mercedes's estimation, his legs were not broken. Geoffrey Elliot III's incessant groans echoed through the forest.

George stared down at him reproachfully. "How could you be so stupid? Don't you realize the value of that animal?"

It took them some time to coax Phantom to his feet. George did the same with Geoffrey, and they staggered back to the mansion. George suggested they send for Martin, the hostler, but Mercedes convinced John that she could nurse the stallion back to health, as she had seen her father do over the years.

Charmaine and the twins were on their way to dinner when they found Dr. Blackford treating a badly battered Geoffrey Elliot in the drawing room. Seated in the large armchair near the hearth, his hair was a tousled mess, flecked with leaves and twigs, one sprig hanging off the side of his head. His face was bruised and dirty. His bleached, starched shirt of that morning was speckled with blood and soiled beyond repair. His right pant leg was split down the seam.

"What happened?" Charmaine asked as the physician pulled the shirtsleeve off Geoffrey's right arm, ignoring his yelp of pain.

"He has fractured his arm," Blackford replied.

"But what happened?" Charmaine asked again.

"That blasted animal threw me!" Geoffrey cursed.

"At least you're not seriously injured," Charmaine comforted, turning reproving eyes on Yvette and Jeannette, who were snickering.

"Not seriously injured?" he protested. "I've never experienced such pain in my life! And the rest of them—why, they're all outside with that vicious beast. One would think it was he and not I who nearly sustained a broken neck!"

John, George, and Mercedes came in from the stables quite late and sat down to eat. The foyer door banged open. A few moments later, Edward Richecourt appeared in the dining room archway.

"Where have you been?" John asked, "I thought you were organizing a search party. We were about to send one out for you!"

"I'm afraid I got lost. Am I too late for dinner?"

Friday, April 6, 1838

"That should do it, Charmaine," Mercedes smiled, securing the last pin on the bodice of her new gown. "We can finish up after lunch."

Charmaine stepped down from the stool, glad to have an hour's respite, equally glad John had taken the girls swimming today. They would have found the morning, as well as the afternoon to come, tedious.

"I'd like you to look over the seating arrangements, before I hand them off to the staff," Agatha was saying to Paul as Charmaine and Mercedes passed through the dining room on their way to the kitchen.

"Where will I be seated?" Anne queried coquettishly, smiling for Paul.

"At the head table, next to Paul, of course," Agatha replied. "You are, after all, our special guest, your invitation written at his request. He will be honored to be your escort for the evening."

As Anne said, "That's wonderful!" Paul glared at Agatha in astonishment.

"Agatha—" he began. Instantly, he thought better of it, his eyes traveling helplessly to his father instead. But the exchange was lost on Frederic, who was absorbed in the newspaper at the side of his plate and hadn't heard a thing.

Charmaine sped up her steps, disappointment rushing in. She could feel Mercedes's regard on her, as well as Paul's, but she didn't dare look around. She declined lunch and fled back to her chambers via the servant's staircase. The new gown was spread out on the bed, but she had no desire to pick up needle and thread. She wanted to cry, but forced herself to the task, lest she give in to the building tears. Now, all her dreams had been laid to waste, again by the inveigling Agatha Duvoisin.

She grimaced when a knock resounded on her door. She could not ignore the second rap and opened it to a grim-faced Paul.

"Charmaine, may I speak with you?" He gestured to the hallway, but as she stepped out of her room, he scanned the corridor, frowning. Voices indicated the approach of guests. "Come," he said, "the gardens will offer some privacy."

He didn't speak again until they were near the center of the courtyard. "I'm sorry about what happened at lunch," he began, his hands clasped behind his back. "I had no idea what Agatha was planning."

She looked up at him, trying hard to conceal her dejection. "Perhaps you could tell Anne there has been a misunderstanding," she offered.

His brow darkened. "I'm afraid that would be in poor taste. Anne would be highly insulted. It could spill over to my guests and spoil the entire affair."

"I understand," she forced herself to say, head bowed.

"Charmaine," he tried to soothe, taking her hands in his, "I'm sorry about this. I really am." When she remained quiet, he felt helpless. He wanted to appease her. "I was looking forward to escorting you. I will make this up to you."

She looked up at him, befuddled, yet hurt, nonetheless.

"Charmaine . . ." he murmured, struggling to find the right words. He started again, fearful of what he was about to say, yet realizing the time was right. "Anne will be at my side tomorrow night, but I want you at my side always. Will you marry me?"

She was flabbergasted. Even though they had spent so much time together over the past months, she never expected this. She couldn't react, so incredible was his proposal. The heart-thumping excitement she should have experienced wasn't there, leaving her acutely confused.

Paul was disturbed by her muteness. He'd anticipated an immediate and unequivocal "yes." *Why is she so quiet?* "Well, Charmaine, you have me in suspense. What is your answer?"

"I—need to think about it," she replied, her face flushed.

"Very well," he muttered curtly, thinking all the while: *She is angry with me.* "I will give you some time."

When she didn't respond, he left the gardens hurriedly, stung that this monumental step had elicited such a tepid response.

Chapter 3

Saturday, April 7, 1838

"WILL you marry me, Charmaine?"

Charmaine woke with a start and stared unseeing at the ceiling above. On a moan, she turned onto her stomach and cried into her pillow. *Not a dream!* The impossible fantasy was no longer a dream. Then why was she weeping?

Stupid, stupid question! You know why! John. The answer was as simple as whispering his name. Mercedes was right. She was in love with him.

Dear God! *What am I to do? What answer am I to give Paul?*

Little more than six months ago, that answer would have been a resounding "Yes!" Last year, she had loved him. Why then had she suddenly turned fickle? Was she no better than he?

The marriage vows are simple, Charmaine, but how can either of us know how we will feel toward each other years from now . . .

Years from now? Again she moaned.

In mere months, her love for Paul had vanished. And if her feelings could change that quickly, could she rely on them? Yes, she yearned for John now, but how could she be certain it was love when so many other emotions were involved: loneliness, sorrow, and empathy. What if it wasn't love at all? What if it was only a tidal wave of commiseration? Perhaps it had engulfed her desire for Paul, and in time, that desire would reemerge.

Yes, that makes sense, she decided.

Her relief was short-lived. She was fooling no one, least of all herself. The elation she had experienced when John returned—the memories of his lips upon hers—mocked all logic. She'd been attracted to him long before Pierre had died. *I love him!* Much as it would be simpler to deny it, *I love him.*

But what of John? *Does he feel the same about me?*

He hadn't given her any reason to think so. Yes, he'd returned, but he'd told her if he extended his visit, it would be for his sisters' benefit. So, where did she fit in? Did she fit in at all? He had walked away from her six months ago. If she had meant anything to him, why had he abandoned her when she had needed him most?

She gulped back her burning misery. Paul had comforted her during those months of agony, had cared and cried with her, held and sheltered her. Could she set aside his compassion so easily—hurt him?

And even if John told her today he loved her, was she willing to gamble on such a declaration? Now she was forced to think about it, she realized she was afraid of loving John. *I'd forfeit every penny for just one more second of her time! I loved her, Charmaine, will always love her . . .*

Fool! Fool! Fool! She could never compete with Colette.

Charmaine wept again.

When she eventually rose, she was grateful she wouldn't be attending the ball, wouldn't have to face Paul. She had a full day to deliberate her dilemma, a full day before Paul would expect an answer; she still had time to decide.

Richmond

Michael Andrews stood in the Harringtons' front parlor, wringing his hands nervously. He'd rehearsed what he would say many times over the past week, and still his pulse raced. Loretta appeared, as surprised as her housekeeper with this visit. "What brings you here, Father Michael?"

"Actually, I had hoped to catch you after Mass the last two Sundays."

"Joshua has not been feeling well for the past fortnight," she offered by way of a hasty excuse. "He's much improved this week, however."

Michael chuckled. "Good Lord, that's not why I'm here," he reassured and, suddenly inspired, plunged ahead. "Actually, it's Charmaine Ryan I've been concerned about. I haven't seen her at Holy Mass for some time now. I had promised Marie, her mother, to watch over her."

"Charmaine?" Loretta queried, bewilderment supplanting her initial surprise. "Why, Father, she left Richmond well over a year ago. She's living in the West Indies now."

"The West Indies?" he asked, astonished.

"She's working for the Duvoisin family," she continued. "They're prominent shippers here in Richmond and own an island in the Caribbean. Frederic Duvoisin and his wife were looking for a governess for their three young children. Charmaine was able to obtain that position."

"Governess, you say?"

The timbre of his voice and his furrowed brow were disconcerting. Loretta attempted to alleviate his anxiety. "She's quite well. My sister and brother-in-law live there. That is how we learned of the job. I'm sorry, Father, but I was unaware of your concern for Charmaine. Had I known—"

"No—no," the priest interjected, belatedly camouflaging his emotions. "Any miscommunication is owing to long hours at the refuge and my thoughtlessness. Over a year, you say?"

"Yes. She was extremely distressed after her mother's passing, especially when her father was never apprehended. I thought distance and new faces would provide a solution, the start of a new life, so to speak."

"You are undoubtedly right. Is she happy there?"

Loretta sighed. "The Duvoisins have endured two tragedies over the past year. Naturally, they were upsetting, but overall, yes, I think she is happy."

"The next time you write to her, please let her know I was asking for her."

"I'll do that, Father."

On his way back to the refuge, Michael's mind was reeling. Charmaine was living with the Duvoisins! She'd been there for the two deaths: the boy, six months ago, and the child's mother. She must have suffered heartache all over again. And John . . . she must know him, and he, her! Michael couldn't focus on anything else for the remainder of the day.

Likewise, the priest's visit perplexed Loretta. If Michael Andrews had promised Marie Ryan to look in on her daughter, why had it taken him so very long to do so? And why had he seemed so emotionally involved? *Yes,* Loretta thought, *very intriguing indeed!*

Charmantes

The fine ore captured the lamplight, a quicksilver glint that traced the delicate engraving within: *My Love, My Life*. The locket snapped shut in Agatha's trembling hand. Gingerly, she placed it on the dressing table and stared at it. The charm had been Elizabeth's wedding present from Frederic.

Bitter memories faded when Agatha beheld herself in the mirror. Elizabeth had not won. The tables had turned in Agatha's favor. Through years of careful planning and maneuvering, she had orchestrated the ultimate victory. Tonight was the culmination of her triumph. Tonight, her genius prevailed. Agatha laughed lightly with the irony of it all. She had won. Elizabeth lay, long disintegrated in the cold earth, a brief six months of marriage the only thing she'd given Frederic. Tonight, the true joy of Frederic's life was the loyal and long lasting treasure Agatha had given him: Paul. He was Frederic's pride this night, carrying on the lofty Duvoisin legacy.

Agatha studied the locket again. She would have been the happy recipient of this fine piece had Elizabeth not interfered. Now, that didn't matter. Yes, time had been on her side. Tonight, she would enter the ballroom on Frederic's arm. Tonight, she reigned victorious.

Dinner was to be served at six o'clock. The twins wore their new chiffon dresses, pale blue with white lace, accentuating their eyes—Colette's eyes. Soon they would look exactly like her. They milled about the nursery, anxious to go down to the festivities. As voices floated up from below, Charmaine decided to humor them. She looked longingly at the lovely gown she would not be wearing tonight. Thanks to Agatha, she would be attending as the girls' governess, nothing more, so she wore her best Sunday dress, as was appropriate. Frederic expected his daughters to attend the dinner and had given permission for them to participate in the first hour of the ball, which was scheduled to begin at eight-thirty. After that, Charmaine would retire with a good book and try not to think about what she was missing.

The twins' new shoes tapped loudly on the marble floor as they crossed the foyer to the ballroom. The doors were open wide, the room as Charmaine had never seen it: splendid beyond description, the crowd clustered and abuzz with anticipation. It was intimidating. She took Yvette and Jeannette by the hand and they passed under the archway together.

Flickering candles in the huge chandeliers cast sparkling light on the place settings of fine china and crystal. The lamps on the wall glowed warmly on the Italian murals. Bouquets of freshly cut flowers crowned four round tables at the far end of the banquet hall. Guests strolled in, with glasses in their hands, gentlemen with ladies on their arms, all elegantly dressed. While they waited to be seated, they ambled about the dazzling room, conversing and enjoying hors d'oeuvres.

As the twins sped over to a waiter with a serving tray, Charmaine eyed the place cards on the tables. She and the twins would be seated with Frederic, Agatha, Edward Richecourt and his wife, Helen, Geoffrey Elliot, Robert Blackford, and a couple from North Carolina.

Paul and Anne London walked into the room. His impeccable formal attire of gray waistcoat and jacket, black trousers and white shirt accentuated his sleek, muscular form. Many women were looking his way. Anne wore an off-the-shoulder gown, skin-tight at the bust with ruffled sleeves, full and flowing from the waist—the newest Paris fashion. The ivory satin was cut scandalously low at the bodice, revealing the generous swell of her creamy white bosom. Delicate lace-trimmed gloves covered her arms, and her ears glittered with diamonds. Her blond hair was meticulously coiffed into tight braids looped high on her head, where a shimmering tiara held them in place. Charmaine knew it had taken her the entire day to dress, for she had not seen Mercedes since breakfast.

John and George appeared next, conversing with the guests from New York and Boston, a corpulent businessman nodding now and then. Charmaine's breath caught in her throat at the sight of John in formal attire. He was dressed entirely in black, save a white shirt and an ivory carnation pinned neatly to the velvet lapel of his jacket. The finely tailored suit accentuated his lean body, catching his broad shoulders and tapering to his slender waist. His hair was combed back, his short sideburns neatly trimmed, his face clean-shaven. He talked easily with the Northern gentlemen, his eyes lively, a window to his keen mind. He was so handsome and projected such confidence Charmaine could not tear her eyes from him.

John, too, had caught the attention of quite a few young ladies. One of them broke away from her mother, who nodded approvingly, and boldly crossed the room, producing a dance card before she reached him. Clearly, these farmers' and brokers' wives had their own agenda. While their husbands sought business partners for their clients, they sought marriage partners for their daughters. In a wave of despair, Charmaine turned away.

The waiters began to usher the guests to their tables, and Charmaine quickly located Yvette and Jeannette. As an attendant helped

Agatha with her chair, Charmaine sat down with the girls on either side of her, but Frederic remained standing, waiting for everyone to find their seats before he himself reclined. As she gestured to his daughters to place their napkins in their laps, she looked up to find his eyes on her. She resisted the urge to look away, only doing so when his attention was drawn to Edward Richecourt. In the corner of the room, a string quartet tuned up and began playing a divertimento. As the first course was served, Charmaine felt her tension ease.

She glanced around the room, noting a Duvoisin family member hosted each table. Paul and Anne were at the table directly opposite hers, where the company was engaged in quiet conversation. Her eyes caught Paul's momentarily, and he smiled at her. Charmaine watched Anne apply the charm, her hand resting possessively atop his. Rose and George were at the table behind her. Though George chatted amicably, his face was forlorn. John was at the next table, which was animated in a lively discourse. As usual, he commanded the banter; all the guests at his table were laughing.

Geoffrey Elliot watched her throughout the endless meal, engaging her in conversation whenever their eyes met. Helen Richecourt chatted with Jeannette and Yvette. They responded confidently, golden curls bouncing on their shoulders as they nodded, their manners exemplary. Colette would have been proud.

As the dishes were cleared away for dessert, Charmaine looked to John again, leaning forward in his chair, arms folded casually before him, a hand clasped to his chin, engrossed in the recounting of some story. He hadn't looked her way all evening. Had he even noticed she was there?

After dessert, the waiters ushered everyone out of the banquet hall so it could be rearranged for the ball. Some of the guests wandered into the drawing room and study for after-dinner drinks, while others left the house to stroll on the lawns or in the courtyard.

Charmaine accompanied the girls to the parlor, where their

father introduced them to several of his guests. All were gracious. Helen Richecourt had learned both girls knew how to play the piano, and she asked Jeannette to play. Before long, a small audience had gathered around to listen as the twins took turns with their favorite pieces. Frederic looked on with pride, and Charmaine was satisfied she could take some credit for these two cultivated young ladies.

"Charmaine? Charmaine Ryan?"

She turned toward a couple she recognized. "Mr. and Mrs. Stanton! It is so good to see you!"

Raymond Stanton was a Richmond merchant and business associate of Joshua Harrington. He and his wife, Mary, had not attended the dinner, so Charmaine assumed they had just arrived for the ball.

"It is good to see you, too, dear," Mary rejoined. "Loretta and Joshua asked us to look for you. They send their love." She smiled, assessing Charmaine from head to toe. This polished young woman could not be the same insecure girl she'd met at the Harringtons a few years ago.

"I'm always pleased with news of the Harringtons. How are they?" Charmaine inquired, ignoring her discomfiture over the woman's blatant perusal.

"Quite well and getting ready for a visit with Jeremy in Alexandria."

"That's wonderful. Travel will be much easier now it is spring."

"Yes, yes," Mary agreed, dismissing the topic, her eyes surveying the room. "My, this house is truly magnificent! What is it like to live in such opulence?"

Charmaine glanced over her shoulder. Frederic was only a few feet away and within earshot. "I enjoy my life on Charmantes, Mrs. Stanton. It is certainly very different than Richmond."

"I'm sure you do. That Paul Duvoisin is quite a handsome fellow. I daresay, he must turn many a maid's eye. Do you see him often?"

"Almost every day, Mrs. Stanton. He lives here, too."

"And I see Mrs. London is with him tonight. That is quite surprising. The talk last year was that she was as good as engaged to his brother, John."

Charmaine was about to speak, but Mary babbled on. "Is *he* here?"

"Yes . . ." Charmaine sighed, as the woman's eyes lit up.

"You'll have to point him out to me. I've heard so much talk about him, but have yet to meet him. Raymond's partners complain he can be quite difficult."

Before Charmaine could respond, the twins came dancing over. She introduced them to the Stantons quickly, as Yvette was tugging on her arm. "Come, Mademoiselle Charmaine, let's find Johnny!"

Mary's eyebrow arched, but Charmaine quickly murmured an apologetic "good evening" and allowed Yvette to draw her into the foyer, relieved to be rescued from the busybody. When John was nowhere to be found, she suggested they return to the nursery to rest and freshen up.

George was miserable. He could not stop thinking about Mercedes and how he wished she were at his side this evening. John had tried in earnest to convince him to propose to her. The widow London's threat of dismissal would be moot, and Mercedes would be free to attend the ball. But last night when George had walked Mercedes to her door, he'd grown cold feet, his tongue thick in his mouth. He knew he'd come off the utter oaf if he managed to stammer those four fateful words, but now, he regretted his cowardice.

As Frederic stepped onto the portico to share a cigar and talk politics and commerce with two gentlemen, he noticed Paul on the lawn with a small group of guests. Anne was still at his side. Frederic had been surprised when his son escorted the widow and not Charmaine Ryan to the dinner table. After his conversation with Paul some weeks ago, he was convinced Charmaine meant more to him than just a casual affair—that Paul intended to squire her tonight. And Jeannette had mentioned something about a new gown. So why had she appeared for dinner plainly dressed and with the twins by her side? Frederic thought back on his affairs with Agatha and Elizabeth and shuddered, uncomfortable his son was so much like him. He could only hope Paul wouldn't make the same mistake.

John knocked on Mercedes's door on the third floor. It opened partway, only her face visible, her eyes red and swollen. "You've been crying," he said.

She looked away.

"I've come to take you to the ball."

"But—I can't," she stammered. "Mrs. London will dismiss me if I dare."

"She won't make a scene. She's trying too hard to impress my brother."

"Really, I mustn't. She will be furious and dismiss me in the morning."

"I have a hunch it won't matter tomorrow, Mercedes," John replied with a crooked grin, "but if it puts you at ease, I will see to it you're taken care of, one way or another. I'm in desperate need of a farrier at my plantation."

She smiled, and the door opened completely. "Really?"

"I owe you this for ministering to Phantom."

"But I haven't anything appropriate to wear!"

"Sure you do," John countered. "The armoire in Mrs. London's dressing chamber must be packed with expensive gowns. Pick one she has never worn."

Jeannette and Yvette began to fidget. The hum of voices and instruments tuning up drifted upstairs, and Charmaine could tell the crowd had grown larger. She and the twins watched from the balcony as carriage after carriage rolled up and men in top hats alighted, lending assistance to elegantly dressed women. The last one pulled away, and it was time to go down. As they stepped out the door, Charmaine took one last look at her lovely gown.

The twins charged jubilantly into the glittering ballroom. Couples were already on the dance floor, and the first number was coming to a close. George was partnered with a very pretty young lady. Her jet-black hair was tied back with a simple ribbon, her dress plain. She had to be an islander. Anne was dancing with Paul, her eyes fixed on his face, her arms ensnaring him whenever the cotillion brought them together. Though the woman irked her, Charmaine was indifferent to the sight of them in each other's embrace. Perhaps she'd grown accustomed to seeing them together.

Robert Blackford stood in the shadows close to the orchestra and watched his sister. As the musicians tuned up for the first waltz, Agatha led Frederic to the dance floor, where she placed one possessive hand on his shoulder and the other on his waist. Her exquisite blood-red gown accentuated a curvaceous figure that every woman her age would envy. Her fine jewelry glittered in the light of the chandelier. Robert admired her anew. She was still beautiful, the most beautiful woman in the room. As Frederic stepped into the waltz, Robert fantasized . . . He crossed the room with an authoritative step, tapped Frederic's shoulder, and took the man's place. But now, as the couple drifted past him, his sister's radiant face shattered his idyllic musings. Though Frederic worked hard at the cumbersome steps, Agatha's eyes were suffused with pride, satisfaction, and love as she looked up at him. Yes, love was the word. After all these years, the truth struck Robert like a full broadside. His sister was, and always had been, in love with Frederic Duvoisin.

As the second waltz began, Yvette and Jeannette took to dancing together, until Yvette caught sight of Joseph Thornfield leaning against the wall holding a tray. She broke away, grabbed the tray, and deposited it on a table. She paired him off with her sister, prodding them to waltz together. They danced off awkwardly, much to the guests' amusement.

A hush and then murmurs near the main archway caught Charmaine's attention. John walked in with Mercedes on his arm. She wore a gorgeous tawny gown, her uncoiffed hair falling to her waist. She was stunning.

Charmaine felt betrayed, consumed with jealousy. Her eyes searched the dance floor to see George's reaction, but he was still partnered with the black-haired girl.

Yvette ran over to her brother and pointed out Jeannette and Joseph. A smile broke across John's face, but Mercedes's gaze was riveted on George.

The music stopped. John grasped Mercedes's elbow and led her to George, who was now quite alone. They exchanged a few words, and George's smile widened when Mercedes fell in at his side. He placed a possessive hand on the small of her back, and Charmaine's envy ebbed. Mercedes was beaming.

The three stood chatting until Rose grabbed John's arm and pulled him into a Scottish reel. She broke into a spry step that belied her advanced years, and John had to work to keep up with her. They danced two more numbers before John wiped the sweat from his brow, and handed her off to George.

Charmaine felt miserable—isolated—anxious for her hour with the twins to be over so she could barricade herself in her room and cry herself to sleep.

Frederic was glad when the waltz ended. It had been a test of stamina, not only of body, but of mind. And now, as he walked off the dance floor and left Agatha with a clutch of prattling matrons and their vacuous conversation, he dropped his constrained smile.

A group of men were arguing heatedly in a corner of the room. He headed their way. ". . . no Percival, I'll leave the first runs to you. You test the waters with *your* goods and *your* money."

"Once Paul has an established market, there may not be space next year."

"I'll take my chances. There are always shippers out there."

"Yes, but at what price? The Duvoisin fees are too gainful to decline."

There were murmurs of agreement, quickly quelled when the first man pressed his point. "Yes, with a five-year commitment. I've heard too much talk of discord. Some say Frederic and John aren't on speaking terms."

"Advantageous to Paul—and anyone using his shipping line. He might very well take charge of his father's fleet one day."

The man grunted. "But in the interim, pandemonium may reign."

Another man said, "I've watched the three of them together throughout the week. I'm not fond of John, but I haven't heard one word that alarms me."

"A word? No. But what about the hostile undercurrents? Even Paul has turned curt. I met him last year at Edward Richecourt's office. He was quite affable then. I get the distinct impression he's annoyed his brother is involved. I also think all three are presenting a grand façade for us."

"When has John ever 'presented a façade,' Matthew? He doesn't care—"

"When it involves money, and his fortune to boot, he cares. He loves to flaunt his wealth. Take that sign above his plantation gate. It must have cost—"

"Excuse me, gentlemen," Frederic interrupted, the small group falling silent. "Allow me to respond to some of your concerns." He looked at the man who was arguing most vehemently and smiled. "You make a good point, Matthew. I would ask the same questions if I were in the market for an intercontinental carrier. John and I have often disagreed—it stems from a desire to be in charge—but those disagreements have never adversely affected Duvoisin business. You see, I respect John's judgment as surely as I do Paul's.

During the ten years he has been in charge in America, my assets have more than tripled there." Frederic paused, allowing his words to sink in. "Nevertheless, John is not the issue here, Paul is. *His* fleet of ships, *his* shipping concern, the routes *he* has set up, are just that—*his*. Everything you have seen this week, he has planned and built on his own. The only help I've provided is financial backing. Neither John nor I will have any dealings with his enterprise, other than to give advice when and if he asks for it. In fact, that should be your primary concern, Matthew—that Paul does, in fact, ask. This area of Duvoisin business is fairly new to him. John has dealt with most of the shipping thus far, and knows, even better than I, the ins and outs that make it lucrative, not only for the Duvoisin family, but for the brokers who utilize his transport. It is the main reason he is here this week—to share his knowledge."

"Frederic, I meant no offense."

"No offense taken," Frederic replied expansively. "Your objectivity in reviewing all aspects of these contracts indicates a sound business mind." He extended a hand to the gentleman, then shook each in turn. "Now, if you have any other concerns, please come to me. That is why you've been invited here."

Anne was incensed. Her personal lady's maid had waltzed by in the arms of her smitten suitor, George Richards, wearing *her* finest gown, a gown she had yet to wear, a gown that had cost a small fortune. Her couturier had designed it expressly for her, and she had been saving it for Mass tomorrow, determined to surpass tonight's stunning effect. That plan was foiled now, and Anne's blood boiled. How dare she? How dare that snip of a girl deliberately flout her mistress's authority? Anne inhaled deeply, holding the violent breath for untold seconds. *Well, Mercedes Wells . . . you will regret coming down here! On Monday, after all the guests have departed, I will dismiss you. Then you shall see how dearly your beau cares for you!*

* * *

John was simmering by the time Charmaine and his sisters left the ballroom. Anne had been his brother's dinner partner and had returned on his arm, obviously his companion for the entire evening. Charmaine was dressed in her drab governess garb, seeing to his sisters. Apparently, Paul's invitation had been rescinded.

The twins were already asleep. Charmaine had changed into her nightgown and had settled into the armchair with a book in hand when there was a rap on her door. She was astounded to find John waiting in the corridor.

"I thought Paul was to be your escort for the evening," he stated directly.

"I didn't lie to you, John."

"I know you didn't lie," he replied. "What happened?"

"Agatha invited Anne London to the ball on Paul's behalf yesterday at lunch. She spoke for him, and he couldn't refuse."

"So *he* lied to *you*."

"It wasn't a lie. He wanted to escort me."

"Right," John remarked doubtfully.

"Agatha threw them together. Paul didn't want to embarrass them."

"I wouldn't have cared about embarrassing them."

"You enjoy embarrassing people, John," she retorted. "Paul doesn't."

"No. Paul enjoys having a woman on his arm while another waits for him in the wings."

Charmaine smarted from his words. "You're wrong. He wanted to take me. He regretted what happened and apologized."

"You humored him and are cheated out of this evening."

Charmaine didn't care to be reminded of her disappointment. Still, she knew the slight had not been intentional and felt compelled to defend Paul. "You don't understand, John, and you are being unfair. He has promised to make it up to me. What does one silly night matter, anyway, when the future—"

She caught herself, certain she'd revealed too much, John's brow already furrowed in swift comprehension. Embarrassed, she turned back into the room, but he followed her.

"Paul proposed to you?" he asked. "Is that what you're trying to hide?"

"Is that so inconceivable?" she rejoined, pivoting round to face him, nettled that he didn't think her worthy.

"What? That he proposed to you, or that you're trying to hide it?"

"I'm not trying to hide it!" she exclaimed. "And, yes, he proposed to me."

"So *he's* trying to hide it."

"No, he's not!" she objected.

John's frown deepened. "So when does Paul plan on announcing this engagement, Charmaine? At the ball tonight, with you in your room and Anne at his side?"

His words stung like salt in a fresh wound. Again, she was baited into saying more than she wished. "We're not betrothed yet. I told him I would think about it."

John's eyes betrayed surprise, but his words were cutting. "How generous of you and convenient for him. One last stand before he's a happily married man!"

"I haven't made it convenient for him!" Charmaine countered defensively, her anger and shame melding into one sickening lump of foolishness. "I've told you, he was embarrassed by Agatha and forced into a situation beyond his control."

John snorted in disgust. "So tell me, Charmaine—if Agatha tells Anne tonight, '*Anne, Paul has asked for your hand in marriage,*' my brother will be too embarrassed to tell Anne, '*I've already proposed to Charmaine.*' Do I have it right now?"

She glared at him furiously. There was no point in responding.

"Now we've figured that out, get dressed. I will take you to the ball."

She hesitated, stunned and thrilled by his offer. She opened her mouth to accept, but the implications of doing so stopped her. "It wouldn't be appropriate for me to accompany another man until I give Paul an answer."

John stood incredulous. "But it's acceptable for him to escort another woman to the ball with a standing marriage proposal to you?"

Charmaine sighed in frustration. "Why does it matter to you, anyway?"

John debated his answer. He must drop talk of his brother if he were to convince her to accompany him. "It matters to me because I know you've been looking forward to this night. You've talked of little else the entire week. I could see how disappointed you were at dinner."

She was surprised. He *had* noticed her. Suddenly, her mood lifted.

"Now, Charmaine," he coaxed, "there isn't a woman alive who wouldn't give her right arm to be downstairs tonight. This opportunity may never come your way again. You can tell anyone who asks we are merely friends."

Her resolve was weakening, even though she knew no one would believe they were merely friends.

"Please come, my Charm," he pressed on. "I've attended many such parties, and it won't matter to me if I miss this one. But I will take great pleasure in seeing you enjoy it. If you don't accompany me, we shall both be disappointed."

Charmaine mulled over his petition. Why should she miss such a splendid affair, perhaps the opportunity of a lifetime? She desperately wanted to go. Then there was her daring side, chuckling inwardly, wondering how the likes of Mary Stanton and Anne London would react when she arrived on John's arm.

"Very well," she capitulated. "I'll go. But I'm warning you now, if you embarrass me even once, I will leave."

"I won't, I won't," he replied, waving off her threat as he headed toward the door. "You have ten minutes," he directed, as he stepped out of the room.

"Ten minutes?"

"Ten minutes." His face was bright with satisfaction. "I'll be waiting."

The door closed behind him, leaving her to her hasty toilette. In a flurry, she was ripping off her nightgown and pulling the evening gown from her armoire. It hugged her bust and waist, flaring out at her hips and falling to the floor. The champagne silk complemented her skin and dark hair, pronouncing her natural innocence, while the sash at her waist accentuated her slim, yet curvaceous figure, and the sheer frill that trimmed her décolletage drew attention to the swell of her breasts. She'd have to get used to the low-cut neckline as well as the feel of the delicate satin slippers on her feet. Already John was rapping on her door. Quickly, she brushed out her hair and swept the curls off her face with ivory combs. Like Mercedes, she left the rest unfashionably loose, a riotous cascade tumbling down her back. With a pinch, she coaxed her cheeks to a rosy hue. Before long, she was standing at the looking glass, wondering if she were the same girl of only twenty minutes ago. She turned from side to side and was pleased with what she saw. She considered her glowing face one last time, then stepped confidently to the door.

John leaned over the balustrade, his impatient eyes on the landing below. At the sound of the door opening behind him, he straightened and turned. The vision of loveliness standing there surpassed any he'd conjured. If he didn't look away, he'd lead her right back into the bedroom and forget the ball. He trained his eyes on her pretty face. She was oblivious to the effect she had on him, for although her cheeks were flushed, her eyes sparkled girlishly.

Charmaine was unnerved by his perusal, which compelled her to speak. "Could it be you of all people are speechless?"

He laughed, glad she had broken the spell. "You are a sight to behold, my Charm," he replied. "A vision of perfection."

His compliment made her feel attractive and feminine. "And you are very handsome this evening," she returned. "Black becomes you."

"Not the first time you've voiced words to that effect."

She giggled, her giddiness rising.

"Be careful, my Charm," he warned, "you are so beautiful tonight, I may have to live up to my black reputation, and we may never make it to the ball this evening."

She smiled with his brash flattery, happy to know he found her desirable. He took her arm and led her to the staircase.

A heady blend of apprehension, joy, and excitement reached its pinnacle as they began their descent. She broke away, and he chuckled when she raced ahead, throwing him a backward glance from the landing. Leaning over the banister, she could see into the ballroom, where the mélange of color, fragrance, and music was irresistible. Hems of gowns flashed past the arched doorway, a kaleidoscope of sight and sound. The waltz was fast and catchy—the newest craze—the Bohemian Polka—the instruments perfectly tuned. Only John held her back.

"Am I not the escort, my Charm?" he smiled wryly as he caught up with her. He extended his arm, and she slipped her hand through the bend of his elbow, reveling in the feel of muscle beneath the fabric.

"I feel like Cinderella," she whispered, "and you're my fairy godmother."

"How can that be, my Charm," he queried devilishly, "when I haven't taken out my magic wand?" He laughed at her confusion, then guided her down the remaining steps and through the foyer. They crossed the threshold of the great hall together.

The music had stopped and Charmaine looked around the room. Her eyes met those of quite a few guests, who considered her with intense interest. She was dressed like an elegant society lady, yet she knew that had little to do with it. The world had suddenly noticed her because she was with John. Two words—"the governess"—passed in murmurs behind her. Undaunted, John led her farther into the room, tall at her side, his gait unrushed and confident. She felt protected next to him, his firm hand at the small of her back.

"Charmaine, you look lovely!" George exclaimed when they reached him. "I'm glad you've returned. Everyone is having a fabulous time!"

With eyebrow arched, Mercedes passed Charmaine a knowing nod.

A bellowing voice called for silence, and the noise of the crowd died down. Charmaine glanced around, and once again, caught many eyes upon her, Mary Stanton gaping from the sidelines. At the center of the room, Edward Richecourt climbed atop a chair, a makeshift platform for his announcement.

John elbowed George. "You slip on the noose, and I'll kick out the chair!"

George's raucous guffaws echoed to the rafters, and people turned to see who was laughing.

"Ladies and gentlemen!" Richecourt shouted magnanimously. "I'd like to propose a toast." He lifted a glass of champagne to Paul. "To our fine host," he continued loudly, "he has treated us like royalty this week, culminating in this exquisite celebration. May this intrepid endeavor become his triumph! Cheers!"

A round of applause gripped the hall. A call went up for Paul to take the platform. As he did, Charmaine felt John's hand slip around her waist, pulling her close, the feel of his sturdy frame quite pleasing.

"Thank you for your kind wishes," Paul stated cordially.

Charmaine stiffened as his eyes roamed over the spectators, arcing in her direction. She tried to step away from John, but his arm was like a vise, holding her in place.

"And I thank you all for journeying here," Paul continued. "I hope this evening will be your best yet on Charmantes—" His gaze alighted on John "—I look forward to a prosperous relationship with each and every one of you—" then settled in blatant astonishment on her. He took them in as a couple, and Charmaine read fury in his eyes, his speech ending between clenched teeth. "My father and I hope you enjoy the remainder of the evening." Though the audience cheered enthusiastically, he didn't seem to notice, for his reproachful gaze never left her.

As the clapping died down, John snatched a glass of champagne off the tray of a passing server. He raised it to propose his own toast, his crisp, resonant voice halting Paul before he stepped down. "To you, Paul," he declared full-voiced. "I admire your persistence. In less than two years, you've kindled a budding empire from a deserted island. When you really know what you want, *nothing* holds you back. Here's to making dreams come true."

Paul's mouth flew open to retaliate, but a third round of applause drowned him out. The crowd closed ranks, shouting good wishes and drinking to his success.

"I'm leaving!" Charmaine huffed, her eyes flashing.

"Not yet," John argued, his voice sympathetic, though he held her fast.

"And how am I to face Paul after this? We both know what he thinks."

"What does he think, Charmaine?" John demanded evenly.

"That we're together."

"And we are," he replied simply. "That's his fault. So why worry about facing him? If you'd left it up to him, you'd be up there—" and he nodded toward the ceiling "—reading some goddamn book, wishing you were down here!"

"Why did you have to embarrass me like that?"

"I didn't embarrass you. He was going to find out sooner or later, wasn't he? He doesn't deserve you, Charmaine."

He released her, acknowledging ultimately, it was her choice to stay or to go. The band tuned up, and the crowd dispersed to clear the floor.

"May I have this dance, my Charm?" he petitioned softly, innocently, prompting her to decide. She wanted to stay, and as her eyes met his, the plea in their soft brown depths gave way to the rogue, chasing the little boy away.

"I'm not sure I remember how," she hesitated.

"I'm not very good at it, either," he smiled, pleased with his second victory of the evening. He held up a finger. "But if we stumble, we can always consult an expert." He nodded in Geoffrey Elliot's direction, where the solicitor looped around a cluster of dancers, writhing and twisting grotesquely before a comely partner, drawing disdainful glares.

Charmaine giggled when the couple whirled past them.

"With Geffey on the floor," John expounded, "nobody will even notice us!"

With that, he opened his arms, inviting her into his embrace. She placed one hand in his and the other on his shoulder. His warm hand clasped her waist as they stepped into the beat of the music. She followed his lead, quickly realizing he knew every step. Her lessons with Loretta came back slowly, and her eyes left her sluggish feet for John's face.

He smiled down at her, and she was bound to his regard until the room and crowd fell away, and there was nothing but the music, the mild air imbibed with the fragrance of tropical flowers, and this man. For months now, not a moment had gone by when some corner of her mind had not coveted precious thoughts of him. Her throat constricted, and a deep flush suffused her cheeks.

She stepped back as the waltz ended, thankful he misinterpreted her crimson face. "It's warm in here, isn't it?" he remarked, leading her to the French doors. "I'll get us something to drink."

She welcomed his departure, for she needed time to compose herself.

Frederic stood on the sidelines of the huge hall watching Charmaine Ryan dance with John. He was intrigued when she'd returned to the ballroom on his son's arm. They were drawing a lot of attention, the room abuzz with speculation. He studied Charmaine's expression, one he'd never seen when she was around Paul, and he understood why that relationship hadn't progressed these many months. *She is in love with John.*

Pondering it now, Frederic realized he'd often thought of the governess and John as a couple. It had started the first time he'd seen them together, the day Agatha had ruthlessly spanked Pierre, that day when he'd been acutely aware of Colette's presence in the house. Then there was the twins' birthday, when he observed John helping Charmaine onto the dappling mare. And the night when Yvette had been gambling at Dulcie's; Charmaine's eyes had flown to John for protection, not Paul. He'd never forget those terrible days when Pierre lay dying, the untold hours they'd spent at his bedside, or Charmaine's compassion for John afterward, her heartfelt tears over his suffering. And only a week ago, her face had brightened with unabashed joy when John returned.

A glimmer of hope heartened Frederic as he watched them now. For the first time in ten long, dismal years, John looked happy. The cynicism John had worn like a badge was gone. Frederic closed his eyes and uttered a silent prayer that his son had finally found someone to call his own.

"So, Mademoiselle, you've rejoined the festivities," Paul commented politely as he came to stand before her. The strains of the next waltz filled the room. "May I have this dance?"

Charmaine nodded charily. John was still off getting drinks, and she knew she could not turn Paul down without embarrassing him. He took her hand, and they walked to the center of the dance floor. There, she stepped into his embrace, not daring to look up. Instead, she cast her eyes aside, noting the scrutiny of many of the guests.

Anne London could hardly conceal her ire when she caught sight of the couple. First Mercedes, now this! *Charmaine Ryan I have underestimated you. You have beguiled not only John, but Paul as well. What is this game you are playing?*

Throughout the evening, Anne had itched to reveal all concerning the rewriting of Frederic Duvoisin's will and John's abolitionist activities. But her father's warning forced her to glumly hold her tongue. Charmaine Ryan had been the least of her concerns. She was a servant girl, riffraff. But here she was—her gown breathtaking, her loose hair a mass of gorgeous curls—squired by John to this high-society affair and dancing with Paul, blushing in his arms! It was time to intervene. Her father hadn't forbidden gossip about the governess; so that was where she'd start. Then, she'd throw caution to the wind and use her experience with men to make Paul forget the woman.

For a few minutes, Charmaine and Paul danced in painful silence. She did not feel the thrill of being in his arms as she had so many times before.

"It didn't take you long to make other plans for the evening, Charmaine."

His words stung. "I didn't make other plans," she countered. "John invited me to join him, and it only happened a short while ago."

She caught sight of Mary Stanton watching amidst a bevy of matrons.

"Why didn't you tell me you were angry, Charmaine?" he asked, drawing her eyes back to him.

"Angry? About what?"

"Obviously you are getting even with me by returning on John's arm."

"Getting even?" she asked, his reasoning beginning to register.

"Because of what happened with Agatha and Anne—to give me a taste of rejection. Isn't that it?"

"No, that is not it!" she refuted, offended he would think her so petty.

Paul chuckled derisively, inciting her more.

"I was not angry, but I *was* disappointed. John saw that, and invited me when he realized I would miss the ball."

"John is very good at stealing other men's women," he replied, his voice low so only Charmaine could hear. "Do you want to be his next victim?"

Her temper flared, but she resisted the urge to tear away. Instead, she looked him straight in the eye, mustered a pleasant voice and said, "He wouldn't have been able to steal me tonight if you had brought me here yourself."

"Then you *are* angry," he rejoined, his minor victory dissatisfying.

"I'm angry now."

They danced the rest of the waltz in icy silence. Paul watched her return to his brother, who was waiting with two drinks.

"You look annoyed, my Charm," John commented as he handed her a glass.

"I don't want to talk about it," she replied.

"Why? Because he scolded you?" John quipped.

"I told you, I don't want to discuss it."

"You should have given him a piece of your mind, Charmaine."

"No! I refuse to make a scene here. This event means too much to him."

"He didn't seem too concerned about that," John scoffed derisively. "He's very fortunate you care."

"Paul has been very good to me," she retaliated. "Although you might not understand it, John, I care for him very deeply."

He relented. Best to drop the subject, though her words "care very deeply" were perplexing. She hadn't accepted Paul's proposal, so what did she mean?

They had danced nearly every dance, and now they were in the lush gardens, where they'd stolen away from prying eyes. George couldn't stop kissing her. How John had managed to coax Mercedes down to the ball, George could only wonder, but whatever he did, George thanked him now. This was the most exciting night of his life. He bent low to kiss her again. On Monday, she'd return to

Richmond. He didn't want her to leave, for he loved her so. "Mercedes," he murmured in her ear.

"Yes . . . ?" she whispered, hugging him close.

"Will you marry me?"

Her embrace quickened. "Yes! Oh yes!"

"May I have this dance with the lady?"

John turned to Geoffrey Elliot, who had tapped him on the shoulder, his avid eyes on Charmaine. "Is your name written on her dance program?" John rejoined.

"Well—actually—no."

"There is your answer." John prodded Charmaine into the steps of the next reel, leaving an insulted Geoffrey alone in the center of the floor.

The next dance was a quadrille. Charmaine squared off with George, and Mercedes with John. Charmaine had thought no one could be as happy as she, but George's eyes twinkled brighter than ever before. As the music died down, Rose once again stepped in and coaxed her grandson away. Charmaine laughed as George tried to keep pace with his wiry grandmother.

Throughout the evening, John had been the perfect gentleman. Like a debutante, Charmaine stole admiring glances at him: his height, the fine tailoring of his jacket, the lamplight playing its color-game with his hair. She was oddly exhilarated when his warm hand lightly brushed hers or their shoulders touched when they sat side by side.

The ballroom was dreadfully hot, and many guests lingered close to the French doors where the air was cooler. Exhausted, Charmaine took a seat close to the doors. John stood nearby, four gentlemen conversing with him. They were embroiled in a debate that, by Charmaine's estimation, had been ongoing over the past week. They could not bend the radical's mind, their discussion spiraling, touching upon an array of current events: the new president (Martin Van

Buren), the dissolution of the Bank of the United States, and inevitably, the slave question. Though the men talked about these subjects with absolute gravity, John remained jocular, his bemusement growing proportionately with their anger. One stalwart Virginian nearly screamed the word "traitor" in his face when he maintained he welcomed protectionist tariffs on foreign imports. Though detrimental to shipping, they would fuel manufacturing in the North and benefit his investments there.

"Well, why should tonight be any different?"

A sandpaper voice caught Charmaine's ear. She turned slightly to find two plump, middle-aged women six feet away, heads tilted together, eyes on John.

"You know, the Palmers were in New York on business last February and he actually had the audacity to bring that quadroon woman along with him to the dinner party thrown by the Severs. Sarah Palmer told me the woman was a slave on his plantation, but he freed her a few years ago and brought her to New York." The woman smiled smugly. "We all know what *she* did to earn *her* freedom!"

The other woman manufactured a scandalized expression. "I've heard whenever he's in New York, she stays with him at his house. It is common knowledge she is his—his—"

"—mistress," the second supplied.

Charmaine was stunned, and her eyes went to John. His futile conversation had taken its toll; he was shaking his head.

"I wonder if his mistress in New York knows he has one here!"

"And the governess of all people!" the first woman exclaimed. "I can imagine the lessons she's taught his sisters!"

Both women shared a hearty laugh at Charmaine's expense, indifferent that she was now looking at them, their heads bent close together, though she caught snippets of their continued abuse. "White trash . . . what can you expect? Imagine, someone like that being hired to such a position?" Their eyes condemned her, while their remarks cut deeply into her dignity.

John's tender voice drew her away from their flagrant condescension. "Pay them no mind, Charmaine." Then he spoke loud enough for the women to hear. "They're two cows who haven't been touched by a man in decades, and they're jealous because you are young and beautiful."

Their mouths dropped open in apoplectic indignation, but they didn't dare utter another insulting word.

Paul found a moment's peace in the cool kitchen, a breeze coming through the open back door. Fatima wasn't there. She was working from the cookhouse behind the ballroom tonight. For as long as he could remember, this was his favorite place to go when he was frustrated. Although it was Fatima's territory, she never shooed him away. She'd been feeding him since he was old enough to beg for her cookies, and understood his moods. So, when he came in search of solace, she'd pile a plate high, pour a glass of milk, and set them on the table before him. Then, she'd turn back to her chores: the potatoes that needed peeling or the dough that needed kneading. In her deep, melodious voice, she'd hum a pitch-perfect tune while she worked, a yearning, soulful strain.

The soothing elixir of childhood memories did not have an enduring effect. Aggravated, he flung himself into one of the chairs, cradling his aching head in his hands. He'd been stupid yesterday, and he'd played the lout tonight. Damn!

Suddenly, he sensed somebody watching him, and he lifted his gaze to the door. He was thunderstruck by the girl standing there. Straight black hair framed the loveliest face he'd ever laid eyes on. Thick, dark lashes hooded her extraordinary green eyes. She stepped into the room, revealing a body that rivaled her face. She was young, more than ten years his junior, he surmised. He wondered why she hadn't caught his eye before. It was impossible not to notice such a comely lass. He stood, uncomfortable with the way she silently assessed him.

Rebecca hadn't expected to find him here; in fact, she was certain she wouldn't find him at all. Now, as she had so often dreamed, they were in a room together, alone, and she was tongue-tied.

"Are you lost?" he asked, the question reverberating foolishly off the walls.

"No," came a husky alto voice.

"Then what can I do for you? Perhaps you are hungry," he suggested, his hand sweeping about in indication of the room.

"No."

The short response left him wondering if she had spoken at all. For all her beauty, she was odd, standing there staring at him. If she were the daughter of one of his guests, why hadn't he seen her before? She must be one of the Caribbean guests who were lodging at Dulcie's, her skin near tawny from the tropical sun.

"I can't say I remember meeting you, Miss . . . ?"

No answer.

"To which family do you belong?"

"None," she finally replied, her voice mellow and sensual. It did not match her youth. "I mean, I'm not one of your formal guests. My brother brought me. He is in your employ."

"Your brother?"

"Wade Remmen."

"Ah, yes," Paul murmured, the light beginning to dawn. "Our impressive Mr. Remmen. I had forgotten he had a sister."

His mind continued to work. What was it now—two years or three—since the indigent siblings had stowed away on a Duvoisin vessel? Amazing, the generosity of time. Or was his memory of a wide-eyed, half-starved, filthy girl deceiving him? "And what might your name be, Miss Remmen?"

"Rebecca."

"A lovely name," he commented gregariously, comfortable now the conversation had begun to flow. "And what brings you to my kitchen, Miss Remmen? Have you a complaint you would like to bring to the cook?"

"I came to see you," she answered simply, much to his astonishment.

"To see me?" he reiterated. "I don't even know you, Rebecca. What could you possibly have to say to me?"

"I love you."

He laughed outright at the ingenuous declaration, the naked honesty that nevertheless gave him pause. *What the hell is this? An adoring adolescent pouring out her heart and soul?* He groaned with the thought of her tagging after him now, appearing at inopportune times, as if her ardent proclamation gave her that right. Well, there was an easy way to deal with this. "You love me."

"Yes."

The green eyes shone brilliantly in the lamp-lit room. If she weren't so young, he'd taste the fruit right here in the kitchen, but he was certain she'd never been with a man. If she had, she wouldn't be standing here laying bare her feelings. He preferred an experienced wench, anyway.

"And what do you intend to do about this?" he asked, commencing a stroll along the perimeter of the room.

"I wanted to tell you," she answered evenly, her eyes following him.

"To what end?"

"To the end of becoming your wife," she declared, eliciting another hearty laugh. Undaunted, she held her head high. He'd never be hers without a fight. The battle would require time, but time was on her side. Tonight was a victory.

"As I pointed out before, Miss Remmen," Paul rejoined, "I don't even know you, and I needn't indicate the difference in our ages. What could you possibly offer me that would make me consider marrying you?" He assessed her rakishly, his eyes boldly running over her body, certain this approach would quell her amorous overtures. However, if she remained open to his advance, he'd be a fool to deny his manhood, especially with such an exceptional prize.

"I don't understand . . ." she faltered in that all too familiar innocence that fanned his ire.

Damn, it was his own fault his pursuit of Charmaine had become so complicated. He'd lost control of the game when he'd begun playing it her way. *We shall see who is the better player.* Had he but stayed the normal course . . . Maybe John *was* the better player. *No—I am!*

He abruptly closed in, towering over the girl. He'd always been victorious in his romantic conquests; she proved it. He could have her now if he wished.

The green eyes were watching him, her head craned back to meet his regard, her composure shaken. But she was too proud, or perhaps wanted him too much to back away. For the moment, he savored this delectable bit of femininity, fought to ignore the young girl he knew lay beneath this deceptive display of blooming womanhood. He leaned forward to kiss her ruby lips, to possess her body, ripe and ready for the plucking.

The door slapped open and the quiet kitchen was violated with a barrage of noise, stale air, and Anne London. With artful timing, he stepped back and was straightening his jacket before she spotted him.

"Here you are!" she bubbled, seizing his arm and prodding him toward the door. "Everyone is looking for you. You've abandoned your own celebration!" She glanced in Rebecca's direction, but turned back to him so swiftly, he wondered if she'd noticed Rebecca at all. He had no chance to protest, and thoughts of Rebecca Remmen were left behind with Anne's fulsome laughter.

Charmaine relished the momentary peace of the terrace. John was perched on the marble balustrade, his arms folded across his chest. He was so close—so alive. A soft breeze tousled his healthy crop of hair so it fell enticingly low upon his brow, just a stroke away from her aching hand, if only she braved the wifely caress. Instead, she stepped into the breeze, moving toward the end of the colonnade where it would be more plentiful.

John grasped her hand to hold her back. "You are lovely tonight, my Charm."

"Thank you," she murmured.

"Why haven't you accepted my brother's marriage proposal?" he abruptly asked, his eyes unusually stormy.

The answer thundered in her head: *Because I'm in love with you!*

Suddenly, someone was calling from the French doors. "Charmaine? Charmaine is that you?"

Charmaine turned. A young woman stood in the archway, silhouetted by the bright light of the ballroom. "There you are!" she exclaimed. "I've been searching for you since I arrived, but nobody knew where you were!"

Gwendolyn Browning stepped into the circle of torchlight.

"Gwendolyn!" Charmaine laughed, rushing forward and hugging her. "What are you doing here? When did you get back?"

"Mother wrote to me, bragging over Father's unexpected invitation, and of course, I wouldn't miss this for the world! We should have been here ages ago, but there was a mix-up at the livery. All the carriages had been dispatched with you-know-who's guests, and we were forced to wait until one returned. Mother worked herself into a dither, telling Father he should have secured a coupé for us. Father insisted he was the hired help and the guests came first. Before I knew it, they were arguing. I thought we'd never get here!"

John chuckled and walked to the end of the terrace, allowing Charmaine some time with her garrulous friend, who gesticulated emphatically with her hands.

"Oh, this is so wonderful, Charmaine, isn't it? This house is beautiful. And look at you! You're gorgeous! Oh, Charmaine, you are *so* lucky!"

"Yes, Gwendolyn, you've said that before. I am very fortunate."

"Charmaine, some of my friends from Richmond are here. They've heard about you-know-who and are jealous."

Charmaine wasn't surprised Gwendolyn's talk turned to Paul. It never took her more than a few minutes to get around to her favorite topic.

"They didn't believe me when I told them the real man is ten times as handsome as the rumor. Anyway, tonight they know I wasn't lying."

"Gwendolyn . . ." Charmaine chided, casting a sidelong glance at John. He was leaning against the railing some distance away, but still within earshot. For the moment, he seemed inclined to allow her this reunion with her friend.

"When word about the banquet started to circulate, I told them I've known about it for months. When they expressed doubt, I told them I could prove my story—my best friend actually works in the mansion where you-know-who lives—and the next letter I received from you, I read to them. You should have seen them turn green with envy!"

"Gwendolyn!" Charmaine expostulated in embarrassment, "you didn't!"

"I did!" she averred unabashedly. "Have you seen you-know-who tonight?"

"Of course, I have," Charmaine answered, "but I—"

"Lord, I nearly swooned when I saw him," she bubbled. "I thought perhaps my memory had exaggerated how fine he is, but I swear, Charmaine, he is the most beautiful man my eyes have ever been blessed to see! His broad shoulders and muscular chest, his narrow waist and finely tailored unmentionables . . . Mother had to scold me three times when my eyes lingered on his manly bulge—"

"Gwendolyn!" Charmaine admonished sharply. "With whom have you been associating? Mrs. Harrington would be appalled—"

"Oh, don't be a prude, Charmaine!" she laughed in naked happiness, ignoring Charmaine's shocked expression. "All my friends whisper about such things, and of course I've told them you-know-who is the most perfect specimen to behold! Why, he's the best part of being home. If only I could dance with him tonight. Oh, those girls would just shrivel up and die! It would be a dream come true for a fat, ugly girl like me!"

"Really Gwendolyn!"

"Ssh . . . !" the girl warned, her eyes cast down the veranda. Charmaine turned round and jumped. John was standing right behind her.

"Are you ready, my Charm?" he asked with a grin, his eyes twinkling.

Gwendolyn became tight-lipped, cowering slightly in John's presence, and Charmaine realized her friend did not know who he was. Likewise, Gwendolyn surmised Charmaine knew this man quite well.

"Miss Browning," John greeted bracingly, his voice sharp and masculine in the stilted silence. "I'm pleased to make your acquaintance."

"How—how do you know my name?" Gwendolyn stammered.

"Oh, I remember you. You're Harold's daughter," he replied. "You used to tag along after your father in the cane fields when you were a little girl."

Confused, Gwendolyn blushed. "Who are you?" she demanded, now feeling quite foolish.

"You don't remember me? Well, now that you've shared your most coveted secrets, introductions are in order."

Gwendolyn's eyes flew helplessly to Charmaine.

"This is John Duvoisin, Gwendolyn."

John's brow lifted devilishly. "You-know-who's brother."

Gwendolyn's eyes grew wide as saucers. Never before had Charmaine seen a face so red, not even in a mirror.

Wiping his hands clean, John returned to Charmaine's side. He considered the couple dancing a few feet away and could scarcely suppress his mirth.

"I can't believe you managed to do that," Charmaine declared with the shake of her head, watching her radiant friend in her glorious moment, dancing in Paul's arms. "How did you get him to agree?"

"He wasn't about to say 'no' in front of two important business prospects and their wives."

Charmaine giggled gaily as Gwendolyn and Paul glided by, Gwendolyn actually tearing her eyes away from the man to smile happily at her. "It was kind of you to do this," she said. "You've made her dream come true."

"I did it for selfish reasons," he confessed.

"Selfish reasons?"

"I'm dying to see her swoon in my brother's arms!"

The statement had barely left John's lips when the room resounded with a loud gasp of: "Dear Lord!" and fell into a hush. The crowd edged away from the dance floor, and the band tuned down, disparate violins carrying fading strains of the melody. The circle of bodies burst open, and Paul labored toward them, a lifeless Gwendolyn in his arms and accusatory eyes leveled on John. Out of breath, he deposited her in a chair. Caroline Browning appeared from nowhere to angrily shoo him away. She produced a fan from her purse and flapped it wildly in her daughter's face. Charmaine's eyes shifted to Paul, who was shaking his head.

"What happened?" someone had the courage to ask him.

"How in hell am I to know?" Paul expostulated gruffly. "Obviously she's of a rather weak constitution."

In the time it took John to snicker, Caroline turned on Paul. "Her constitution was fine until you accosted her! She is of fine stock, sir, descended from an established bloodline!"

"Do you have her papers?" John demanded loudly. "Fine breeding requires official certificates. My brother always demands certificates. He loves the little seals, you see."

If there were a hole nearby, Charmaine would gladly have crawled into it, for each and every eye had turned upon them. Even Caroline Browning was speechless. Mercifully, Gwendolyn sighed.

"What happened, Gwendolyn?" Charmaine probed.

The bewildered girl sighed. "I swooned!"

John's hearty laughter brought the unfortunate episode to an end. Taking Charmaine's arm, he led her back to the dance floor, muttering, "I told him his pantaloons were too tight."

"I wanted to prompt your recollection, John. You will permit me to call you John, won't you?" Geoffrey Elliot asked rhetorically. "I'll be making my departure tomorrow and do require your autograph on the legal instruments I proffered to you on Monday."

"Did you write those contracts?" John asked.

"Why, yes, I did."

"I gave them back to Richecourt," John lied.

"To Mr. Richecourt?" Geoffrey asked. "Why?"

"They need to be translated."

Geoffrey's face twisted into a confused frown. "Translated?"

"Into English."

"But—they *were* in English," he stammered. "I don't understand . . . ?"

"Neither did I, Geffey. But, that's neither here, there or anywhere. There's a lovely young lady I'd like you to meet. Her bloodlines rival your own . . ."

They'd danced their last dance of the evening, and John escorted Charmaine to her bedchamber door. The clock tolled one, but music and voices still resounded in the corridors. She stood against the door with arms clasped behind her. "Well, my Charm," John said, "I suppose this is goodnight."

"Yes, I suppose it is," she replied with a smile. "I have to check on the girls," she added, suddenly nervous. "I hope they've stayed in their room . . ." The words caught in her throat as John closed the short distance between them, looking down at her, so very silent. "Thank you," she murmured, her head tilted back.

"Thank you?"

"For a wonderful evening—for escorting me."

"You're welcome."

His voice was low, his eyes inviting as his head dipped forward, his lips stopping shy of hers, his breath buffeting her face. She closed her eyes to the moment, awaiting his touch. His hands closed over her shoulders and she fell willingly against him, her heart throbbing when his mouth initiated a long sultry kiss that tied a knot of pleasurable pain deep inside of her. With limbs trembling, she savored the pleasing warmth of his body, the strong arms that held her, his wet lips moving over hers, and without thought or hesitation, she grasped him tightly. Regret marred the sweet sensations when his arms dropped away. "Goodnight," she whispered hoarsely.

In a rush, she pushed into her room, closed the door between them, and collapsed against it. By dint of will, she held rigidly to that spot, for the urge was strong to turn around and fall back into his embrace.

With the sweet memory of Charmaine in his arms, John escaped to the stable and settled on a bale of hay in the corner of Phantom's stall, a bottle of wine in hand. The injured stallion watched him impassively as he took a swig. But the spirits had little effect.

After a time, he stepped out of the barn and looked up at the house. Lights still burned bright in the ballroom and on the terrace. His eyes found Charmaine's room. A lamp glowed there, softly penetrating the leaves and branches of the oak tree. *Is she awake? Best not to think about her or you'll never sleep tonight.*

He slumped back against the doorframe. Seconds accumulated into minutes, and he willed his mind blank, breathing deeply of the cool night air.

Paul and Anne stepped out of the house and ambled along the portico, descending to the lawns. When they were a discreet distance from any onlookers, Anne wrapped an arm around Paul's waist, and pressed her hips and breasts into his lean body. She raised a champagne glass and toasted his success. He bent down and kissed her long and passionately. Her hands moved over him brazenly, intent upon bringing the evening to the close she desired. Paul pulled her to him again. Abruptly, they stopped. "Not here," he muttered. "There's a boathouse not far away." He grabbed her hand, and they rounded the deserted north terrace, disappearing into the night.

"Damn you!" John cursed, walking back to the house unnoticed.

Charmaine had no desire to retire once she had slipped into her nightgown. She turned the lamp down, and sat in the wing chair, wide awake as seconds grew into minutes and minutes approached a full hour. Why hadn't she let him in?

Ashamed, astonished, and ultimately dismayed, she set her mind on the ball, reliving every splendid moment of it. She could feel John's warm hand on her back, see his crooked smile, hear his resonant voice, smell the pleasing scent of light cologne and flesh, taste his kiss. Each sensual recollection evoked such sweet yearning she jumped from the chair and stepped through the French doors.

Two figures emerged from the veranda below. In the torchlight, she recognized Paul and Anne, arms entwined. Anne raised a glass of champagne and lavished him with blandishments. "You are the toast of the evening, the envy of the shipping world." She tossed her glass aside and boldly looped her hands around his neck. On the tips of her toes, she drew his head forward, kissing him squarely on the mouth. He responded by pulling her hard against him. The sound of heated kisses and murmured endearments soon punctuated the rhythmic chirping of crickets. Charmaine's cheeks burned as Anne touched him in places a wife might hesitate to venture. "Not here," he murmured, "there's a boathouse not far away."

Charmaine stepped back. No need to watch. She knew where they were headed. At first, she wanted to cry, not out of disappointment, but innocence lost. And then, even that impulse vanished. She was a woman now and ready to leave the naïve girl behind.

She turned her face into the breeze and luxuriated in the cool night air. She had already recovered from the lascivious scene, for she knew the truth about Paul. Hadn't he told her so himself? *I'm a rogue, Charmaine . . .* But it didn't matter! She didn't care! A half hour passed, perhaps more. She didn't know how long she stayed there, reveling in the lightness of her mind.

She returned to her room and paced the floor, once, twice, and once again. She was still wide-awake; the fresh evening air had dusted all the cobwebs of sleep from her head. She settled into the chair, but she couldn't close her eyes. Not now . . . not tonight . . . She sprang up and circled the stifling, oppressive room again, this room where she didn't feel whole.

John couldn't sleep, so he started reviewing Geoffrey Elliot's contracts. They took his mind off Charmaine. The thought of her accepting his brother's marriage proposal would drive him mad if he dwelled on it any longer.

He came up from his contemplation with the rap on his door. The rap came again. Who could be knocking at this hour? The ball had broken up long ago. He left the bed and the many papers strewn over it and opened the door, indifferent to the fact he was clad only in his swimming breeches. It was more than likely Paul, back from his romp.

He was astounded to find Charmaine there. "What is it?" he queried softly, worried by the look on her face.

She stood mute, then breached the distance between them, encircling his waist in a tentative embrace. Her cheek caressed his naked chest, triggering a quickening in his loins.

They stood that way for a time; she, apprehensive, yet savoring the sensation of his sturdy body against her own; he, dumbfounded, wondering what had prompted this uncharacteristic display of sensual affection. Was this what he thought it was? He stroked her hair and asked again, "What is it?"

"Nothing," she said, oblivious to anything save his embrace.

She didn't know what force had drawn her to his chamber; she didn't have a purpose in mind, other than her need to see him. And, unlike his cavalier brother, John was in his room, alone. When she beheld him half-naked in the doorway, all rationality fled and animal instinct took over. Now, here she was, in his arms.

John was aroused, her soft breasts pressing into his chest, sweet agony. Did she know the trouble she was courting with her hands stroking his back? When she turned her head the other way, laying a cool cheek against his skin, he silently groaned, his resistance rapidly dwindling. Throwing caution to the wind, he clasped her shoulders, stepped back into the room, and pulled the door shut, turning the key in the lock. He no longer hesitated, his hands coursing the length of her, firmly grasping her buttocks and pulling her hard against his manhood.

She was surprised, but not displeased. Looking into his eyes for the first time, she wrapped her arms around his neck and met his mouth halfway. Like before, his lips brushed over hers ever so lightly, barely touching, playing. His kiss deepened, and he pulled her closer yet, his tongue finding hers in an erotic, catapulting caress.

He pulled away and stepped over to the bed. Hastily, he began to gather the papers, depositing them unceremoniously into the armchair. She looked on in expectation, so when he gestured toward the bed, she walked to it straightaway and climbed in, ignoring the rational voice that screamed: *Return to your room!* It was of no use to her now. The sensible Charmaine had been left there to contemplate right and wrong. This Charmaine wanted to know, touch, become part of the flesh and blood John. She lay back against the pillow, trembling, yet alert to his every movement.

Aware of her inexperience, John used the task of clearing the bed to cool his ardor. Yes, she was here with him, but was she ready for intimacy? Unless he had sorely misjudged her, this was her first time. Better to approach the encounter delicately, slowly. He wouldn't undress yet.

Her rapt eyes followed him as he moved about the room, lowering the lamp, drawing the curtains, and securing the dressing room door. A strange exhilaration was building inside as she freely perused the inviting expanse of his back, the muscles in his shoulders where they met sinewy arms.

He settled into the bed next to her, and their eyes met. Surprisingly, she found voice to speak, something to break the awkward silence of anticipation. "Do you always wear your swimming breeches to bed?" she asked.

"When it's hot," he smiled, noting she had pulled the coverlet up to her neck, clutching it with white-knuckled fists. Not that she needed such fortifications; she was wearing a robe over her nightgown. "Do you mind?" he queried softly with a gesture he'd prefer to leave the blanket down.

"No," she replied unsteadily, releasing it.

She caught his grin as he pulled the coverlet aside and sized up her amply clad body. "Aren't *you* hot?" he asked. In fact, the chamber was suffocating. Realizing how silly she appeared, she doffed her robe.

They lay there, not touching, he with his back resting against the pillows and headboard. His eyes took on a pensive gleam, and he regarded her quizzically. "Why are you here, Charmaine?"

"I don't know," she answered honestly.

"Are you sure you want this? You won't be crying in the morning?"

"Should I be? Crying, I mean?"

"No, my Charm. I'd never intentionally make you cry. I can make you very happy. I want to make you happy."

"I couldn't stand being apart from you for another second," she murmured, lost to her love for him. "When you were away, I missed you terribly."

He pondered her response and smiled. "I've fantasized about this moment many times. Now it's arrived, I feel like a little boy let loose in Cookie's kitchen after she's spent the entire day baking nothing but treats."

He raised his arm and invited her closer.

She snuggled in, laying her head against his hard shoulder,

slipping her arm over his bare chest. The feel of his flesh, his solid body next to hers, sent a pleasing thrill into her soul. Ever so lightly, he pulled her hair to the side, his fingers brushing her neck and playing with the thick, unbound locks.

They remained that way for minutes on end, quiet, yet communicating all the same. She closed her eyes to the ecstasy of his hand sliding over her back and shoulders, caressing her arm. She knew he was enjoying it, too, for she could feel his heart racing under her palm. Suddenly, he seemed agitated, as if this closeness were not enough. He tugged at her nightdress. She looked up at him.

"Charmaine," he murmured, "why don't you take this off?"

Had she been anywhere else at this moment, she would have shrunk back at the bold request or scurried away like a frightened rabbit. But here she was, pulling the garment away, watching bashfully as he did the same.

It was close to dawn when they consummated their love. Charmaine was anxious, but John calmed her with tender words and kisses, his rough cheek brushing hers as his lips moved to her ear and the hollow of her neck. His hands moved freely over her now, stroking her breasts, her bottom and thighs. His touch evoked erotic sensations she had never experienced before. A sweet ache throbbed in her belly, leaving her quivering with lust and wondering why she had avoided this for so long. He explored the most intimate of places, places she should have been embarrassed to permit, and yet, she was certain if he stopped, she would beg him for more.

He held his passion at bay as he covered her body with his and penetrated her slowly. She whimpered, and he perceived her pain across his own elated revelation that she *was* innocent to a man and had chosen him to be her lover. She was his alone; he wouldn't have to share her with anyone. As he pressed deeper, she went rigid beneath him, and he reined in his heightening urge to climax, holding still for her, allowing her time to adjust to these new sensations, time for the pain to ebb. "It's all right, Charmaine," he whispered, his hands cradling her face, his thumbs caressing her tears away. "I love you. Let me show you how much I love you . . ." He kissed her again. She responded with parted lips, her tension yielding to passion. Unable to hold himself in check any longer, John began to move above her.

Charmaine was hostage to pleasure—the indescribable oneness she felt with him. The chaffing discomfort was gone, and she pulled him closer with unbridled abandon, as even in their intimacy, she couldn't have him close enough. For the first time, she understood her desperate yearnings and felt complete. As she breathed deeply, tiny tentacles tantalized her from within, intensifying her desire, until she was writhing beneath him. John accelerated slightly, the persistent rhythm so sensate it evoked a deeper need within her: a mystical unity, a divine splendor, an unfathomable crescendo that crested without warning. Her body contracted with one tremendous jolt, then relaxed in the bliss of the sweet tremors that followed. John groaned and hugged her tightly, breathless and satiated.

They lay entwined, quiet for many minutes, basking in ebbing ecstasy. Charmaine's sigh drew John's attention, and he propped up on an elbow, his eyes sparkling. She was ready for any number of comments, but to her amazement, he held silent. He relieved her of his weight, then lifted a strand of her hair and played with it between thumb and index finger, before letting it fall on her breast. She resisted the urge to pull up the coverlet and allowed him to behold her naked body, glowing in the soft lamplight. His hand caressed her shoulder, moving over the curve of her hip and coming to rest on her thigh. She shivered in anticipation, incredulous she wanted him all over again.

He plumped the pillows and drew her to him, so her head rested upon his chest and his arms encircled her. As they lay with eyes closed, a potent contentment settled over her. He stroked her hair and her shoulder again. "I have my life back . . ." she heard him murmur as he drifted off to sleep.

Tears of joy trickled down her cheeks. "I love you, too, John," she whispered into his chest. She reached up and, at long last, ran her fingers through his tousled locks. Almost immediately, she succumbed to slumber.

Closing her sitting room door, Agatha sighed in deep satisfaction. The evening had been magnificent. She couldn't be happier. Paul had been brilliant, a star that outshined her sister's son in every respect. And Frederic—he had been the perfect host, as handsome as the day they had first met. Tonight, she had claimed the coveted place by his side.

There was only one flaw in the entire week. She'd been unable to tell everyone Paul was her son, too. But at least he knew the truth, and was not, as Frederic had predicted, offended by it. They should have ended the deception years ago. She longed to speak to him, to proclaim her love for his father and explain the unfair twists of fate that had deprived him, until now, of his birthright and everything he deserved. She shook her head of the troublesome thoughts. She'd give it a bit more time. Tonight was too glorious to waste on sad memories, not when it was *she* who had danced in Frederic's arms. Tonight, she would seek his bed.

She undressed slowly, donned a sheer nightgown, brushed out her hair, and dabbed perfume behind her ears. Frederic hadn't made love to her since the day she had spanked Pierre, and though she'd attempted to seduce him since then, he'd set her aside. But not tonight. Tonight, she'd break down the fortress he'd once again erected around his heart. She had done so before and could do it again.

She was surprised to find him standing beside the French doors, staring down into the gardens. He turned as she closed the door behind her.

"It was a wonderful week, an exquisite evening," she praised. "You've made our son very happy. You've made him proud to be called a Duvoisin."

"Yes," Frederic murmured, turning back to the glass doors.

"I'm proud to be your wife," she whispered in a husky voice.

Coming up behind him, she looped her arms around his waist and leaned her cheek against his back. "I love you."

Frederic pulled away, placing distance between them before facing her again. The ball was over, the week behind him. He could stop pretending.

"Agatha," he began, "I don't love you. I thought perhaps something akin to love could grow between us—companionship, perhaps—but we've grown apart these past nine months."

"I don't understand."

"Don't you? You despise my children even though they are a part of me."

She bristled at the statement. "I love Paul."

Frederic was saddened by her lame defense. "Exactly. You love *your* son. As for John—your own nephew—time and again you've set out to alienate him from me. This last time, the worst of all."

When she started to speak, he held up a hand, and she wisely let him finish.

"I know you have always wished to legitimize Paul's birth. God knows I've wished the same. But to usurp John's rights because of what happened between us—that, I cannot understand, refuse to accept. I thought our marriage would heal your pain, but sadly, it hasn't. You're filled with bitterness and hate."

"I can change, Frederic, I promise I can!" she pleaded.

"Then there are my daughters," he pressed on. "We both know how you feel about them. And when Pierre was alive—"

"Is this still about that spanking?"

"No, Agatha. The spanking was a manifestation of your true feelings for my children. It is something I should have taken the time to notice, to realize would never change."

"I'm sorry if I've hurt you," she whimpered softly. "I never meant to hurt your children, especially Pierre. As for the girls, I thought a school for young women would be best for them."

She hung her head, and he realized she was crying. He hadn't intended to inflict pain, not tonight when she'd been so happy. But he *was* through pretending. "Agatha, I'm tired," he said softly, compassionately. "It has been a grueling week. Let us await our guests' departure. Then we can talk again—with Paul."

She looked at him lovingly. "Yes, Frederic," she eagerly agreed. "We *should* speak with Paul and explain everything to him." She crossed to him, stood on her toes, and kissed his cheek. "I do love you," she whispered, "more than you will ever know." She quietly left his room.

He closed his eyes to agony, the agony he read on her face. He turned back to the French doors. Perhaps Colette would come to haunt him tonight.

Agatha leaned against the door, breathing deeply, allowing the stabbing sorrow to subside. She'd pushed Frederic too far, too fast. But she loved him and, in the end, that love would vanquish his disillusioned heart. She'd gained too much to think otherwise. Wasn't the prosperous week and triumphant evening testimony to that fact? Frederic might be upset, but she'd weathered setbacks before. Now that John was removed from the will, she would back off. In time, he would be banned from Charmantes. She must concentrate on getting back into Frederic's bed. He would come around.

Frederic lay abed, listening to the silence. One year . . . it had been one year since he had held Colette in his arms, one year ago tonight he had prayed for a miracle that never came. She had breathed her last while he slept, his arms wrapped protectively around her. Now, a year later, he closed his eyes to the piercing pain he'd experienced when he'd awoken to find her cold in his embrace, when he had cuddled her for hours and wept for the love he had chastised, the happiness he had thrown away. *Colette, I'm sorry, and I promise, if it's the last thing I do, I will make amends. I love you,* ma fuyarde . . . *I will always love you.*

He did not remember sleeping.

Chapter 4

Sunday, April 8, 1838

PAUL awoke at the crack of dawn with a splitting headache. He lay in bed considering the week's accomplishments, yet he felt disenchanted and depressed. His tryst with Anne London had satiated his manly need, but in every other way, it had left him empty. She'd wanted to accompany him back to his bedchamber, but he turned her down flat, relieved when she rushed to her rooms in an insulted huff. If he had made love to Charmaine in the early hours before dawn, he would now be sound asleep, content with her in his arms.

Charmaine—therein lay the rub, the root of his depression and the headache that awoke him. He should never have allowed himself to be manipulated into escorting Anne to the grand gala, not when he had already invited Charmaine. What had he been thinking? He had proposed marriage to her! He should have used the event to present her as his future wife, but that opportunity had slipped through his fingers. Now, when he announced his betrothal, he would really appear the fool. He could hear the gossip already: *You know, the governess. No, Paul didn't escort her to his ball; he was with Anne London all evening. Remember? Yes, the young woman who tended to his two sisters. The woman who returned on John's arm! Isn't that curious?*

Damn! Last night had been a debacle. And John had certainly made the most of it. Paul couldn't understand why Charmaine was smitten with him, but he should have read the signs. They'd been obvious all week long. Still, nothing rankled him more than seeing her rejoin the festivities with John. It was his own fault. If he had proposed sooner, Agatha would not have dared meddle.

Paul left the rumpled bed, dressed quickly, and headed to the dining room, grateful no one was there. He needed peace and quiet.

Unfortunately, his sisters came out of the kitchen, bright and bubbly.

"Good morning, Paul," Jeannette greeted. "Wasn't the ball magnificent?"

"Magnificent," he answered gruffly.

"Have you seen Mademoiselle Charmaine?" Yvette asked.

"No," he said. "Isn't she with you?"

"We haven't seen her since last night," Yvette replied in exasperation.

"She's not in her room," Jeannette added, "and her bed is made, so we thought she'd already come downstairs, but Cookie hasn't seen her either."

Paul was intrigued. It had been well past midnight when Charmaine left the banquet hall with John. Why would she have risen, made her bed, and left her chambers so early? And if she had, why hadn't she let the twins know of her whereabouts? Suddenly, he was uneasy and suspicious.

"I have an idea," he said. "Let's find John and see if he knows where she is. Yvette, I'll pay you five dollars if you can get him to open his bedchamber door and come out."

Yvette eyed him dubiously, but she wasn't about to turn down a sum like that, no matter how odd the request. She'd worked harder for a lot less.

Once they were at John's door, Paul nodded for her to go ahead and knock.

Charmaine awoke slowly, the room bathed in the early light of dawn. She was lying on her side, with her knees curled up, and John cuddled behind her, his chest pressed against her back, his warm legs tucked under hers, an arm draped possessively across her shoulder. She could feel his even breathing close to her nape and sighed contentedly. She had slept for only a short time, but it had been a deep and satisfying slumber. She belonged to John now. *Please, Dear Lord, let him belong to me as well.*

As if she'd spoken, he stirred, and his arm tightened around her. He kissed her neck, and she could tell he was smiling. They reveled in the warm cocoon until he broke away and rolled onto his back. When Charmaine turned to face him, he plumped up her pillow, tucked it under his arm, and beckoned to her. She had just snuggled in when someone knocked on the door.

Startled, she bolted up in the bed, clasping the sheet to her breasts. The knock came again, but John put a finger to his lips. "Who is it?" he called.

"It's me, Johnny," Yvette answered in a loud whisper. "Can I come in?"

"What do you want?" he asked, rising from the bed and pulling on his swimming breeches, suppressing a chuckle when Charmaine turned away in embarrassment.

"Jeannette and I are looking for Mademoiselle Charmaine," she answered.

John helped Charmaine slip into her robe, then led her into the dressing room. "Stay here," he whispered, brushing his lips across hers, "and don't leave this room without me."

He pulled clothes from his armoire, grabbed his boots, and stepped back into the bedchamber, closing the connecting door behind him.

". . . she's not there, either," Yvette was saying as he yanked on his trousers. "Have you seen her?" The silence behind the door annoyed her. "Open up!"

"I'm getting dressed," he called. "Did you look downstairs?"

"I told you—we can't find her. Open up!"

"I'm coming," he said, pulling on his shirt.

Yvette snatched the five-dollar note out of Paul's hand and pocketed it before John opened the door. He was astounded to find Paul there, too.

"Good morning, Paul. Are you looking for Charmaine as well?" he inquired nonchalantly, fastening the buttons at his neck.

"In fact, I am," Paul replied, peering over John's shoulder and into the empty room. "We're concerned. Apparently, she didn't sleep in her bed last night."

"And you suspect she slept somewhere else," John remarked sarcastically, glaring at his brother in disgust. "Is that it?"

Paul thought better of responding.

John returned to the bed. "Did you check in the chapel?" he asked as he sat and pulled on his boots.

Yvette wrinkled her nose. "It's too early to be there."

"Well, that's where I'll look," he stated, his eyes on Paul as he stepped out of the room and closed the door. "Perhaps she was upset about something and went there to be alone." He turned to his sisters. "Why don't the two of you check upstairs? Maybe it was too noisy last night, and she decided to sleep there. And Paul, why don't you check the boathouse?"

Paul's eyes narrowed. John must have seen him with Anne last night.

"The boathouse?" Jeannette asked. "Why would she be there?"

"Just a thought," he said with a shrug. Then, with a wicked smile and lighthearted gait, he left them.

The twins headed toward the servants' quarters, but Paul hesitated at John's door, his eyes riveted on the knob. Charmaine might have taken cover in the dressing room. Indecisive, he contemplated going in, but decided against it. If Charmaine had slept with his brother last night, John would have flaunted the conquest. Besides, she wouldn't do something that dimwitted.

Suddenly, he was very hungry. Dismissing the thought of Sunday Mass, he went back to the dining room for breakfast.

Not a half-hour later, John returned to the dressing chamber with fresh bed linens and clothing for Charmaine. He found her working out the tangles in her hair with his comb. He hadn't thought to retrieve her brush.

She turned quickly when he entered the room and blushed, memories of their night together rushing in.

She was radiant, and John's heart missed a beat as her shy manner swiftly aroused him. There would be time for that later. He smiled joyously, knowing he would have limitless nights with this woman.

"The coast is clear, my Charm," he said, taking her in his arms. "The girls are searching for you upstairs, and I'm to find you in the chapel, awaiting Mass."

He wondered if she had heard his brother's voice in the hallway, but didn't ask. Instead, he cupped her chin and kissed her tenderly.

It served as a stirring reminder of their lovemaking and left her so incredibly giddy she grabbed hold of him for support.

"It was worth the wait, my Charm."

He stepped out of the dressing room so she could dress. When she returned to his bedchamber, she found him spreading a clean sheet over the soiled one and looked at him quizzically. "You'll understand tomorrow," he explained. Without a word, she helped him make the bed.

"Now, come with me," he commanded, scanning the hallway before he led her from the bedroom.

They descended to the foyer and walked through the messy ballroom. The staff had retired late, and the tedious task of cleaning up hadn't begun. The lavish hall was empty and quiet.

"It's early for Mass," Charmaine said as John led her to the chapel doors. Like a bolt of lightning, a new thought struck her, and she froze.

"What is the matter?" he queried.

"I'm in a state of mortal sin," she moaned, bringing her hands to her mouth. "Everyone will know when I refuse communion."

"Don't fret, Charmaine." Though his voice was kind, she was certain he would mock her religious conviction. Instead, he said, "We haven't come for Mass. We've come to exchange marriage vows. That is—if you'll have me?"

Charmaine was dumbfounded. When John had left her this morning, cold reality set in, and she'd chastised herself for succumbing to her physical yearnings. She was a good girl, had always been a good girl! Not even the memory of their intimacy—that crowning moment when she had been one with him—could assuage her belated misgivings. Yes, she had given herself to this man, but until this very moment, she had been afraid to hope he wanted her as completely as she wanted him.

"Have you?" she asked incredulously. "Surely you jest?" But one look at his earnest face, quietly waiting, and she knew he was dead serious. Her joy burst forth, and she threw herself into his arms. "Of course, I'll have you!" He lifted her clear off the floor and whirled her around. By the time he set her back down, she was shaking all over, tears streaming down her cheeks.

They stepped into the chapel and found Father Benito preparing for a large congregation of worshippers. John grasped her hand and pulled her to the altar with him. When he explained his reason for being there, the priest immediately objected, contending he could not officiate over the holy sacrament of matrimony during the solemn Lenten season. "Today is Passion Sunday. It is entirely inappropriate. And there is the matter of confession," he continued. But before he could finish protesting, John fanned a wad of ten-dollar notes under his nose. Charmaine gaped in disbelief as Benito snatched them and, without so much as one repentant word from either of them, made the sign of the cross and intoned a general prayer of absolution.

The chapel door opened, and George and Mercedes stepped in.

"Our witnesses, my Charm," John explained.

In less than five minutes, they had spoken their vows and were husband and wife. Charmaine thought she was dreaming.

"Where to now, my Charm?" John asked. "Mass doesn't begin for another hour, and we can't hide here forever."

"No," she agreed, "and the girls are probably still looking for me."

"Why don't we go back to the nursery?" he suggested. He wanted to take her back to his room, but that would have to wait until tonight.

They passed a few guests as they made their way upstairs, all too exhausted to pay them much notice. Still, Charmaine breathed a sigh of relief when they reached the nursery. She didn't fancy coming face-to-face with Paul just yet. It was short-lived, however; Paul's chamber door swung open, and he stepped into the hallway.

"So, you've found her," he said.

Charmaine wondered what he meant. Paul's assessing eyes raked her from head to toe as if plumbing for secrets, making her terribly uncomfortable.

"She was precisely where I said she would be," John replied, "in the chapel, praying."

Yvette's voice rang out from the north wing. "There you are! Jeannette and I have been looking for you everywhere."

"Where have you been, Mademoiselle?" her sister asked, rushing forward. "We were worried when we didn't find you in your room."

Charmaine looked at each of them, quickly formulating an answer under Paul's scrutiny. "I couldn't sleep after all the excitement."

"You didn't go to bed at all?" Paul interrogated.

To John's amazement, she looked him in the eye and replied, "I was upset by something I saw from the balcony last night."

Paul appeared shaken.

"What was it?" asked Yvette.

"Nothing important," Charmaine answered laconically, turning to the girls and reminding them they had best get ready for Mass.

A short while later, she entered the chapel again, this time with Jeannette and Yvette on either side of her. It was empty.

They had just finished their prayers when John appeared in the doorway. Yvette saw him first. "What are you doing here?" she whispered incredulously as he lifted Jeannette over his lap and placed her to his right so he could sit next to Charmaine.

"Attending Mass," he stated simply, a twinkle in his eyes.

Charmaine was astounded as he took her hand and cradled it affectionately on his warm thigh. He had left them to bathe and shave, and she'd assumed she wouldn't see him again until breakfast. But now, here he was beside her, feeding her pride. Blissful beyond measure, she looked up at him with a brilliant smile. In reply, he raised her fingers to his lips and kissed them tenderly. The twins exchanged glances and giggles.

Charmaine could only wonder what the other family members thought when they saw John there. She kept her head bowed, more in thanksgiving than to avoid suspicious eyes. John, however, gave a friendly nod to anyone who looked his way. Frederic's brow rose, Agatha's eyes narrowed, Anne stuck her nose high in the air, Rose's lips curled with a knowing smile, and Paul simmered.

The entire congregation stood as Father Benito entered the sanctuary. Charmaine hardly heard the opening prayer, but her pulse quickened with the pronouncement: "This Mass is being offered for the repose of the soul of Colette Duvoisin at the request of her husband and her children."

Charmaine's eyes closed in silent agony. *One year ago today! How could I have forgotten?* John grasped her hand and squeezed her fingers. She stole a glance at him; he was smiling. The sorrow passed, and her heart grew light.

She couldn't concentrate on the Mass, her mind possessed of her incredible experience the night before. She blushed, and noticing John studied her, the color in her cheeks deepened.

During the Consecration, she began to fret over taking Communion. But when the time came, John nudged her up and out of the pew, his hand under her arm. He remained close and prodded her toward the altar. Unable to protest without making a scene, she found a spot to kneel with John beside her. Father Benito reached him first, and with great reverence, the host was placed on his tongue. John bowed his head and waited for Charmaine. They rose together and rejoined the twins in the pew. As she knelt down once again, she offered up her petition and asked the Lord to bless her new family this day, most especially her husband. *Forgive me for receiving your precious gift while in a state of mortal sin*, she silently whispered, *but I do love him so.* John's head remained bowed long after she had finished.

Later, she asked him why he had prompted her to receive the Holy Eucharist. He looked at her with a mischievous smile. "Of all the grave sins in this world, my Charm," he replied, "making love to you will never be one of them." His wise words were a tender absolution.

The ceremony ended, but Father Benito detained the assembly a moment longer. "Godspeed to our guests who will be journeying home. Before you leave, John would like to say a few words."

To everyone's surprise, John stood and walked to the front of the chapel. "Good morning," he greeted, glancing over the congregation. "Because you are all here, family and friends alike, this is the perfect time to introduce you to my wife—the woman I love—Charmaine Duvoisin."

Charmaine heard her married name pronounced for the first time, and her heart leapt.

His eyes rested momentarily on the twins. "We were married earlier this morning, and we want to share our happiness with all of you."

He gestured for Charmaine to stand, and though disconcerted by the large, attentive crowd, she proudly rose to her feet. He went to her side and took hold of her arm. Someone started clapping and the twins immediately joined in gleefully.

"Oh, Johnny, oh, Mademoiselle Charmaine, is it true? Is it really true?"

"Yes, Jeannie, it's really true."

They were stopped numerous times as they wended their way to the chapel doors, guest after guest stepping forward to offer congratulations. The family held back until the end. Rose shook a crooked finger at John, but hugged him close, a long, heartfelt embrace. George nudged his grandmother along, giving John another hearty clap on the back. Mercedes hugged Charmaine again. Paul was next. His eyes were dark, and Charmaine shivered. He had to be told sooner or later, and this was the best way for him to find out. He said nothing, but glared at John, who, undaunted, stared him down. Agatha extended them cordial good wishes.

Frederic was the last to leave the sanctuary, offering his hand to John. To Charmaine's surprise, John took it. "Congratulations, son," he said, his voice husky, "may you be truly happy."

"I intend to be," John responded without acrimony.

"And you, Mrs. Duvoisin," Frederic added, "welcome to my family. I hope you know what you're entering into," he quipped.

"I think so, sir," she said timidly as he bent forward and embraced her, his lips lightly brushing her cheek.

"Shall we break the fast?" He gestured toward the dining room, allowing Charmaine and John to lead the way.

The twins remained by his side, bantering happily as they skipped along. "Isn't it wonderful, Papa? Charmaine is part of the family now! We told you it would be a good thing to invite Johnny home. We were right, weren't we?"

"Yes," the man breathed expansively, "you were both very right. Come now, I'm famished. Let us see what Fatima has prepared for us."

Charmaine enjoyed Cookie's reaction most of all. Choking back tears, she exclaimed, "Only thing could've made me happier today, Master John, would've been if you'd have married me."

John gave her a huge hug, and Fatima had all she could do to contain herself.

"Master John, you know better than to kiss me like that. Now look what you've done—you've gone and made me cry! Now you get out of here and save your hugs for Miss Charmaine."

If there was any talk about the early morning wedding, Charmaine was unaware of it. Throughout the day, she received many warm wishes, and John happily introduced her over and over again to anyone who approached them.

She saw little of Paul. After breakfast, he left with two of his guests. She was thankful he kept his distance, but she dreaded the inevitable confrontation.

For the first time in years, John and Frederic carried on a cordial conversation at the table. Charmaine looked away when she caught their eyes on her. If she could have read Frederic's thoughts, she would have been abashed.

He wondered about the hasty marriage. Had John seduced Charmaine last night? Her crimson face led him to think so. But no matter; John had chosen well, and Frederic felt a fondness for his son as never before. John had finally buried Colette and was willing to accept Charmaine's wholehearted love. Frederic knew Paul was angry. Nevertheless, Paul wouldn't have allowed Charmaine to slip away if his feelings ran as deeply as John's. Frederic hoped Paul would accept the marriage without interfering—that history wouldn't repeat itself.

As the day drew on, the guests departed, sent off with endearing farewells. They would get settled for the night on the *Falcon*, the *Raven*, and two of Paul's new merchantmen, setting sail for home at the break of dawn.

Agatha breathed a sigh of contentment when the last carriage pulled away. The week had been well worth her grueling efforts. This was her destiny. For the first time, she was truly recognized as the mistress of the Duvoisin manor. John's marriage to the governess was the icing on the cake, a balm for her little setback with Frederic last night. When John left Charmantes, perhaps in the next few days, Charmaine Ryan would go with him. Perhaps they'd even take the twins. Then she'd send Paul to Espoir and have her husband all to herself, reliving those days of blissful rapture before cruel, twisted fate had wrenched him from her all those years ago. It was time to pay her brother a visit and relate the good news . . .

Robert expected to a find a desperate patient on his doorstep, but was surprised to see his sister instead.

"Oh, Robert," she declared as she stepped over the threshold, "the gods have smiled down upon us this day!"

She spun around to greet him, a brilliant smile lighting the whole of her face. But he had already returned to his bedchamber where he had been busy before she came calling. Agatha followed him. Something was amiss. A trunk was open at the foot of his bed, packed with clothing.

"Are you going somewhere?" she queried in consternation.

"Yes. I'm leaving."

"Leaving? You can't be serious. The past few days have been fortuitous. Our plans—"

"Your plans, dear sister, not mine," he said softly.

"What do you mean, *my* plans? You've shared in all my dreams and desires."

"Yes, *your* dreams and *your* desires."

"Now, Robert," she soothed, "what is that supposed to mean?"

"I have desires, too," he sneered, his eyes meeting hers. "I thought you understood that. You led me to believe I mattered. But last night, after watching you *admire* your husband, I realized I've been a dolt these many years, a simpering dolt, happy with the scraps you've tossed my way."

She bristled, but he continued. "Frederic offers us security," he mimicked in an effeminate pitch. "I must right the wrongs perpetrated against me—and then, Robert—then we will be together." Suddenly, his voice was no longer mewling, but hard and clipped. "You've no intention of leaving Frederic, even now when you have everything you want, even after all he has done to you. You love him! Have always loved him, even when you've hated him!"

"Yes, I love him!" she screamed.

"Then why pretend with me? You used me. I know that now. That was why you kept me around. You used me for your own conniving ends."

"Now, Robert," she purred, coming close to him, "that's not entirely true. And you yourself conspired in the beginning."

"Because I loved you—and cursed the man who nearly destroyed you!"

"And I shall always love you," she whispered, brushing her lips across his sallow cheek. "You are my brother, after all."

"Enough! No more games!" He shoved her aside and grabbed more clothing from his armoire. "You don't need me anymore. And I think I've finally had enough of you. Like your guests, I shall be aboard the ship that departs for Richmond tomorrow. And I shan't be back."

"But how will I explain your departure?"

He eyed her with a crooked smile and snapped shut the trunk. "You don't need me to come up with ideas, dear sister. After all, duplicity suits you."

She did not press him and left without a backward glance.

Through the slit between curtain and window, Robert watched her go, combating tears as she climbed into the carriage. All hope she would beg him to stay faded as it lurched forward and rolled away.

Agatha Blackford, the other half of his soul, was gone—forever. But he had never really possessed her. He'd spent the whole of his life convincing himself she loved him, that someday, when she was completely healed, when she was vindicated, she would belong to him. But in his heart of hearts, he knew the truth. He sat hard on his bed and, with head in hands, looked back on the thirty years that had brought him to this despicable moment.

As children, he and Agatha had been close, even into

adolescence—too close, as their father would say. But their mother indulged that "love"; they were twins after all. Lucy Blackford idolized her eldest children and spurned her daughter, Elizabeth, five years their junior and the apple of their father's eye. Lucy turned a blind eye to the ridicule Elizabeth endured at Robert and Agatha's hands.

Robert Blackford senior had been a merchant on the Mersey River in the heart of Liverpool, a modestly wealthy man. And so, he could afford to send Robert to university to study medicine. But only men went to Oxford, and Robert missed Agatha terribly while he was away. He did not know one of their father's wealthiest suppliers, Frederic Duvoisin, had caught her eye, or he would have hastened home earlier and put a stop to the blossoming love affair. Even now, he was consumed with jealousy as he remembered those first few months when Agatha's eyes lit up at the mere mention of Frederic's name.

"Don't be silly, Robert," she'd cajoled. "I'm a spinster, for heaven's sake, and people are talking about us! I don't love him, and I will always have you close. Marrying him will keep up appearances and afford us security at the same time. Besides, someday I may wish to be a mother."

Soon they were planning a wedding. Frederic Duvoisin loved her, Agatha averred. In truth, Frederic was sealing a business deal with Robert senior, forging a robust family enterprise. The two men had included Robert in a late night conversation, tallying the benefits both sides would reap from the union. Frederic would supply the imports; Robert senior would secure buyers and distributors.

"So much the better if Agatha fancies herself in love with Frederic," his father confided that night as they left the inn where Frederic was lodged.

"She is not in love with him, Father," Robert bit out.

"How would you know that, son?"

"She told me."

"She is a woman, Robert, and a beautiful one at that. She's held many a swain at bay, but now it is time. Frederic and she make a handsome couple. It is wise for the family business. With Agatha as his wife, Frederic will not think of negotiating with other merchants in England. Medical practice is a dubious undertaking. The family business, on the other hand, is established. You'll have something to rely on after I'm gone. And there is Elizabeth to consider."

"I don't need something to rely on, Father. I can care for Agatha and myself. And if you're so worried about Elizabeth, why don't you offer *her* to Mr. Duvoisin? It's obvious he's charmed by her, and she, him."

When his father did not comment, Robert knew he had noticed the attraction, too. At that precise moment, the idea of sabotage took root, and Robert silently vowed Frederic and Agatha would never be married.

But the wedding date was set, and Frederic invited the Blackfords to his Caribbean home for a glimpse of the paradise island where he and Agatha would live as man and wife. They spent five months abroad and a fortnight on Charmantes. Agatha had fawned over Frederic, while he played the role of an eager groom-to-be, his hand always possessively under her arm, pretending interest in her every word.

But Robert saw how he watched Elizabeth, and how his younger sister reacted. He had had enough. The night before their departure for England and the impending nuptials, Robert cornered Elizabeth alone in the mansion's gardens. For nearly a week, he had carefully planned exactly what he would say. But then, the plot had been simple really, thanks to Frederic and his announcement that he would not be returning to England with them—that he had business to attend to both in Virginia and New York, and would follow on a separate ship.

"Oh, Robert," Elizabeth sighed when she saw him. "I'm going to miss Charmantes. It's so unlike our rainy England."

"Are you sad we're leaving or Frederic is remaining behind?"

"Why ever would you say that?"

"Isn't it obvious? You're smitten with him."

She squirmed on the bench, and he continued. "I daresay, Frederic has eyes for you, too. And, I think you know it."

She objected. "He's in love with Agatha—is going to marry Agatha!"

"A shame, really," he pondered aloud.

"What do you mean?"

"She doesn't love him," he stated sourly. "She's going through with this marriage for Father's sake and the business connections it will secure for him."

"You're wrong, Robert," she countered. "Agatha loves him dearly. I've seen them together. She dotes on his every word."

"As a good wife should," he bit out, smarting with the remark.

Elizabeth studied him curiously, and his anger settled into one enormous knot of jealous resentment. It fueled his zealotry, the focus he needed to execute his plan. "She's told me she does not love him," he declared. "In truth, she does not wish to marry at all."

Elizabeth shook her head. "I can't believe that."

The resentment grew. *Let her see how it feels—let the ax fall!* "Here you are, attracted to him," he continued, "wishing you didn't have to leave, yet you are to be taken home and wed to that pompous fop, Henry Davenport."

"What?" Elizabeth went white, and Robert delighted in her anguish. Evidently, thoughts of the odious man could make her physically ill, for her hands reflexively clasped the edge of the bench as if to steady a teetering world. Fat, bald, and thrice her age, Henry Davenport had asked for Elizabeth's hand in marriage on a number of occasions. Even Robert senior had been repulsed.

"That's right," Robert proceeded, prepared to drive the last nail in the coffin. He knew her well: She would claw her way out, then act impulsively. "On the eve of our departure, he bent Father's ear at the tavern, and Father relented."

Her hand flew to her mouth. "Father would never do that! He knows I despise that man!"

"Yes, but Mr. Davenport has made an impression on Mother, and she refuses to let the matter rest. Father has grown weary of her nagging. It's a shame you and she don't get on well. She is bent upon getting you out from under her roof, especially now that Agatha will no longer be there."

"Well," Elizabeth said, her chin slightly raised in a burst of defiance, "I'll speak with Father and let him know—"

"And what if your pleas fall on deaf ears, Elizabeth? Father has to live with the woman, after all. In the end, Mother always triumphs."

Grim reality seeped in, and she buried her face in her hands and wept. "What am I to do? Dear God, Robert, what am I to do?"

"There, there," he soothed compassionately, as if he'd gladly shift the burden of her anguish to his shoulders, his hand placed gently on her arm. "You know . . . there might be a way."

Her head lifted slowly. "What do you mean?"

"You could remain behind!" he declared, as if thunderstruck.

"Remain behind? But—"

"Just think," he hurried on, "you'd be alone with Frederic, have him all to yourself."

"Remain behind?" she muttered again.

"Yes—when we leave. Without Agatha here, you could confirm his feelings for you, perhaps save Agatha and yourself from a dismal and unjust future."

Robert studied her vacuous expression, certain the amber-brown eyes were deceiving; her quick mind was turning furiously. And then she spoke. "But if he has no feelings for me, my reputation will be ruined."

"Exactly. And if nothing comes of this 'experiment' with Frederic, Mr. Davenport will surely withdraw his proposal. That sort of man would never consider marrying a maid who'd been compromised, soiled or not."

A sudden smile broke across Elizabeth's face. "You are right," she said, clearly relieved. Just as abruptly, her manner changed, and Robert knew her conscience had intervened. "But, what about Agatha?"

He answered dispassionately. "I would say you are doing her a service."

"Even so—" she wavered "—this is so very devious. What if—"

He didn't allow her to finish. "Better to make your own decision than have it made for you."

"But how—how do I remain behind? I can't announce I'm not going. I will have to board the ship along with everyone else."

At last! "You have a point . . ." he said, pretending at deep concentration, settling his chin atop his fist, even though he'd formulated an elaborate solution days ago. "Vessels are always bustling before departure, and I can distract Father and Frederic. It shouldn't be terribly difficult to slip off unnoticed. As for Mother and Agatha, they will be preoccupied in their cabins and assume you've remained in yours."

"But what if a sailor waylays me?" she asked, dismay heavy in her voice.

"Simply tell them you left something behind in the carriage."

"And what happens when Mother and Father discover I am missing? Surely they'll demand the captain turn back."

"All the more reason not to dally. Make the most of this opportunity—*quickly*."

"I should tell Agatha," she suddenly decided.

"Do that, and I guarantee she will speak to Mother," he replied coldly, having expected such a thought. "You know she resents you and would cut off her nose to spite her face if it meant making you miserable as well." He smiled to himself when she grimaced; she knew he was right. Agatha despised her.

How she carried out the plan, he never really knew. He distracted Frederic and his father as promised, and later, when the ship was under way, he went to Elizabeth's cabin. It was empty. He'd been correct in counting on his family's disinterest in his younger sister. Meals had been served up in the cabins, and nobody even noticed her absence.

To ensure the vessel would not turn back, he executed the next phase of his scheme. Just before daybreak, he hoisted a ballast stone over the ship's railing and into the ocean. Immediately, a cry went up from the rigging, "Man overboard!" Within an hour everyone, except Elizabeth, was accounted for. Dinghies were dispatched, but the search was futile. They concluded she'd gone above deck to see the sunrise and had somehow fallen to her death. A funeral service was held, and they spent the remainder of the voyage in mourning. Even Agatha did not suspect the truth, not until three months later, when Frederic stepped off the ship with Elizabeth on his arm.

Never had Robert seen Agatha turn so ugly, lashing out like a cornered beast. But Frederic was unmoved and broke the banns, vowing to marry Elizabeth instead. When Robert senior objected, Frederic told him he'd compromised Elizabeth's reputation. Agatha wailed her good name had been compromised first, but Frederic pointed out Agatha's visit to Charmantes had been chaperoned; no one need ever know of their tryst as long as she kept her mouth shut. She was outraged and maintained she was carrying Frederic's child. Frederic hesitated, then called her a liar, scrutinizing her slim form. She prostrated herself at her father's feet, demanding he hold Frederic accountable. But Robert senior was in a difficult quandary. Agatha was capable of lying, his dear Elizabeth could be pregnant as well, and he didn't fancy alienating his most lucrative trade partner. Frederic's marriage to either of his daughters achieved the same economic ends he'd been cultivating all along.

The next day, Agatha enlisted Robert's aid and showed up at Frederic's lodging, confident if she were alone with him, she could win him back. But Frederic, though contrite, remained resolute. He loved Elizabeth. And so, he gave Agatha a sizable sum of money, promising he would provide for any child she produced within the next five months. When she cried at his feet, he offered to raise the baby himself, but she refused, vowing to revile him for all time.

For two weeks, she wallowed in anger and despair, refusing to eat. Elizabeth, in turn, lamented the part she had played. Robert turned mediator, interceding whenever Elizabeth seemed on the verge of forfeiting Frederic for Agatha's happiness.

Then, quite suddenly, a glimmer of hope punctured Agatha's black despair. Elizabeth vanished. She'd gone off riding, and hours later, only her horse trotted home. Anticipation flickered in Agatha's eyes as day after day, no one, not even Frederic, could uncover a trace of her. A week passed, and she was found—left for dead at the side of a road. Still, Agatha waited with bated breath, smiling when she learned Elizabeth had been raped repeatedly at the hands of a band of highwaymen. She was soiled—had gotten precisely what she deserved.

It didn't matter to Frederic. He remained by her side and nursed her back to health. Seeing her great shame, he broached the subject of his own disgrace—his lust for Agatha and the babe she might carry to term outside of wedlock. Later, Elizabeth told Robert this single admission, accompanied by his vow to take care of Agatha's child, alleviated her humiliation. Weeks later, they wed and returned to the Caribbean, leaving behind a hollow, disillusioned Agatha.

Agatha was indeed carrying Frederic's child, and so, the Blackfords closeted her away, determined to keep her dishonor a secret. She seemed impervious to rebuke, speaking to no one, not even Robert, who delivered the baby.

After months of apathy, a ray of happiness lit her eyes. The babe was handsome, a miracle amidst such anguish, and she cradled him so tightly it was often difficult to pry him from her arms. It soon became apparent she was not in her right mind, and their parents only made matters worse. Appalled, they refused to even look at the infant. *A bastard! A scandal!* they swore. He would not remain under their roof! Despite Agatha's wailing, Robert whisked him away. It was for the best, he decided, as he set off with a wet nurse and the tiny bundle, boarding a ship bound for the Caribbean and the boy's father. *We will be together when I return, Agatha. I will make you forget Frederic.*

Such was not to be the case. Robert arrived on Charmantes to find Elizabeth heavy with child. The couple took in Paul with open arms and asked Robert to stay and deliver Elizabeth's baby. He longed to return to Agatha, but could not refuse Elizabeth's pleading, and so, he was there on that bleak night that brought one life into the world and snuffed out another.

He did everything in his power to save Elizabeth. God knew he didn't want Frederic left a widower. The man might repent and marry Agatha after all. The delivery was torturous, the babe breech, and Robert could not stem the hemorrhaging. Elizabeth succumbed hours later with Frederic at her side.

Robert thought his own life would end in those hours before dawn, as Frederic's grief congealed into a feral rage. "Man, you are a butcher—a murderer! You delivered Agatha safely, but not my wife!"

Though Robert quailed, a new, more potent loathing took hold, its ferocity paramount to any terror he suffered. How could Frederic so hardheartedly wish Agatha dead? It had been satisfying to point the finger of blame on the men who had raped Elizabeth. In so doing, Robert cemented Frederic's latent fear the baby was not his. "I did everything I could!" he protested. "She was not fit to deliver a child after her ordeal!" With Frederic's darkening scowl, he added, "The baby is most surely born of their seed."

Frederic blanched and turned away, but as the days passed, his anger gave way to grief again. Remorseful over his irrational accusations, he apologized to Robert, asking him to stay on Charmantes; the island needed a physician. Robert declined the offer; his beloved Agatha awaited him in England. When Frederic entrusted him with a letter for her, Robert's worst fear was realized. Frederic intended to set things right: he would marry Agatha and legitimize Paul's birth.

On the voyage home, Robert worried over what to do, indecisive to the end. It didn't matter. Robert senior had married Agatha off to Thomas Ward, a former suitor who did not know about her confinement and thought she loved him. Despondent, Agatha had accepted the man's proposal, obedient to her parents' demands for the first time in her life. Robert couldn't say why he gave her the letter, but it evoked a poignant response: she cried on his shoulder, then allowed him to make love to her completely that night.

Later, when they lay entwined, she had whispered, "We are not defeated, Robert. We will build on this—you must build on this. I cannot be with my son right now, but you can. Elizabeth must pay for her deeds. What better way than to make *her* son suffer? Go back to Charmantes and set up your practice. Watch over Paul and never fail to remind Frederic *he* is the firstborn, the rightful heir. He must shine while Elizabeth's babe . . ."

Robert gazed incredulously into her tormented face. Noting her faltering sanity, and guilty over the part he had played, he told her what she wanted to hear. "For you, my love, I will do anything."

"I love you, Robert," she had sighed, "will always love you. You are the only one who has ever cared about me. Someday, I will come to you, and we shall be together . . . someday . . ."

Her earnest pledge seized hold of his heart, and his shallow promise became a quest. He returned to the West Indies, where he carried on her mission until yesterday. But last night, he embraced the truth he had doggedly brushed aside for all those years: she was obsessed with Frederic.

With a final sigh, he dragged his trunk to the door.

John shut the door and faced his father. He didn't relish meeting in this room. Some of their most damaging confrontations had taken place here.

"Be civil, John," Charmaine had cautioned. "Your father is making every effort." Though he placated her, he was not pleased. *Why do all the women in my life champion my father?*

"Come in, John," Frederic beckoned from the desk.

They were alone. "Richecourt is late?" John asked.

"Not late," Frederic explained. "I wanted to speak with you first."

John braced himself for the worst. Frederic lifted a sheaf of papers and handed them to him. "I believe they're all in order," he stated, "however, before you read them, I'd like to explain my decisions to you."

"Your decisions? I thought everything had been decided."

"By you, perhaps, but not by me."

John began to object, but Frederic waved him off. "John, I'm not about to get into a row with you; I only ask that you listen to what I have to say. Then, if you object, we can discuss it."

Shaking his head, John slumped into a chair.

"First, custody of Yvette and Jeannette will be turned over to you upon my death. Doing so makes a great deal of sense, especially now that you are married to Charmaine."

That's the good news, John thought. *Now for the bad.*

"As for the plantation and Richmond holdings, they will be left to Yvette and Jeannette. I know your misgivings concerning an impending civil war; however, the land is there, and at present should be accounted for. The girls will soon be women, and when they are introduced into society, it will likely be with you, in Richmond. When they come of age, the properties can be divided equally. However—" he drew a long breath "—the property needs to be managed until then. I ask you to remain on as guardian to their interests."

"No."

"John, hear me out. I believe this Underground Railroad business is dangerous for any plantation owner, but I cannot fault you for upholding your ideals. It is a trait I honestly respect in you."

John was taken aback. Certain he was being manipulated, he said nothing.

"Obviously, this escape system involves more than smuggling runaways aboard a Duvoisin ship. I gather Freedom is a stop on this 'railroad.' Can it afford to do without you?"

John hadn't considered this. He was, after all, Freedom's mainstay. Brian and Stuart might elect to remain on, but a new manager would not give them the protection he did. He'd discounted switching the station to Wisteria Hill long ago. Freedom was ideally situated on the Appomattox River, making hound tracking nearly impossible. "What exactly are you saying, Father?" he asked. "You *want* me to run your plantation as a stop on the Underground Railroad?"

"Run it however you wish—until your sisters come of age," he said simply. "And lastly," he went on, as if the previous matter were settled, "Charmantes—"

What was the score now? John wondered.

"—I didn't know what to do about that until this morning. Paul has Espoir, and I will give George Esprit. He deserves it for his many years of dedicated service to this family. However, Charmantes will be left to your children, my grandchildren. If you refuse stewardship, I will place it in Paul's hands until your sons come of age."

John swore fiercely. "You're still vying for the upper hand, aren't you?"

"I'm not surprised you see it that way, John. I've never given you a reason to think otherwise. However, there is only one reason I've made these adjustments. Leaving you and your children a piece of my estate is the only thing, other than life, I have been able to give to you." Frederic struggled for words. "I wish that were not so, but for you and me, it is too late for many things."

John didn't know what to say. He was uncomfortable with his father's naked emotion, and his anger ebbed. All these years, he had craved approval—affection—from this man. Now it was offered to him, the feeling was alien and disquieting. He changed the subject. "And what of the ships?"

"Upon my death, they will be left to Paul, with the stipulation that any transport you require is free."

John snorted. One more point for him. He'd sooner find another carrier than rely on Paul's generosity. "What of all your investments?" he pursued.

"They will be divided equally between you and Paul."

"I told you I'd—"

"Do whatever you wish, but they will be equally distributed by week's end. I have more than enough money to see me content until the end of my days. I don't want the Duvoisin fortune to dominate and undermine our relationship any longer." He paused for the moment it took to swallow against the lump in his throat. "I invited you home to start anew, John. I'm sorry about Agatha and Stephen. She got exactly what she wanted, and now Paul is angry with me, too."

"Angry?" John asked bemusedly. "With you?"

"He learned Agatha is his mother."

"You can't be serious," John chuckled, his incredulity fanned by his father's grim expression. But he didn't need Frederic's affirmation. In its insanity, it made sense—perfect sense. Agatha championed Paul because he was her son.

"I knew Agatha before I met your mother. After I pledged my troth to her, we became lovers. For her, it was love, for me, another business proposition. Then I grew to know your mother and experienced love for the first time. In the beginning, I held fast to my promise—attempting to ignore my feelings for her. But eventually, the idea of sacrificing that love became incomprehensible, so I broke the banns with Agatha, and married Elizabeth instead, even though I knew Agatha was carrying my child."

John was shocked. "No wonder she hated my mother . . ."

"And you," Frederic finished.

"So Paul *is* older than I am."

"By three months," Frederic answered.

The rest of the story unraveled slowly, Frederic speaking plaintively. When he finished, John inhaled. "Why didn't you tell Paul the truth?"

"I was ashamed."

John was astonished. To him, Frederic was only a bitter, vindictive man with a hardened heart. "But why was I promoted as your heir?"

"Because you were the son born into wedlock, because you

belonged to Elizabeth, and because, as you got older, I thought it was the only way to make amends for your childhood—my scorn."

Strange words, John thought. "So now, Paul knows, and he's upset."

"Yes, though he presented quite a front for his guests this week. But what is done is done, and it had to be told sooner or later. I thought you should know."

John nodded. After a moment, Frederic gestured to the documents he still held. "Are you agreeable to them?"

"Not really, Father," John smirked, "but what does it matter?"

Yvette tried to ignore the giggling in the hallway. She had promised to be good and stay in the nursery with Jeannette until Charmaine or John came for them. After all, the morning had been so wonderful, the news that John had married Charmaine so gratifying she truly intended to keep her word. John had gone off to speak with Father, and Charmaine was napping. Yvette turned her back to the door, which was slightly ajar, and stared hard at the book in her lap. Not a moment later, a man's devilish chuckle echoed outside the room. She glanced at Jeannette, who was deep in concentration at her desk, practicing her script. Yvette crept to the door and peered through the crack.

John gathered up the last of Geoffrey Elliot's papers. Except for one, he hadn't signed any of them. The contracts, which should have been simple renewals, had been completely rewritten, and now each one had a mistake.

John met Travis in the foyer. "Is Richecourt still with my father?"

"No, John," the manservant replied. "He was quite alone when I left him."

"Wonderful," John muttered, "now I'll have to ride into town to catch him."

"No, you won't, Johnny," Yvette called from the stairs.

John walked over to the landing. "You've seen Richecourt, then?"

"Maybe . . ."

He let out an exasperated sigh. "How much do you want, Yvette?"

"Ten dollars."

"You're mad."

"One dollar."

"Not worth it."

"Yes, it is," Yvette countered in a singsong voice. "You'll see."

John canted his head as if to read her mind. "Very well—one dollar."

"Oh goody!" she exclaimed. "With the five dollars Paul gave me this morning, that's the most money I've ever earned in one day!"

John eyed her in astonishment, the implications of her declaration and Paul's curious behavior that morning sinking in. "So, where is Richecourt?" he asked, mindful of the more pressing matter at hand.

Yvette's lips curled into a smile. "In Felicia's room. When do I get paid?"

John threw open the door to Felicia's room. There was Edward Richecourt suspended on all fours above the maid, his bare buttocks soaring high in a sea of blankets and discarded clothing, his manhood dangling in all its decrepit glory. In a panic, he dove under the covers, pulling them up to his neck.

"Holy coconuts, Pitchfork!" John exclaimed.

"This is not what you think!" the solicitor sputtered, his face flaming red.

"Far be it from me to jump to conclusions," John expounded, stepping into the room, his shock giving way to a crooked grin. "I suppose if you're providing legal counsel, there are as many ways to get paid as there are to get laid. Ah . . . I knew I'd get to see your horn one day, Pitchie."

"I have no horns!"

"Then you're bound to disappoint Felicia over there."

"I hardly think it proper to barge in on us like this!" Richecourt growled. "Was there something you wanted?"

"I've finished with Junior's papers," John replied, displaying the contracts. "I thought you'd like to look them over before you throw them out. They need a little work."

"Give them here," Richecourt ordered, arm outstretched.

"Come and get them."

The lawyer glared at him, then shifted uneasily. "Leave them on the bureau. I'll read them later."

"No, I've made some notes I want to show you now." John smiled devilishly, waving the documents in indication that Richecourt come and get them.

Felicia, nestled quite comfortably next to the flustered barrister, giggled.

Richecourt glanced around the room in search of his clothes, but they were piled on the floor next to John's feet. He hesitated a moment and swung his hairy legs over the bed, clutching the linens about him. Reluctantly, he stepped across the room until he ran out of covers just shy of John's extended hand. He reached out to grasp the papers, but John pulled them back. Humiliated, Richecourt took the last three steps and the coverlet fell away, revealing sagging shoulders, flabby arms, and a paunchy middle.

With an exaggerated grimace, John considered the specimen, then regarded Felicia in disbelief. "You went from my brother to this? You've lowered your standards, Felicia—or dropped them altogether."

"Give me those!" Edward barked and, snatching the papers out of John's hand, quickly lowered them to his groin to cover himself.

"Junior would be shocked to learn his papers have been reduced to fig leaves hiding the shriveled up—I mean—forbidden, fruit."

"Get out! Just get out!"

Despite her short nap, the heady day caught up with Charmaine, and her eyes grew heavy after dinner, burning when she blinked.

The twins were exhausted, too. She coaxed them upstairs, leaving John with George and Mercedes, who were celebrating their engagement, in the drawing room. She was startled when the nursery door opened behind her and Paul stepped in.

"Yvette, Jeannette, I want to speak to Charmaine—alone," he stated sharply. "And if you know what is good for you, you won't go running to John."

They sent anxious eyes to Charmaine, intimidated by his dark demeanor.

"It's all right, girls," she said. "Please wait for me in my room."

When they were gone, Paul studied her for a moment. She braced herself for the worst, but it was best to get this over with.

"What happened last night?" he asked.

She was surprised and heartened by his even tone. Perhaps this discussion wouldn't be as unpleasant as she anticipated.

"I don't know what you mean," she answered softly. She was not about to tell him she had spent the hours after the ball in his brother's arms.

"You know damn well what I mean," he snarled. "I thought we had an understanding. I proposed marriage to you. I thought that was what you wanted, have always wanted!"

Charmaine bowed her head. "I thought I wanted it, too."

"Thought? Didn't you know?" He was seething. "Let me understand this, Charmaine. You spend week after week in my company. You allow me to kiss you, to caress you, to make plans with you. You lead me to believe you desire me, too, but because of your morality, you require a commitment before you'll come to my bed. And then, when I give you that commitment, you marry my brother instead? Have I been taken for an idiot here? What is going on?"

"I couldn't sleep last night," she began, hoping to provide answers that would not widen the rift between him and John. "When I walked out onto the balcony, I saw you with Anne London."

He inhaled. "So, you ran to my brother's arms. Is that what happened?"

"No!" she railed, insulted he was making light of his tryst, while scorning hers.

Paul was satisfied with the response. He'd been right in assuming if John had bedded her, he would have bragged about it. No, his brother had simply capitalized on her vulnerability when she grew disillusioned with her fiancé's dalliance. "Don't be a fool, Charmaine," he proceeded. "John is never going to make you happy."

"And you will?"

"I've been honest with you," he reasoned. "I'm a flesh and blood man. You refused me time and again. Last night meant nothing to me."

"How can you say that? How can you stand there and say that to me?"

"Really, Charmaine, you are very naïve about men. Do you think John hasn't taken a woman to his bed since he left here last fall?"

"But he wasn't the one who proposed marriage to me. You were! If you cannot be faithful when you are engaged, how will you be faithful when you are married?" *And John was alone in his chambers last night,* she thought, *not cavorting with the loosest woman at hand.*

"Be a fool then. But you are the first and only woman I've ever loved. John, on the other hand, will *never* forget Colette. You know that, and I know it."

"You're wrong!" she objected vehemently.

"Am I?" he shot back, further annoyed when she turned her back on him. But when he realized she was crying, his anger abated. "Charmaine," he cajoled, "let us set this situation straight, right now. Let us go together and find Father Benito. The vows have not been consummated. The marriage can be annulled."

"No!" she sobbed, wrenching free of the hands that closed over her shoulders, free of the lies he was spinning to confuse her. She whirled around to face him. "I love John! I don't love you!"

She saw the pain in his eyes and softened her words. "I thought I loved you, Paul. But when John was gone, I missed him so. If he hadn't come back, I would have believed I meant nothing to him. But he did come back, and he loves me, too. He *does* love me! Last night when I saw you with Anne, I should have been hurt, but I wasn't. If it had been John in her embrace, I would have cried myself to sleep."

Her remarks cut deeply. "You're lying," he snarled, his anger barely in check.

"No, Paul. Truly, I don't want to hurt you, but I do love John."

He didn't hear her, for his mind was racing. "You saw me with Anne last night, but you say that didn't upset you. Yet, John finds you praying in the chapel this morning and claims you were very upset . . ." His thoughts trailed off as he pieced the puzzle together. Then he glared at her through smoldering eyes. "You spent the night with him, didn't you?"

Her silence was affirmation enough.

"You little fool! You've thrown away the happiness we could have shared! John knew you were vulnerable. Can't you see he's using you to get to me?"

When she shook her head in denial he pressed on, determined to hurt her as she had hurt him. "Do you know he came to me and suggested I marry you before he left here six months ago?" He smiled in satisfaction at her stunned face. "It's true. Ask him. He doesn't love you, Charmaine. He's just using you. And when he's had enough—"

"Stop it!" she screamed. "I hate you! Get out!"

When he didn't budge, she flew at him, pummeling his chest with both fists. "Get out, I tell you! Get out!"

Frederic heard the cries coming from the nursery and pushed into the room to find Charmaine in hysterical tears. "What goes on here?"

Paul spun around. "I was leaving," he bit out.

"It's best you do," Frederic warned, catching hold of Paul's arm as his son attempted to brush past him.

Paul stopped, looked down at his sire's hand, then met the man's eyes. "Charmaine is John's wife now," Frederic said. "Remember that."

Paul had no intention of heeding his father like a scolded child, and he tore away. Frederic watched him leave, then turned to Charmaine.

She fought to master her emotions, wiping away her tears. "I knew I was going to have to face him. But it was terrible. I've hurt him deeply."

"Perhaps," Frederic offered, walking over to her. When she wouldn't meet his gaze, he placed a finger under her chin and forced her to look at him. "I would say it's more a matter of wounded pride."

"I wish it were so simple," she murmured.

"Do you love my son, Charmaine?" he asked.

She knew he meant John. "I love John deeply."

"Good, because he needs that love, and I believe he loves you just as much. He has had many hard knocks in his life, but because of you, his future looks very bright. This marriage has made me very happy today."

John was highly agitated to find them together. It was apparent Charmaine had been crying. "What is this all about?"

She went to him in relief. "Paul and I had words. Your father intervened."

John's eyes darkened, but he said nothing. After Frederic bade them goodnight, he put an arm around her and led her back to his room. Once there, she reveled in a soothing bath, leaning her head back against the rim of the tub and closing her burning eyes. Perhaps the water would wash away Paul's bitter remarks.

John left her to tuck the twins into bed, but returned long before she was finished. He sat on the rim of the tub. Embarrassed, she sank modestly into the water to conceal her breasts. But he wasn't looking at her, his thoughtful gaze cast beyond the room. "Will you tell me what Paul said to you? I know you were crying."

She closed her eyes and whispered, "It was terrible. I knew it would be."

"I'm sorry, my Charm," he said. "I had hoped to spare you his wrath. When he disappeared today, I thought you were safe."

"If it hadn't been today, it would have been tomorrow," she said, though she knew Paul had cornered her in the hope of sabotaging her wedding night.

"Did he hurt you?"

"Only with his words, but I hurt him, too. John—what he said doesn't matter. I don't want it to come between the two of you."

"It matters to me," John replied heatedly. "We must understand each other if this marriage is to be a success. What did he say?"

She studied him, then plunged ahead. "He called me a fool—said you could never love me as he could—that your heart would always belong to . . ."

"Colette," he supplied.

"Yes," she whispered.

"Damn him," John swore, but to Charmaine's chagrin, he did not deny the assertion. She looked at him with tear-filled eyes, and John read her pain. "You don't believe that, do you? Charmaine, you can't possibly believe that."

"I don't think I do," she choked out. "I don't want to."

"Charmaine, I love you, and only you. Colette is dead. Yes, I loved her, but I had resigned myself to a life without her before I came back last August. Still, the love I shared with her has made me a better man, one who understands what is valuable in life. I'm not about to lose you now that I know you love me in return."

"Is it true you told Paul to marry me before you left for Virginia?" she asked, dreading the answer.

John regarded her pensively. "I suggested he marry you *before* Pierre died, when I knew I had to leave. I had feelings for you, but I was afraid—afraid I'd only hurt the children if I stayed—afraid I'd hurt you. When Pierre died, all those fears were confirmed. I left because I had interfered in everyone's lives: my father's life, Paul's life, the twins', yours, and most important, Pierre's, and the consequences were devastating. I didn't want to live that way any longer, to do the very things my father did to me, be the hypocrite."

"Then why did you come back?"

"I came back because a friend persuaded me. I came back because I missed my sisters, because I missed you."

"Would you have returned without an invitation?" she asked apprehensively.

"I would have stayed away," he confessed. "As I said, I didn't want to interfere. I missed you, Charmaine, but I didn't realize I loved you until I walked up to the house a week ago and saw you standing there. I was amazed Paul hadn't married you yet. I was *happy* he hadn't married you."

"And you didn't interfere last night?"

"When I took you to the ball, yes, I interfered," he replied. "I was angry at Paul—the way he was treating you. He had six months, Charmaine, six months with you all to himself, and still, he threw away his opportunity to have you!"

"And after the ball?"

"You came to me, Charmaine. I asked you if you were sure before we even started. So, you tell me—did I interfere?"

"No," she murmured, the color rising to her cheeks again.

His eyes searched hers, then he asked, "And you, Charmaine, did you come to my room last night because you saw Paul with Anne?"

She was astonished, uncertain if he were serious. "Self-assured John Duvoisin needs to ask me that?" she teased, but when his eyes remained earnest, she realized he was as vulnerable as she. "No," she answered honestly, "I wasn't upset. I came to you because I love you, John. I suppose I realized it when Paul proposed, but I didn't know how to tell him, or how to tell you. I was frightened to tell you. When I watched Paul and Anne go off to the boathouse, everything became clear. Paul's walking away didn't matter. But I would have been heartbroken if you walked away. I don't want you to ever leave me again. I love you, John."

His heart expanded jubilantly, and he leaned forward to kiss her.

"One more thing," she interrupted, forefinger to his lips.

"Yes?"

"Do you really have a mistress in New York?"

His brow lifted innocently, but his smile turned raffish. "Not anymore."

The water was growing cold, and she shivered. "Come," he coaxed, "it is time you were about your bath."

He rolled up his sleeves and lathered the sponge. When she leaned forward to take it from him, he held it out of her reach, chuckling when she blushed. He lifted a shapely leg out of the water and washed her ankle, her calf, then her thigh. He started on the other leg, and she could feel her tension falling away. He moved behind her and pressed the sponge to her back, massaging it over her shoulders, down one arm and up the other, a soothing caress. He nudged her forward and washed her back. She felt his lips on her neck, then on her shoulder, sending a shiver of pleasure down her spine. He discarded the sponge, and his hands traveled down her arms, moving to her breasts, cupping them, brushing his thumbs over her nipples and coaxing them erect with desire. Charmaine groaned and closed her eyes to overwhelming, burning passion. His hands traced over her belly and stroked the inside of her thighs.

When she could stand it no longer, she pushed up from the tub and stepped out of the water. John grabbed the towel off the armchair and, coming from behind, draped it over her shoulders. She was shaking uncontrollably, but not from the cold. He dried every inch of her slowly, then turned her around so she faced him. Using the towel, he pulled her naked body to him, dropping it as he encircled her in his arms and kissed her. His hands roamed freely, finding her womanhood, where ever so lightly, his fingers stroked and teased until she was moist with anticipation. Her loins pulsed with desire, and when he drew away, she looked up at him and pleaded, "Don't stop."

He quickly stripped off his own clothing and led her to the bed, pressing her gently into the soft mattress as he rolled on top of her.

"I do love you, Charmaine," he affirmed in a husky voice.

"I know you do." She smiled, relishing the ecstasy of being in his arms, yet certain his lovemaking couldn't be better than the night before. She was thrilled to learn she was wrong.

Monday, April 9, 1838

When they awoke the next morning, they were still in each other's embrace. Much later, they rose and John stripped the clean linen off the bed, revealing the stained sheet beneath.

"Let them think what they will," he stated with a wry smile.

"I'd prefer no one see that," Charmaine stated anxiously.

"Then the gossips in this house will have reason to whisper, my Charm. You are my wife, and I want them to treat you with respect." With that, he opened the door and glanced up and down the hall. No one was about. He took the clean sheet with him, depositing it in the laundry service room.

When he returned, she smiled warmly at him. "John?"

"Yes?"

"I didn't thank you for all you did yesterday: the way you treated me, your concern, our wedding, attending Mass and your beautiful announcement afterward." Her eyes welled, and her voice grew raspy. "You never cease to amaze me. The day was perfect in every way, and I shall cherish it always."

He inhaled contentedly, his happiness compelling her to say more. "Only your lovemaking surpassed it."

His expression turned wicked, lips curling deviously. "I told you long ago I'd not let your first ride end in failure—that I'd go to great lengths to ensure its success. We've given new meaning to Passion Sunday!"

They arrived at the dining room in time to watch a gratified George chastise an indignant Anne London. "I'm afraid you'll have to pack your own trunks. I won't permit my future wife to do so for the likes of you. It would be far below her rank in society." Anne marched away in a fulminating huff.

John chuckled. "Well, George, she hates all three of us now." He pointed to himself, George, then Paul's empty seat. "Shooed, booed, and screwed."

When they had finished eating, John gave Charmaine a quick peck on the cheek and headed toward the study, where he knew he'd find his brother. As he closed the door behind him, Paul lifted his eyes from the paperwork on the desk.

"We need to talk, Paul."

Paul pushed back in his chair and folded his arms across his chest. "I'm listening."

"I want you to leave Charmaine alone," John stated directly.

"Do you now?"

John didn't respond.

Annoyed, Paul added, "In other words, the game is over, and you've won. Is that it, John?"

"It hasn't been a game for a very long time. Maybe if you had realized that, Charmaine would be your wife right now instead of mine. However, she is my wife, and you will respect her as such. So, no more cornering her when she's alone, no more making her feel she wronged you when, in fact, it was the other way around."

Paul snorted. "What I said to Charmaine was between the two of us."

"No, Paul, you hurt her with your accusations, accusations that included me, and I won't allow it to happen again. I realize you were upset, but you've had your say, and there won't be a repeat performance."

"Aren't you a fine one to talk?" Paul roared. "When Father married Colette, you couldn't keep from tormenting her—even on the night the twins were born!"

"Colette has nothing to do with this," John stated softly, controlling the anger his brother was desperately trying to incite. "And if you think you can shake Charmaine's feelings for me by throwing Colette in her face, you're wrong. She knows Colette is in the past—that my love belongs to her alone."

"You're awfully sure of that, John. But I'll be right here when your 'love' fails her."

Agatha studied the portrait of Colette Duvoisin. Over the past week, many who entered the manor marveled over its opulence. Amongst its palatial splendors, this one item, this exquisite painting, rendered each and every guest momentarily speechless. She recalled their open admiration—the comments, the questions. *Oh my, isn't she breathtaking! Who is she?* Once again, the bile rose in Agatha's throat. She had forced a stiff smile, then uttered Colette's name nonchalantly, unprepared for the final insult: the astonished eyes, the perceptible nod that measured the third wife against the second in the space of one awkward moment. She would never suffer such humiliation again!

Agatha confronted her adversary—the woman who taunted her, even in death. *You frivolous little whore . . . the father and the son! Why do men always fall for trollops like you?* The blue eyes stared back, so lifelike, they condemned her from the lofty perch upon the wall. *Condemn all you like, but this is the last time you will harass me.* Like the wife, it was time for the painting to go.

She rang for Travis Thornfield. "I want that canvas removed," she stated blandly, her arm sweeping upward in a dismissive gesture, "immediately."

The butler hesitated. The portrait had hung in the foyer for nearly a decade, serenely greeting those who entered the mansion, and he knew how ferocious Frederic could be in all matters concerning the Mistress Colette.

"Immediately!" Agatha shrieked. "I said immediately!"

Frederic had come abreast of the upper staircase and heard the strident command. "What is this?" he seethed as he labored downward.

"Why, Frederic," Agatha replied bracingly, "this painting should have been removed a long time ago. After all—"

"Leave it alone!" he barked over his shoulder to Travis as he grabbed hold of Agatha's arm and marched her into the study.

Paul and John were there, but before Frederic could ask them to leave, Agatha pulled free of his grasp and allied herself with her son. "Tell your father I am the mistress of this manor."

Paul scowled and looked away.

"Agatha," Frederic began, "I have made a grave mistake."

Oddly, she seemed placated, but when he continued, she grew horrified.

"A year ago, I thought to right the wrong I perpetrated against you long ago, but I have only made a sad situation worse. Had I married you when Paul was a baby, things might have been different. However, we are two very different people now. I cannot continue with this ruse."

"Ruse? You call our marriage a ruse?"

"Agatha, I told you Saturday night—I don't love you. I have directed Edward Richecourt to draw up the documents required to—"

But she didn't allow him to finish, her long-contained agony erupting. "Now let me tell you something! You ruined my life! I loved you! I gave you everything! You proposed to me! *We* were betrothed! And then, oh God, you took Elizabeth instead—first to your bed and then to the altar! How could you do that to me? How could you turn your back on me when you *knew* I was carrying your child? *How?*"

Paul paled, and John surmised Frederic hadn't told him the entire story.

"Do you know how it felt to have my baby ripped from my arms because he was a bastard—because I had shamed my parents—" she accused, genuine tears streaming down her face "—how it felt to be called a whore because I had loved you? And Elizabeth, your *precious* Elizabeth, she knew my heart was breaking, but she stole you anyway. I hope she's rotting in hell!"

"Enough!" Frederic roared, his eyes glassy. "Any pain you endured was my doing, not Elizabeth's."

She abruptly composed herself, wiping away the moisture with the back of her hand. "That's right, Frederic, you excuse her, but I know what she did. *She* was the whore, for she did not have your vow when she went to your bed."

"Damn it woman!"

"I'm already damned," she pronounced proudly, chin raised. "You remember the money you threw at me?" When his brow gathered in confusion, she continued. "You said it would provide financial security for my child. You do remember, don't you? Tell Paul you remember!" She looked directly at her son. "Your father didn't intend to raise you as his own. He thought to buy me off—abandon us in England so he would never have to look at us—at you." She turned back to her husband. "I took that money, Frederic, and I invested it."

"Invested it?"

"I used it to bribe some men. They did not refuse my hefty purse."

Frederic felt the blood drain from his limbs. "What are you saying?"

"I can inflict pain, too." Her eyes turned maniacal. "I took great pleasure in knowing Elizabeth was raped over and over again. Those ruffians were only too glad to take your money. If only it could have purchased her life as well!"

Frederic descended on her in a deranged fury, his hands around her neck before anyone could react. Paul shouted, then grabbed hold of his arms, John, Agatha. It was all they could do to tear them apart, Frederic's burst of strength dissipating the moment he was disengaged. He slumped into a chair and buried his head in his hands. Agatha collapsed into the sofa, sobbing pitifully.

"I'm sorry, Frederic, but I love you!"

"Get out! Get out, damn you, and never come back!"

"But, Frederic, I'm your wife!"

"Not anymore!" he snarled, his face set in stone, her future inexorable.

"But, Frederic! I love you!" she implored. "Truly I do!" When she got nowhere, she turned pleading eyes on Paul. "I only did it for you . . ."

With great pity, Paul went to her. He knew his father would not change his mind and resentment consumed him. Placing an arm around his mother, he coaxed her up. "Come with me. You'll be comfortable on Espoir."

"But I'm the mistress of *this* manor," she objected, her expression strangely blank. "Frederic needs me here. He doesn't know what he's saying. He'll realize his mistake and . . ." Her words trailed off as Paul ushered her from the room.

John shook his head and sat opposite his father. "Are you all right?" he asked, amazed he felt sympathy for the man.

"Dear God," Frederic groaned. "I've made such a mess of things."

"From the deepest desires often come the deadliest hate," John murmured.

"She has every right to hate me."

"And my mother as well," John said, suddenly understanding why Agatha had despised him all these years.

"No, Elizabeth didn't do any of those things," Frederic insisted. "I was enamored of your mother just as my affair with Agatha began. Elizabeth had no idea we had been intimate until after she and I were lovers." Frederic bowed his head again. "But for Agatha to have wanted her dead—to have hired those men to . . ." His words fell away under the weight of the incomprehensible, the realization he'd seriously underestimated Agatha and her pernicious animosity. "She fostered more evil than you can imagine, John. For the first ten years of your life, I thought you were born of that vile crime against your mother, and I believed the rapes caused her death. Blackford convinced me of it. I suppose he was avenging Agatha."

John was astonished.

"It's no excuse," Frederic said, his hand massaging his forehead.

"You were only a baby; it shouldn't have mattered. But I missed Elizabeth desperately, and you were an easy scapegoat." He breathed deeply, and the minutes gathered before he spoke again. "What is wrong with me? Will my decisions ever prove sound? When will my family know peace?"

John had no answers. Hadn't he often asked the same questions of himself, cursed his propensity for hurting those closest to him? Unexpectedly, he was beginning to understand his father and was uncomfortable with the realization they were alike in many ways.

Yvette protested when she learned she and her sister were not invited to the newlyweds' picnic. "But we want to go, too!"

"Charmaine and I are on our honeymoon," John attempted to explain.

"I know what that means: you want to be alone so you can hug and kiss."

"Exactly," John affirmed, sending her into a pout.

Charmaine's face was beet-red. "They know we've been kissing, my Charm," he chuckled.

"In your bedroom," Yvette interjected. "Does it have to go on all day, too?" She spoke to her sister. "I liked it better before they were married, Jeannette."

"I think it's wonderful they're married," Jeannette countered.

"I have an idea," John offered. "Father has had a bad morning and could use a bit of company right now. If the two of you cheer him up, we'll take you on a picnic tomorrow. How would that be?"

"I guess it's better than nothing," Yvette relented.

With John's smile of encouragement, they went off in search of Frederic.

Charmaine enjoyed having John all to herself. He told her about his father's will and all that had happened with Agatha. "Paul's mother for Christ's sake," he muttered, still incredulous. "All these years, all the times we pondered it, and I never thought of Agatha."

Although astounded, Charmaine was happy to learn the woman would no longer reside at the house.

"That makes you mistress of the manor," John quipped. "You're Mrs. Faraday's boss now!"

Charmaine smiled wickedly. She'd never been anybody's boss!

"And you must look the part," he continued. "It's time for the governess garb to go. Tomorrow morning, I'm taking you to the mercantile to select a more appropriate wardrobe."

"I don't think we will find anything grander than what I've been wearing."

"We shall order them out of Maddy's catalogs. My wedding present to you." He kissed her then, a long, delicious kiss.

The twins awaited their return, having prepared them a wedding gift. "You are going to be so happy!" Jeannette bubbled from the steps of the portico.

"Oh, yes!" Yvette agreed. "It's the best present you'll ever receive!"

"Really?" Charmaine asked as they stepped inside the house and Jeannette nudged them up the stairs.

"Truly!" the girl gushed. "And best of all, *we* can enjoy it, too!"

The declaration drew a swift glare from Yvette, but it did not succeed in stifling Jeannette's jubilance. "They're going to see it anyway," she reasoned.

Yvette rushed ahead and stopped at Charmaine's dressing room door.

"Is this where your gift is hidden?" John asked, eliciting wide-eyed nods. "Well, what are we waiting for? The suspense is killing me."

Jeannette giggled, but Yvette scowled. "Go ahead and make fun of our present," she dared, "but you'll see how unique it is!"

"Unique? Why don't you let me be the judge of that? Open the door."

Jeannette led them into the immaculate room. Not one piece of furniture was out of place, not one speck of dust marred the polished wood floor. Nothing was out of the ordinary. The twins snickered at John and Charmaine's confusion.

"Well?" he demanded.

"Well, what?" Yvette inquired innocently.

"Where or what is our wedding gift?"

"Can't you see it, Johnny? It's right before your eyes." Yvette turned to Charmaine. "Maybe Mademoiselle Charmaine knows what it is."

"Yvette, this isn't fair," Jeannette interjected, "we haven't shown them everything." She opened the door to Charmaine's bedchamber and gestured for them to step in.

John's large armoire sat opposite them, against the wall that abutted the nursery. "How did you get that in here?" John asked Yvette.

"Joseph helped us push it along the balcony so nobody would see."

"And what is it doing here?" he probed curtly, his eyes narrowing. "And I hope it's not the reason I think it is."

"It's part of your present, silly!" Yvette giggled, unaffected by his stern regard. "Both rooms are your present."

"Isn't it wonderful, Mademoiselle Charmaine?" Jeannette asked. "Just think, you'll be right next to us again, and so will Johnny!"

"That's right," Yvette piped in, "now we can bring you breakfast every morning and keep you company during thunderstorms and—"

"Damn it, girl! Don't you know when you've gone too far?" John's heated query sent Jeannette scurrying to Charmaine's skirts, tears welling in her eyes. Yvette stood her ground, pretending confusion, though her eyes blazed brightly. "Whose idea was this—" he growled "—as if I really have to ask?"

"A fine brother you are!" Yvette spat back. "This gift took us all afternoon to organize! You'll never get another one from me! That's a promise!"

They matched scowl for scowl. Finally, John strode to the bell-pull, and yanked it violently. When Travis appeared, he instructed him to install a lock on the adjoining nursery door, then he asked for George.

"He's in the drawing room with Miss Wells," the manservant informed him.

"Can you send him up here?"

As Travis left, Jeannette looked at John woefully. "I thought you'd be happy with our present, Johnny," she lamented. "We could have so much fun."

John was at a loss for words in the face of the girl's innocence. Yvette, on the other hand, had ulterior motives.

George appeared in the doorway. "You wanted something?"

"I need help moving this bed into the dressing room. Yvette has decided the wedding present we need most is a new bedroom—this one in particular."

"How cozy," George chuckled under his breath.

"Aren't you taking this a bit far?" Charmaine interjected.

John looked at her in disbelief. "My Charm, on some future morning when we are 'occupied,' you will be thankful the door is bolted."

Charmaine blushed. "I wasn't talking about the lock. I don't understand why you want to move the bed into the other room."

"Why don't you ask Yvette how many glasses she has hidden in the nursery?"

When the bed had been moved and all was in order, Charmaine sighed in relief. She didn't relish the idea of sleeping with John in the room he had more than likely shared with Colette, the room with so many sad memories, Pierre's death the most potent. In this room, they would make their own memories.

John came up behind her. He must have sensed what she was thinking, for he said, "That should do it, my Charm. I didn't fancy sleeping in the other chamber, anyway."

Edward Richecourt turned his face into the wind, heaved a deep sigh, and looked at Helen. She stood at the railing with friends.

They certainly had plenty of gossip to bring back to Richmond. The ship lurched in the turbulent sea, and the ladies grasped the railing or clutched an arm to steady themselves. Helen . . . In her younger days, she had been the belle of Richmond. But they had drifted into middle age together, Helen more so than he.

It had been convenient, practical to marry Helen Larabbie. She was the eldest of three daughters, and her father, Neil, ran a respectable law firm in Richmond. Edward was young and ambitious, so when he began to pay court to the eldest Larabbie daughter, Neil couldn't have been more pleased. The family firm could be passed along to a son-in-law. Edward had an amiable relationship with the man, both professionally and personally. And Neil Larabbie was content with the two grandchildren Edward and Helen had given him, especially his grandson, who was studying law. Neil trusted Edward, expecting only that he uphold the firm's good name and keep his daughter happy.

Edward was always discreet about his infidelities. And what harm? Helen had little interest in the marital bed, and he'd found relief with youthful damsels who viewed him as distinguished and worldly.

Paul Duvoisin's triumph . . . It could well be Edward's waterloo! Old man Larabbie had at best ten years left. *Ten years!* God, what if he found out about the Duvoisin domestic? What if Helen found out? He didn't want to think about it, hated the fact it all depended on the whim of one man: John Duvoisin. Would he tell Larabbie? Edward hadn't even consummated the adulterous encounter, and yet, he'd literally been caught with his pants down. The last time this happened, John had extorted information about Paul's shipping venture. But John didn't seem to care about Paul's business plans anymore. Now Edward could only pray he'd come up with something to offer John in exchange for his silence. His future depended on it.

Chapter 5

Tuesday, April 10, 1838

JANE Faraday appeared in the bedroom doorway. "May I have a word with you, ma'am?" she asked.

Charmaine nodded, disconcerted by the woman's formality.

"As you know, Mrs. Duvoisin—Agatha, that is—hired a temporary staff for last week's festivities. She indicated the five most competent employees would earn permanent positions on Espoir. I'm assuming she has chosen from the servants that are already there."

Charmaine listened patiently, wondering, *Why is she telling me this?*

"There is one girl working here who is most deserving, and I recommend she be added to *our* staff."

The monologue ended, and Jane seemed to be waiting for a response. Puzzled, Charmaine said, "I suggest you bring the matter to Master Frederic."

"No, ma'am. He told me to bring it to you—you are the mistress now."

Charmaine was flabbergasted. *You're mistress of the manor now!* Evidently, Frederic thought so, too. It was incomprehensible! She rubbed her brow. "If you feel she is qualified, Mrs. Faraday, I trust your judgment."

The woman smiled and turned to leave, stopping shy of the doorway. She pivoted around, hesitant. "Ma'am, I apologize for what I said to you last fall."

"Apologize? I'm afraid I don't understand."

"I was in the laundry service yesterday when Felicia and Anna collected the bed linen—" Charmaine felt her cheeks grow warm, but Jane talked on "—and I want you to know I was wrong, terribly wrong. I hope you won't hold it against me."

"No, Mrs. Faraday," Charmaine whispered. "I won't hold it against you."

A few minutes later, John found Charmaine humming happily to herself.

"Something I did?" he roguishly laughed.

"If only you knew!" she giggled.

Sunday, April 22, 1838

Benito St. Giovanni stood before Frederic Duvoisin, having demanded this meeting directly after Mass, but now found it difficult to begin. Agatha had not kept her weekly appointment last Saturday; the reason confirmed first thing this morning. Her husband had literally banished her to Espoir. But why? Benito didn't fear exposure. If Frederic had knowledge of his unscrupulous dealings with the woman, *he* would have called this meeting. Even so, Agatha's exile could potentially prove disastrous.

"You wanted to speak with me?" Frederic prodded.

"Yes." Benito cleared his throat. "There have been rumors circulating, rumors concerning your wife. As your spiritual adviser, I think you should apprise me of your intentions."

"Do you?" Frederic queried laconically.

Benito cleared his throat again. "I do."

Frederic leaned back in his chair, a faint smile tweaking the corners of his mouth. "Very well. Perhaps you can be of service to me, Father. I have renounced Agatha as my spouse and have had legal documents drawn to that effect. Of course, we are still united in the eyes of God. I would like you to write to Rome and obtain a dispensation that will dissolve the marriage entirely."

"I can't do that!" Benito objected. "She is your wife. You spoke the words 'for better or for worse, until death do us part.' Rome will refuse. You will face excommunication if you proceed further."

Frederic merely chuckled. "Then the legal document will stand as my repudiation of the marriage. In either case, she'll no longer be called my wife."

Benito's eyes narrowed. This was not going well at all. He'd hoped to sway Frederic, reinstate Agatha to her post of mistress, and continue with his extortion. One more year, and he'd have accumulated enough wealth to retire comfortably. Suddenly, his source of income had been cut off, and the fervor of Frederic's declaration left no doubt it would remain that way. The only option open to him now was to leave Charmantes. He had no reason to stay. Nevertheless, he must carefully disengage himself, lest his departure raise suspicion. Best to set that in motion now.

"I am extremely displeased," he remarked condescendingly. "The lack of morality . . . Paul's gala celebration during the solemn Lenten season . . . A disregard for all that is holy . . . I tell you now, Frederic, I intend to retire by year's end. I've received word from family in Italy, a nephew who is ill. If you wish, I can write to my superiors in Rome and request a replacement."

Frederic grunted. "Do as you like Benito." He refrained from adding he doubted the priest would be missed.

Tuesday, May 1, 1838

The days fell in on themselves, a heady blend of lovemaking, picnics, and laughter, all of which left Charmaine glowing. Paul had moved to Espoir, venturing home only twice, and then for only a night. He had three reasons to keep his distance: Agatha, his father, and her. He barely acknowledged her during those visits, so she was glad he stayed away.

This morning they were breakfasting together—a true family—for Frederic was at the table, along with the girls, Rose, Mercedes, and George. Charmaine marveled over the change between John and his father, their discourse no longer baiting and angry. Yvette told a joke that left everyone chuckling. The girls were benefiting most from this newly won harmony.

Fatima bustled in with coffee and biscuits, frowning when she reached Charmaine. "Miss Charmaine, you ain't touched a bit of your food."

"I'm sorry, Cookie, but I'm not feeling very well this morning."

John leaned forward. "Are you all right, my Charm?"

"I'll be fine once this queasiness passes." She pushed her plate away.

John's eyes lifted to his father, who was smiling at them, a shared look that bewildered Charmaine. "Sir?" she queried, as if he had spoken to her.

"Charmaine," Frederic said, "you are part of this family, and I'd be pleased to have you call me Frederic."

"I wouldn't feel comfortable—" she began. Then she was muttering an apology, overcome by a wave of nausea. She pushed away from the table and ran for the kitchen, reaching the washtub in time.

"Miss Charmaine," Fatima soothed, "are you all right?"

In the next moment, John was there, placing a hand to her back. Another significant look passed between the cook and her husband. "Come, Charmaine," he coaxed, "why don't you sit down?"

"I'm fine now, really I am."

"Yes, I'm certain you're fine," John chuckled.

"Stop laughing!" she snapped.

"I'm not laughing. After all, I feel responsible."

"Responsible?" Charmaine asked, completely baffled. "For what?"

"Your condition." Then, he bent close to her ear and whispered, "Do you think it will be a Michael or a Michelle?"

She blushed a deep crimson, her innocence warming his heart.

"I love you, Charmaine Duvoisin!" he shouted. "Come! Everyone will want to hear the good news."

"John—wait!" she protested. "Are you certain? How can you be sure?"

"I suppose nine months or your tummy will tell."

Fatima laughed robustly.

Monday, May 7, 1838

When Frederic arrived at the tobacco fields, John was already there. John wiped his soiled hands on a rag and walked over to him. "What are you doing here?" they asked simultaneously.

Frederic chuckled, but John answered first. "Charmaine doesn't fancy leaving for Richmond yet, so I thought I might lend a hand. And you?"

Frederic tethered his stallion to a tree. "I ride out every day now. It does me good to work."

John nodded in understanding.

His father turned and gazed critically across the terrain. "I'm thinking of turning the ground over. The first crop wasn't what it should have been. Paul's initial assessment was correct; the fields need to breathe for a while. Then we can go back to sugar."

John frowned. "I thought Espoir's bumper crop flooded your market."

"Paul has done very well," Frederic agreed.

"It would be a shame to abandon this investment," John continued, gesturing toward the tobacco fields. "Perhaps the first yield was poor, but Harold says the tracts due for planting have lain fallow for four years. The crop should flourish in that soil, and I know a few tricks that will bring top-dollar at auction."

Frederic was inspired. "What do you suggest?"

"Fire-curing for one," John responded. "Add a little charcoal, and your tobacco will have a distinct smoky aroma and flavor. We'll have to build a couple of barns, but that shouldn't be too difficult."

"Let's do it. Where should we erect them?"

John was astounded. Frederic hadn't challenged his expertise. As they walked off to find a spot for the barns, he realized it was the first time they had worked side-by-side in over ten years—not since the day Colette made her choice.

Saturday, May 12, 1838

Paul sat alone in the study of his grand new mansion. It had been a month since the life he had known had crumbled. His triumphant ascent into the world of commerce had been tainted from the outset. He reflected on John's return, the confrontation that had removed his brother from Frederic's will and revealed the truth about his own parentage. Agatha was his mother. Even after a month, it was hard to believe. For years, he had longed to know the details of how he had been placed in his father's custody. Today, he wished he didn't.

He had achieved more than he'd ever dreamed possible, stood to inherit much of his father's fortune. Yet, it left him empty. John was legitimate, John had Charmaine, and John was man enough to stand on his own. What had John called him months ago? A pathetic fool? Yes, he was pathetic. He had revered his father, but had it earned him the man's admiration or respect? No—just his money, and *that* only when John had turned it down.

Then there was Charmaine. She had been lovely the night of the ball. He'd allowed himself to be manipulated and distracted, taking it for granted she'd always be there. But John had been man enough to pass up frivolous temptation and claim what he truly desired. Paul was certain this had played a part in Charmaine's decision to marry him, John's apparent propriety set in counterpoint to his incontinent behavior with Anne London, confirming he would always be a rogue. He rubbed his brow, remembering how she'd pummeled his chest and screamed her hatred of him. He could have loved her, but now she, too, was lost to him.

John, who had nothing, now had everything, even his father's love. Frederic might storm and rage, but in the end, he really loved his legitimate son. As for his bastard son? Frederic was willing to pay Agatha to raise him in some far off place, choosing never to know him. After all these years, Paul understood why he had never measured up.

A great shame laced with pity seized him. How often had he scorned Agatha, and still, she had championed him? Yes, she had done some terrible things, but he could empathize, and therefore, forgive. She had been egregiously wronged, had suffered at his father's hands. He would never allow her to suffer again.

Voices from the hallway brought him up from his contemplation. Agatha was talking to someone. "Go away! Frederic loves me! He'll be coming soon, and I don't want him to find you here!"

Piqued, Paul strode to the doorway, only to find her staring off into the distance. "Agatha?" he queried, uncomfortable with calling her "Mother." "To whom are you talking?"

She spun around and smiled at him. "Paul, you're here," she breathed. "When will your father return?"

"Father?" he asked in growing dismay. "My father won't be coming here, Agatha. He's in his home on Charmantes. Are you feeling ill?"

"I'm well, Paul. But he'll be here shortly, and I have to explain things to him. Once I do, I know he'll understand."

"Agatha," Paul cajoled, "why don't you retire? I'll call for a maid to assist you."

"No, no, I'd rather be awake when your father arrives," she stated resolutely, sweeping into the study.

It was the last straw. His father was to blame for this situation and had yet to answer for his ignominious actions. It was time they talked.

"Are you feeling better now, Charmaine?" John asked. She had reached the water closet just in time. The last week and a half had been very unpleasant.

"This is going to be a terrible nine months if I feel this way the entire time."

"Rose says it will only last a month or two," he reassured.

"That's easy for her to say!" she moaned, sitting hard on their bed. When he snickered, she fumed. "Go ahead and laugh! You had all the pleasure—"

"All the pleasure, my Charm?" and he raised a brow that set her cheeks crimson. "You're still blushing."

"Out!" she ordered, pointing to the door.

"Before I leave, I have something to discuss with you."

She eyed him apprehensively, his change of demeanor disconcerting.

"I've been here for six weeks now," he began, "but I have other matters to attend, both in Virginia and New York. I'd like to take you and the girls with me when I go. I spoke to my father yesterday, and he'll allow them to accompany us. I also want to show you our home."

She had stiffened even before he'd finished. Richmond . . . home . . . it did not beckon to her at all. Yes, she would be able to see the Harringtons, proudly introduce her husband to them. But thoughts of John Ryan raised the hair on the back of her neck. He was still out there. Charmantes was her haven; she did not have to worry about him here. "I don't think I could go right now," she replied, shaking her head. "I'm afraid I'd be ill the entire voyage."

"Very well. We shall wait a bit longer and see if Rose is right. My father should be pleased. He's beginning to realize how much Paul accomplished each day."

"You won't be overworking, I hope?" she asked, mindful of the grueling schedule Paul had always kept.

"Me? Never. But we won't be picnicking every day, either." He studied her for a moment longer. "Shall we take a walk together? The sunshine should do you some good."

Charmaine accepted John's invitation, but no sooner had they reached the foyer, and Paul strode in. His punishing gaze immediately settled on her. "John," he acknowledged caustically.

"Paul," John rejoined, stepping behind her and placing a reassuring hand on either shoulder. "We have a bit of good news. Charmaine is expecting."

"Congratulations," Paul bit out, his day turning more sour. "Where is Father?"

"In town with Yvette and Jeannette. Isn't that right, Charmaine?"

"Yes," she murmured, her eyes fixed on the floor.

Paul swore under his breath. He had hoped to corner Frederic at home; now he had to ride back the way he had come. Without another word, he was gone.

"Charmaine," John chided softly, squeezing her shoulders, "you must stop giving him the satisfaction of upsetting you."

Goose bumps rose on her arms, and her blood ran cold. "John," she murmured, dismissing his comment entirely, "would you take me into town?"

"Why?"

"I have a very bad feeling about Paul going there."

He stepped in front of her and canted his head. "Very well," he said.

She chose to take the horses; they were faster to ready. In less than ten minutes, they were on their way. She quickly set aside any concern the mare's jostling might endanger the baby; she felt no different than at any other time she had ridden and began to enjoy being out in the fresh air.

In town, they found Yvette and Jeannette shopping at the mercantile. The girls hadn't seen Paul, but Frederic had ventured to the dock; they were to meet him at Dulcie's in a half hour. Leaving Charmaine with them, John promised to do the same. He headed toward the harbor.

"Haul them off with the nets, then," Frederic commanded, "I'll stay down here and direct you when they're ready to lower the boom." The worker went off quickly, leaving him alone on the pier.

Frederic was enjoying himself today. He was thankful for his improving health, that he had not died as he had once prayed. John and he had come to a truce, and though they would never be completely reconciled, he was glad the interminable acrimony had subsided. His son had a wife, a baby on the way, and a future. This grandchild would be welcomed into the family with joy, rather than sorrow.

His two beautiful daughters were growing lovelier each day. In a few years, they would be turning many a young man's eye. For this reason, he had agreed to let John take them abroad. It was time they saw the world beyond Charmantes' shores. He would miss them, but John would bring them back, granting him more time to mend their healing relationship.

Despite his clash with Agatha and Paul's anger over it, it had been years since he'd felt this optimistic. Regrettably, he couldn't change the circumstances surrounding Paul's birth. Still, if he and John could take a positive step forward, Paul would certainly come around.

Frederic had wasted so much time, but here on the wharf, watching the men unlading the *Black Star*, he had a purpose once again. If only Colette were alive, waiting for him at home, life would truly be complete.

A large net was hoisted off the deck of the merchantman, cinching around nearly a ton of grain sacks. The vessel had weathered rough seas. Casks in the hold had collided and split open. The crew had bagged the grain that could be salvaged, but unlike the barrels, this cargo couldn't be rolled off the ship and had to be discharged with a boom and net.

Frederic cringed as the frayed ropes pulled taut, wondering why the crew hadn't divided the haul. Suddenly, the boom let go of its tether and swiveled wildly over the wharf in a one-hundred-twenty-degree arc, slamming into the foremast rigging. Puffs of dust exploded from the sacks as the spinning net bobbed back and forth, the mast's tapered yards puncturing the burlap with each collision. Amid the shouts of deckhands, the tether was slowly reined in, grain trickling onto the decks below. Frederic eyed the tattered, yet bulging net, certain the load was too heavy. "Buck!" he shouted, "You need to—"

"Father!" Paul approached, scowling darkly, his teeth clenched.

"Paul, I didn't know you'd—"

"We need to talk," Paul cut in, dispensing with false greetings.

"Come back to the house and have dinner with us. We can talk there."

"I don't have time, but I would like to clear up a few things."

Frederic took courage to say, "Paul, I know you are angry with me—"

"You can't begin to imagine how I feel about you!"

"I'd like the chance to explain," Frederic insisted, "but not here." Mindful of the dangerous work overhead, he took hold of his son's arm to lead him away.

"A chance to explain?" Paul laughed insanely, yanking free, appalled his father was still determined to keep the secret. "I'd say you've had over twenty years to explain! Now, when you're cornered, you want more time?"

"Paul, I never meant to hurt you. You are my son and I will always—"

"Don't—don't you dare say it! When I wanted your love—your acceptance—your approval, what did I get? Name calling, nothing more!"

Seeing the rampant confusion on his father's face, Paul stormed on, all the angrier with the realization the man was unaware of the ridicule he had endured as a young boy, even into adulthood. "It was easier for you to turn a blind eye to the taunting than to be honest with me. 'Oh, Paul Duvoisin,' " he mimicked, " 'the bastard Duvoisin? No, he doesn't know from where he came—but his father must have had one hell of a lay with his whore of a mother if he took her bastard under wing! All that money, but he's a bastard still!' That's what I heard day after day, and why? Because my 'well-bred' father wouldn't marry her. No, he sent her away with a hefty purse and wed her sister instead! How did you live with yourself all those years, Father—looking at me, knowing what you had done to my mother—*to me?* Answer me that? Did you think taking me into your home absolved you? That telling me she was dead legitimized my birth? That I—"

Suddenly, there was a shout from above. Frederic and Paul looked up as the boom swung over them, one rope rapidly unraveling down to a single ply of hemp. The strand snapped and the netting broke open, touching off an avalanche of fifty-pound sacks. Some of the punctured bags exploded with the forceful shift, showering their meal below. The rest fell in rapid succession, hitting the quay with thundering thuds, most splaying open and spilling forth a mountain of grain.

Charmaine and the girls stepped out of the mercantile and into the bright sunshine carrying two bundles of goods. "The two of you go on to Dulcie's," Charmaine directed, passing her purchases to Jeannette. "I am going to find your father and John. We shall meet you there."

Frederic fell on the settling heap of grain. Not a hand, not a boot, not a trace of Paul. He cast his cane aside, digging barehanded into the pile. He cried out for help, yanking at the heavy sacks, clawing at the fluid mass that caved in upon itself as quickly as it was cleared. Surely Paul was unconscious—would suffocate. Pray God, he wasn't dead already! He cursed his feeble arm, less hale than he'd thought, and cried out for help again. Did no one hear him? Would no one come? The longshoremen were suddenly there beside him, tackling the pile in the same frantic frenzy.

John felt a series of shudders rumble the wharf. Charmaine's earlier premonition took hold, and he broke into a run along the boardwalk, swiftly coming upon the disaster. Pandemonium ruled, then he heard George's voice: "What is it?" followed by his father's: "Paul—he's buried under all of this!"

"Good God!" George exploded, and seeing John running toward them, he let out a blood-curdling yell that incited anyone within earshot to come post-haste. "It's Paul! He's buried alive!" He, too, jumped into the fray.

Men were grabbing sacks and tossing them aside, some landing with huge splashes in the water, others splitting open on the quay. Still, there was a mountain of grain to clear away.

John spun around. Spotting Charmaine, he shouted to her. "Ring the bell at the meetinghouse and raise the alarm!"

Propelled by fear, she pressed herself to run. She looked back only once, remembering a similar accident long ago. Everyone had escaped injury then. Today, she prayed for the poor soul trapped beneath.

Paul was breathing. Through God's mercy, they uncovered his head first. Slowly, they cleared the remaining meal away.

"Paul, can you hear me?" Frederic beseeched, but his son lay unconscious. "Damn it, where's Blackford?" he snarled.

There was a murmur before Buck stepped forward. "He's gone, sir."

"Gone?"

"Yes, sir, left a month ago. But we sent for Doc Hastings."

Charmaine's fist flew to her mouth when she reached the scene. "Is he—?"

"Alive," John answered, breathing easier. "We're waiting for the doctor."

"Oh John, I knew something was going to happen. I just knew it!"

Frederic hobbled a few feet away and slumped torpidly on a cutoff pile at the pier's edge. John wondered how much more the man could endure in his life. John had to give him credit; somehow, he always managed to pull through.

Dr. Hastings arrived, and Paul was placed on a makeshift stretcher. Broken ribs, he concluded, which could be wrapped once Paul was home.

As the litter was raised, Charmaine picked the grain from Paul's hair, a gesture that disturbed John even in its seeming innocence. Paul groaned, and John noted the relief that swept over his wife's face. Before they began their trek down the boardwalk, Paul's eyes opened, and he slowly scanned the crowd that had gathered around, reading the concern on their faces. He attempted to sit up.

"Lie still," Charmaine admonished, chasing more granules from his shirtfront.

He grabbed her hand and pressed it to his lips, then lost consciousness again, his arm falling away.

"Don't be cross, John!" Charmaine beseeched as they rode home together. "He was hurt, and I was frightened for him."

"So was I, but I didn't brush his hair clean for him."

"You're jealous!" she accused and then laughed.

John squeezed Phantom's flank, nudging the stallion into a gallop. Charmaine was left behind to ponder his ill humor.

When the doctor deemed Paul fit for visitors, Frederic seized the moment. He had almost lost his eldest son, the son he had taken for granted. He was not about to squander this second chance. "I'm sorry, Paul," he whispered, standing over the bed.

Paul closed his eyes to the pain on his father's face. He knew what had happened on the pier, the effort everyone had exerted to pull him out alive.

"You gave us a fright," Frederic continued, searching for words. "Son—I don't know what I would have done if . . ." He faltered. "You have every right to hate me, but I *do* love you, and I'm proud—have always been proud—to call you my son. If you ever doubted that, then I'm sorry. I only kept the truth from you because I was ashamed of myself. I hope someday you can forgive me."

Paul could not open his eyes for the tears that burned there. Though he fought to suppress them, small rivulets chased down his cheeks and into his hairline. His throat was dry, and it was painful to swallow, to breathe. He opened his eyes, only to find his father's countenance mirrored his own. As Frederic turned to leave, he rasped, "Father—I'm no longer angry."

Charmaine eyed John surreptitiously from her mirror on her dressing table. He hadn't spoken two words to her since they had arrived home. His morose mood was quite amusing, and she thought to have a bit of fun with it.

"How is Paul?" she asked sweetly.

He only grunted, provoking a smile that danced in her eyes. But he wasn't looking her way. He sat hard on the bed, pulling off a boot.

She arranged a serious expression on her face and stepped in front of him. "You wouldn't object if I nursed Paul back to health, would you?" she asked nonchalantly, stooping to help him with the second boot and tossing it aside.

"The hell you will!" he exploded, nearly coming to his feet.

She ignored the outburst and pushed him back onto the bed. Propping herself atop him, she giggled. "John Duvoisin—the man who's so good at getting everyone else's goat—can't take a bit of teasing himself."

As his eyes narrowed, her fingers traced his hairline, and she studied every feature of his handsome face. "If you don't know by now my heart belongs only to you, then you *are* a fool, Mr. Duvoisin!"

Before he could reply, she kissed him passionately, entwining her hands behind his head.

His arms encircled her and he rolled over with her in his embrace. When he lifted his head, his eyes sparkled with mischief. "You saucy, brazen wench." He kissed her again and all other thoughts fled him.

Saturday, May 19, 1838

Paul spent the next two days trying to cleanse his body of the grainy odor that permeated his hands, his hair, and his nose. His throat was parched and he couldn't drink enough to quench his persistent thirst. His body ached from head to foot, his chest raw and throbbing. Dr. Hastings had bound the ribs tightly, and the wrap offered support, but he grimaced every time he moved. Still, he counted himself lucky to be alive. Everyone in the household bent over backward to see to his comfort, and he soon grew weary of their hovering.

Charmaine used the time he spent recuperating to carve out a new friendship with him. Though John might not understand, she liked Paul and regretted their estrangement. He had been her protector—a fortress, and she was ashamed she'd told him she hated him.

Near the end of the week, she caught him alone in the study, sitting in an armchair with a newspaper. When she stepped in, he rose as quickly as his mending ribs would allow.

"How are you feeling?" she asked.

"Much better. And you?" he inquired, aware she suffered with morning sickness. Even so, she looked radiant; pending motherhood brought a new beauty to her face.

"I'm fine."

The room fell into an awkward silence. He moved closer, putting her ill at ease. When he was but a breath away, he spoke again. "You're happy now, aren't you?" he asked, as if it were very important for him to know her marriage to John was what she really wanted.

"Yes," she sighed, "I'm very happy."

"I could have made you happy, too."

"Yes, you could have, had I never met your brother."

Paul nodded slightly, realizing again what he had lost. Charmaine belonged to John, and he would do well to remember that. He raised a hand and gently tucked a stray lock behind her ear.

She did not cringe. Inexplicably, she wanted to cry. "I would like for us to be friends, Paul," she whispered.

"I'll always be here for you, Charmaine," he said, "all you have to do is call." With that, his hand dropped away.

Friday, May 25, 1838

John was livid. He had stewed for the better part of the afternoon, and now it was time to have it out.

Charmaine jumped when he slammed the bedroom door shut behind him. "What is the matter?" she queried with concern.

He paced back and forth, then abruptly stopped. "I'm very angry."

Instantly, she realized his ire was directed at her, but she was at a loss as to what she had done to upset him so. "What is the matter?" she asked again.

Her seeming innocence riled him more, and he raked a hand through his hair twice. "Don't pretend ignorance!" he stormed.

"I don't know what you are talking about!" she responded in kind, annoyed with his childlike behavior. "Why don't you tell me why you're upset?"

"I was coming out of the stable this afternoon," he bit out. "I saw Paul's arms around you—the two of you were laughing together!"

Charmaine let out a relieved giggle, but John did not find her sudden gaiety humorous. "*This is funny?*" he choked out.

"No," she said, "but you mistook what you saw. I tripped on the top step of the portico. I was running to help Jeannette with the heavy lemonade tray, and I tripped. Paul was right there, and he caught me. I knew I looked foolish, so I started to laugh. He laughed, too."

The explanation did not put him at ease, and she was at a loss as to what to say. "Surely you're not upset over an innocent stumble? The girls were right there, John. I slipped!"

"Yes," he muttered, his eyes still simmering, "that's how it starts—with a slip, an innocent slip."

Charmaine considered the strange remark. "What are you

saying?" she asked, her eyes narrowing. "Is that how your affair with Colette began? She stumbled into your arms?"

He was uncomfortable with her swift comprehension and turned away. Charmaine tore after him. "Well, let me tell you something, John Duvoisin!" she shouted, standing in front of him now. "I am not Colette! And I will not meekly stand by while you compare us!"

"Charmaine—" he started, his voice soft and repentant.

"No! I don't want to hear it!" She charged from the room, slamming the door behind her.

John sighed, feeling quite the buffoon. Clearly, his wife would not be bullied into feeling guilty over something quite innocent. *I must learn to trust her; otherwise, our marriage is a farce.*

Quite abruptly, he realized his worry had little to do with his faith in her and quite a great deal to do with his mistrust of Paul, who seemed bent upon pursuing her, even though she was now married. Suddenly, he was ashamed of his own behavior, not with Charmaine, but with Colette.

Grace Smith, Paul's head housekeeper, was glad when he returned to Espoir. Though the manor was back in order, and things were running on an even keel, Agatha Duvoisin had been rattling her nerves, roaming the mansion and talking to herself. Even more disturbing was the voice Grace heard answering. The moment Paul stepped through the door, she confronted him with the news of his mother's condition.

Tonight, he sat alone in his library, sipping a brandy. He felt like a different man; he should have been dead. Charmaine was lost to him forever. Earlier today, he'd almost come to blows with his brother. John had cornered him in the stable, incensed that he'd touched his wife. The stumbling incident had been spontaneous and innocent, but Paul could still hear the blood thundering in his ears as he hugged her, holding her a moment longer than necessary. She had laughed with embarrassment, he with happiness. John had had a right to be angry with him. To avoid another such encounter, he would stay far away from Charmaine—best to remain on Espoir. With a sigh, he drank the last of his brandy and rose for bed.

Voices in the hallway drew him to the door. Agatha stood in the foyer: her hair knotty, robe askew, eyes vacant. Grace's disquietude appeared warranted. Two weeks ago he'd attributed his mother's condition to duress, but now he was really concerned. She wasn't talking to herself, but to people she believed stood before her: her brother, Elizabeth, and, he suspected, Colette.

"Agatha, what is wrong?"

"Frederic," she sighed, "there you are. I heard the baby crying, but I can't find the cradle where Robert has put him. Help me find him."

"Agatha," Paul implored. "It's me—your son—Paul. Agatha?"

Her head was cocked to one side, straining to listen. "Do you hear that?" she queried, oblivious to what he had said. "I think . . . I think I hear *two* babies crying. You haven't brought Elizabeth here, have you?"

"Agatha—"

"I'll not allow her bastard in this house!"

Paul was beside himself. He grabbed her shoulders and shook her hard, forcing her to look at him. "Agatha! Mother!"

Recognition dawned. "Paul?"

"Yes, it's me," he said, relieved. "I think you've been sleepwalking. Why don't we get you to bed?"

"Yes," she murmured, "I'm quite tired. Tell your father I'm in my chambers when he's ready to retire."

"I'll do that, Mother."

John found Charmaine in Pierre's bed, cuddled under the light coverlet. He had searched most of the house, overlooking the most obvious place. Now, he felt the dunce. "Charmaine?" he whispered.

When she didn't stir, he scooped her up and headed to the door. She murmured something in her sleep and, with a sigh, shuddered deeply, the kind born of many tears. He was ashamed he had made her weep. He cradled her close, kissing her head. Before he got to their room, he realized she was awake. He laid her gently on the bed, and she looked up at him through heavy eyes.

"I'm sorry," he said, his voice thick, "I won't—"

She put her fingers to his lips, not wanting to hear Colette's name again. He grabbed her hand and kissed it. Settling next to her, he drew her close. They lay quietly, Charmaine sad, yet content with the feel of his chest rising and falling beneath her cheek, he relishing her arm wrapped around his waist, a sense of forgiveness. He stroked her hair and kissed her head again and again, then pressed back into the pillows and closed his eyes.

She awoke at dawn, not knowing when she had fallen back to sleep. John's arms were still around her, his breathing deep.

When he rose, he found she remained annoyed with him, and even though he apologized again, she had to speak her mind to put the event behind her. "I chose you, John," she said, "not Paul. I waited for *you,* even though Paul was here while you were away. Why would I turn to him now? I love you."

He believed her and vowed never again to brood over Paul. Still, he was happy his brother had returned to the other island.

Paul threw himself into work on Espoir. There was plenty to keep him busy, and he'd ride home at dusk exhausted, unable to think about anything but sleep. If he wasn't overseeing the planting or nurturing of a field of sugarcane, he was directing the clearing of the first harvest. It had taken nearly twelve months for the stalks to grow a full twenty-four-feet high. He had staggered plantings to pace the yield. Though the harvest should have heralded the end of the grueling labor, it was, in fact, the beginning of another brutal phase. After the cane was cut, it was hauled and shredded. Lastly, the stalks were immersed in water and passed through large rollers to express the sugary extract that ran into casks that were sealed and carted to the warehouse for transport.

He had many valuable workers. His father had suggested he take three of the best men from Charmantes, indentured servants who had paid their time of service. He put them in charge of planting and weeding, cutting and shredding, pressing and transport. Others had ventured from Charmantes on their own, those without families, eager to work harder in the hopes of carving out a more elevated position on the fledgling island.

Although the plantation could run itself, toil helped Paul forget. His drive and ambition inspired the laborers, and he got more out of them than before. After three months, he was able to stand back and smile. Three shipments had already left port—not bad, considering his crew had tarried through the rainy season of May and June, and this was still a virgin undertaking.

He threw a party to celebrate at the end of July, giving all the freed men a bonus. Presently, most of them were living in tents, so he encouraged them to build cabins near the harbor, supplying the lumber at a nominal fee.

As busy as he was, he checked in on his mother almost every day. She seemed to improve for a while, but if he missed a visit, Grace Smith would give him a disturbing report. It was almost always the same: she heard voices. Agatha usually carried the conversation, but Grace often heard a whisper from the other side of the room. Paul laughed off her superstitious speculation, until one day, she claimed she'd had enough of the frightening episodes and quit.

Saturday, June 10, 1838

Mercedes was radiant when she stepped into the chapel.

George had the jitters waiting for her at the altar. Paul and John were with him, doing little to calm his frazzled nerves. Paul kept teasing him it wasn't too late to back out: plenty of good years of bachelorhood left, no more late nights at Dulcie's, no more flirting with the barmaids, no more courting the maidens in town who pined for him. "No more hoarding all your money," John added.

When Mercedes followed Jeannette and Yvette up the aisle, George was beaming, and Charmaine was certain the smile would be permanently etched across his face.

A small group of friends had been invited: Wade Remmen and the Brownings among them. John and Charmaine stood as witnesses for the bride and groom. After the ceremony, they were the last to congratulate the newlyweds. Charmaine kissed Mercedes on the cheek and gave George the fiercest hug she could muster.

At the luncheon reception on the portico, Caroline Browning approached Charmaine. "My dear Charmaine, you are looking well!" Her eyes darted to Charmaine's stomach.

"I *am* well, Mrs. Browning," Charmaine replied cautiously.

"Harold and I are so happy for you, dear. I *knew* I was right in convincing my sister to bring you here. And look how well you have done for yourself, marrying such a fine gentleman!"

Charmaine was astounded, recalling the woman's scathing remarks about the Duvoisin brothers. "I'm very fortunate, Mrs. Browning, and very blessed."

"I can see marriage agrees with you." The fulsome compliments continued to pour forth as Caroline assessed Charmaine from head to toe.

"Good day, Charmaine," Harold Browning greeted as he walked over to them. "Congratulations to you, too! John is a smart man choosing you for his wife."

"Of course he is!" Caroline exclaimed, clapping her hands together. "You must bring him over here, Charmaine, so we can congratulate you properly."

Charmaine reluctantly called to him.

He broke away from George and Mercedes and joined them.

"Welcome to our family, John," Caroline purred sweetly.

"*Your* family?"

"Why, yes! Charmaine is practically a daughter to my sister and a niece to Harold and me. She is family, John. I may call you John, yes?"

"That was my name this morning."

Charmaine could see the devil in his eyes, but Caroline was oblivious.

"I was just telling your wife if it weren't for me, she wouldn't have learned about the position of governess here. It took some coaxing, but I convinced my sister Charmantes was the right move for her."

"Then we have you to thank for bringing us together, Mrs. Browning."

"Please don't be so formal. We're family now. Do call me Caroline."

Harold fidgeted uncomfortably with his collar as Caroline blabbered on. "I owe you a thank-you, too, John. Gwendolyn writes that the distinguished Mr. Elliot has come calling on her. If it weren't for you—"

"Oh, don't thank me," John replied with a magnanimous wave of the hand, "that was an accident—I mean—match just waiting to happen."

"Oh, but I must!" Caroline gushed effusively. "It was precisely what my dear Gwendolyn needed—a handsome young man to pay her court . . ."

And so it went. Mercifully, Rose glided by, announcing it was time to cut the cake. Charmaine and John fell in behind the Brownings as they headed toward the small crowd that had gathered around Fatima's splendid concoction.

"What do you think she wants, Charmaine," John muttered when Caroline was out of earshot, "a ship, a plantation, or a loan?"

Charmaine giggled and hugged him close.

For the next few months, John kept busy helping his father. In the evenings, the family dined together, then retired to the drawing room. Frederic, John, and George taught the twins a wicked game of checkers, and, when Yvette begged enough, poker. "I promise never to play outside of the family," she had implored one night, her liquid-blue eyes beseeching her father. He relented. To their amazement, neither girl needed much instruction.

Charmaine continued to complain of morning sickness, though she wasn't as ill as she had been at the onset of her confinement. Still, John did not press her concerning his need to travel abroad. She seemed so content, and surprisingly, so was he. He was enjoying his days on Charmantes as he never dreamed possible. Before he knew it, July melted into August. He could hardly believe a short year ago, his life had been about to change.

Friday, August 24, 1838

Agatha stared across her lovely room. Thanks to Paul, she wanted for nothing, and yet, she wanted nothing but Frederic. *Frederic, how can I convince you I did what I did because I love you?* She cursed her many misfortunes: Elizabeth, her parents, her marriage to Thomas Ward, Colette, and now, this! But it all stemmed from Elizabeth, revolved around Elizabeth, and ended with Elizabeth. Elizabeth, Elizabeth, Elizabeth! *How I hate you, Elizabeth!*

Life with Thomas Ward had been the same as her life now. He had been a British naval officer, the only son of a modestly wealthy family, destined to one day inherit his father's small fortune, for Commodore Thomas Wakefield Ward Sr. had no intention of leaving any money to his five daughters. Thomas junior had adored Agatha for many years, and when his frigate made port, courted her in a bashful sort of way, long before she met Frederic. Because he was at sea during her time of confinement, he knew nothing of the dashing rogue who had captured her heart. When they wed, his good name cleansed the stain of her humiliation. He worshipped the ground upon which she walked, and with him, she enjoyed a comfortable life. But her heart was scarred, and she passively submitted to his lovemaking, leaving him to wonder over her melancholy moods.

Her parents were another matter. Even after Robert had departed with her illegitimate son, their contempt persisted, and they refused to look at her. Agatha's despair turned to resentment. Only her maternal grandmother, Sarah Coleburn, defended her, later convincing her to accept Thomas Ward's marriage proposal.

"You have been through a great deal, Agatha. Learn from it. Thomas is a fine young man. As his wife, you shall want for nothing, and someday, God willing, you will be a widow with resources. You are at the mercy of your parents now. Is that what you want?"

So Agatha stepped into the role of wife, departing her parents' home without a backward glance. It didn't matter. They were relieved to be rid of her and showed no remorse the day Robert returned to Liverpool with Frederic's letter. When she learned he had been willing to marry her after Elizabeth's death, her resentment festered into unmitigated hatred. If they hadn't driven her from their home, she could have wed the man she loved.

She began to believe she was cursed. By the time she had received Frederic's letter, she had been Mrs. Thomas Ward for nearly six months, and though no one knew it, she was pregnant again. The fate of her unborn child was sealed with Frederic's second proposal. She cried on her brother's shoulder, insisting he return to Charmantes and become Paul's guardian. She kissed him, took him to her bed, and pledged undying love for him, all in the name of revenge.

The day he departed, Agatha aborted Thomas's baby, refusing to be bound by his offspring. If Thomas were to die, she would be free to pursue her heart's desire: Frederic. She nearly bled to death from the resulting miscarriage. Thomas was granted a leave of duty to minister to her. He remained by her bedside for nearly a month, and, quite unexpectedly, she grew fond of this tender, compassionate man. He never learned she had destroyed his baby.

When she recovered, she resigned herself to a life without Frederic. As with Paul, he was lost to her forever.

"There will be other children," Thomas had promised, finding succor in her genuine embrace. But the months turned into years, and she never became pregnant again. Agatha knew she had done irreparable damage when she'd jabbed the sharpened twig between her legs and terminated the life of his unborn child.

"I worry for you, my dearest," he fretted over the years that followed. "My father wants a grandson to carry on his name and has threatened to leave his fortune to my sister's son should I die without an heir. We must get you in the family way again. Let us seek the advice of a physician."

Fearing her husband might discover the cause of her infertility, Agatha pacified him by insisting she take the matter up with Robert. "During your next voyage abroad, I shall travel to Charmantes," she suggested. "Robert will know if something can be done."

That was the summer of 1813, and Paul had just turned five. He was growing into a fine lad. If she was apprehensive over her reception on Charmantes, she needn't have been. Frederic welcomed her into his home and insisted she stay as long as she desired.

As handsome as ever, he remained aloof. She valiantly kept him at arm's length, resisting his magnetism. She should hate him, she reasoned. He had stolen Paul away, and now, she would never know the joys of motherhood. She was irrevocably barren; there would be no other offspring. When she passed from this life, only Paul and the children he would someday sire would mark her existence. Paul became her obsession.

Then there was Robert, always sniveling at her feet. She knew he still adored her in his own possessive, repugnant way, so, occasionally, she allowed him to make love to her. He repaid the favor by denouncing John and promoting Paul as Frederic's flesh and blood. Because of Robert, Frederic believed the lie, doting on Paul and scorning John. Though she basked in that knowledge, she could not rest until Paul was the sole heir to the Duvoisin fortune—his birthright.

When she left Charmantes, she resigned herself to three things. First, her struggle to forget the past was futile. She was hopelessly in love with Frederic. When she returned to Charmantes she would seduce him. Second, she would not leave Thomas. Sarah Coleburn was right; he would be a well-off man someday, so long as he outlived his father, and if she remained by his side, she would benefit from his wealth. She would always desire Frederic, but she'd learned not to rely on his love. He had used her and discarded her when she'd been most vulnerable: in love, pregnant, and alone. If she were widowed tomorrow, she could not bank on a proposal from him. His guilty conscience had prompted the last one. Never again would she be without resources. Third, time was on her side. With Elizabeth dead and John spurned, she could bide her time.

By the following summer, she was living two very different lives: a respectable British officer's wife when in England and a sultry seductress when her husband's naval obligations took him far from British soil. She ventured to Charmantes as often as possible, and she and Frederic became intimate again, resurrecting all those glorious feelings. Leaving him grew more and more difficult, but Thomas's father was growing feeble, and it was only a matter of time before Thomas inherited his estate. When Thomas died, she could count herself an independent woman, something she deserved after all she had suffered and sacrificed. No matter what the future held, she'd be secure.

Thus, the years slipped by, and she and Frederic remained lovers. But this satisfactory arrangement was most unexpectedly annihilated.

In the spring of 1829, Agatha met Colette Duvoisin. Paul had been off to university in Paris, and she hadn't traveled to Charmantes in nearly four years. She was horrified to find Frederic had married this young woman, thirty-four years his junior. A whirlwind wedding they called it. Robert surmised it was something else, for Colette had come to the West Indies on John's arm. But Agatha's raging intuition dismissed his assertion. She shuddered with the memory of that introduction, Frederic's desperate, consuming love for his child-bride branded on his face. He had barely looked

Agatha's way, and she was on fire with covetous hatred. Elizabeth had returned, the battle for him resumed.

She turned to Robert. But he made light of her predicament with a shrug. "Frederic is married to her now. There is nothing you can do."

"Nothing? She is Elizabeth reborn, can't you see that?"

Robert laughed incredulously. "Don't be ridiculous!"

"I tell you, she *is* Elizabeth. Frederic knows it, too. I can see it in his eyes! She's come back, I tell you, she's come back to—to—"

"To what, Agatha?"

"To curse me—and Paul—to patch things up between Frederic and John!"

"You are wrong, my dear, very wrong."

"Can't you see? John stole her away, and John has brought her back!"

Robert laughed at the preposterous premise. "John and Frederic's questionable kinship has finally ruptured. John loathes his father now, his departure permanent. I should think this would please you, my dearest. So, if you hate Frederic as much as you say you do, let *this* be your revenge. Frederic may very well disinherit John if you use Colette as the wedge between them, and then Paul *will* have it all. It stands a better chance at succeeding than any of your other mendacious schemes."

Agatha was desperately forlorn when she returned to England, and Thomas was at a loss. His father's death and mother's widowhood distracted him, however, affording Agatha time and space to ponder this newest adversity.

Her sour disposition abated when news arrived all was not well between Frederic and Colette. *She cried out for John over and over again during her labor,* Robert had written, *though Frederic was there.*

Agatha eventually recognized the potential in exploiting the discord between Frederic and John, but first, she had to get back into Frederic's bed. It was easier than she had imagined. Robert set the stage with three simple words that he repeated like a mantra to both Colette and Frederic: *No more children.*

Another visit and it became obvious husband and wife were no longer intimate. Agatha couldn't quite piece the puzzle together. Frederic obviously lusted for his young wife, and intuition told her Colette desired him as well, yet they remained estranged. Why? Was John truly to blame?

Agatha capitalized on Frederic's frustrated desire and seduced him before he returned to Colette's bed. Then Colette had her affair with John. Betrayed, Frederic never made love to his wife again.

So where had she failed? Somehow, Elizabeth had won; even in death, then in life and in death again, she had won.

Agatha rubbed her brow with both hands, her torment manifest in an excruciating headache that threatened her sanity. She closed her eyes, and her sister's caramel-colored eyes swam before her, taunting her as they turned smoky blue.

Elizabeth, the war is not over. I am not defeated! Frederic belonged to me first. I've shared his bed more times than you and Colette combined. Very soon, he will realize I did what I did for him, our son, and our undeniable love.

Saturday, August 25, 1838

Paul scoffed down a light dinner and had retired to his study when the door banged open. His mother stood silhouetted in the low lamplight.

"Frederic?" she asked timidly. "Is that you?"

She stepped deeper into the room, and the light illuminated her face. Her cheeks were pale, her eyes vacant, yet searching, as if he weren't there.

Paul stood. She attempted to compose herself, sweeping the disheveled hair from her brow, smoothing the wrinkles from her robe.

"Frederic," she sighed, "it *is* you."

"No, Agatha, it's not Father, it's me—Paul."

"Frederic—I need to tell you, I need to explain. You'll understand—"

"Agatha, you're still asleep. Let me—"

"—I'm going to explain everything. Then you will love me again . . ."

Chapter 6

Sunday, August 26, 1838

THE house was quiet. Everyone was at Mass, and John was catching up on paperwork. He couldn't put off a trip to Richmond much longer, but he didn't have the heart to tell Charmaine. She still suffered from morning sickness, but intuition told him she was avoiding Richmond because of her fugitive father. Still, he'd have to leave soon if he hoped to be back before she delivered.

The study door opened, and John looked up, astonished to see Paul. He'd only visited Charmantes once since their confrontation in the stable: for George's wedding. *He's grown tired of Agatha and is returning her to Father,* John snickered to himself.

Paul took the chair opposite the desk, his face somber.

"What brings you back here on a Sunday morning, Paul?" John asked, refraining from a barb about not being able to make a go of it without Father.

"John . . ."

Something was wrong. The man was perturbed: his face ashen, his eyes turbulent, his demeanor shaky.

"What is it?" John demanded. "You look as though you've seen a ghost."

"Agatha," he began. "It's Agatha. She's deranged—gone mad."

"You're just now realizing this?" John quipped.

"I'm not joking, John. She's been grief-stricken since Father cast her out, and last night, she snapped. She's in a state of delirium—she thinks *I'm* Father. She makes little sense, but she's saying things . . ."

John's eyes narrowed. "What has she been saying?"

"She goes on and on about meeting Father before your mother did. She rants about Elizabeth stealing him away."

John sighed. "We know all this. Why is she still crying about it. She managed to bring Father around to her way of thinking. You have your fair share now, so what else does she want?"

"She wants Father! She's insane, I tell you! She's confusing your mother with Colette, and she's been saying things. I don't know if they're true, but . . ."

"What has she been saying, Paul?" John reiterated.

"Things about Colette," Paul replied, his eyes searching John's.

"What about Colette?"

"She claims she and Robert saw to it Colette was—removed."

Dumbfounded, John leaned back in his chair. *"Removed?"*

"John," Paul murmured, dreading what he was about to say. "That last year when Colette was so ill . . . Agatha set herself up as Colette's personal companion, maintaining she was not well. She had Robert here treating Colette every week, then twice a week, and finally, every day. In the beginning, Colette tried to avoid him, complaining about feeling worse after he left. He changed his compounds, or so he said, and she seemed improved. After Christmas, I was away, and I assumed I'd find her completely recovered when I returned. But Charmaine contends she only grew worse. Blackford blamed it on a lung infirmity, but now, now I don't know . . . Colette's death enabled Agatha to become Father's third wife. John—" Paul's face went white, and he hesitated to state his next horrific speculation. "Pierre was in Father's will. He was named as successor to the estate after you. Agatha found out and was very upset, probably furious."

Like the light rushing into a darkened room, comprehension dawned, and Paul's words melded with a kaleidoscope of incidents that were suddenly most logically connected: Agatha's persistent efforts to alienate him from Frederic, her triumphant face when he'd removed himself from his father's will, Blackford's abrupt departure, a demonic Phantom escaping his stall, Pierre getting past all eyes to make it to the lake—even his nightmares! *I followed Auntie . . . She gave him a pouch. I think there was jewelry inside . . .*

John jumped to his feet and headed for the door, but Paul caught his arm before he reached it. "Where are you going, John?"

"To church!"

The Latin phrases of the consecration echoed in monotone off the walls of the chapel. The coolness was rapidly dissipating as the heat of summer penetrated the sanctuary on beams of sunlight plunging down to the nave and altar. With the small congregation behind him, Father Benito sped up his lengthy recitation. Grasping the host, he held it up to the crucifix before him, uttering the Latin intonation: "*Hoc est enim corpus meum . . .*"

The chapel doors banged open, and though he held a reverent silence as he cast the bread heavenward, he cursed the inopportune interruption at the pinnacle of the holy celebration. Footsteps echoed hollowly on the floor, but Benito resisted the urge to look back, lowering the bread to the plate. He raised the chalice when a shadow loomed behind and his arm was violently wrenched away from the altar, knocking the cup from his hands. It spiraled off the table and clattered to the floor, splattering wine across the white linens. He was brutally twisted around and came face-to-face with a livid John. "What do you know, old man?"

Charmaine cried out as Benito's vestments were abruptly gathered in two balled fists, his face pulled up close to John's. From the corner of his eye, the priest saw Paul draw up behind his brother. "What do you know?" John demanded full-voiced.

"I don't know what you're talking about!" Benito sputtered.

"You know goddamn well what I'm talking about, and let's have it out before I choke the life from you right here and now!"

Charmaine jumped to her feet, but Frederic grabbed her arm, holding her to the spot, his eyes riveted on the scene unfolding in front of the altar. "What are you doing, John?" she cried. "What is going on?"

But John's eyes were locked on the petrified priest, his grip tightening around his neck. "You were taking payments from my aunt! Why?"

"They were contributions for my mission for the needy," Benito croaked.

"Do you want to *die*, old man?" John shouted, his hold so fierce Benito's eyes were beginning to bulge from their sockets.

"John, stop it! Stop it!" Charmaine screamed, her horror increasing. She looked to Paul. *Why is he here? Why isn't he intervening?*

"You have one choice right now," John snarled. "Tell me what happened, and I won't kill you. Understand?"

Benito's face took on a bluish hue. The tableau held for what seemed endless minutes, the clergyman's cyanotic complexion now ghastly. Charmaine's desperate gaze traveled helplessly from Frederic to Paul; both were equally bent on facilitating this inquisition, refusing to intervene. The gaping congregation was standing, frozen, the chapel deadly silent. Just when Charmaine thought the priest would pass out, he rasped, "Your aunt and uncle poisoned Colette . . ."

Benito's eyes rolled back in his head and his eyelids fluttered shut.

"The rest, Benito!" John seethed, adjusting his grip enough to revive him. "Speak up, you bastard!"

"Blackford . . . abducted the boy . . . and drowned him . . . in the lake."

The terror on the priest's face climaxed as John, insane with fury, twisted the garments ferociously, lifting Benito St. Giovanni up and off the floor.

Charmaine screamed again, but Paul had already grabbed hold of his brother, and George was charging the altar. John shoved Benito away, the man tumbling backward to the floor. "I should kill you, you greedy charlatan!"

Paul was between them now, allowing the gasping Benito to rise to his feet. "George," he directed, "take Bud with you and lock Benito in the bondsmen's keep."

"No!" Frederic countermanded. "Take him to the stable and wait for me there."

George shoved Benito toward the back of the church. The grooms who had attended the service fell in alongside him, then they were gone.

Jeannette had begun sobbing uncontrollably, her arms flung around Charmaine's waist, her head buried in her bosom. Yvette remained silent, standing ramrod straight, her eyes clouded in disbelief.

"John!" Charmaine implored desolately, rushing to his side when Frederic released her. "Oh, John!"

But he wasn't hearing, his mind racing. He headed toward the chapel doors.

"Where are you going?" she called after him.

He didn't answer, and she looked helplessly to Paul again.

Paul chased after him. "Where are you going, John?"

"To see Westphal," he replied. "Come with me."

When Paul did not return, the austere company migrated to the drawing room. Frederic settled into an armchair and cradled Jeannette in his lap. She buried her face in his shirt and whimpered pitifully, hugging him fiercely. He stared beyond the walls, stroking her hair and patting her back until the tears subsided.

Charmaine closed her eyes to the piercing pain in her heart. It was as if Colette and Pierre had died all over again. Poisoned! How had she not seen it? No wonder Colette had been so ill! All the signs were there. And Pierre! His death had not been a horrible accident!

Charmaine groaned. *I didn't protect him! Dear God, I didn't protect him!* But why murder an innocent, beautiful boy? Agatha had much to gain from Colette's death, but Pierre—*why?*

"Why, Papa?" Yvette asked, her voice quivering. "Why did they kill Mama and Pierre?"

"Because they are evil," he said quietly, his voice hard and heavy. He nudged Jeannette's chin off his chest so she would look at him and gently wiped away the tears that smudged her cheeks. "Better now?" he tenderly asked.

"I think so," she heaved.

"Good. I have to speak with Father Benito. Will you be all right if I leave you with Charmaine and Nana Rose?" When she nodded, he kissed her forehead and rose, setting her back into the chair. He patted Yvette's head. "They will be punished, Yvette. I promise you that."

She smiled up at him mournfully. "Be careful, Papa," she warned.

"I shall."

He looked across the room at Rose and Mercedes. The old woman shook her head sadly. He walked to the doorway where Charmaine stood. "I won't be long," he told her. He squeezed her shoulder and was gone.

The greater the wealth, the deeper the pain . . .

John and Paul rode into town together. Westphal's house was directly across the street from the bank. They dismounted, and John rapped on his door. Finally, it opened.

"What is it?" Stephen asked, astonished to find both Paul and John there.

"Get your keys and open the bank," John stated flatly.

"Open the bank? It's Sunday!" Stephen objected. "I'm eating right now!"

"Open the bank."

The banker looked at Paul.

"Stephen, do as he asks," Paul said.

They waited at the doorstep as the man went inside to retrieve his keys. They crossed the street to the bank.

"What is it you want?" Stephen queried, clearly annoyed as he fumbled with the lock.

"I want to see Blackford's account," John answered.

"I can't do that!" Westphal roared. "It would be a breach of privacy!"

"Blackford is a murderer," John replied. "He left the island in April, and he's not coming back. He had to have taken all his money with him. I want to know how much and to which bank you endorsed his money."

"You can't be serious!" Westphal objected.

John considered him for a moment. "Westphal, what I've told you is true. Benito Giovanni corroborated it. Now, I'm losing my patience. Will you give me Blackford's file, or do I have to get it myself?"

Westphal's eyes went helplessly to Paul. "It *is* true, Stephen. We need to find out where he headed after he left in April."

Shaking his head, Westphal entered his office. He retrieved the file and handed it to John, who flipped it open and settled into the desk chair to study it.

After a few minutes, John looked up at Paul. "Agatha paid her brother well for his work. He made a few hefty deposits, starting in April of '36. I would imagine that's when the poisoning began. But the big payoff didn't come until the week after Pierre's death. That's when she signed Thomas Ward's entire estate over to this account."

John paused, rubbed his forehead, and turned to the banker. "This shows Blackford drew all his funds in a voucher, signed by you, Westphal, to the Bank of Richmond. I doubt he remained in Virginia. Did he tell you where he was headed?"

"No," Westphal replied. "He only said he planned on retiring comfortably. But perchance this will help."

John was surprised when the financier handed him a letter from Benito Giovanni. "Benito entrusted it to me for safekeeping," Stephen explained. "I was told to pass it on to your father should anything happen to him."

John didn't need to read the letter to know it was the clergyman's insurance against an untimely death.

George and Gerald stood guard over Benito, who sat on a crate with his hands bound behind his back. Both men were scowling at him when Frederic entered the stall. "Leave us alone," he ordered.

"We'll be outside," George said.

Frederic waited until the stable door closed, then he lifted a horsewhip off the peg from which it hung and stepped closer to the priest. Benito's head lifted for the first time, and he cringed.

"Now, my *good* man," Frederic growled, slapping the butt of the whip across the palm of his hand, "I am going to ask you a few questions, and unlike the last time, you are going to answer every one of them, or you will hang for your corrupt deeds before sunset. Do you understand?"

The priest nodded slightly.

"Good. Now, how did you come by the information you just revealed?"

"Overcome with guilt, Agatha confessed her sins, then sought to appease her conscience by offering me money for the needy."

Frederic's eyes narrowed. "One more lie, Benito, and I'll tie the noose myself."

Benito swallowed, the seconds accumulating. He had run out of options. "When you called me to your chambers that night, after Colette's death, I realized lies were being spread about her."

"Lies?"

"Although years ago she had confessed her affair with John, on her deathbed, she did not confess any other adulterous liaisons. Therefore, I concluded she had not been unfaithful to you." He hung his head and waited.

"And yet, you led me to believe otherwise!"

"I never claimed she had committed adultery," Benito objected obliquely. "If you think back on that night, I merely refused to reveal her private confession."

The whip whistled through the air, missing its mark by inches. "Liar!" Frederic shouted, outraged. "You led me to believe there was a secret to keep, and when you escaped my chambers unscathed, you used that information to extort payments from Agatha and Blackford! Now—be truthful."

"On the contrary," Benito whispered to the floor, "I didn't request money from Agatha until she had married you." When the whip did not crack again, he bravely looked up. "It was only after she succeeded in bringing you to the altar that I surmised her motives. Until then, I thought she and her brother had lied to you to save your life!"

"Really? And I suppose you, too, meant to save me by guarding that lie?"

"Actually—yes. If it could bring you to your senses—"

"Don't!" Frederic snarled. "If you want to live, you'd be wise to drop the act, *Father*. Your pretense at piety is revolting. Now—when did you find out Colette had been poisoned? The truth man, I want the truth!"

"I only guessed that," he admitted. "It was strange Agatha paid as willingly as she did, despite her protests. It became clear she had something more important to hide. So, I was prepared for the day she told me it was her last visit, claiming you knew the truth—that Colette had not been unfaithful. I gambled on my speculation and told her I knew Colette had been poisoned. Agatha accused me of not having proof, but she didn't deny it. When I said Pierre's death was a strange coincidence, her face went white. Only then did I realize how unscrupulous and heartless they were."

"You are an evil beast," Frederic sneered, appalled by the man's candor. "If you had come to me with this information, Pierre would still be alive."

"No, I wasn't certain! Not until it happened—*after* the boy's death."

"But you had your suspicions. You enjoyed the luxuries my money could buy at the expense of two innocent lives!"

The priest eyed him meekly, his brow raised in contrition, fanning Frederic's ire. "How dare you attempt to excuse yourself now?"

Frederic jerked the crop back and delivered a blistering *thwack* across Benito Giovanni's face, slicing open his cheek and the bridge of his nose.

The priest yelped in agony. "I'm sorry!"

"How much did she pay for your silence?" Frederic demanded.

When Benito didn't answer, Frederic launched the whip again, the bloodied thong lashing across his shoulder and neck this time. *"Was it worth this?"*

Again, the priest screamed. "Mercy! Please, have mercy!"

"My sons saved your life, you ungrateful, despicable bastard! What kind of priest are you? Or have you been pretending all these years?"

"No, I am a priest. I swear, I am!"

"Worse for you, you demon!"

Frederic raised the whip again and Benito winced, curling into a ball. "Please, no more!" he implored.

"Where's Blackford now?"

"I don't know—he just left!"

"Why? Why did he leave? Was he afraid of you? Was he unable to pay? Did you push him too far?"

"No—I mean, I don't know! Agatha was paying for both of them," he attempted to mollify. "I don't know why he left Charmantes! He just did!"

"You know more than that!" Frederic countered. "You'd better tell me something, man! Why was Blackford involved? His sister had plenty to gain, but what was in it for him?"

"Agatha said he despised you for blaming him all these years."

"Blaming him?"

"For your first wife's death."

"Retribution? He was driven by retribution? No, that's not it," Frederic refuted. "Why harm the boy? *Why?*"

Benito was quaking. "I—I don't know. He didn't say anything else. I only know he was receiving money from Agatha as well."

"Yes, Agatha was behind it all, but what hold did she have over her brother that he was willing to murder for her? He was well established on Charmantes. Why did he risk everything for her?"

"I don't know, I tell you!"

"And you weren't interested in finding out? I find that hard to believe!"

"Believe what you will, but I don't know!"

Frederic coiled the thong again and Benito quickly added, "It must have been for the money!"

Frederic's eyes narrowed with his lame reasoning. "Then why flee?"

"I swear, I don't know! Perhaps he was frightened it would come to this."

"Come to what, Benito, the moment of truth?" He studied the crop, then disgusted, flung it into a stall.

Benito looked up, an ugly welt running down his forehead and joining the blood that oozed from the bridge of his nose and his right cheek. "What will you do with me?" he beseeched.

"John saved your life. I think he should decide how it will end."

Frederic called for George and Gerald. "Take him to the bondsmen keep and make certain he's well guarded. John can *visit* him later."

John was a maelstrom of emotions: despair, helplessness, guilt, anger, and loathing. *Colette and Pierre were murdered. I didn't protect them.* Blackford's tidy escape fed his torment. How had his father allowed this to happen? Paul had an excuse. He had been toiling and then was abroad, but his father had been there—right next door—as the sinister plot was being executed. His hatred for his uncle did not rival his searing contempt for Frederic.

They rode home in silence. Paul knew what John was thinking and fearlessly said, "John, I know you blame Father, but he was as ignorant of what was happening as we all were. He had no idea Colette was being—"

"Really?" John bit out, not allowing him to finish, looking him in the eye. "Would it have happened if either you or I were married to her?"

Paul inhaled. *John loved her—had loved her deeply.*

"*Would it have?*"

"I don't know, John."

"*Don't you?* Well, you keep making excuses for him—protecting him. I, on the other hand, will remember everything I've suffered at his hands, to this very day. I've been a fool these last months," he said self-deprecatingly, "pretending the past was behind us. But here it is—right in my face again."

"John, he's tried to right those wrongs."

"Has he?" John growled. "How—by throwing me a bone now? What about last summer, when it would have made a difference? No, Paul. He was jealous of my love for Pierre, and he was out to destroy it. He set me up to abduct Pierre—to tear him away from his sisters and Charmaine, just so the boy would grow to hate me. By proving I was as terrible a father as he, he could feel vindicated. That was his objective, nothing more and nothing less."

"You're wrong, John. I know there are some things Father can never change, but he didn't want to hurt you anymore. When he realized you were leaving, he wanted to make amends. He signed custody of the girls and Pierre over to you the morning you were to leave. I saw the papers—signed *before* Blackford ever laid a hand on Pierre."

John's eyes betrayed great surprise, but before he could retaliate, Paul pressed on. "During the ordeal with Pierre, Father stayed away out of respect for you and your grief, not because he didn't care. I went to see him each time I left Pierre's bedside. He didn't eat or sleep. He was suffering as much as you were—was beside himself with guilt. He loved Pierre and still blames himself for what happened." Paul turned away, his anguish poorly concealed.

The minutes gathered, the only sound the clip-clop of horses' hooves. Paul wrestled with his thoughts, wondered whether it was wise to voice them. "Father loved Colette, too, John. You may not believe that, but it's true, and though you may not want to hear it, she loved him as well. She told me so. The last thing Father wanted was to see her suffer. He was devastated when she died."

John clenched his jaw in renewed rage. *Is this what he allows to happen to those he loves?* But his rebuttal withered away when he read the desolation in his brother's eyes and realized Paul was only stating the facts as he saw them.

"I don't know what tore them apart, John, but I realize now, it transcended you and Colette. I suspect my mother was involved in that, too." Bearing his own burden, Paul could say no more, and they rode the rest of the way home in silence.

"You cannot be serious!" Charmaine exclaimed. "You cannot mean to leave me alone here when our baby is on the way!"

Her eyes followed John around the dressing chamber, as he pulled clothing out of drawers and threw them into a knapsack on the floor. He did not respond and doggedly continued packing. She couldn't stand his silence and stepped in front of him to block the path he was beating.

"This is pure folly!" she protested. "It is far too dangerous!"

"The man murdered my son, Charmaine," he replied, stopping to regard her. "He is not getting away with it."

"You will never find him! He is long gone!"

"I *will* find him. If it's the last thing I do, I will find him."

"John, it could take years to hunt him down. Why won't you let the authorities apprehend him? They are better equipped to do this than you are!"

"Like they apprehended your father, Charmaine?" John asked derisively. "If you could find your father and make him pay for what he did to your mother, what would you do?"

His question left her momentarily mute. "And what of the life we've made together?" she murmured. "You can walk away from it that easily?"

He strapped the knapsack shut. "There is no life if I do nothing."

She turned away, head bowed, tears stinging her eyes. "I will be alone here, worrying for your safety."

"You won't be alone. You have the twins, you have Rose, George, Mercedes. You will be fine. *I* will be fine. I will send word." He came up behind her, placing his hands on her shoulders, but she pulled away.

"You love her more than me," she choked out, "still—you love her more."

"Don't do this, Charmaine . . ."

"If you loved me more, you wouldn't leave!" she cried.

"Don't make this a choice between you and a dead woman, Charmaine."

"Then don't leave," she whispered.

John reached out and turned her in his arms to embrace her, but she pulled away again, setting her face in stone as he bent down to kiss her cheek. He stepped back and considered her for a moment longer. He grabbed his cap off the dressing table, placed it squarely on his head, and left the room.

Charmaine ran into the bedchamber and threw herself on the bed, burying her face in her pillow, fighting her tears, swearing she would not allow herself to cry over him. She lay there for minutes on end. The reality he had left consumed her. *He will be in great danger. Will he return unharmed? I may never see him again!*

She sprang from the bed, flew out of the room and down the

stairs, through the foyer and across the lawns to the stable. She entered the dim enclosure and ran headlong into Gerald.

"What is it, ma'am?"

"John—is he still here?"

"He's already left, ma'am—gone a good five minutes now."

Travis had just finished packing Frederic's trunk, saying, "That should do it, sir," when Frederic's outer chamber door banged open. Charmaine stood in the archway, out of breath, tears streaming down her cheeks.

"He's leaving!" she sobbed, casting beseeching eyes to Frederic, then Paul. "Please stop him!"

"This ship is setting sail for Richmond in thirty minutes," John pronounced, as he boarded the *Raven*.

One look at John's face and Captain Wilkinson knew there was no point in objecting. "May I ask why?" he queried, wondering when his cargo would ever reach England.

"I'll explain later," was all John would say.

Taking heed, Jonah began barking orders to the crewmen who were milling about. Grumbles went up, unhappy they were returning to the States without so much as a layover on Charmantes. But Jonah brooked no resistance, and they dutifully fell in with John, preparing the ship for departure.

When the last of the staples had been hastily loaded, Jonah gave the order. The mooring was released, and the vessel pushed off.

A shout from the quay brought all eyes around. Jonah frowned in consternation when he saw Paul, running down the pier, frantically waving both arms at the ship. The men standing on the boardwalk began to shout after the *Raven* as well. John came to the railing next to Jonah.

"We'd best throw out the ropes," Jonah said.

But John only called to his brother, "What is it?" thinking Paul had uncovered something pertinent relating to the monstrous revelations of a few short hours ago.

"Bring the ship back in!" he called. "Bring her back in!"

As Jonah looked from John to Paul, he caught sight of Frederic, laboring down the wharf. "Bring her back in!" Frederic demanded.

John had seen him, too. Swearing under his breath, he turned on the captain. "Keep going! *Do not* turn back!"

"But, John—" Jonah faltered.

"Go! Just go!"

Jonah Wilkinson looked across the water to Frederic, who was ordering him to return, then back to John. "Throw out the lines!" he commanded.

The crew scrambled to do his bidding.

"Damn him!" John swore, punching the railing. His rage smoldered when the ropes were cast to the dock and secured round the pilings on the quay. The ship clapped against the pier, the gangway was lowered, and Frederic boarded.

"What are you doing here?" John snarled in his face.

"Charmaine sent me," he replied. "She doesn't want you to leave, John. She's frightened for you."

"This is something I must do. I've explained that to her."

"She's your wife. You shouldn't be leaving her, not now."

"Don't you dare tell me what I should or shouldn't do!" John shouted. "Now, if you'll get off this ship, I'll be about my business."

"Don't do this, John. No good will come of it!" Frederic implored.

"Do you really think I could live knowing the man who killed my son and *your wife* is out there—living, breathing? What kind of man are you, Father? How can you let him get away? Did Colette mean nothing to you at all? And what of Pierre? He was an innocent child who had the lousy luck of being born into this rotten family."

"You are right," Frederic breathed dolefully, startling John and momentarily quelling the fire in his eyes. "I want you to stay here and allow me to do this—on my own."

"What?"

"You heard me. You have a new life, John. Charmaine doesn't deserve this. She's carrying a child—your child. She needs you by her side right now. I have nothing to tie me to Charmantes. I will see to it Robert Blackford is apprehended. I promise you that."

"No!" John stated vehemently. "This is something I have to do. Someday Charmaine will realize it's the only way to bury the past."

Frederic sized his son up and nodded in understanding. "Very well, we'll do it your way."

"We'll?"

"I'm coming with you."

"No, you're not," John refuted.

"Then we are at an impasse. This ship is not sailing without me." Frederic ordered his trunks carried below deck.

John turned away in chafing frustration; as usual his father held the upper hand. No matter. He would dump the man when they reached Richmond and pursue Blackford on his own.

"Set sail, Jonah," Frederic commanded. Then he shouted to Paul who waited on the pier. "Tell Charmaine I will bring him home safe and sound."

With Paul's dismal nod, the *Raven* cast off a second time.

Yvette and Jeannette watched Charmaine pace the portico, arms crossed, brow knitted, and tears still smudging her cheeks. Yvette looked to her sister in silent communication. Jeannette shook her head when it seemed she would speak.

"Johnny will be all right, Mademoiselle," Jeannette comforted, "you'll see."

"Only if he drops this foolhardy idea and comes home!" she agreed hotly.

"He's *got* to find Dr. Blackford," Yvette declared. "I hope he kills him for what he did to Mama and Pierre!"

Charmaine was aghast. "And if Dr. Blackford kills him first . . . ?"

Neither girl had considered this. Earlier, when they were alone, Yvette had accused Charmaine of not loving Pierre or her mother. "Why else would she be angry with Johnny for what he wants to do?" Now she felt ashamed and grew concerned.

Jeannette was more optimistic. "Don't worry, Mademoiselle Charmaine. Papa will protect him. Please don't be upset."

A rider approached, and they soon recognized Alabaster. Paul rode directly to the house, dismounted, and climbed the portico steps. He shook his head to Charmaine's unasked question. "They're gone—both of them."

She turned her back on him, her rage caving in to anguish, her anguish rekindling her rage.

"Charmaine," Paul placated. "He'll be fine. Father is with him. He promised to bring John home to you." When she didn't answer, he continued. "It's something John felt he had to do. Surely—"

"No, Paul," she bit out over her shoulder, "you were right. He will never love me as he loved her. That's why he's gone, and I hate him for it!"

Yvette and Jeannette stole quizzical glances at each other. One look at their faces, and Paul spoke sharply. "This is neither the time nor the place to discuss it, Charmaine. You'll feel differently when John gets back."

She began to cry. "He's never coming back! I feel it—I just feel it!"

Paul came up behind her and turned her in his arms. He held her until she calmed down, his head resting atop hers. "Dwelling on this cannot be good for the baby," he said. "Come, let us find a distraction." He led them into the house.

Monday, August 27, 1838

The ocean was so blue Frederic could not distinguish it from the sky. It was the color of Colette's eyes. How had he allowed this to happen to his beautiful wife? To sweet, innocent Pierre? With an aching heart and paralyzing remorse, he looked at John. Like yesterday, his son had not moved from the bow, his eyes fixed on the sea ahead, as if he could spur the vessel on simply by staring into the distance. Frederic knew they must talk, and breathing deeply, he joined John at the railing. They stood silently for many minutes.

"What are you thinking about?" Frederic asked.

John gritted his teeth. He had no intention of talking with the man. Their camaraderie of the past four months had been a farce. They'd only turned a blind eye to their hatred for each other, but it was there, would always be there. Today, John loathed him more than ever.

"John?" his father pursued.

John dragged his eyes from the cerulean sea and, wearing a twisted, satanic smile, turned on Frederic. "Thinking about? You want to know what I'm thinking about? I'm thinking about my aunt and uncle, and how it took them nearly a year to poison and kill Colette. And I'm thinking about her husband, who stole her from his son, loved her so dearly he set her up for a love affair, and then punished her for being unfaithful, yet didn't suspect a thing." John shook his head in revulsion. "Your own daughter sensed what was taking place."

Seeing Frederic's surprise, John pressed on, all the more disgusted. "That's right. Yvette told me her mother always seemed worse after her visits with the good doctor. She was so suspicious she even took to spying on him and Agatha. But her father—my father—no, *he* didn't suspect a thing—had no idea anything was amiss. Or did you? Was that how you punished her, Father? By offering her up to the executioner?"

The heated remarks, raised to near shouting, had caught the ears of the crew, and they began milling nearby, pretending not to listen.

"Is that what you think happened?" Frederic queried plaintively.

"Not what I think—what I know!"

"John, I had no idea—"

"Shut your goddamn mouth! There will never be an end to your evil! I blame Agatha and Blackford, yes. But I blame *you* more!"

His agony increasing, unbearable now, Frederic exploded. As John turned away, he grabbed his shirt and threw him back into the railing. John gaped at him, unable to react. "Let's get one thing straight," Frederic growled, "Colette was *my* wife. Accuse me of turning a blind eye to what was happening, but you were just as blind! Where were *your* eyes when Pierre was snatched from the house? I'll tell you where. on that damn horse of yours!"

"I should kill you for that!" John snarled, fists at the ready.

Frederic stepped forward, his face inches from his son's. "I'm sick and tired of your self-pity—your vicious ridicule—your tantrums!"

John laughed diabolically. "Tantrums? Ridicule? Self-pity? You wrote the book, Father! They're the only reason Colette didn't leave you!"

"You'd like to believe that!" Frederic fired back. "But if she really loved you, she wouldn't have given me a backward glance when you begged her to leave!"

"Damn you! Damn you to hell!"

John lunged at him, but Frederic caught him by the wrists, warding off the assault. John shoved harder, and they staggered across the deck, crashing into the capstan with such force the gears shuddered.

"Enough!" Jonah Wilkinson shouted, jumping into the escalating brawl. The sailors took his lead and pulled them apart. "Are the two of you mad? Save your fight for the murderer!" he admonished, planting himself squarely between the two men, knowing they'd go at each other again if he stepped aside. "What's gotten into you?" he demanded of Frederic. "He's your son, man. And you—" he said, turning his eyes on John in a deep scowl "—this is your father. You'd best respect him."

"He'll never gain my respect," John vowed tightly, "not while there's a breath left in my body!"

They stared each other down, and not another word was spoken that day.

John fumed over his father's declarations, and they turned his mind inside out. *If she really loved you, she wouldn't have given me a backward glance* . . . He picked up the chair in his cabin and slammed it into the wall, wood splintering in all directions. His anger spent, he studied the rungs he clutched. *Your vicious ridicule, your tantrums* . . . He sat hard on the cot and put his head in his hands. *Damn the man! He will not have the final say!*

The sky was dark when he left his cabin, but the deck was bathed in moonlight. He couldn't sleep, and the sea breeze might clear his churning mind. At the stern, a skeleton crew cast lots while they kept vigil under the star-studded sky. Their banter and the serenity of the ocean provided a peace he'd not enjoyed for two long days. Leaning on the rail, he contemplated the choppy water, the small waves catching the moonlight and sparkling brilliantly as they clapped together.

He was surprised when Jonah Wilkinson drew up alongside him. He respected the man and made an effort to smile.

The minutes gathered before Jonah spoke. "Why do you hate him, John?"

"You know why, Jonah." John swung round and leaned back. "Some things will never change."

"But you have a wife now and a baby on the way, possibly a son. Isn't it time to bury the past?"

"If only it were that simple," John murmured, his chin tucked to his chest, arms folded. "You know what's gone before and what's happened over the past two days. The wound has been opened again. It was left untended, and now it festers with poison, waiting for the kill."

"The two of you have made it so," Jonah said. "Why can't you accept the fact your father loved this woman—deeply—and she loved him as well?"

John's head came up. "Why is everyone trying to convince me of this? She didn't love him—not ever."

"That's not how I saw it," Jonah countered. "When I returned to Charmantes after they were married, I watched them together, in town and at the estate. Frederic invited me to dinner, as he always did back then. Colette was radiant; there was no doubt she was in love with him. And your father, he doted on her as if she were a princess—acted like a young man again."

John's turbulent eyes did not faze Jonah. He had known John since he was old enough to climb the *Raven*'s gangplank and had weathered this expression before. Suddenly, it became imperative to make the younger man see reason. The resentment that ate away at his heart would destroy him if he didn't let it go. "I know you loved her, John," he continued, "and perhaps she loved you. But she loved your father as well."

"If she loved him," John ground out, "why did she turn to me?"

"I don't know," Jonah replied. "Why don't you ask your father? But when you do, *listen* to his answer. Your father is a good man, John. It would be a shame if you left this world not knowing that."

Tuesday, August 28, 1838

Paul swore under his breath as he dumped out the last drawer and tossed it to the cabin floor. George kicked a stool aside and, wiping his hands together, said, "That's it. He must have spent it all, like he said."

Paul shook his head and rubbed the back of his neck. "I doubt it. Yvette said Agatha handed him jewelry. He wouldn't have been able to pawn that so easily—not here on the island."

George sighed. "Well, there's nothing here."

"I don't trust him, George. I'm going to move him out of the bondsmen's keep to a place where he'll be isolated, where it will be difficult to escape."

"What do you think your father will do with him?"

"I don't know. But I want him alive and well when he and John return."

Paul strode to the window and stared at the wooded grounds beyond. "I can't go back to Espoir," he murmured. "If I do, I might strangle her."

George walked over to his friend and placed a reassuring hand upon his shoulder. "It's not your fault, Paul. None of this is your fault."

Paul nodded, tears stinging his eyes. "I know it's not. But I'm so goddamn angry, I feel like—"

"We're all angry, and we all feel helpless," George reasoned. "Give it some time. We'll recover. You'll recover. As for Agatha, Jane Faraday will keep an eye on things there. And, if you'd like, I'll venture over every so often."

Paul faced him. "You're a good friend, George. I'm lucky to have you here."

John found his father at the rail, leaning forward, contemplating the vast Atlantic. He steeled himself for another confrontation. He doubted Jonah's words. His father had raped Colette. How could she have loved such a man?

"So, Father," he said as he came abreast of him, "she didn't love me?"

Frederic turned around and folded his arms across his chest. "I shouldn't have said that to you."

John was not happy with his answer. "So, you're saying you were wrong."

"No. I'm saying I shouldn't have said that to you."

"If she didn't love me, Father, why did she come from your bed to mine?"

Frederic didn't answer, and John pressed on. "And unlike you, I didn't have to force her. She came to me of her own volition."

Frederic bowed his head, and John reveled in the delicious pain he was inflicting. "So what was it, Father?" he smiled crookedly, virulently, "you tired of forcing her or—"

"You're not ready for the truth," Frederic cut in.

"Try me."

Frederic eyed him speculatively. "Colette chose you because I hadn't made love to her for five long years. She was lonely."

John laughed outright, the comment insane, but his father's sober eyes gave him pause. Shaken, he blurted out, "I loved Colette!"

"That is where you and I are different, John. For I love her still."

"How touching!"

"But true," Frederic responded, turning back to the ocean. "I was also hurt."

"*You* brought it down upon all of us—not I!" John accused.

"Yes, I did," his father ceded, "but not for the reasons you think."

"Then why?"

Frederic inhaled deeply, held the breath, then released it, all the while staring across the water as if he could see beyond the barriers of time. "The moment I saw Colette, I was struck by her resemblance to your mother—not in her looks, but in her mannerisms: the way she walked into a room, her self-confidence, her smile, the mischievous fire that lit up her eyes. Even the small things: the sweep of her hand and the lilt of her voice. They disturbed me, and though I struggled to ignore the similarities, the attraction only grew."

"So, because she reminded you of my mother, that gave you the right to rape her?"

"No," Frederic replied softly.

"Then why did you force her? Why did you steal her away? Do you really hate me that much?"

"I don't hate you, John!"

"No?" John cried, spurred on by the malice he'd endured and suppressed the whole of his life. "Were you so angry I took Elizabeth from you that you took Colette from me? I loved her, couldn't you see that?"

Frederic stood stunned, moved by his son's unmasked torment. *Dear God, is that what he thinks?*

"How could you do that to me?" John demanded.

"I didn't do it *to you*, John," Frederic refuted. "And though you may never believe it, I *am* sorry." He paused, at a loss, fearful of saying more. John continued to stare at him, his disbelief and misery increasing, an awesome front. For Frederic, it was now or never. "I misjudged Colette," he began hesitantly, his chest constricting. "I was certain she was playing you for the fool—me for the fool. I'd overheard a few conversations between her and her friend and could see her mother's fear of poverty. So I assumed Colette didn't love you at all, that she was simply out for a rich husband. That night, I only thought to confront her, to make her realize she was playing with fire. But that fire got out of hand. Once I'd kissed her, the years fell away, and it was as if I had your mother back in my arms again. I know it's not an excuse, but I was lost to desire."

Frederic breathed deeply, the ache in his breast acute now. "She didn't fight me. I realized later she was too frightened to fight. But when it was happening, I believed I was right about her: she had had other lovers. I couldn't stop. I didn't want to stop. I didn't hurt her, John, not physically, anyway."

He gulped back his pain. "When it was over, I realized my mistake. She *was* pure and innocent, and I was ashamed over what I had done. At the same time, I was elated my speculations had proven wrong. The next day, I couldn't concentrate for thinking about her. That night, I went to her and offered marriage. I promised to help her family. Yes, I wanted to set things right, but more than anything, I wanted her to be *my* wife. I convinced myself what happened between us was destiny: she belonged with me and not you. You were young, I reasoned, too young to be married. You weren't in love, merely infatuated. Eventually, you'd find another.

So, I brushed your feelings aside." Frederic closed his eyes, struggling valiantly to rein in his rampant emotions. "I convinced Colette this was true and warned her she might already be with child, my child. She realized she couldn't go to you a soiled bride and agreed to marry me."

He regarded his son, wondering how his words had been received. The ignominious story had to be as difficult to hear as it was to tell. "It wasn't planned, John. It just happened."

"I don't want to hear any more," John sneered.

"Very well," Frederic rasped, grabbing hold of John's arm before he could walk away. "Answer me this: If I am willing to accept your love for Colette—forgive your affair—why can't you consider that I loved her, too?"

John yanked free, unmoved by his sire's beseeching voice. "I'm not asking for your forgiveness, Father! I didn't do anything wrong. I took what belonged to me in the first place."

Frederic shook his head, knowing John couldn't possibly believe that. "I should have released her," he murmured. "I tried to deny loving her for those five years. It would have been easier to let her go."

"Then why didn't you?"

"*Because* I loved her," he said simply. "I loved her, and I couldn't bear to see her walk out of my life. Having her there, even without her love, was preferable to never seeing her again."

"So, you admit she didn't love you," John rejoined.

"I *thought* she didn't love me," he corrected softly. "The first year we were married, we were happy—I was happy, happier than I'd been in a very long time. I had a reason for living again. I thought Colette was happy, too. Though she never said it, I felt in my heart she'd grown to love me.

"Then she was expecting and we were overjoyed, until the night the twins came into the world. It was a terrible ordeal, the labor long and hard. Blackford gave her something for the pain. I stayed with her, frightened I was going to lose her all over again, as I did the night you were born. Then the laudanum took effect and she became delirious. She called for you over and over again, leaving no doubt as to whom she really loved."

Frederic bowed his head with the painful memory, and John recalled the fierce argument he'd had with Colette that night, one that had induced her labor, perhaps ravaged her mind.

"I begged God to spare her, John—vowed I'd never touch her again if He'd just let her live. And so, when she recovered, I stayed away. At first, I was able to accept my promise, but as time passed, I began to pray she would come to me. When she didn't, I ached with the belief she had never loved me.

"I threw myself into work—first on Charmantes, then on Espoir. Then you came home, and things went from bad to worse. I don't blame you, John, and I don't blame Colette, I blame myself. At that time, however, I wanted to blame everyone *but* myself.

"After the stroke, I prayed to God to take me, so you and Colette could be together. But death never came.

"The years passed, and suddenly, she was gravely ill. I was going to lose her all over again, and I damned myself for the pain I had caused her, the time I had wasted. I bared my heart to her—told her I had always loved her and asked her to forgive me. She said she'd forgiven me years ago—said she loved me, but thought I hated her for what she had done—thought I no longer wanted her. Dear God, how could she think I wouldn't want her?"

His eyes grew glassy, his hoarse voice nearly inaudible. "She died in my arms that night, John. When I awoke the next morning, she was gone. She died in my arms . . ."

Frederic's tears fell freely now, and John, with eyes stinging, walked away.

Wednesday, August 29, 1838

In less than four days, the *Raven* reached Richmond. John threw his knapsack over his shoulder and rushed down the gangplank, bent on abandoning his sire. He glanced back to see Frederic laboring far behind him, trying his level best to keep up. *It wasn't planned—it just happened . . . That's how it starts—with a slip, an innocent slip . . .*

"Shit!"

John hailed a carriage, then turned back to his father, grabbed his bag, and helped him into the conveyance.

"Good luck!" Jonah Wilkinson shouted after them.

"Don't leave port until I speak with you tomorrow!" John called back. "We may need the packet."

The bank was busy for a Wednesday, but John and Frederic went straight to the platform and inquired for the bank manager, Thomas Ashmore, an acquaintance of John's. "I need some information on a Robert Blackford," John stated, once his father had been introduced and handshakes exchanged.

"Well, John," the bank manager proceeded cautiously, "what kind of information are we talking about?"

"Robert Blackford left Charmantes four months ago," he offered. "At that time he had closed out a sizable account with the island's bank and had a promissory note drawn up payable to this bank. We are trying to track him down. Therefore, I need to find out when he deposited that note, if, in fact, he still holds an account here, or whether the money was endorsed to another bank."

"Well, John," Thomas Ashmore replied, "you're asking for personal information. Can you give me a good reason why I should release it to you?"

"The man is a murderer."

"Well, John, why don't you go to the authorities?"

"Because I want to track him down myself, Ash-hole," John replied through clenched teeth, missing Frederic's snigger.

"Well, John—"

"Is 'well John' the only thing you know how to say?" Frederic interrupted.

Thomas gave Frederic a sidelong glance. "Well, sir—"

"Obviously, it is," Frederic bit out. "Mr. Ashmore, this institution was one of the few unscathed by last year's bank panic, was it not?"

Thomas nodded, but his eyes grew wide as saucers.

"I daresay, I had a lot to do with that, considering my substantial backing here. Now, if this bank wishes to avoid another such panic today, you had best go and find the information my son has requested. If you are not back here in ten minutes' time, information in hand, I will close out every account I have in this establishment, and demand each balance in cash. Do you understand?"

"Yes, sir," Ashmore gulped out before fleeing his desk.

Very good! John thought.

Joshua Harrington overheard the dispute at Thomas Ashmore's desk and was taken aback when John Duvoisin turned around and flopped down in the nearest chair as the banker scurried away.

"Mr. Duvoisin?" Joshua inquired, determined to speak to him.

John looked up and, canting his head, tried to place name to the man's face.

"Mr. *John* Duvoisin?" Joshua asked again.

"What can I do for you?" John responded. Frederic looked on in interest.

"I'm Joshua Harrington. We met quite a few years ago . . . I was wondering if your wife was with you—here in Richmond?"

"Charmaine?" John asked in bewilderment. *Who is this man?* His name sounded familiar.

"Yes, Charmaine lived with my wife and me before becoming governess on Les Charmantes."

John rubbed his forehead. *Of course!*

"We are concerned about her," Joshua rushed on. "Her last letter—well, we'd love to see her and make certain she is—in good health."

"Yes," John breathed, irritated by the tacit message Charmaine was in peril married to him. "Unfortunately, she did not accompany me. I had urgent business to attend, and she wasn't able to make the voyage in her condition."

Joshua's brows raised in what appeared to be ghastly comprehension.

"She is fine," John quickly added, "but preferred to stay behind."

Thomas Ashmore returned, and with a nod, Joshua retreated.

Frederic and John left the bank with the information they needed. Blackford had deposited the monies on the fifteenth of April and drawn on the new account immediately. The family's finances had facilitated his escape: The Charmantes' seal guaranteed the note and the Duvoisin funds were held against it. He had taken a quarter of the money in cash and the remainder in another note payable to a New York bank.

They headed back to the harbor to check the ships' manifests for the month of May and ascertain exactly when Blackford had headed to New York City.

The carriage was quiet. John stared out the window. Frederic watched him. "Do you love Charmaine?" he abruptly asked.

John faced him, brow creased. "What do you mean, do I love her?"

"It's a simple question, John."

"Yes, I love her."

Frederic turned and looked out his window.

"That's it, Father?" John queried. "That's all you wanted to know? I know you better than that. What was your real reason for asking that question?"

"You certainly didn't give Mr. Harrington the impression you love her," Frederic replied, ignoring John's dismissive grunt. "The man was obviously concerned. You did nothing to alleviate his disquiet. In fact, he appeared more worried when he walked away."

"He'll get over it," John replied dryly.

"Yes, but what of Charmaine? Do you think she'll get over it?"

He gave John a moment. "You may have told her you needed to do this for Pierre, and I understand that. But on the ship, your anger was about Colette."

"My *anger*, Father," John ground out, "was directed at you, no one else. Do you want to hear how I hate you for robbing me of the three short years I could have spent with my son? If you had seen Agatha for what she was, Pierre would still be alive, wouldn't he?"

"Yes, he would," Frederic capitulated softly. "But Charmaine sees only one face when she thinks of you running off and leaving her, and that face is not Pierre's. You should go back home and allow me to find Blackford."

"No," John snarled. "You're not going to deprive me of the satisfaction of seeing *his* face when I confront him. He will wish he had died and gone to hell."

"We're of a similar mind, but are you willing to forfeit Charmaine for that?"

"Charmaine has waited for me before, Father. She will wait for me again."

"Are you certain?" Frederic probed. "Your brother loves her, too, you know. I've seen it in his eyes."

John grunted again, and again Frederic paid him no mind. "*Your eyes,* when you looked at Colette after I married her."

"My eyes were filled with loathing."

"And deep pain and longing," Frederic finished. "Strange how one can desire something the most when it is no longer his to claim."

"Charmaine doesn't love Paul," John reasoned, "or she would have gone to him long before I returned."

"I pray you are right. But she has a woman's heart now, one that you've broken. In her pain, she may turn to the nearest arms that offer her solace."

John was ill at ease with Frederic's words, but as the carriage drew near the docks, he refused to be deterred. He resolved to write Charmaine that night and let her know he loved her despite their strained good-bye.

* * *

Charmaine sat at the piano, absentmindedly picking out a disjointed melody. Mercedes and George had taken the girls into town, for she had been dismal company the past five days. Even the news of Mercedes's pregnancy had not lifted her spirits. In the quiet solitude, her mind wandered to the sea and Richmond. Any hope John would change his mind and turn back dwindled by the day. She had been a fool to ever love him—a stupid fool! She did not hear Paul step into the room.

He considered her momentarily, her sorry state. Nobody could make her see reason. His assertion on her wedding night had met its mark. How easy it would be to exploit it now, to side with her and bolster her doubts.

He walked over to the piano and put his hands on her shoulders. "It is quiet now," he said when she turned to face him. "We need to talk." He drew up a chair and took both of her hands into his. "Charmaine, I know you're angry with John, but you can't go on like this. He and my father may be gone for weeks. Do you really want to be miserable the entire time they're away?"

"You are right," she said. "Why should I sit here pining for John, when I know he hasn't given me a second thought?"

Inspired, Paul agreed. "Exactly! I told you I'd always be here for you, Charmaine. When you've had enough of this, my arms are wide open."

She was aghast and jumped to her feet. "If you think I could forget John that easily, you insult me! I may be angry with him, but—"

Her anger instantly ebbed, for Paul's eyes were laughing up at her. "I thought you hated him," he said.

"I do," she sputtered, sinking back down to the bench. "I *do* hate him and when he gets back, he's going to hear it! But—"

"—you love him, too," he finished for her, "so much so you hate him for leaving you in pursuit of Blackford. And there's nothing wrong with that."

"But what if he doesn't come back, Paul?" she implored, voicing her darkest fear. "I'm so worried for him."

"Charmaine, nobody is as slick as John. He knows what he's doing. If he can't find Blackford, no one can. And Father is there to watch out for him. I doubt anything will happen to either of them." He paused for a moment and added thoughtfully, "Don't you find it strange they've been thrown together to set this terrible thing right, as if it is meant to be? Providence perhaps. Maybe they will come home reconciled, not only with the past, but with each other."

Charmaine listened quietly, wishing his wisdom true. Clearly, he had been pondering the nefarious events almost as much as she and cared enough about her to offer comfort. She lifted her hand to his rough cheek. "I pray you are right," she said softly. "And I promise not to be so very miserable from now on."

He took her hand and pressed her palm to his lips. "I want you to be happy, Charmaine."

The Duvoisin ship manifests revealed Blackford had left Richmond on the *Seasprit* on the sixteenth of May, which put him in New York by the eighteenth. He'd had over three months to dissolve into the hubbub of the burgeoning city.

With Frederic waiting on the wharf, John boarded the *Raven* and spoke to Jonah. They would set sail on the morrow, and the cargo of tobacco and sugar intended for England would be sold at auction in New York instead.

They settled back in the cab, and John turned to Frederic. "I would like to make one last stop. It won't take long."

Frederic nodded, wondering what John had in mind.

Joshua Harrington arrived home, heavy of heart. He entered the front parlor with head down, wondering how he would tell his wife what he had learned.

Loretta immediately knew something was wrong. "What is it?"

"I encountered John Duvoisin at the bank today."

Her face lit up. "Was Charmaine with him?"

"I'm afraid not, my dear, and I fear things are not good between Charmaine and her husband. She was left behind because she *is* expecting. I knew no good would come of this."

Loretta wondered if he meant Charmaine's marriage to John or her idea to send Charmaine to Charmantes. Over the last two years, the letters they'd received from Charmaine often conveyed a disconcerting gloom. She wrote of Colette's death, Frederic's marriage to Agatha, the prodigal son's return, and little Pierre's terrible drowning accident. Both Loretta and Joshua surmised something more dreadful than Pierre's death had happened to this family, and they had second thoughts about Charmaine living there. Yet, she gave no indication she wanted to return to Richmond. Instead, she wrote of her resolve to stay by the twins' side, John's departure, Frederic's slow recovery, and Paul's preparations for the unveiling of his fleet of ships and island. Obviously, she was spending a great deal of time with Paul, though she never mentioned her feelings, nor speculated where that relationship might lead. Loretta worried often, but Charmaine was a woman now, twenty years old, certainly old enough to make sound decisions.

Michael Andrews's peculiar visit nearly five months ago rekindled their concern. Not two weeks later, Joshua and Loretta entertained Raymond and Mary Stanton, just returned from Charmantes and Paul Duvoisin's commercial debut. Mary was burning to recount the most unexpected and quiet wedding that had capped the week's events.

"You knew nothing about this, Loretta?" Mary had exclaimed, reading Loretta's surprise, ravenous for more gossip. "Surely Charmaine wrote she had feelings for this man—that he was courting her? No?"

When Loretta remained speechless, the woman rushed on, tickled to tell what she knew. "It was so strange—the whole thing." Then she paused, reliving the grandiose event. "Oh, it was a most impressive affair. Charmaine, however, was there in the capacity of governess, nothing more. I spoke with her before the ball. She was plainly dressed, with the children at her side. She said nothing about having an escort for the evening and disappeared not two hours later, settling the girls for the night, no doubt. I can assure you no one expected her to return—certainly not on John Duvoisin's arm, anyway, and so elegantly garbed! She remained at his side for the rest of the evening, danced nearly every dance with him. As for Paul—he may have squired the widow London to the festivities, but everyone could see he was preoccupied with Charmaine. He appeared highly agitated. Either he did not want her there or he disapproved of her partner." Mary shook her head as if she could not fathom it. "My, you should have heard the talk when *he* danced with her! Something was amiss to be sure!"

Loretta shuddered, displeased Charmaine was the subject of much Richmond gossip. Though she dreaded the rest of the scandalmonger's narrative, her desire to know was greater than the woman's humiliating glee, and so, Loretta allowed her to prattle on.

"I heard that, at Mass the following morning, John was seated beside her again, a most unexpected sight, as everyone who is anyone knows he *never* attends church services. They say Charmaine's head remained bowed for the entire time, feeding speculation as to her involvement with the heir to the Duvoisin fortune. But nobody was prepared for the announcement John made at the conclusion of the service. They were wed not two hours earlier! And I have it on good authority Paul was furious."

"What of Charmaine?" Loretta probed worriedly. "What was her reaction?"

"Anne London maintains she couldn't stop blushing, as if—" Mary lowered her voice to a whisper "—as if she had something to be embarrassed about."

"Mary," Loretta chided sharply, "you don't know that. After all, Mr. Duvoisin must feel strongly for Charmaine if he proposed marriage to her."

"Really?" Mary rejoined. "Well, if he feels *strongly* for her, why didn't he arrange a proper ceremony and celebration? He can well afford it, can he not?"

Why indeed?

For weeks, Loretta and Joshua fretted over Mary Stanton's news.

Eventually, they received word from Charmaine, the correspondence lively and gay. She *had* married John. *I know this will come as a shock to you and Mr. Harrington*, she wrote, *but nearly two weeks ago, I married John Duvoisin. Tell Mr. Harrington not to worry. I am very happy. As I insisted some months ago, John is not the man I thought him to be when first we met.*

Though Loretta remained confused, she was at ease with Charmaine's decision to wed. She had no reason to feel otherwise. The young woman had, in fact, done very well for herself, even if the man she had chosen was notorious.

But today, all of Loretta's concerns were revived. She was dismayed Charmaine was already pregnant and left behind while her spouse traveled abroad. She considered her husband woefully. "What has happened, Joshua?" she whispered. "What do you suppose has happened to our dear Charmaine?"

"I'm afraid to guess," Joshua bit out, "but I intend to find out."

"How?"

"I will book passage to Charmantes," he said determinedly. "And if you're willing to brave the voyage, my dear, you are welcome to join me."

"Do you think I'd allow you to travel there without me?"

The carriage pulled to a stop in front of the St. Jude Refuge, and Frederic allowed John to help him down to the cobblestone. "What are we doing here?" he queried in surprise.

"A bit of investigating," John explained, as they entered the sanctuary. "I have a friend here who may have the means to provide information on our good Father Benito. We mustn't forget the part he played in this atrocity."

A nun opened the door. John pulled off his cap, and she led them into a tiny interior room, a makeshift office with sparse, worn furniture. They were seated for only a few minutes when a tall priest entered. His face brightened when John stood to greet him with a handshake. "John," he breathed, belatedly noticing Frederic. "This must be your father."

Frederic read the priest's stunned expression and surmised he knew of their stormy relationship. As John introduced them, Michael stepped forward to shake hands. Something in his manner, his directness perhaps, put Frederic at ease.

"Please, have a seat," Michael offered, pulling up a chair close to them. "I'm glad you decided to stop by. I've tried to get in touch with you for months now."

"We've just arrived in Richmond," John said.

The priest's eyes returned to Frederic. "I gather your visit went well?"

"At the onset," John answered grimly, "but this is not a social call, Michael. We learned the deaths of my son and Colette were not accidents. They were murdered."

He recounted the evil plot that had taken the lives of Colette and Pierre. Michael listened without a word, reading the pain on each man's face. "May God rest their souls," he murmured compassionately when John had finished. "I'm very sorry. What can I do?"

John marshaled his emotions. "We're seeking information on a Father Benito St. Giovanni. He shipwrecked on Charmantes almost twenty years ago and, when he recovered from nearly drowning, was asked to stay on as the island priest."

"He claimed to be a missionary," Frederic explained, "his destination another Caribbean island. During his recovery, he grew adamant about 'converting' Charmantes, assuring me the Vatican would approve such a mission, eventually boasting he'd received papal blessing from Rome. Of course, his work on my island could hardly be called missionary, but suggesting it afforded us a priest."

John snorted. "If you could call him a priest."

"Why do you say that, John?" Michael queried.

"He knew of the murders and was blackmailing my aunt."

"Are you certain?"

"Oh, I'm certain," John affirmed. "He confirmed all of Agatha's mad ranting and raving. We even have a letter, penned in his own hand, as proof."

"Dear God," the priest sighed. "I'll do what I can. It may take some time to receive word, but I'll write to the Vatican and find out whatever I can about Father Benito St. Giovanni of Italy. When do you think you will return to Richmond?"

"That depends on how long it takes me to find Blackford in New York and—" John stopped short, but his manner and the fire in his eyes shook the priest.

"And?" Michael pressed, but John would say no more. "You don't intend to take the law into your own hands, do you?" The silence collected and Michael looked to Frederic. "You're not planning to murder this man, are you?" With Frederic's muteness, Michael grew alarmed. "John, you must not do this! You may think retribution will satisfy you, but I promise, it will not. Please tell me you will not seek revenge on this man."

"I can't promise you that, Michael."

Michael shook his head fiercely. "John—track him down, call the authorities, but leave it in their hands and in the hands of the Good Lord."

"The *Good* Lord," John bit out venomously, "allowed that man to take my innocent son, hold his head under the cold water and callously watch his arms and legs flail in unfathomable distress until the life was snuffed out of him." Suddenly, he was crying. "Don't tell me seeking revenge won't satisfy me—bring me peace—because, goddamn it, I won't know peace until the very last breath is snuffed out of him!"

Again Michael looked to Frederic. "You have to talk him out of this. He'll be a wanted man—a murderer!"

"I can't," Frederic stated solemnly. "I want to see Blackford suffer as much as he does."

"You are not in your right minds! Can't you see this man is not worth your own souls? He's already damned. Do not damn yourselves!"

Silence.

When the answer congealed into a knot of cold dread, Michael implored, "Is there nothing I can say to change your minds?"

"Pray for us, Father," Frederic replied.

Michael shook his head, and John hurriedly stood, wanting only to end the meeting. "Depending on how long we're in New York, we may head directly back to Charmantes. When you receive word from the Vatican, I'd appreciate it if you would send it to Stuart. He'll make certain it gets to me."

"I may deliver the correspondence myself," Michael said softly, still shaken.

The statement piqued John's curiosity. "Why?"

"I need to check on someone there," Michael replied. "Actually, someone in your employ, Frederic."

"Who?" Frederic asked, equally befuddled.

"The governess to your daughters—Charmaine Ryan."

Though Frederic was surprised, John's confusion ran rampant. "Charmaine?" he queried. *How does Michael know her?*

The priest was smiling again. "I took your advice, John, and contacted Loretta and Joshua Harrington shortly after you left for Charmantes. Charmaine was working for them when Marie passed away."

Michael had never seen John speechless, let alone dumbstruck. "John, are you all right?"

"He's in a bit of shock," Frederic interjected. "You are the second person today who has inquired about his wife."

"His wife?" Michael uttered. Impossible! The incredible coincidence had instantly grown fantastic. "But you never told me you knew her!"

"You never mentioned her name!" John rejoined.

"But surely you knew she was Marie's daughter?" the priest pressed.

"I never knew," John murmured, his memory jarred. That first morning he had come home, Charmaine had looked familiar. Marie—Charmaine was Marie's daughter! His mind raced—John Ryan had killed Marie! His eyes darkened once more. "My God," he breathed as all the pieces fit together. *John Ryan isn't Charmaine's father!* The insanity of it all hit him full force, and quite abruptly, he threw back his head and laughed. "Wait until Charmaine hears this!"

"No, John," the priest warned, eyeing Frederic, intent upon keeping the story confidential. "You mustn't tell anyone! I want to see her first."

"Not tell her?" John queried in waxing glee. "Of course you've got to tell her! She hates the man she thinks is her father."

"John, please," Michael cut in, searching Frederic's face.

John's eyes traveled to his father as well. "Your little secret won't shock him, Michael. He's done plenty of things of which he's not proud. Believe me, he keeps secrets better than you keep confessions."

Later, as John and his father traveled to his town house, Frederic asked him about Charmaine's mother.

"I met her a few years ago. She was working at St. Jude's and came to my aid when I no longer wanted to live. Like Charmaine, she was my savior of sorts, and through her, I befriended Michael. Together, they turned my life in a new and, I think, better direction. If I had known about Marie's hardship, I would have helped her. But I'm ashamed to say we only spoke of me."

He looked out the window, introspective with the wrenching revelation. He thought of Charmaine and realized how much he missed her.

They spent a quiet evening together. After dinner, John withdrew to his desk and wrote to her, carefully choosing the words he put to paper, telling her he loved her and longed to put this ordeal behind him. He then penned a quick letter to Paul. When he was finished, he said goodnight to his father.

Frederic stayed awake long into the night, contemplating all that had gone before, all that had been revealed today, and all they had yet to face. He walked to the hearth and studied a small sketch tacked there. It was a picture of a black horse rearing high in the air with the words: *Fantom misses you, Johnny! So do we! Love, Yvette.* With a sad sigh, he traced a finger over the drawing. It was faded and curled at the edges. *What was I thinking when I tore this family apart?* He retired, praying to God that, for once in his life, he was doing the right thing.

Michael prayed fervently that night as well, kneeling before the crucifix that hung above his bed. By dawn, he had come to a decision, inspired by his prayers. He found Sister Elizabeth, told her about his plans and, throwing some clothing into a threadbare satchel, left St. Jude's.

Silence stalked the halls, cloaked the rooms, and seeped into the cracks and crevices, joining the darkness in an eerie, unholy communion. It was near midnight. Agatha crept up the staircase, her head cocked to one side, listening, groping, grasping the balustrade. "Frederic?" she whispered. "Is that you? Robert! Where are you? Is it accomplished?"

She found a lamp on a table and blindly lit it, chasing the dark away to lurk with the shadows. "Who is it?" she cried. Sensing a movement far off to her left, she whirled around. "Elizabeth—is that you?" Undaunted, she stepped closer. "I told you never to come back here! Frederic is mine now!"

A cold gust of air swirled about her lithe form, carrying upon it a whisper. "He's gone now . . . never to return . . ." Her eyes darted about the corridor, tracking the breeze back down the cavernous flight. It was true; Frederic had left days ago, hadn't returned since she'd explained everything to him. She thought he would understand, but now, she was apprehensive.

Paul hadn't awakened. He should be hungry by now, should have wanted to nurse. Panic seized her. Had Frederic taken her babe away? Or had Robert taken him again? She'd told him to take Pierre! The air whispered from below, as if reading her thoughts. "Pierre, *mon caillou* . . ."

Agatha flew down the stairs, tripping on her robe and nearly dropping the lamp. She followed the wraith into the drawing room, her eyes distended in recognition. There stood Colette, grasping the hand of her small son.

"You!" Agatha hissed. "Where is Robert?" she demanded, searching the room. "He was supposed to take your boy away!" She laughed truculently. "Frederic will now know how it feels to have a child ripped from his arms!"

"My boy is safe," Colette whispered, "with me."

Again Agatha's eyes darted about. "Where's Robert? Where is he?"

Colette smiled. "He's gone . . . with the other babe . . ."

"Elizabeth's bastard?"

"No, John is with Frederic . . . is safe with his father."

Fear seized Agatha. "Paul?" she cried, flying to all corners of the room and out to the foyer. "No! Robert promised me! He promised to make me happy—promised he'd never take Paul from me again!"

"But you didn't make *him* happy," Colette breathed. "He's angry with you."

It was true; Robert hated her now. Agatha had used him, and he knew it.

The front door flew open and the night air beckoned to her. "Where did he go?" she pleaded. "Where did he take my baby?"

Colette led the way. "You told him to drown the boy . . ."

Instantly, Agatha knew. Desperate, she ran after the apparition that remained out of reach. "Oh God!" she sobbed.

"Agatha . . . you deserted Him long ago . . ."

"Please!" she shrieked. "Not my son! Please, not my son!"

The dock was just ahead, and Agatha flew across it, possessed. She could see a dinghy bobbing in the waves. "Robert! No! Please! You have the wrong boy!"

There were cabins near the wharf. The men inside thought they heard a cry, but they stepped out too late, rubbing sleepy eyes. They heard a splash. Or was it the clapping waves? They shrugged and returned to their quarters.

Thursday, August 30, 1838

The Richmond harbor was already buzzing when John and Frederic arrived at the *Raven*. Jonah was on the quay with Stuart Simons, and John was pleased. He thought it would be months before he saw Stuart again.

"John," he greeted, "I was expecting the *Destiny* to land today, but certainly not the *Raven* and you." He noticed Frederic and politely extended a hand. "You must be Frederic," he said jovially. "I'm Stuart Simons."

John let Frederic reply, then took Stuart aside, walking the length of the boardwalk with him.

"Jonah told me what happened," Stuart said. "I'm sorry, John."

"I'm dealing with it," John replied, abruptly brushing the matter aside. "Remember when you made inquiries about John Ryan?"

"Yes. What about it?"

"Have any of the longshoremen seen him?"

"I don't know." When John frowned, Stuart added, "I never really pursued it, so he may have been around."

"Spread the word I'm offering a reward to anyone who can identify him. When you know who he is, pay him so well he can't *wait* to come to work each day."

"Why?" Stuart asked in bewilderment.

"Once he's consistent about showing up, promote him to a better paying job on board a Charmantes-bound packet. When he's on that ship, notify me."

"But how am I to know where you are?"

"Send the information with the cargo invoices. If I'm not on the island, Paul will be there and know what to do. I've written to him." John pulled two letters from his shirtfront. "Make sure these are on the *Destiny*."

"But she's headed for Liverpool. We're packing her hold with tobacco."

"Load only half," John directed. "The *Raven* will return to Richmond by next week, ready to take on a full cargo. As for the *Destiny*, Paul can fill her hold with sugar." He handed Stuart the letters. "It's important these get to Charmantes."

John didn't know Michael Andrews had boarded the *Raven*. Frederic told him to stay below deck until they were far from port. When he did emerge, John was annoyed. "What's this?" and he looked from his father to Michael. "Now I have two fathers with whom to contend?"

"You're stuck with me," Michael said, casting his eyes heavenward. "Rant and rave all you like, but I've been sent by a higher authority."

"I hope you can walk on water, Michael. Any preaching, and I'm throwing you overboard."

The news of Agatha's death reached Paul when he arrived in town early that morning. In less than an hour, he stepped onto Espoir. The corpse was left as it had been found on the beach, with a blanket draped over it. With a mixture of disgust and guilt, hatred and sadness, he looked down at Agatha's bloated body. His heart heavy, he ordered two men to construct a pine box for the burial.

That night, he sat in his grand mansion, alone and lonely. So this was what commercial success meant. In the past four months, three vessels had departed his island; their cargo would fetch tidy purses. Yet today, he didn't feel the deep satisfaction he'd always experienced when he'd worked hard for his father. He retired, the empty hallways echoing his desolation. He could not sleep.

* * *

Michael knocked on John's cabin door, then entered the cubicle on an indrawn breath and a prayer. John was seated at a small desk, his brow furrowed. "I'm not here to preach," Michael promised. "I'd like to talk about Charmaine."

John leaned back and propped his feet atop the desk, inviting him to sit on the small cot. He was smiling now. "I love her," he said decisively.

Michael returned the smile and asked, "How did this happen?"

"God, Michael, I don't know. When I returned home to find Colette had died, Charmaine was already there caring for the children. I didn't like her at first. Actually, I misjudged her." *I misjudged Colette . . .* John frowned with the unbidden thought, rubbed his brow, and addressed Michael again. "We were thrown together day after day. I wanted to spend as much time as possible with Pierre, and of course, she was always there. She was a mother to him. When he died, she was as devastated as I was, and yet, she comforted me. Looking back on it now, I know I was in love with her when I left last fall, but with everything that happened, I wasn't ready to admit it until I went back home last April and saw her again." He grinned with the heady memory. "It was a taste of heaven to find she felt the same way about me."

John grew thoughtful. "If your God *is* out there, Michael, he planned this one pretty well, didn't he? And I promise you this: we couldn't protect Marie, but you needn't ever worry about Charmaine."

"What of Colette?" Michael mused. "You said you couldn't love another."

"I didn't believe I could," John murmured. "But I do."

"Enough to forgive your father and yourself?"

John's face hardened. "I don't know."

"He's forgiven you, hasn't he?" Michael probed.

John was uncomfortable and rose swiftly from the desk. Michael wisely changed the subject. "When were the vows spoken?"

"On the island, after Paul's party. It was very private with

Father Benito—" John's words broke off, and Michael followed his thoughts: *What if the priest isn't a priest at all?* "When we are finished in New York," John decided, "we will have a ceremony on Charmantes with you presiding this time, Michael."

"I would be honored."

"There is something else you should know. You are going to be a grandfather."

Michael wondered if the surprises would ever end, but this was the sort of announcement he could capitalize on. "A baby on the way," he pondered softly. "When is he or she due?"

"Around Christmastide."

"And you think it wise to be away from Charmaine at such a time?"

"You sound like my father," John pronounced as he began to pace.

"We're concerned for you, as well as for your new son or daughter."

"Yes, I'm sure you are," John muttered, then he stopped in his tracks. "So—is the sermon coming now or are you still leading up to it?"

"John—"

"You're wasting your time, Michael."

"John, you are one of the most honorable men I know. For that reason alone, my time is not being wasted. But you are also married to my daughter now. I can't keep silent. We each have our missions here."

John's tumultuous eyes mocked his crooked grin, but he did not argue.

Friday, August 31, 1838

Agatha Blackford Ward Duvoisin was not buried beside Frederic's other two wives. Paul had her grave dug on the far side of the cemetery. Charmaine, George, and Mercedes were the only ones attending the small funeral, for the girls had refused to go, and even for Paul's sake, Charmaine could not force them to pray for the woman who had murdered their mother and brother.

Without a priest, it fell to Paul to offer a eulogy, one sad sentence that chilled Charmaine's soul: "May God forgive you and bring you the peace you never found in this life." With bowed head, she allowed her tears to fall, not for Agatha, but for her son.

Late that night, Charmaine found Paul in the dark library; he'd allowed the lamp to burn out. She stepped into the room, the hallway sconces sending a shaft of light across the chair in which he lounged. As she moved closer, she found he slept. Her eyes filled with tears again. It would have been easier to love this man, she realized. Today, he had desperately needed someone to love him. Her mind wandered back to that time of innocence, when a bare chest and a lazy smile made her legs go weak. She'd always treasure those profound feelings of first love.

"Paul," she whispered. "Paul?"

He stirred, his eyes fluttering open, and then, almost in a daze, he realized where he was. He rubbed his brow and then his eyes. "I must have fallen asleep."

"Why don't you go to bed? You've had a draining day."

"No, no," he dissented. "I wouldn't be able to sleep if I retired."

He stood, stretched, and went to the decanter to pour himself a drink. "Would you like some?" he offered, but she only shook her head.

"I felt the baby move today," she said, attempting to break the melancholy.

His half-smile told her she hadn't succeeded. "And how have *you* been feeling?" he asked.

"Better. Rose was right. The first few months were the worst."

"You look beautiful, Charmaine," he told her, his smile finally reaching his eyes as if he'd read her thoughts, "even if you are in the family way."

Why this silly small talk? She inhaled, then plunged headlong into the source of their misery. "Paul, we haven't spoken about this, and perhaps now is not the time, but John told me everything about your father and Agatha, and—" she paused, searching for the right words "—you should know you're one of the finest men I've ever known. I hope you don't hold yourself responsible for what's happened to this family. I don't, and I'm certain John doesn't, either."

He was listening intently, but she was uncertain of his reaction.

"I've lived with that terrible feeling of helplessness," she continued, "and I've finally realized I could never have changed my father or prevented what he did. Agatha is only a bad memory now, but she did bless this world with something very good—you."

Chapter 7

Sunday, September 2, 1838
New York City

WHEN Frederic and Michael stepped off the ship with John, they were awed by the bustle on the docks and the throngs in the street. They hailed a carriage and headed for John's row house near Washington Square. Manhattan made Richmond look like a country village.

"This is where the future of shipping is, Father," John said as the conveyance rolled through the streets.

They settled into the vacant row house on Sixth Avenue, opening windows and lighting the lamps. The next day, they set up house with supplies and foodstuffs, and began planning how they would track down Robert Blackford.

The bank where he'd deposited his small fortune proved to be a dead end. The account had been closed as soon as the Richmond banknote cleared. The financier yielded little information. Robert was shrewd. The money had not been transferred; he'd taken his funds in cash. There was nothing to do but start scouring the city, hoping for a clue or a lead.

They agreed Michael would accompany Frederic, and John would go out on his own because he knew New York better.

"I'm sure he's taken an assumed name," John said.

Frederic concurred. "But how do we begin to guess what that might be?"

"Start with the obvious ones," Michael suggested, "Smith, Jones, Brown . . ."

"He won't go from Blackford to Brown," John quipped derisively. "Is there anything darker than black? That's what he is."

"No, John," Michael replied grimly. "Black is as dark as it gets. Try then the names Black and Ford."

They grew quiet, discouraged by the daunting mission ahead of them.

"I want to know why he did it," John muttered. "It wasn't for the money, I know it wasn't. There was something else."

Frederic looked up, not surprised that his son had come to the same conclusion.

Their eyes locked, and John addressed the other problem they would have to face. "What do you intend to do with Agatha when we get back?"

"I don't know, John. From what Paul told me, she is in her own private hell already."

That night, John had his recurrent dream of Pierre, lost in the streets of New York. But this time, after Pierre disappeared in the crowd, John found himself in a dark factory, where veiled black figures shoveled coal into large ovens. The flames flared up and burned brightly, greedily devouring the coal.

Friday, September 7, 1838
Charmantes

They had fallen into a routine. Paul and George made a point of being home before dinner, and the table was laid for seven each night: Paul and Charmaine, the twins and Rose, Mercedes and George. Charmaine marveled at how the girls were maturing. They showed an interest in nearly any topic and participated in each conversation; Yvette in particular often questioned Paul about his workday. She continued to be an asset to the mill operation, the only bookkeeping about which he didn't have to worry. Her knowledge of the family business astounded him, and as his respect grew, so, too, did the camaraderie that had sprung up between them.

Tonight was the same, and when the dishes were cleared away, everyone stood to retire to the front parlor. Yvette and Paul were involved in a heated discussion concerning the benefits of building a sugar refinery on Charmantes. "It can't be done!" Paul argued. "Purification must be accomplished abroad."

"But the ships could carry far more condensed extract than raw, and you could charge a higher price for a nearly finished product."

"Fresh water is limited here, Yvette, and there's the wood supply to consider. We'd be burning a great deal each day just to fire the plant."

"Then what about cocoa?" And so it went.

Charmaine exchanged a chuckle with Rose and, seeing one last plate on the table, turned to the kitchen to deliver it to Fatima. Pots and pans were piled high in the middle of the wooden table, and the cook was shuttling dishes and cutlery to the new girl, Rachel, who was scrubbing them in the adjacent scullery.

"Oh, Miss Charmaine," Fatima scolded lightly, "let me have that plate."

"Cookie, where are Felicia and Anna?"

The woman grunted. "Seeing to Master Paul, I suspect."

Charmaine felt her ire rising. Evidently, this was not the first time the duty of washing the dishes had fallen to Fatima. "But this is their job, isn't it?"

"With Missus Faraday minding Master Paul's house and Mistress Agatha gone, they've been getting out of a lot of work they ought to be doing."

"Have they?" Charmaine mused before marching from the room.

She'd suspected the two lazy maids had been slacking off, but that wasn't the only reason she was furious when she entered the front parlor. Two days earlier, she had overheard their whispers behind the doors of John's old room.

". . . and now he's away, you see how she fawns over Paul?"

"Even with John's baby growin' inside of her."

"Well, maybe it ain't John's at all!"

The room echoed with vicious giggles.

Charmaine had turned away, not allowing them the victory they would certainly savor if they knew they had hurt her. But not tonight! Tonight she was armed for battle.

Sure enough, she found the two at the liquor cabinet, Anna pretending to wipe up, while Felicia strolled across the room with hips swaying, presenting a glass of port to Paul, who looked up and smiled.

"Felicia, Anna," Charmaine called from the doorway, her arms crossed.

The two women turned to face her.

"Have you finished with the dinner dishes already?"

"Fatima said she'd see to it," Felicia lied.

Charmaine responded sternly. "I told *Mrs. Henderson* she is not to do dishes, pots, pans, knives, forks, spoons, or utensils of any sort. She is our cook, not the cleanup help. However, if I do find her cleaning up after a meal, I will give her a day off, and the chore of cooking will fall to you. Understood?"

Both maids appeared shocked, but when Anna opened her mouth to speak, Charmaine rushed on. "Now, if I were you, I'd run to that kitchen and make myself busy. You're not being paid to pour drinks."

Felicia's eyes flew to Paul, as if to say she'd only take orders from him, perhaps hoping he'd come to her rescue, and Charmaine held her breath. But one look at his face told her he was of no mind to interfere. Felicia must have recognized it, too, for she stomped from the room in an insulted huff. As she passed through the door, Charmaine added, "In future, we won't be requiring your services after dinner. This is family time."

When they were alone, Yvette and Jeannette began to laugh, and George quickly joined in. "What was that all about?" Paul asked.

"If I am mistress of this manor, it is time I start acting the part."

Paul raised his glass in a toast and winked. For the first time in two long weeks, Charmaine felt happy.

Three days later, Felicia was sent packing. Charmaine hadn't a clue why.

Paul fired the trollop on the spot and didn't give her a backward glance as she scurried from the house. Returning to the study where he'd been working, he thought back on the morning. Anna and Felicia had been making his bed, thinking him gone for the day. They were also talking about Charmaine.

"My blood boils every time I think how that hussy sauntered into this house," Felicia was saying, "wormin' her way into the family by playin' the virgin."

"You'd best get over it," Anna advised in a whisper.

But Felicia could not curb her temper. "I'd rather have Agatha back."

"Charmaine's not that bad. You're jealous, is all."

"Jealous of what? Her big belly? I think that baby was growin' inside of her long before she snared John."

"Felicia, you saw the bed linen, same as I did!" Anna stated.

"She probably cut herself and bled on them sheets just to trick everyone, John included. You see the way she's sprouting? It won't be long before Paul is disgusted by the sight of her, and then he'll be looking my way again."

Paul had heard enough and barged in, slamming the door behind him.

"Master Paul!" Anna shrieked.

His scowl was directed at Felicia, and she recoiled. "Pack your things," he growled. "You'll not spend another night in this house."

"But where will I go?"

"Your parents live in town, don't they? Maybe they'll take you in. If not, there's always Dulcie's. You're more suited for that type of work, anyway."

Felicia blushed and fled the room.

Paul turned on Anna, and she unconsciously took two steps backward. "Sir," she implored. "I didn't like listening to her."

"You had best make me believe that," he warned, his jaw still clenched. "I don't want to hear that Charmaine has had to speak to you again. And she had better not be the subject of any of your conversations. Is that clear?"

"Yes, sir," she murmured meekly and, with a swift curtsy, flew out the door.

Tuesday, September 11, 1838

Paul was in town when the shout went up that a ship was docking. He stood on the wharf as Matt Williams navigated the *Destiny* to the pier. Once the ship was moored, he jumped aboard. "What brings you to us, Matt?" he queried. "I thought you'd be running shipments for John out of Virginia."

"That was the original plan, but according to Stuart Simons, John and your father changed all that. They've taken the *Raven* on to New York and sent me to deliver these." He handed Paul two letters, the envelopes addressed in John's scrawl. "I'm carrying only a half-cargo of tobacco. John thought the trip could be salvaged if I filled the remainder of the hold with sugar."

"Rest for now," Paul said. "We should be able to get her loaded tomorrow, and you can set sail in two days' time."

Matt nodded, then informed his crew. With a whoop of appreciation, they quickly finished securing the vessel, motivated by thoughts of Dulcie's and an afternoon of leisure.

Paul went down into the captain's cabin and tore open his letter. When he'd finished reading it, he looked at the envelope addressed to Charmaine and abruptly decided to postpone the work he had planned for the afternoon.

Charmaine was sitting on the swing listening to the girls as they took turns reading to her. The weather was mild and the day too beautiful, so she had suggested they finish the novel in the shade of the oak tree. She was surprised to see Paul ride through the gates and rein Alabaster in their direction.

He dismounted quickly, tucked both hands behind his back, and suggested she pick one. Bewildered, she chose the right, but when it came up empty, he quickly presented his left. "A little present," he said with a debonair smile.

Charmaine recognized John's handwriting and gasped in relief. She turned the envelope over, carefully broke the seal, and sat absentmindedly on the swing.

"Is it from Johnny?" Jeannette asked.

"What does it say?" Yvette demanded.

Paul put a finger to his lips and motioned the girls to follow him to the stable. Without an argument, they fell in step beside him, Alabaster in tow. When they were a distance away, he said, "Give Charmaine some time alone. She needs a few moments of happiness."

They smiled up at him.

"Besides," he continued, "John wrote to you in my letter."

"Truly?" they queried in tandem. "What did he say?"

"He wrote he misses you and will be home as soon as possible."

"That's all?" Yvette asked. "Did he say if he killed Dr. Blackford yet?"

"No, Yvette—" Paul frowned "—he didn't write about that. According to his letter, he's still searching for him."

"Well, he's sure taking his time, isn't he?"

"What about Papa?" Jeannette asked. "Did Johnny write if he's all right?"

"I don't know," Paul admitted, "but I'm certain Father is fine."

"I just hope they're not fighting," Yvette proclaimed. "That will surely slow things down."

Paul shook his head with his sister's words of wisdom. "Let it be, Yvette."

Charmaine feasted on John's letter from the tender opening: *My dearest Charm*, to the poignant closing: *Tell our beautiful baby I love him as much as I love his mother.* She learned his pursuit of Blackford was taking him and his father to New York and he'd unexpectedly met Joshua Harrington. Then came his love words, words that melted Charmaine's heart.

I apologize for the way I left you that day. Please understand I am compelled to seek justice. I could never live with myself knowing the murderer of my son was still at large and I did nothing. And, yes, I am also doing this for Colette. I would be a liar if I didn't admit that to you or myself. But it is not because I harbor a fierce love for her. She was a good and kind person who didn't deserve to die so young—to be murdered. If she were alive today, I would still choose you. You are more woman than I could ever hope to love me. I learned something incredible today—something that made me smile amidst all this gloom, but that news will have to wait. This revelation made me realize how much you mean to me, my Charm, and how very much I love you. It's so lonely here tonight. I long to hold you in my arms and make love to you. I promise when I return, we will make up for all the time these weeks have stolen from us.

Blinded by tears, Charmaine pressed the signature to her lips and savored the contact, as if she could drink in John's presence through the kiss. She closed her eyes to bittersweet happiness and breathed deeply. When she had composed herself, she looked up and realized she was alone.

Later that evening when Yvette and Jeannette were asleep, Charmaine wrote her first love letter. She poured out all her emotions and found herself crying before she had finished. Like John, she, too, apologized for the things she'd said before he left and told him how much she longed for the day he'd return home to her. When she was finished, she kissed the missive. Paul promised to put the post on the first vessel bound for New York. Thanks to George, they knew John's address there.

Thursday, September 13, 1838

Robert Blackford stood behind a middle-aged woman who spoke softly to the clerk at the apothecary counter. He smiled to himself when she asked for a small vial of arsenic, and he wondered whose demise she was planning, most likely her husband's or perhaps a lover's. The clerk produced a ledger he asked her to sign. She paid him, and he handed over the poison.

Simple, Robert thought, *so very simple.* If Colette had lived on the mainland, Agatha wouldn't have needed his services. But the mercantile on Charmantes stocked few medicinal items, and she had had to rely on him to procure the arsenic from Europe, which he did after she'd given Colette that first, nearly fatal dose in the early spring of 1836.

Robert stepped out into the bright sunshine moments later. He breathed deeply of the unusually brisk autumn air—crisp, but not clean. The booming factories soiled the afternoon breezes with thick smoke. Ah well, he couldn't have everything.

As he walked along the bustling streets, his mind returned to Charmantes, that faraway place where he'd passed the better part of his life. Agatha had neatly sewn up the future for him, situating him here. He remembered his joy when she had arrived on Charmantes to stay. He thought it was the beginning for them; in reality, it was the beginning of the end.

Her husband had died, and even now, Robert wondered if Thomas Ward was the first of her victims. She had left Britain with enough arsenic to kill Colette overnight. But her rush for revenge was thwarted. Perhaps Colette was stronger than she realized, perhaps the entire draught was not consumed. Whatever the reason, Colette recovered, and Agatha had little poison left. When she confided in Robert, he upbraided her.

"You fool! What if Frederic were to find out? He'd have your head!"

She threw herself into his arms and cried on his shoulder. He basked in her embrace. When her tears subsided, she cajoled him, and promised she loved him as well. "I must rid Charmantes of any memory of Elizabeth. Please help me, Robert!" she implored.

She was determined to do away with Colette, marry Frederic, and effect John's disinheritance, ensuring Paul the security that had been robbed from him on the day of his birth. Only then could they be together and enjoy the wonderful life Frederic's money could buy.

He believed her. And because he loved her fiercely, he took command of the murder plot. He procured the arsenic and administered it in minute doses. "So it will be a slow, unexplainable death," he reasoned. In truth, he dragged his feet for a full year before he killed Colette, hoping Agatha would change her mind and return to him.

"Yes," her eyes glittered. "Let it be painful."

When Colette began to complain about her "illness," her mistrust of Robert apparent, it was easy to allow Agatha to take over. A strict schedule was developed, doses carefully calculated. A dash of poison was sprinkled on Colette's food three days prior to Robert's appointment, a tad more the following day, and a full measure the day after that. Colette was so ill by the time Robert arrived she welcomed his visits. Agatha withheld the poison on the days he came, and Colette would feel better after he left, as the severe side effects of the arsenic were wearing off. After three days, Agatha began the dosing all over again.

For months, she took enormous pleasure in watching Colette suffer, gleefully describing the grisly details: the headaches and dizziness, the vomiting and soiled undergarments, the ghastly face and hair loss. But in time, Agatha grew anxious to be done with the act, accelerating their routine to two appointments per week.

Colette should have died sooner, but pneumonia made poisoning difficult. Though arsenic was undetectable in food and liquids, Colette consumed very little of either, and when she did, there was always someone hovering over her: Gladys, Millie, Rose, and on occasion, Frederic. Toward the very end, Robert grew apprehensive; both Paul and Frederic were asking too many questions, and he prayed the pneumonia would kill her. When Colette pulled through, he seized the moment and liberally laced her broth and coffee with a lethal dose. But he wasn't allowed in her room, and the tray he carried from the kitchen was left with Frederic. He feared the worst: what if Frederic sampled the poisonous fare?

Robert was lucky. Colette swallowed every drop and, within the hour, was violently ill. He was surprised she lasted the day, more amazed no one ever contemplated her many symptoms. But then, they had been gradual and endured over a long period of time.

His cunning had worked in their favor; their treachery met with only one hitch: Benito St. Giovanni. The island priest had been just as clever and ruthless. It could not be helped, but Robert let Agatha handle that. Benito's extortion did not deter her. She was certain she'd find a way to shake him off. Besides, there was more to do: Pierre was next.

"He is in the will," she complained. "Pierre may inherit it all, and Paul won't get a red penny of his birthright. We must set this injustice right, Robert! Help me, my dearest, please! I promise we shall be together as soon as we've taken care of this one last detail."

"John is first in line," he'd reasoned. "I thought *he* was the problem."

"Of course he is! But I want him to suffer as I did. It's only a matter of time with John, anyway. I guarantee this event will be his undoing. I'll make it so."

Her hollow pledge haunted him still. Unconsciously, he'd embraced the truth: she was only using him. He didn't want to believe it, and so he agreed to the diabolical deed, praying that in the ensuing turmoil, Frederic would suffer a fatal stroke and Agatha would finally realize how much *he* loved her. But just in case she didn't, just in case he needed to flee Charmantes, he set a high price for the part he would play.

The fateful night arrived. Agatha swept into his abode, a hungry gleam in her eyes. The perfect opportunity had unexpectedly presented itself. Pierre had set the stage at dinner. "We must strike while the iron is hot," she eagerly declared, her mind racing, "now, while Frederic is furious with John—before John returns to Richmond. We must stoke the rage into an inferno!"

Robert shuddered at her maniacal euphoria. "How much are you willing to pay?" he inquired coolly.

She was momentarily deflated, but quickly recovered, signing a promissory note that turned Thomas Ward's entire estate over to him.

The next morning, she slipped a minute dose of arsenic into the boy's milk. He became ill within the hour, complaining of stomach cramps and a headache, and as Agatha had predicted, John was asked to mind him while the family attended Mass.

In the meantime, Robert visited the stables. Few were about; most of the hands were also at Sunday service. His greatest fear that morning had been the great black stallion, but even that was easy. Phantom greedily devoured the mango he had pitted and filled with lye. Within seconds, the horse was writhing in agony. Robert unlatched the stall door, and the stallion bolted, knocking him over as he galloped out of the stable. He jumped to his feet and fled through the rear door, charting the shouts and high-pitched neighing that rose from the front lawns.

Within minutes, he reached the second floor of the manor, taking the back stairway that originated behind the ballroom and opened on to Agatha and Frederic's chambers above. He watched John run from the nursery, and before the front door slammed shut, he was at Pierre's bedside, scooping him up. The boy's eyes were closed, and Robert looked away, racing back the way he had come, out across the rear lawns, and into the safety of the tree line. Capsizing the boat and the actual drowning took longer than anticipated. He was distracted by shouts in the distance. "The lake—my father said the lake!"

He fled and watched from the boathouse, petrified when he realized the boy was not dead. What if he awoke? What if he talked? For three agonizing days, Robert could only pace. There were no ships in port—no means of escape. He waited to be called upon; he'd waste no time finishing what he'd begun. But Pierre died all on his own.

Even today, the memories remained vivid. Robert breathed a sigh of relief. Fate had smiled down on him eleven months ago. It was just as well he had left Charmantes. Here, he was far from Benito, even Agatha, and he was safe. No one, neither Frederic nor John, could ever track him down. Smiling smugly, he ambled down the busy road with a lighthearted gait.

Saturday, September 15, 1838

Maddy Thompson shook out the last lovely dress. The wardrobe John had ordered for Charmaine had arrived from Europe. But the new garments held no joy for Charmaine. The dresses didn't fit, and even if they did, John wasn't there to see her in them.

"What's the matter?" Jeannette asked. "Don't you like them?"

Even Yvette was disturbed by Charmaine's apparent dissatisfaction. "They're all beautiful," she said.

"Beautiful, yes," Charmaine murmured, "but I'll not be wearing them for quite some time."

Maddy returned the garment to its box. "Your condition won't last forever," she said. "By springtime you'll have your figure back. For the moment, however, I think I could sew something a bit more comfortable than that." The widow's eyes rested on Charmaine's protruding belly and tight bodice. Every dress Charmaine owned had been altered, each pleat, each seam, let out, and soon, not a one would fit. "If you stop by my house in an hour's time, I will take some measurements and have a few dresses ready for you by next week. How would that be?"

"It would be wonderful," Charmaine replied gratefully.

The bell sounded above the mercantile doorway and Wade Remmen stepped in with a beautiful young woman at his side—the girl George had been dancing with the night of the ball. "Good afternoon, Yvette," he greeted. "I left this week's invoices at the warehouse a few minutes ago."

She nodded, but like her sister, her eyes rested on the woman.

"This is my sister, Rebecca," he offered, seeing their interest. "Rebecca, this is Yvette and Jeannette Duvoisin, and this is Charmaine Duvoisin, John's wife."

Charmaine extended her hand, but received only a hostile glare.

Later, outside the general store, Wade berated his sister. "What was that all about?"

"What?"

"You know what, Rebecca! Charmaine was being friendly, and you were downright rude to her."

Rebecca raised her nose. "I don't like her, that's all."

Friday, September 21, 1838

Paul was determined to accomplish some work. Riding out at dawn, he headed to Charmantes' tobacco fields.

He'd spent a week on Espoir. One man in particular had proven an asset. With Peter Wuerst in charge, Paul was confident he could reside on Charmantes and venture to Espoir once a week. Her sugar crop was hardy, and his laborers had been through the production routine a number of times.

Tobacco, on the other hand, was a time-consuming and tricky business: transplanting early in the season, pests and mold to manage, and painstaking fire curing over a three-to-twelve-week period. The curing barns had been constructed. But now, with another harvest upon them, each field required a half-dozen pickings, starting from the bottom of the stalk up. After curing, the tobacco needed to age for a year before being sent to market. The leaves were bundled into "hands" and warehoused in town near the wharf, where they were regularly inspected for insect infestation. Charmantes' tobacco hadn't turned a profit yet, making Paul wonder why he'd ever gotten involved with it. At the time, he'd reasoned if John had been successful, it had to be easy. *Easy?*

He arrived at the southern fields not a half-hour later and cursed as he looked out over the sloping terrain. The paid help and indentured servants were milling around. Paul urged his horse forward. "What's going on here?" he demanded.

"We're waitin' for Mr. Richards," one man answered. "He said he'd come out first thing this mornin' to show us what needed doin'."

"What about Mr. Browning?"

"He took some men with him into town. They're stackin' the kegs from yesterday's cane pressin' in the warehouse."

"So because he's not here, and Mr. Richards hasn't arrived yet, the lot of you don't know what to do?" Paul growled, jumping down from the saddle.

He strode through the nearest row of tobacco plants, plucking off several dark green leaves, bending each one over, noting they were brittle. Returning to Alabaster, he pulled up and into the saddle and shouted out to all the men. "I want the remaining leaves of this entire tract gathered and bundled. Tomorrow, I want them hung in the curing barns."

The workers began to grumble, "We went through this field a day ago."

Though irritated, Paul knew losing his temper wouldn't get the work done, especially if George remained absent. "I know John has shown you what to do. These leaves are ready. If they are reaped by sunset, I will grant a day off for every man here—after the harvest. For those of you who've paid your time, an extra day's wages!"

A whoop of approval went up, and the men threw themselves into the toil.

Paul turned Alabaster around, intent upon locating George. He checked the mill next and found the same situation there. Unsupervised, the men were taking advantage. "Have any of you seen George Richards?" he queried in rising agitation.

"No, sir, he don't usually drop round 'til noon."

"Where the hell is Wade Remmen?"

"He's normally here by now, sir, but he was feelin' poorly yesterday."

Paul swore under his breath. "Very well, Tom, how would you like to be in charge for the day?" When the man frowned, he added, "Double wages if you mill as much lumber as Wade usually does."

"Yes, sir!"

Paul spoke to the other men who had gathered around. "Tom's in charge. Follow his orders, get the work done, and there will be a bonus at sunset."

Before Paul had mounted up, Tom was barking orders.

What to do? He had been lax lately, and the word had gotten out: Frederic and John were gone, and he was rarely around. Had everyone gone on holiday because he wasn't breaking his back? He had no idea where to look for George, but Wade Remmen was going to find out he couldn't take a day off on a whim. The man was paid well to be reliable.

Twenty minutes later, he was riding along the waterfront road on the outskirts of town, where the cottages were humble. Near the end, he reined in Alabaster, dismounted, and tied the horse to the whitewashed fence that enclosed the bungalow's small front yard. Of all the abodes along the lane, this one was the most charming, with flower boxes under the windows and a fresh coat of paint on the front door. Paul smiled despite his foul mood.

He knocked and waited. The door opened. There stood the young woman who had approached him in Fatima's kitchen on the night of the ball. *Of course! She is Wade's sister.* Even in her plain dress, she was stunning. "Is your brother here?" Paul inquired curtly, attempting to camouflage his surprise.

"Yes," she said softly.

"May I speak to him?"

"He's not well."

"I would still like to speak with him," Paul persisted. *It would be nice if she invited me in.*

"He's sick with fever," she argued. "I don't want him disturbed."

Paul snorted in derision. Obviously, she was lying. Her manner alone branded her guilty, for she refused to budge.

"May I come in?" he bit out, quickly losing patience.

When she protested again, he placed palm to door and pushed it aside. As he strode into the plain but tidy room—a kitchen and parlor of sorts—the young girl tracked him, spitting fire over his audacity.

"How dare you? This is our home and if you think you can barge in here because you're the high and mighty Paul Duvoisin, you've got—"

Paul headed toward one of the bedroom doors.

Just as swiftly, Rebecca scooted past him and flattened herself against it. "I told you—Wade is ill! You can't disturb him!"

"Miss Remmen—step aside, or I will move you."

"You just try it!" she sneered through bared teeth and narrowed eyes.

She was a little vixen, but he wasn't about to be deterred, or worse, ordered around by a sassy snip of a girl, lovely or not. In one fluid motion, he swept her up in his arms and deposited her unceremoniously in the nearest chair.

Astounded, she scrambled to her feet, but he'd already entered the bedroom.

The curtains were drawn and someone was abed. Wade's breathing bordered on a snore. As Paul's eyes grew accustomed to the dim light, he could see beads of perspiration on the young man's brow. He placed a palm to his forehead. Wade's eyes fluttered open, and he murmured something in delirium. "He's burning up," Paul stated irately. "Why didn't you summon the doctor?"

"Doctors cost money," she defiantly whispered. "Now, please, he's resting. You will awaken him, and then I'll have him arguing with me as well."

"Arguing with you?" Paul declared incredulously. "He's delirious! I pay your brother decent wages. He can afford a doctor when he's this ill."

"Wade insists on saving his money."

Paul glowered at her, and she added, "So we don't ever go hungry again."

The last remark brought her shame, and she turned away, glad when another knock fell on the outer door.

Paul followed her out of the bedroom, somewhat contrite. He, too, was grateful for the distraction. George was standing on the threshold.

"Where have you been?" Paul demanded.

"Looking for you," George replied. "When Wade sent word he wouldn't be going to the mill, I figured one of us would have to oversee his work. You left the house before me. I missed you at the tobacco fields, then I went to the mill—"

"All right, George, I understand," Paul ceded. He rubbed the back of his neck, the day's work less pressing than Wade.

George volunteered to fetch Dr. Hastings, and before Paul knew it, he was once again alone with Rebecca. Her face remained stern.

"You were far more fetching at the ball," he commented with a lazy smile. "Remember—in the kitchen—when you were in love with me?"

"Mr. Duvoisin," she responded flatly, feigning disinterest in his flirtatious compliment, "I told you my brother won't waste his money on a doctor. Thanks to you, he has a fever. With a bit of rest, he will heal all on his own."

"Thanks to me?"

"Yes. You see, Wade kept on working in the pouring rain last week—to make things easier for you. He caught a chill, and now he's paying for it."

Paul ignored her statement. "Why didn't you tell me you had sent word?"

"I thought that was the reason you were here." When he seemed confused, she continued, "I thought you were going to force him to work, anyway." She bowed her head. "I love my brother. He's all I have."

"And that is why George is fetching Dr. Hastings," Paul interjected. "You needn't worry about his fee. I'll take care of it."

"Wade wouldn't like that," she argued, her head jerking up, eyes flashing again. "It would be like taking charity."

"Miss Remmen," Paul countered, "if your brother remains ill for days on end, I will lose a great deal more money than the cost of a doctor. Right now, I'm shorthanded. I need Wade up and about. He's invaluable."

She looked at him quizzically, and it occurred to him she didn't understand. "I can't do without him," he explained, distracted by the sparkling green eyes that changed on a dime, speaking volumes.

Apparently, his reasoning met with her approval, for she was smiling now, the orbs even more captivating with this new expression. She was lovely.

"Would you like a cup of coffee or perhaps tea?" she offered, grabbing the kettle and swinging it over the embers in the hearth.

"That would be nice. I'd like to hear what the doctor has to say."

Rebecca grew dismayed. "You don't think it *is* serious, do you?"

"No, you are probably right. Wade will mend all on his own."

She sighed, her smile returning. Then, as if suddenly shy, she began to stoke the fire. Paul sat back and watched her.

Dr. Hastings's diagnosis was similar to Rebecca's: overwork and a chilling rain had brought on the fever, bed-rest and nourishment, the cure. Paul told her to keep Wade home until Monday and he wanted to know if there wasn't an improvement. Then he and George were saying their farewells.

As they turned their horses onto the main road, George spoke. "Rebecca is smitten with you."

Paul snorted.

"It's true! You should have seen her at the ball. I danced with her once, but she couldn't keep her eyes off you the entire evening. If you hadn't been so damn busy, I would have introduced you."

Again Paul snorted. He didn't tell George Rebecca had introduced herself.

George pressed on. "Whenever I go to the cottage, she always brings the conversation around to you."

Paul's brow arched, and though he tried not to, he smiled. "She wasn't too happy with me this morning."

"She can be a regular spitfire," George confirmed. "She bullies Wade like no man's business. But she is quite lovely."

"And young—she can't be more than sixteen."

"Just seventeen, I believe." He paused for a moment. "You know, Paul, a bit of a diversion is what you need—take your mind off things."

Paul scoffed at the idea. "The last time I had a 'bit of a diversion' I lost the one thing that meant the most to me."

"Maybe Charmaine wasn't yours to find," George replied evenly. He let the remark sink in before saying, "John will be home before long. And when that happens, you'll be nursing a broken heart—again."

Paul looked away. "Is it that obvious?"

"Yes, it is."

Paul shook his head. "When did things become so complicated, George? I remember when we were young. Everything was so very simple. We enjoyed life, and the women were free for the picking."

"I guess we grew up," George supplied.

"I guess we have."

Another knock resounded on the Remmen door. Rebecca collected herself and walked slowly to the door. Perhaps it was Paul again. She lamented his departure, treasuring the private moments she'd had with him. But when she opened it, she frowned in disappointment. Felicia Flemmings stood in the doorway. "What was Paul Duvoisin doing here?"

"My brother is not well," Rebecca answered. "Paul was checking on him."

"Paul is it?" Felicia asked as she pushed into the cottage.

Rebecca eyed her speculatively. She didn't think she liked the older girl, though Felicia had tried to ingratiate herself with Rebecca from the moment she'd moved back into her parents' home next door. Rebecca suspected it was because Wade was so good-looking. But she had allowed Felicia her visits over the past few days because the older girl was willing to divulge a plethora of information concerning the goings-on in the Duvoisin mansion, details about Paul the most interesting of all. Felicia had told her she'd quit her domestic job at the manor because she couldn't tolerate John's new wife, Charmaine, an opportunistic trollop, who was intent on ensnaring Paul in her husband's absence. "I couldn't watch it any longer," she had complained. "Poor John!"

Poor Paul, Rebecca had thought.

Presently, Felicia was assessing her, chuckling perspicaciously. "You have your sights set for Paul, don't you?"

"I'm going to marry him."

Felicia guffawed until she realized Rebecca was serious, the girl's tight expression giving her pause. When Wade didn't appear, she wished her luck with another flippant chuckle and promptly left.

Rebecca tucked the woman's ridicule in the back of her mind and indulged in memories of Paul: his rough hands on her, strong arms lifting her up, carrying her . . . She was alone; her brother slept soundly. Intoxicated, she entered her bedroom and, with heart accelerating, closed the door.

Friday, September 28, 1838

Yvette and Jeannette's tenth birthday dawned bright and warm. But the brilliant day did not lift Charmaine's spirits. She left her bedchamber with a heavy heart, dwelling on cherished memories of last year. She wondered where John was and what he was doing. Did he remember what day it was? Was he thinking about their wonderful picnic one short year ago?

The girls were sad, too, making no inquiries about gifts when they reached the dining room.

Mercedes and George were there. "Why the glum faces?" George asked. "I thought everyone was happy on their birthday."

"We don't feel like celebrating," Yvette grumbled. "Not without Johnny."

"Is that so?" he queried. "Mercedes and I thought the two of you would like to try out the new saddles and tack Paul purchased for your ponies." He was smiling now, noting their faltering sadness. "That's right. Mercedes placed the order. And I've taken the day off so we can go riding."

Sparks of happiness lit the girls' eyes. Soon they were departing. Charmaine couldn't join them in her condition. Instead, she sat with Rose on the portico and thought about John. Tomorrow, he'd be spending his birthday with his father . . .

Monday, October 1, 1838

The days melted into weeks. Frederic and Michael spent them visiting the city post office and the shipping offices, combing address listings and immigrant registers for Blackfords. Though common sense suggested the man *had* changed his name, they couldn't be certain, and with nothing to go on, they were compelled to track down every Blackford, Black, Ford, and eventually Smith, Jones, and Brown they came across. Frederic exerted his influence on the owners of other shipping lines to gain access to passenger manifests. Not one listed a Blackford leaving New York recently, but they found a number of Blacks and Fords in the post office registry. Though it did not provide a street address, the public roll did help narrow down the neighborhoods where these men lived. Frederic and Michael passed hours scouring the streets and visiting places of business in the hopes of turning up the fugitive doctor. Even with the most remote of leads, they often waited an entire day for the resident to return, only to head home disappointed.

John wore street clothes like the immigrant factory workers, making the trip every day to the shipping wharfs downtown, the mercantile exchanges on South Street, or the textile factories on the lower East Side, talking to dockworkers, visiting taverns, and casing houses of ill-repute. He asked passersby if they'd seen anyone meeting Blackford's description, or if they knew anyone who went by that name. He'd inquire of local doctors and mention the names Black and Ford, Smith and Brown. He'd walk the residential avenues of redbrick row houses and meander through the slums south of Wall Street, hoping to get lucky and spot his uncle.

He liked this face of the city: the immigrants pouring off the merchant ships, longshoremen heading home for dinner after twelve hours of grueling labor. He watched children playing in the streets and mothers doing laundry in wooden tubs and hanging the clothes out to dry. New York was where they all wanted to be, and he enjoyed being in their midst, even though his own privileged life was so different from theirs. As hard as the labor was, they all tarried with such purpose, leaving hopeless existences in Europe for the chance at something better. John was sure the city would one day be the jewel in the crown of the nation, for the Erie Canal had made the city the gateway to the West, a merchant's magnet.

Tonight, he sat at the desk writing a letter to Charmaine. In his rush to press on to New York, he hadn't given her the address where he could be reached. George knew it, but John wanted to send it along, just to be sure. How ironic that tonight his father was in this house with him. He'd scrupulously kept the residence a secret in the hopes that one day he, Colette, and the children could start a new life here. If they fled to New York, nobody, especially Frederic, would ever find them. Last year, it had taken George weeks to track him down, resorting to staking out the Duvoisin shipping offices until, one day, John stopped by.

A month had already passed since he'd last written to Charmaine. Tomorrow, he'd put this letter in the mail to Richmond, and

Stuart would place it on the next Duvoisin vessel bound for Charmantes. He had held off writing, hoping he'd have encouraging news. But at least he could write they were ruling out each Blackford one by one. He was anxious for news from Charmantes.

The parlor was chilly. He left the desk to stoke the fire with fresh logs, pushing them back with the iron poker. The logs hissed, throwing out angry embers that lit the hearth like tiny fireworks. Frederic and Michael reclined in the armchairs on either side of it.

Frederic considered John in the tranquil room. He had been pensive, distant all day. A year ago this week, Pierre had died. Obviously, the bleak anniversary was on his son's mind.

He looked above the mantel. John had tacked a small drawing there. *I gave Mama and Pierre the hug and kiss you sent* Jeannette had written below a picture of five figures standing on a beach. Frederic remembered Yvette's sketch in John's Richmond town house, and he bowed his head regretfully.

"All these empty houses, John . . . in Richmond—here. All these empty, lonely houses."

Michael looked up from his bible, as did John from the fireplace. "I'm in Richmond and New York frequently, Father. Houses are more comfortable than hotels," he replied placidly, wondering over Frederic's thoughts.

"You wanted to bring them here—always hoped that someday you'd bring them here, didn't you?" Frederic mused more than asked.

Michael stood up to leave.

"You can stay, Michael," John said, his eyes fixed on his father, astonished by his parent's acuity. He looked away and stared into the hearth, propping an arm against the mantel. Perhaps for the first time, he really understood Frederic, the deep regrets the man harbored. If his father could turn back time to that fateful day five years ago—the day of their vicious row and Frederic's debilitating seizure—he would let Colette go, just so she could be alive today. Suddenly, everything was very clear. Frederic hadn't coveted Colette to smite him, or to exact revenge. His father had done so because he loved her and couldn't bear to let her go. Now remorse plagued him, and he desperately needed to be forgiven. But there was no one to offer comfort, no one to comprehend his pain. The room had fallen silent, and the minutes gathered.

"When I came back here after Pierre died," John murmured, "I asked myself a million times: Why didn't I protect him? How could I have left him alone that morning? I should have realized he'd wake up, find me gone, and go looking for me. He'd told me at dinner what he was going to do. I should have seen it coming."

John sighed against the crushing pain in his chest. "I wasn't in the room the night he died, either. Charmaine found me and told me. She was as devastated as I was. She could have blamed me, but she didn't. Instead, she was compassionate. I held on to her words for months afterward, remembered them when I didn't want to go on anymore . . ."

John stopped to collect his rampant emotions. "No, Pierre didn't go looking for me," he rasped, "but if I'd taken him seriously, I would never have left that room, and Blackford wouldn't have been able to snatch him away. Sometimes it can be right under your nose—so damn obvious—and still, you don't see it." John looked back at Frederic, struggling for words. "Colette's death wasn't your fault, Father. I was furious when I found out what happened, but I shouldn't have blamed you. Agatha and Blackford are to blame—not you."

John went back to the desk, sat down, and picked up the pen.

Michael was astounded. He looked at Frederic. The man's face was awash with relief and hopefulness, and Michael's heart swelled with pride for Charmaine. Her influence was at work here with these wounded, but healing souls. His own soul rejoiced with a gladness he hadn't experienced in three long years. Marie was gone, but her kindness and empathy lived on. *This* was why he'd become a priest, remained a priest even through his apathy and self-doubt. Michael closed his eyes and offered a prayer of thanks.

Tuesday, October 2, 1838

When Jeannette heard a carriage approaching, she scampered to the balcony, and her sister quickly followed. Charmaine's heart caught in her throat and the baby gave a violent kick. She, too, rushed out the French doors. *John! He's injured and they're bringing him home in the carriage because he can't . . .* She refused to entertain the horrific conclusion.

An unfamiliar coach had passed through the front gates. She watched a moment longer, then composed herself and followed the girls downstairs. They stepped onto the front portico as the carriage door swung open and Joshua Harrington stepped down, turning to assist his wife.

"Mrs. Harrington!" Charmaine gasped, consumed with relief, disappointment, surprise, and joy. "Mr. Harrington! What are you doing here?" She rushed down the portico steps and fell into Loretta's embrace.

"My dear!" Loretta exclaimed, tears brimming in her eyes as she held Charmaine at arm's length and assessed her from head to toe. "So it *is* true?" she said, her gaze resting momentarily on Charmaine's middle.

Charmaine blushed. "Yes, it's true. Didn't you receive my letter?"

Loretta shook her head, but seeing the happiness in Charmaine's eyes, felt reassured things were not as bad as she and her husband had feared.

Yvette and Jeannette stepped forward and were reintroduced.

Charmaine clicked her tongue. "Where are my manners, having you stand out here in the blazing sun? Let's go inside where it's cool."

Joshua turned to retrieve their luggage, but Charmaine scolded him. "Leave that, Mr. Harrington. I'll have Travis get your bags." She led the company up the porch steps, instructing the butler to see to the Harrington's belongings. "Take them up to John's old room. Our company should be comfortable there."

"Very good, Miss Charmaine," the manservant nodded with a smile.

Loretta and Joshua exchanged astonished glances. Charmaine had regally assumed the title of Mrs. John Duvoisin. But was Frederic's wife, Agatha, happy with the young woman's air of authority?

They settled in the drawing room, and Charmaine rang for lemonade. She joined Loretta on the settee, her eyes sparkling, still astounded Loretta was truly there. "What has brought you to Charmantes?"

"We were concerned for you," Loretta began, glancing at the twins.

Charmaine understood and addressed the girls. "Since we have visitors, why don't we postpone your lessons for the day?"

They eagerly agreed. "May we visit the stables and curry our ponies?" Jeannette asked. With Charmaine's assent, they said goodbye and hastened happily from the room.

"They love you very much," Loretta commented when they were gone.

"And I love them," Charmaine whispered, and then, "Oh my, I still can't believe this! I'm so glad you're here! Where is Gwendolyn? Did she accompany you? Is she visiting with her mother and father?"

"No, she remained in Richmond with Cal, insisting that our housekeeper would grow lonely with no one in the house. In truth, Mr. Elliot is the reason for her disinterest in Charmantes. He has been paying her court."

Charmaine giggled, envisioning the budding romance.

"Are you well?" Loretta pressed, brushing the topic of Gwendolyn and Geoffrey Elliot aside and leaning forward to clasp Charmaine's hand.

Charmaine noted the worry in Loretta's voice and replied, "When I first found I was expecting, I was ill most mornings. But that passed, and I've been feeling much better."

Loretta and Joshua exchanged looks of relief.

"Joshua met John in Richmond," Loretta offered.

"Yes, I know. John wrote that you'd spoken at the Richmond

bank." She looked up at the older man with a smile, then back to his wife, reading her misgivings. "Mrs. Harrington, I'm fine. I don't know what you've heard, but truly, I'm fine."

"But are you happy?" Joshua asked.

Charmaine tilted her head, trying to read him. "Yes, I'm happy . . ."

"But?" Loretta probed.

"But," Charmaine breathed, "I miss my husband."

"And the only reason you're not with him in Richmond is because of your morning sickness?"

"That is not the reason," Charmaine admitted. "And John is no longer in Richmond. He's traveled to New York."

"Charmaine," Loretta began slowly, not wishing to alarm the young woman, but determined to make sense out of all she had heard. "There is idle talk in Richmond, and it concerns your hasty and most surprising marriage to Mr. Duvoisin."

Charmaine grew dismayed. "What are they saying?"

"It is not what they are saying, it is what they are insinuating. And as much as I hate to admit it, some lies often stem from truths." When Charmaine didn't respond, Loretta pressed on. "Were you forced to marry this man?"

"No!" Charmaine denied, aghast with the canards that had obviously prompted the Harringtons' trip. "John was my choice. I love him."

Loretta was happy with the vehement answer, but Joshua wasn't convinced. "Then why has he left you alone at a time like this?"

Charmaine studied the hands in her lap. "Something terrible happened here a month ago." Slowly, painfully, she told them about the murders.

"But why is your husband tracking down this doctor?" Joshua asked. "I thought he and his father didn't get along."

Charmaine grappled with an excuse, for the truth could never be revealed, and Loretta realized there was a great deal more to the story.

"There, there, Charmaine," she soothed, "we don't mean to upset you." She eyed her husband and added, "After all, it's not good for the baby. I would like to freshen up and rest a bit. The voyage was extremely unsettling. Could you show us to our room?"

"Certainly," Charmaine said, grateful Loretta understood. "How long will you be staying?"

"For as long as you would like," Loretta offered with abundant love.

"At least until the baby is born," Charmaine hoped aloud.

"I'm certain we could manage that, now couldn't we, Joshua?"

Monday, October 15, 1838

John's second letter to Charmaine was delivered to the Duvoisin warehouse in Richmond. One of the employees paid the mail dispatcher the postage fee. Seeing the post was sent CARE OF STUART SIMONS, he tossed the envelope atop a pile of mail for the man. Stuart wasn't due in Richmond for another fortnight.

Friday, October 26, 1838

The jeweler handed John the ring for his inspection. He'd fashioned it precisely to his customer's specifications. It had taken weeks to locate the diamond, a difficult task, since Mr. Duvoisin wanted a flawless stone weighing at least three carats. The jeweler watched John as he examined it. Even in this dim room, the stone flashed with fire and light. It was set on a thick, unadorned band, engraved inside with the simple sentiment, FOR MY CHARM, WITH MY LOVE, J.D.

The jeweler could see his client was satisfied, so he placed the ring back in its box. John paid for it in cash, tucked the box into the pocket of his overcoat, and stepped out of the shop into the overcast day.

Nearly two months had passed since they'd arrived in New York and their efforts had proven fruitless, all their leads dead ends. His father had begun suggesting they take their search to London or

Liverpool. After all, Blackford's roots were in England. But John was adamant they stay in New York, certain Blackford had not gone any farther than the anonymity and the work the large city had to offer, especially with the burgeoning immigrant population. He had only his intuition to support this hunch, but he could not shake the certainty of it, nor ignore the recurrent dreams of Colette and Pierre that reinforced those assumptions every night.

He walked to the post office. He'd received a letter from Charmaine earlier that week and had been relieved to hear news from home, the most important: Agatha was dead. It was one less thing to plague him, to have to face. He was happy to know the twins were well, Mercedes expecting, and Charmaine had forgiven him his hasty departure. She'd written she could feel the baby moving. He longed to put this crusade behind him so he could return home; he was missing so much. The letter he'd send off today admitted they hadn't uncovered anything new concerning his uncle's whereabouts, but reassured her it was only a matter of time until he was holding her again.

Like his last letter, he'd placed it within another envelope addressed to Stuart in Richmond with instructions for its immediate delivery to Charmantes. With Paul's packets running supplies to Charmantes at least once a month, John was certain Charmaine would receive the correspondence by early December.

That night, John showed Michael the ring. "Beautiful," the priest admired.

"I know what you're thinking," John said. "I should have given the money to the poor."

"No, John. Charmaine deserves to be happy." Michael looked at the ring again, turning it over in his hand. "This should make her very happy."

John smiled, watching as his friend read the inscription.

"My Charm?" he asked.

John's grin widened, his eyes lighting up as well. "My pet name for her," he explained. "She used to hate it when I called her that, but I'd say it again and again just to see her eyes flash."

Michael could tell John relished the memory.

"Like Marie's eyes . . ." John mused.

Michael nodded. "Yes," he breathed. "I remember that look . . ."

He handed the diamond back to John, who replaced it in its box, then locked it away in his desk. "If anything should happen, Michael, please make certain Charmaine gets it."

Michael's heart lurched with the tenebrous request.

November 1838

Charmantes didn't have a jail, so Benito Giovanni had spent the last two months incarcerated in the storeroom beneath the town's meetinghouse. The cellar had been used for petty infractions in the past, and, so, Paul had transferred the priest from the bondsmen's keep three days after his arrest to keep a better eye on him.

The edifice was built into the side of a hillock, and those attending Sunday Mass climbed eight steps up to a small wooden platform that opened into one large room. Inside, a staircase led down to a dark, cool basement, where perishable items were stored. The chamber was six feet deep with an earthen floor, its front wall constructed of rock and clay mortar, the rear wall, little more than heavy stones embedded in the hillside. Three rows of shelves lined the back of the cellar. They were stacked with preserves, wine, vegetables, and exotic fruits. The priest was pleased to discover the farthest shelf was set about two feet away from the stone and dirt wall. It was tight, but there was room to move behind it.

Giovanni had spent the first two weeks of his imprisonment cursing his rotten luck, his scheme to leave Charmantes at the end of the year, foiled. He'd prepared for the possibility of betrayal from the start, but when Blackford departed and Agatha was banished, that ceased to be a concern. Certainly, he never expected this! Before he could escape from the island, he had to escape his cell. As long as he had time, there was a chance. Within two weeks, he had formulated a plan.

Twice a week, either Paul or George would check in on him.

Sometimes the door would open, other times he'd hear their voices on the other side and knew a sentry stood guard. He wondered why John or Frederic had not come to confront him again, concluding they had left Charmantes in search of Blackford. He wondered what had happened to Agatha and puzzled as to how the truth had been unraveled and their treachery revealed.

Twice a day, he was brought food: breakfast early in the morning, and around five, supper. At that time, his chamber pot was removed and returned clean. Buck Mathers had been taken from the docks and charged with delivering these meals and any other needs. The priest knew better than to attempt an escape when Buck came through the door. Giovanni used the time to strike up several conversations with the man, however, gradually putting him at ease. Buck religiously attended the Sunday noon Mass with his wife and five children. Like everyone else on the island, he was astonished a man of the cloth could be guilty of blackmail, blackmail over two murders.

"I don't know how this happened," Benito murmured humbly one evening.

Buck looked up from the chair he had posted near the door.

"Surely Frederic realizes I'm bound by the Holy Father's precepts to hold confessions secret." Giovanni stole a glance at Buck and was pleased with the Negro's look of consternation. He softly added, "It pained me to hear Agatha Duvoisin's confession, but I was not allowed to divulge her terrible sin."

"The way I hear it," Buck bristled, "there wasn't a confession. You were blackmailin' her."

"I am sad to say she was very sly," the priest admitted, head bobbing forward. "She attempted to bestow gifts upon me, perhaps to ease her guilt. If only I had known she was tricking me into sharing the blame . . ."

He said no more for a week, allowing Buck to mull over his remarks.

One day, he managed to steal a spoon off his food tray and was pleased it went undetected. That evening he calculated where he would dig and how he would conceal the hole. Using the utensil, he pried the first stone of the rudimentary foundation free, and like unraveling a knitting stitch, the rocks next to it dislodged easily. When the hole was big enough, he lifted the rocks back into place. He wasn't quite ready to begin digging. The shelves would help to conceal the breach, but a rearrangement of goods was necessary first. He moved a sack of fruit one day, a few jars the next, a bucket or a crate after that, until slowly and imperceptibly, the excavation site was concealed. Then he began to dig, spending hours in the dim room, timing his work on the light that came through the narrow, barred window, stopping a half hour before meals were delivered. He'd fill an empty bucket to the top and sprinkle the loose dirt evenly on the ground, trampling it under foot until it compacted with the earthen floor. He prayed he'd break through to the other side before time ran out.

His contrition had garnered Buck's sympathy, and Giovanni read pity in the black man's eyes every time he delivered meals. The Negro was speaking freely to him now, and the priest learned John and Frederic had indeed left the island in pursuit of the evil Robert Blackford. Paul was in charge while they were away, and Agatha had committed suicide, or so everyone assumed.

It could take months, possibly years, to track down Blackford. Benito had plenty of time to tunnel his way out of his prison, recover his stash of jewels, and flee Charmantes on the skiff he'd hidden near his cabin. Of course, Paul might discover he was gone before he was off the island, but the man would search the ships in the harbor first. Giovanni had practiced an escape. His maps were stowed with the rowboat. The nearest uninhabited landmass was tiny Esprit, half a day's trek in the skiff. No one would think to look for him there, but with the jars of fresh water and foodstuffs he'd stored on the isle, he could survive for two weeks, if necessary. From Esprit, six hours rowing and a good wind would take him to any of three inhabited Bahamian islands. He would melt into the populace and leave for civilization when it suited him. All he needed was calm seas, grit, and some luck. Thanks to Agatha, he could kiss the priesthood goodbye.

Thursday, November 15, 1838

John was dreaming. He was at home—on Charmantes—in his room. Colette was beckoning to him from the French doors. This time he followed her: out onto the balcony, across the side lawns, behind the manor and to the edge of the woods and the small, unbeaten footpath to the lake.

He was on the shore when he noticed Colette was gone, her only trace the faint scent of lily. A dark, faceless figure loomed beyond his reach at the water's edge. Even though the sun shone high in the sky, everything was shrouded in darkness. Shards of light flashed on the rippling water.

Then he saw the boat and the boy in it, bobbing perilously on the churning lake. Predictably, it capsized, toppling its passenger out. He started forward to save Pierre, but he could not lift his feet. It was as if they had sprouted hearty roots, holding him fast. There was no time to lose, yet he watched, horrified and helpless. His eyes went desperately to the morbid specter, standing an easy distance from the tumult, but it only backed away, dissolving into the tree line.

John awoke with a start, a cry shattering his nightmare. He jumped up, rushed into the dimly lit hallway, and crossed to his father's room. As he reached for the knob, the door opened.

Frederic was standing there, bleary-eyed. "What is it?" he asked.

"I heard you cry out."

"I heard *you* cry out," Frederic rejoined, baffled.

"It wasn't me," John replied. "Maybe it was Michael." He walked down the corridor and opened the door to a third bedroom, but the priest was snoring loudly. "Perhaps that's what we heard," he quipped lightly, quietly closing the door. "The windows are rattling." He walked back to his room.

Frederic followed. "I had a dream about Pierre," he offered in a low voice. John stopped dead in his tracks. "First he was at the lake," Frederic continued, "in the boat. It was very dark. The dinghy capsized—" Frederic's voice cracked.

"And?" John pressed.

"I was powerless to get to him, just like the morning Blackford—"

"You've had this dream before?"

"No," Frederic muttered. "I was awake the morning Blackford abducted Pierre, wide-awake when Colette came to me. She led me out onto the balcony, then evaporated. I thought I was going mad, until I saw a movement in the tree line. I was gripped with dread. That's why I sent Paul to the lake."

John stared at him in mute consternation. He'd never learned why his brother had gone to the lake, assuming Charmaine had returned to the nursery, found Pierre missing, and had sent Paul in search of him. Vexed, John exhaled. He turned toward his room, but Frederic halted his step. "There's more."

John frowned, facing his father slowly.

"The dream changed. Suddenly, I was here, in New York. I saw Pierre. He was lost in a busy street, but when I tried to reach him, he was swallowed up by the crowd."

John gaped at him in utter disbelief. "What happened next?"

"There were furnaces and flames—burning coal. I thought I was going to fall into them. Maybe that's when I cried out in my sleep."

"Does burning coal mean anything to you?" John asked, gooseflesh raised on his arms and up the back of his neck.

"Why?"

"Because I've had the same dream."

Frederic's eyes widened. "I don't know," he said. But as he lay in bed, an oblique memory hit him: Elizabeth's mother's maiden name had been Coleburn.

Friday, November 16, 1838

Stuart Simons swore under his breath when he found not one, but two letters from John addressed to him at the warehouse. Sickness at Freedom and Wisteria Hill had kept him away from the Richmond harbor for over a month now, but he had left explicit instructions that any correspondence from John should be opened and forwarded to Charmantes as appropriate. He was relieved when he read John's notes to him and realized there was no news to tell. John just wanted to make certain the accompanying letters reached his wife. She wouldn't have to wait much longer. The ship dedicated to Charmantes was due in port any day now.

Stuart smiled. Although John's search had proved futile thus far, Stuart's had not. John Ryan had surfaced nearly two months ago.

Saturday, December 1, 1838

Charmaine's birthday was a short two weeks away and the twins wanted to get her a present, something special, they told Paul. He agreed to take them into town. Charmaine declined to accompany them, reluctant to appear in public in her condition. "I'll rest," she said. "I didn't sleep very well last night."

When Loretta showed concern, Charmaine reassured her, saying, "I had dream after dream. My mother was there—" she laughed hollowly "—talking about John, of all people!"

After Paul and the girls left, Charmaine remained contemplative, wondering whether her dreams meant more. She had not received word from John since his letter ten weeks ago and, as the days accumulated, she grew more and more worried, a gnawing dread plaguing her late into the night. Loretta sent Joshua off with George, and stayed with Charmaine all afternoon. It was then Loretta learned about John and most of what had happened on Charmantes.

* * *

Leaving the livery, Paul draped his arms across Jeannette's and Yvette's shoulders and they strolled down the thoroughfare, drinking in the sunshine despite the brisk breeze.

"Aren't Sundays pleasant now that we don't have to attend Mass anymore?" Yvette mused.

Paul raised a dubious brow. "Charmaine had better not hear you say that or she'll be sending for a new priest." His mild warning ended in laughter. "I have to admit, I don't miss Father Benito's sermons, either."

"But what will happen if someone wants to marry?" Jeannette asked.

"I suppose the couple will have to travel to America or Europe," Paul speculated, guiding them toward the mercantile, "or do as father's sister did and exchange vows before a ship's captain."

They met Wade and Rebecca Remmen inside the store. Paul and Wade conversed for a few minutes, but Rebecca pretended disinterest, turning her head aside. Paul noticed her coy reaction and found it appealing. He spoke to her directly. "You see, Miss Remmen, your brother is no worse for the fever he suffered a few months ago."

"It's as I told you, Mr. Duvoisin," she replied levelly, though her legs were like liquid and butterflies fluttered in her belly, "all he needed was bed rest."

"And a tender touch," Paul added with a dashing smile, his eyes holding her captive. "Now, if you'll excuse us, we have some shopping to do."

"Paul is helping us pick out a gift for Mademoiselle Charmaine," Jeannette explained. "It will be her birthday soon."

Wade nodded, not interested in the least, but Rebecca was miffed.

Less than a half hour later, Paul and his sisters left the mercantile carrying a box of sweets and a new book of poetry. He had ordered a rocking horse months ago, and although it had arrived, it would be delivered to the house later that day.

The girls teased him. "The baby won't be able to ride it until next year!"

"Nevertheless, it will be in the nursery when he's ready," Paul rejoined, "and I'm sure the two of you will be eager to teach him how to rock on it."

"You're as bad as Johnny!" Yvette chided.

"I'm taking that as a compliment."

"It was."

Paul laughed as they crossed the busy street, turning around when shouts resounded from the wharf, heralding the arrival of a ship.

As always, the pedestrians pressed toward the landing stage, and soon, the pier was a sea of people. Paul hastened to the boardwalk, guiding his sisters through the throng that obligingly parted for them. They passed unimpeded until they were standing abreast of the huge ship. Paul cautioned the girls to wait for him on the wharf. He saw no sign of John or his father, but was anxious for news. The ship had most likely come from Richmond. Before the last mooring lines were secured, he was boarding the vessel.

The captain rushed over, clearly relieved to see him.

"What is the matter, Gregory?" Paul queried anxiously. "You haven't brought us bad news from my father or John?"

"No, sir, no," he reassured. "But I do have some important documents Stuart Simons instructed me to hand over to you as soon as we made port." He produced the shipping invoices. They confirmed what Paul had already guessed: John Ryan was on board.

"Excuse me, gentlemen!" Paul shouted, waiting for the crew to quiet down. "I'm looking for a Mr. Ryan."

John Ryan was not surprised to hear his name called. According to Stuart Simons, Paul Duvoisin was looking for efficient, reliable laborers. Having learned of John Ryan's exemplary work in Richmond, Paul wanted to meet him as soon as he reached Charmantes. Ryan snickered to himself. *How dim-witted could the man be?* Snickering again, he confidently stepped forward.

"Mr. Ryan?" Paul queried through narrowed eyes. "Mr. John Ryan?"

"That's me," Ryan nodded, his chest puffed out like a bantam cock.

"You're just the man for whom I've been looking," Paul said, hiding his revulsion behind a smile. "These documents tell me you've been an invaluable help to my brother. I believe I can use you up at our meetinghouse."

"Oh, I'm valuable all right," Ryan boasted. "I just hope this job pays what I'm worth."

"It does better than that," Paul confided, placing an arm around the man's shoulder in fraudulent camaraderie. "It includes free meals, room and board."

Astounded, John Ryan happily allowed Paul to lead him down the gangplank, eager to learn about this unprecedented windfall. His ship had finally come in!

Yvette and Jeannette suspiciously eyed their brother's motley companion as the two men approached. "Girls," Paul called, "let us lunch at Dulcie's. I'll be there in ten minutes time."

"Who is he?" Yvette asked, when Paul offered no introduction.

"The name's Ryan," the man blurted out. "John Ryan."

Paul swore under his breath. Recognition had dawned on his sisters' faces.

Yvette overcame her surprise and studied her brother. A fleeting scowl had crossed Paul's face, accompanied by a barely perceptible shake of his head. Reading his signal, she grasped Jeannette's arm and began to nudge her down the pier. "Very well, Paul, we'll meet you at Dulcie's."

Paul thanked God she was maturing and turned back to John Ryan. "My sisters," he explained nonchalantly, noting the man's interest. He indicated the boardwalk. "Shall we?"

Ryan nodded, and Paul struck up some small talk as he escorted the older man to the meetinghouse. They climbed the steps, and

Paul allowed John Ryan to step in first, closing the door behind him and leaning back against it.

"Well," Ryan began when it seemed as if Paul would not speak, his eyes darting around the empty room. "What work do you want me to do here?"

"Prayer work," Paul said softly.

"Prayer work?" the elder asked, laughing outright at the inane suggestion.

"Yes, Mr. Ryan," Paul pronounced rigidly, his brow suddenly furrowed. "You'd best start praying, because I believe you're a wanted man." Seeing John Ryan's stupefaction, Paul continued, arms folded across his chest. "I have it on the most reliable authority you murdered your wife."

The older man did not like this conversation and grew belligerent. "I mighta hit her on occasion, but she had it comin'."

"Had it coming?" Paul asked incredulously, his jaw clenched.

"She was a mouthin' off hen-pecker who needed to be put in her place. And that's what I did—put her in her place."

Paul's hand shot out, grabbed a fistful of shirtfront, lifted Ryan clear off the ground, and sent him sailing. He hit the floor with a loud oomph, his legs and arms splayed in four directions. "Why'd ya do that?" he demanded from where he lay, astonished. "Why'd ya bring me here?"

"So you can pay for your crime."

John Ryan jumped to his feet, but Paul rushed him, grabbing his forearm and yanking him around. He squealed in pain as Paul guided him down the stairwell, wrenching his arm ever higher behind his back. The guard unlocked the door and swung it open, and Paul shoved him inside. Again, he stumbled to the floor.

Paul eyed Benito, who had scrambled to the center of the room. "The two of you should be great company for each other," he commented wryly, wiping his hands on his trousers. "Tell your new inmate to whom my brother is married. Mr. Ryan should be very interested to know."

When the door was bolted, Paul cautioned the burly guard to remain alert.

By the time he reached Dulcie's, his sisters were already eating. After he'd ordered his own meal, Yvette bluntly asked, "Was that Charmaine's father?"

"Unfortunately, yes," Paul admitted. "But you mustn't tell her he's here."

"Why *is* he here?" Jeannette asked, her eyes clouded with worry.

"John wants to deal with him. He's responsible for his wife's murder."

"What will Johnny do to him?" Yvette asked.

"I don't know, Yvette."

"What would you do?" Jeannette queried.

Paul raked his fingers through his hair. "I don't know that, either. I'd have to think long and hard on it. Will the two of you keep quiet about this?"

"If that is what you want Paul, that's what we'll do," Yvette promised.

"Thank you," Paul said with a warm smile. "And thank you for heeding my warning on the quay. I wanted to make certain John Ryan was locked up with our good Father Benito before he learned why he was here."

Yvette smiled wickedly. "I'll wager he had the surprise of his life."

"That he did," Paul affirmed. "That he did."

New York

After a long day walking the streets of lower Manhattan, Frederic had grown weary and Michael, hungry. They hailed a ride near the harbor and headed back to Washington Square. Frederic had had enough of New York City. After weeks of scouring her streets, their paltry leads had turned up nothing. Even their breakthrough with the name Coleburn had led nowhere. He stared out the window of the quiet cab, contemplating their futile search, frustrated, angry, and homesick. It was growing dark, and people were spilling onto the streets, stopping along the way to buy bread or a slab of meat for dinner.

He closed his eyes and dozed to the lull of the rocking carriage. It rolled over a hole as it negotiated a turn, jolting him awake. He shifted and looked out the window, the silhouette of a man about a block ahead snaring his attention. Tall, dark, and slender, he was just now reaching the street corner. His black overcoat billowed against a stiff breeze. One hand was planted on his top hat; the other toted a black bag.

Frederic's heart leapt into his throat. Their carriage was turning away! He pushed the door open with his cane, shouting up to the driver to stop. He scrambled out of the conveyance, nearly falling as the cabman yelled at him to wait. "Get back here, man! You ain't paid the fare!"

Bumping shoulders with pedestrians, Frederic ignored the indignant voice that followed him and leaned hard on his cane, dodging the hogs and goats that wandered the road, scavenging street refuse for food scraps. When he reached the next corner, heaving and breathless, the man was nowhere in sight. Had he continued straight ahead, turned left or right? Frederic wheeled in all directions, straining to see beyond the press of people, hoping to catch a glimpse of the dark figure again. It was useless; he was gone. Downhearted, Frederic turned back to the cab in mute resignation.

Even though Michael was convinced he'd imagined it, Frederic thought about the incident for days. Every evening afterward, he left Michael at the town house and headed downtown, strolling the streets in the same neighborhood. When night fell, he would step into a local tavern for dinner, sitting near a window with a tankard of ale as he watched people walk by.

Tonight, the waiter had just set a plate of hot food before him when a commotion erupted two tables away. A barmaid was screaming at two men, who had shot to their feet. "You told me you loved me, you lyin' bastard!" she spat at him, her face red, tears streaming down her cheeks. "I ain't doin' this, I seen other girls bleed to death!"

When one of them shrugged sheepishly, she hurled a crumpled piece of paper into his face and flew at him. The patrons nearby scrambled from their tables, and two waiters rushed over to break up the fracas. Frederic came to his feet as well. The barmaid was hissing and spitting fire at the longshoreman, even as the waiters pulled her away. The dockworkers threw a few coins on the table and fled the tavern. The proprietress put an arm around the sobbing girl and, with comforting words, led her into the kitchen.

Frederic sank back into his seat and lifted his fork, noticing his napkin had fallen to the floor. As he reached down for it, he saw the crumpled paper under his chair. He picked it up and smoothed it open, his heart nearly stopping when he read: COLEBURN CLINIC. 27 WATER STREET.

According to John, the address was in a seedy section a few blocks from the wharfs. He would check it out the next day. Frederic insisted on going with him, but John objected. "We'll be too conspicuous together."

Frederic capitulated reluctantly. "If it is Blackford, promise me you won't take action on your own. We must decide together how to proceed."

John nodded placidly, but Frederic was unnerved.

The next day, John went to the address. It was a row house with a continuous stream of people going in and out. He approached a woman with two young girls as they left. "Is this the doctor's office?" he asked.

The woman looked at him quizzically. At first, he didn't think she spoke English. "Yes," she finally replied in a thick Irish brogue, "it's Dr. Coleburn. Why do you ask?"

"I wasn't sure if I had the right address. Thank you."

She nodded and nudged her children along.

John waited in the street until long after dark. As dusk fell, the clientele changed. Mostly young women and tarts entered the building, hesitating before their hands alighted upon the knob, their eyes darting surreptitiously to and fro to be certain nobody saw them enter. Eventually, the last patient left, and the lights in the first floor windows went dark. A few minutes later, a tall dark figure appeared in the doorway and descended the steps, setting a brisk pace up the street. John followed, keeping a safe distance behind, walking gingerly so his footfalls would not call attention to his presence. The man turned a corner and walked a few blocks farther, turned again and ascended the steps of another row house. John marked the address.

Before dawn the next day, he was seated on the steps of the row house across from 13 Stone Street, his collar drawn high around his neck, his cap cocked low over his forehead. At exactly eight o'clock in the morning, Robert Blackford stepped out of the door and headed toward his clinic.

"We can have a ship ready. Now that we know his address, all we have to do is corner him. He'll be no match for the three of us, and we can take him to the ship straightaway."

"I agree with your father, John," Michael offered, stirring his tea. "This is the least dangerous way to handle it." Though John did not argue, his dissatisfied frown bolstered Michael's dismay. Clearly, the man was keeping his own counsel. "Once he's on Charmantes," Michael continued, "your father will have free rein to punish him however he sees fit."

With hands clasped behind his head, John leaned back in his chair and looked from his father to Michael, deliberating. Michael could read a hundred thoughts flashing in his eyes. "All right," he replied, his face suddenly stolid. "When do we start?"

"We'll make arrangements for the ship tomorrow," Frederic replied. "The next Duvoisin vessel in port will be rerouted to take us back to Charmantes."

"I plan on keeping an eye on Blackford while we wait," John interjected. "He's not going to get away again."

"Fair enough," Frederic agreed.

John pushed from the table and turned to retire. Michael stared after him, very uneasy. He couldn't shake the feeling John had plans of his own. "John, while your father arranges for the ship tomorrow, I want you to show me where Blackford lives."

John faced him. "It's too risky. He might spot us."

"We can go after he opens his clinic. It's just a precau—"

"Fine," John interrupted sharply. "I'm going to bed."

Wednesday, December 5, 1838

The evening air was raw, and it was going to rain. Lily Clayton made her way up Washington Square past the elegant row houses of Greenwich Village and turned toward Sixth Avenue. Even though it was Wednesday, her employer had allowed her to go home early, an extremely rare act of generosity, and for that, Lily was grateful. Now she had two hours to spare before her sister, Rose, who was minding her children, expected her home. That free time brought her here.

She stopped on the walk outside of John's row house and noticed the lamps were burning inside. She smiled. The lights meant John Duvoisin was back in New York. She missed him, for she hadn't seen him since February. Over the past months, she had worried about him, because he never stayed away from New York this long. Now she wondered when he'd gotten back and why she hadn't heard from him. He always came by to check on her as soon as he arrived in town.

Lily and her sister, Rose, had been house servants at the Duvoisin plantation in Virginia. They were quadroons and became the property of John Duvoisin when he purchased Wisteria Hill, the plantation adjacent to his father's, in late 1834. They were thrilled when they heard John was interested in buying the property, because they knew all the slaves at Freedom had been set free. On his first visit to Wisteria Hill, she'd been attracted to him. He was young and handsome and, unlike other plantation owners, he had spoken to her, even though she was a slave. Within months of purchasing Wisteria Hill, John freed her and Rose. She moved to the plantation house at Freedom and became the resident housekeeper there, while Rose remained at Wisteria Hill for the same purpose. Rose was a mere two miles away.

Lily was beautiful, her skin a light, creamy tan. She was tall and lithe with straight dark hair, black eyes, sensual lips, and an aristocratic nose. Lily had twin sons and a daughter by her husband, Henry, who had been sold south to a North Carolina cotton planter before John had purchased Wisteria Hill.

Henry was a mulatto, so their children were also light-skinned; the casual observer would never suspect their black ancestry. John had tried to purchase Henry to work at Freedom, but his owner, a viciously stalwart Southerner, was unwilling to sell him for any price, for Henry was big and strong and worked hard. Furthermore, his new master held great disdain for border-state plantation owners who liberated their slaves, and bristled at the thought of even one more black, especially a mulatto, being freed.

Lily knew she would never see Henry again. Over three years ago, she had received word he'd been "crippled" during an unsuccessful escape attempt. Three runaways had made it as far as Freedom, delivering into Lily's hand a short letter from Henry. According to the runaways, Henry had been brutally mutilated, the toes on his right foot hacked off so he would never run again. Lily became resigned to life without him.

When John began making frequent trips to New York, she begged him to take her, Rose, and her children there. She wanted to start over, to be independent. She wanted her children to be more than emancipated, she wanted them to be educated. In New York, they could go to school. John was reluctant to bring her north. Lily and Rose kept the plantation houses running smoothly when he wasn't there, which was more often than not. But with her incessant begging, he eventually relented, and nearly three years ago, she arrived with him in New York.

John helped both women find jobs as housekeepers for affluent

New York merchants; for the first few months, Lily worked for his aging aunt. He located a tiny house for them in lower Manhattan, gave her money for a full year's rent, and accompanied her when she enrolled her children in a New York public school. The schoolmaster assumed John was her husband and the children, white. When he asked John where he was employed, he simply said the Duvoisin shipping line, which satisfied the schoolmaster and wasn't a lie. So, even without Henry, Lily's life had never been better.

Lily loved Henry and longed to be with him again, but Lily also loved John. She loved him because he treated her with a respect other white men reserved for white society ladies. She loved him because she could tell him anything and he always listened without passing judgment. She could cry about missing Henry, and he understood, because instinctively, she knew he also had been separated from somebody he loved. She loved him because he was kind to her children and he made her laugh. She loved him because he had never forced himself on her, as every one of her other white owners had. Even so, she had shared his bed many times. John had joked if Henry ever found out, he'd overcome his infirmity and escape bondage solely to find and kill him.

Tonight, she would seek out John. He'd relieve her gnawing need, one that hadn't been satiated since February. After her children were fed and put down to sleep, she would leave them with Rose and return to John's house.

John pulled his collar up high around his neck and his cap down low on his forehead, his back to the hallway as he rapped on the landlady's door. The building had been sectioned so each floor was a two-room apartment. The ground floor corridor was shrouded in darkness, as evening was falling and rain pounded on the muddy street outside. Most of the longshoremen had already arrived home, the connecting houses resonating the sounds of clattering dishes, muffled voices, and children's play.

The landlady opened the door. She was a stout, middle aged

woman, her greasy, gray-streaked hair tied back into a ponytail that reached her hips. She looked up at him, chewing on a mouthful of her dinner.

"Whaddaya want?" she asked before swallowing, one front tooth missing.

"I am looking for Dr. Coleburn."

"Did ya knock on his door?"

"There was no answer. When does he usually arrive home?"

"Who wants tuh know?" she boldly asked, sizing him up. He'd probably knocked up his girlfriend and needed the doctor's services.

"A patient."

She eyed him skeptically.

He flashed her a one-dollar note.

"He gets back late. After nine o'clock, gen'rally. You'd best come back then." She snatched the bill from his hand.

"It's raining. I've come a long way, and I'd rather wait for him here, in his apartment."

Though suspicious, she didn't object. "What's it worth tuh ya?" she asked, fingering the keys that hung on a chain at her waist.

John extended his hand again; a crisp five-dollar note sat neatly in his palm. Her greedy eyes grew wide. "How's about two of those?" she replied.

Frederic pushed through the front door and found Michael in the parlor reading a newspaper next to the burning hearth. Dusk had fallen and all the lamps were lit. It had been a long, yet gratifying day.

Late last night, the *Heir* had reached New York. Frederic had spent the hours after dawn closeted in the captain's cabin while John showed Michael where Blackford lived and worked. In the two hours they were gone, Frederic explained to Will Jones, the *Heir*'s captain, what had happened and what he planned to do. By the time John and Michael arrived at the wharf, Will knew if, for any reason,

Frederic, John, or Michael had not contacted him in three days' time, he was to sail back to Charmantes without them. There he would tell Paul that Blackford had indeed been found under the assumed name Coleburn, and Frederic and John had attempted to apprehend him on the sixth of December. Frederic was confident nothing would go wrong, but it was best to be prepared for the worst.

The *Heir* carried a letter from Charmaine, and Frederic had watched as John eagerly ripped into it, the third he'd received. He'd been happy with all her news, especially pleased to learn the Harringtons had decided to remain on Charmantes until the baby was born. He was befuddled as he read on; Charmaine had not received any of his letters, save the first one. Frederic had assured him that mattered very little now. By tomorrow, everything would be resolved and they'd be on their way home, arriving a month before the birth of his child.

The remainder of the morning had been grueling. Frederic and John unloaded the ship's cargo onto a partially laden vessel that had berthed in New York en route to Liverpool. They had hastily commissioned the other carrier while the cargo space was still available, and threw themselves into the laborious task of shifting goods, since hired help was short that morning. In this way, the *Heir* could return directly to Charmantes, and the sugar and tobacco promised for Europe would arrive on time. Frederic had felt extremely lucky that morning. He'd been certain they'd have to wait at least a fortnight before a Duvoisin vessel reached New York.

A crew had been hired by lunchtime, and Michael realized he was of little use standing around. He was only getting in their way. So, he left them and spent the afternoon and early evening walking the streets, visiting a myriad of churches and buildings, many of them magnificent. In the weeks they had been there, he'd rarely gone exploring, and by tomorrow, they'd be traveling to Charmantes, so this was his last chance. When it began to rain, he headed home.

He'd been at the house for nearly two hours and looked up when Frederic entered, pulling off his wet overcoat, shaking it out, and hanging it in the foyer. "Where is John?" he asked when the door did not reopen.

"What do you mean?" Frederic queried. "I thought he was with you. He said he was going to meet you when he left the merchant's office a few hours ago."

Their eyes locked, and Frederic's face grew stormy. "What is Blackford's address, Michael?"

"13 Stone Street," he answered, praying John had taken him to the right building and hadn't purposefully misled him. "It's just south of Wall Street."

"Thank God."

"I should go with you."

"No. Wait for me here—in case we're wrong."

Michael looked at him skeptically. "I should check the clinic. Something may have happened there. We will meet back here."

Frederic agreed, then rushed upstairs, taking the stairs as swiftly as his lame leg would allow. Riffling through his trunk, he found the revolver and bullets he'd purchased their first week in New York. He hastened back down to the foyer, where he pulled on his coat, loaded the firearm, and shoved it deep into a pocket. Grabbing his cane, he threw one last look at Michael, who was also ready to leave. Together, they set off, hailing two cabs.

Robert Blackford climbed three flights of stairs to his cramped rooms. The cry of a baby and the couple fighting on the floor below echoed upward, the odor of food fried in rancid suet melded with the must of the damp hallway. Although the row house afforded him anonymity, he eschewed such squalor whenever possible. Practically every evening, he visited the affluent neighborhoods north of this hovel, where he could enjoy the finer things in life the city had to offer. Tonight, he was returning from dinner at the Astor House Hotel. Tomorrow, he would go to a playhouse. He liked it here in New York. Indeed, life was better than he imagined it could be, even without his beloved Agatha.

He walked to his door, put the key in the lock, and turned it. He tried to push the door open and realized he had locked rather than unlocked it. Funny, he always locked up when he left.

He stepped into the dark flat and groped his way to the lamp on the table. Finding the tinderbox, he struck the flint and lit the wick, the flame flaring up in the lamp and illuminating the cold room. He rubbed his hands briskly together to warm them against the chill and decided to leave his cloak on. After thirty years in the Caribbean, he would never grow accustom to the penetrating cold.

It wasn't until he turned to light a fire in the stove that he saw the shadow of a man sitting in the chair next to it. Recognition spurred him into motion, and he swung around swiftly, flying to the door.

John was out of the chair in an instant, reaching out and clutching his billowing cloak. Robert managed to pull the door open before he was forcefully jerked backward. John immediately threw an arm around his neck and grabbed his wrist, yanking it high behind his back. Robert howled in pain.

"It's reckoning time, Blackford," John growled against his ear, pushing him toward a large wooden dish tub set on the floor next to the stove.

As they got closer, Robert could see it was still filled with the morning's dishwater. John wrenched his arm even higher, then violently kicked the back of his legs so they buckled under him, and he fell to his knees before the tub.

John followed him down. "Tell me why you did it, Blackford."

"I don't know what you're talking about, John," he croaked, as he felt his nephew's hand move to the back of his head. "There must be some kind of mistake. What is this about? Can't we talk about it?"

"Tell me why you did it, and I'll let you live."

"I don't know what you're talking about!"

"Then why are you hiding here under an alias?"

"Please, John . . ."

John ignored his pitiful appeal and began pushing his head slowly, purposefully down toward the water. "How do you think it felt, Blackford?" John cried. "How can you live with yourself knowing what you did to Pierre?"

Robert resisted, struggling to turn his head aside as his face met the cold water. Then he was totally submerged, held fast, immobile. He concentrated on mustering all his strength to throw his body backward, but that effort proved futile. John finally released his head, and he came up sputtering and gasping for air.

John took tighter hold of him, pressing a knee deep into his back. "Are you ready to tell me why you did it now?"

"It wasn't my idea—it was my sister's! Paul is her son, *he* should have been the heir."

"That's not good enough, Blackford!"

John propelled his head toward the water again. "Do you think this is how it felt, you evil fiend?" he sobbed. "Did you take great pleasure in drowning an innocent child? I want *you* to know how it felt, you Satan!"

He plunged Blackford's head deep into the tub again, pressing down upon him for endless seconds. Great air bubbles churned violently to the surface, and water sloshed over the sides of the tub. Blackford's legs thrashed and kicked across the slippery floor, catching the chair and toppling it over. His free arm flailed in every direction, blindly grappling for anything within reach. John released his head, and Robert emerged, heaving and gulping in air.

"Are you ready to tell me now?" John sneered, his fingers entwined in the man's hair. "It wasn't just for the money. So tell me—why did you do it?"

"I loved my sister. Your father ruined her life," Robert wheezed, gasping to catch his breath, the water dripping off his face and hair.

"Not good enough, Blackford!"

Robert's head dipped toward the water a third time, the room deathly silent, save his desperate struggle to wrench free of the strong hands guiding him forward. "All right, John, all right!" he begged. Then came the murmured admission. "I was *in love* with my sister . . . I would have done anything for her."

John felt the blood drain from his limbs and, with a tormented curse, relaxed his grip. Robert instantly threw himself backward, and John staggered, slipping on the wet floor. Robert rolled over to face his attacker. But John was up and on him again, straddling and pinning him down, hands around his neck. Robert's head was cocked at an awkward angle, shoved against the side of the tub. He sputtered for air, and his fingers furiously clawed at John's hands. But the vise continued to constrict. John was going to strangle him.

He had one last hope. Straining to the right, he groped inside his boot for the knife he carried for protection against the street thugs who loitered around his clinic. The tips of his fingers brushed against the smooth handle. Stretching farther, he loosed the dagger from its sheath, pulling it free. He drew it back and plunged it viciously into John's flank.

John cried out and, clutching his side, collapsed next to him.

Choking, Robert's hands shot to his throat, the knife clattering to the floor. He threw his head back and closed his eyes, inhaling rapidly, his pulse thundering in his ears. When he could breathe again, he fumbled for the knife at his side. He knew he had to finish John off—slit his throat quickly and flee.

As he opened his eyes, a tall shadow loomed above him, and he found himself looking up the barrel of Frederic Duvoisin's revolver.

Frederic looked away and pulled the trigger. There was a flash and a loud report. He glanced down at the grisly sight, threw his cane aside, and dropped to his knees beside John.

"John! Get up!" he urged, nudging John fiercely. "We have to get out of here—now!"

"Father . . ." John groaned, pushing himself onto his knees.

Already the room reeked of fresh blood. Frederic hurriedly looped his arm around John's waist and shouldered a portion of his weight. Then he struggled to his feet, dragging John with him.

Somebody screamed, and Frederic looked up, the pistol concealed in the folds of his coat. A young woman stood in the doorway, gaping at them. "Murderers!" she shrieked, raising the alarm. "Murderers! Police!"

He advanced, his arm tight around his son. The girl blocked their path. "Move aside," he demanded. When she didn't, he pointed the firearm at her. She stepped back quickly, but screamed again after they passed. More voices sounded from the dark hallway below.

Frederic forced himself calm. "John, you have to walk down the stairs. You must help me." Trembling, Frederic released him, his hand covered in thick, syrupy blood.

John grabbed hold of the railing and started down, enduring the searing pain that radiated into his chest and down his leg.

Frederic followed, gun drawn.

John managed the first two flights, fighting to breathe, each aspiration shallow and excruciating. Three steps farther, and his knees buckled beneath him. He tumbled down the last flight, landing in a crumpled heap at the foot of the stairwell.

Frederic raced after him. The landlady's door cracked open as he reached the bottom, and she peered out. Frederic dropped to one knee, but swiftly straightened as two men confronted him. He flashed the pistol again, and the two backed off. "Get up, John!" he shouted, holding the firearm level against them. "You must get up!"

His father's command echoed as if at the end of a tunnel. Though everything was fading, John grabbed the railing and pulled himself to his feet.

Frederic put an arm around him again, and John leaned heavily into his body, forcing Frederic to carry most of his weight. Staggering across the foyer, they pushed through the doors and out into the rainy night.

Thankfully, the hired carriage was still there. Frederic had promised the driver a double fare for the return trip if he waited. He shoved John in and climbed onto the seat across from him, directing the cabby to make haste uptown. The old man set the horses into a brisk trot, and at last, they were rolling away. As they turned the corner a few blocks up, they passed two mounted policemen heading toward the row house.

John moaned and his head fell back against the seat cushions. Frederic crossed to his side and pulled him into his arms. John jerked forward, then slumped across his lap, shivering uncontrollably, his clothing soaked through.

"Hold on, John," Frederic pleaded in a whisper, enfolding him in his cloak, his anxiety rising in proportion to his hammering heart.

"How could he, Papa?" John beseeched, his voice a strained sob, his face contorted in pain. "How could he murder my little boy?"

"I don't know, John," Frederic murmured, pulling John closer, gathering the dry cloak tighter around him. "I don't know."

"Is he dead?"

"Yes, he's dead."

John looked up at his father. He hadn't heard the answer, for the world was slipping away. "Is he dead?"

"Yes, John, he's dead."

John closed his eyes. "Charmaine . . ."

"Hold on, John. Just hold on. You're going to be all right. We'll get you a doctor." Frederic looked at the blood on his hands again, his own coat stained red, and was petrified his son was going to die in his arms.

The carriage rolled up to John's row house, the driver glancing furtively back into the enclosure of his cab.

Michael heard them and ran outside. He'd been back all of ten minutes, having found the clinic closed. Frederic had already alighted, his expression imploring Michael to keep silent.

Frederic addressed the coachman, pulling the double fare from his wallet. "You'll get twice this tomorrow night if you keep your mouth shut," he enjoined, pressing the coins into the man's hand.

The cabman nodded, and waited as Frederic and Michael pulled an unconscious John from the vehicle. They struggled a moment, throwing his arms over their shoulders, then dragged him inside and up the stairs to his bedchamber.

"What happened?" Michael asked, alarmed by John's blood-splattered coat, horrified when Frederic removed it to reveal his blood-soaked shirt beneath.

"They were in a scuffle," Frederic replied brusquely, ripping open the shirt and pressing a handkerchief to the wound. "Blackford knifed him."

"Is he alive?" Michael asked fearfully, placing a hand on John's chest in search of a heartbeat.

"Yes, but there is no time to lose. He needs a doctor before he bleeds to death. I'll find one as fast as I can. Lock the door behind me and douse the lights."

"Why?"

"Blackford's dead. There were witnesses. The police will be looking for us."

Michael regarded Frederic in dismay. "Did John—?"

"No. I did."

A knock on the front door silenced them.

"Damn!" Frederic cursed, moving to the window. To his relief, a woman was on the stoop. "Probably a meddling neighbor. Can you get rid of her, Michael?"

Michael hurried to the first floor. *Sweet Jesus, how did I wind up here, aiding and abetting a murderer? What lies will I have to conjure now?* Closing his eyes, he drew a deep breath and intoned a Hail Mary. He opened the door, stunned to see a woman he recognized. They had met in Richmond nearly three years ago when John was bringing her to New York. *"Lily?"*

"Father Andrews? What are you doing here?" Lily queried.

"Come in, come in," he insisted, gesturing emphatically for her to step inside quickly and out of the rain.

"Where is John?" she asked, looking across to the parlor, disconcerted by the priest's white face and disquietude.

"He's been hurt."

"Hurt?" Her eyes shot back to Michael. "How? Where is he?"

"Upstairs."

Lily flew up the stairs and charged into John's bedroom, running headlong into Frederic. He grabbed her arms, keeping her from the bed. "Who are you?" he demanded as she struggled to pull free, her eyes riveted on John.

Michael stepped through the door.

"My God!" she cried.

"Who are you?" Frederic demanded again.

"I'm his friend!" she replied, trying to wrench free, looking for the first time at Frederic. "John brought me here from Virginia. Who are you?"

"John's father."

Frederic read her astonishment. He released her, and she ran to John, clutching his cold hand. "John! John! Can you hear me?" She brought his hand to her lips and kissed it. "Sweet Lord!" she cried, caressing his face and stroking back his hair. "There's so much blood! Wake up, John! Please wake up!"

She looked over her shoulder at Frederic and Michael. "He's soaking wet. We have to get him out of these clothes and warm him up! And the blood—this cloth isn't working. We have to stem the blood!" She started to pull the shirt from John's arms. "Get some clean towels!"

"I will do this, Miss," Frederic declared, uneasy with her familiarity. John and she were obviously more than friends. "Do you know a doctor who can help us? We need one right away. Neither of us know the city well enough—"

"Yes, I do."

"Can you get him to come here tonight?"

"I think so."

"Then please take Michael, go find him, and bring him back

here," Frederic implored. He handed Michael his wallet. "Spend whatever it takes, Michael, but bring him back as quickly as possible."

Frederic followed them downstairs. Without another word, Lily and Michael slipped out into the dark city.

After they left, Frederic locked the door and doused the lamps in the parlor. He returned to John's bedchamber, pulling the curtains shut, leaving only a single candle burning on the floor as he tended to his son.

Within the hour, the clopping of horses' hooves resounded from the street and men's voices carried up to the quiet bedroom. There was a rap on the door. Frederic snuffed the candle. The rap came again, louder this time, and he peered through a crack in the curtains down to the street. Two men in uniform, carrying nightsticks, stood at the door. The cabdriver must have ratted on them. Frederic prayed they would not try to enter. The police rapped again and waited, and he worried Lily and Michael would return while they were there. A carriage rattled up the street, slowing as it passed the row house, but then it lurched forward, turning a corner a few blocks up. The officers paced around the yard a few times, glancing up the façade of the building. Shrugging, they mounted their horses, and trotted away. Not long afterward, the same cab of only minutes before pulled up to the house, and Lily, Michael, and another man alighted.

Lily returned to John's side as Dr. Hastings came away from the bed and washed his hands for the last time in a bowl of water on the dresser. Grabbing a towel and his medical bag, he motioned for Frederic to step out of the room.

They descended to the first floor, where Michael stood sentry in the darkened foyer, waiting for the police to return.

"It's just as well he's unconscious," the doctor stated, their only light the small candle Frederic carried. "Stitching a deep wound can be very painful."

"Will he be all right?" Frederic asked.

"He has lost a lot of blood, but the bleeding has stopped, and I don't think any important organs were damaged, else he'd be dead already."

Frederic sighed in thanksgiving.

The doctor noted his relief and was compelled to speak again. "I am concerned about his left lung. It may have been punctured. And there's the greater danger of infection. I saw this in the wounded in 1812. The infection will eat beyond the wound. It can kill him. He's likely to become very ill in the next few days."

Frederic's alarm was rekindled. "Then what are we to do?"

"Keep the fever down. Keep a tub of water and some ice on hand. If he gets very hot, submerge him in an ice bath. It's my own remedy. I've found it works. Other than that, there's nothing to do but wait. It all depends on how strong he is. It doesn't help that he's lost so much blood."

Frederic closed his eyes in dread. He'd hoped to leave on the *Heir* first thing in the morning, but now that was too dangerous. "What will it take to keep this between us, Doctor?" he pursued in another vein.

"Nothing," Dr. Hastings replied. "Your son is a good man, Mr. Duvoisin. He helped my nephew set up a practice—on your island. I hope he recovers." He removed his cloak from the coat rack and pulled it on. "Send for me if you need anything else."

Frederic returned to the bedroom once the physician had left. "We have to move him," he declared. "The police will be back."

"You can stay at my house," Lily offered. "It's small, but we'll make room."

Frederic nodded, and once again, Lily and Michael went out into the gloomy night, this time in search of Lily's friend, who owned a livery service. She would borrow a carriage to transport John downtown.

By dawn, they had settled John into her humble, two-bedroom home. Lily's children and Rose were moved to the tiny parlor, leaving the second bedroom to Frederic and Michael.

Michael caught a few hours' sleep before setting out in search of ice. He got lucky when he went to a neighborhood tavern. The proprietor gave him the name of an ice supplier, and by the afternoon, a buckboard had pulled up in front of the house. Curious neighbors paused to watch as the massive block was unloaded. It had been cut out of a lake well north of the city in Rockland County and floated down the Hudson River. Now it sat on a wooden pallet in the backyard of the small house, covered in burlap. The December weather had turned mercifully cold, snow blowing in, and the ice would stay frozen.

Friday, December 7, 1838

Frederic came away from John's bedside early, nodding to Michael who now took up the vigil. As he stepped into the front parlor, he found Lily hastily tying her daughter's shoelaces, her twin brothers impatiently waiting.

"I can do it, Ma!" she complained. "We're gonna be late!"

Lily stood, gave both sons' coats a final tug, nodded her approval, and shooed all three out the door with the words, "No stopping along the way and come directly home after school!"

"We will, Ma!"

She sighed, then turned around, surprised to find Frederic studying her.

"You love them very much," he said.

"Yes," she admitted with a smile, "my pride and joy. How is John?"

"The same: still sleeping, no fever."

"Good." She moved toward the hearth. "Rose has already left for work. Can I make you something to eat?"

Frederic waved away the offer. "Not just yet. I'd like to talk, if you can spare the time."

"My time is my own. Rose will make my excuses at work."

She settled into an armchair and motioned for Frederic to do the same. When he had, he rubbed his brow, wondering how to broach the subject that had plagued him since Lily had rushed into John's bedroom not two days ago.

"You're quite a woman, Miss Clayton," he began. "Again, I thank you for your hospitality—what you've done for my son."

Lily smiled knowingly. "I'm also a woman of color, Mr. Duvoisin—a quadroon." She chuckled deeply at his astonishment. "You're surprised."

"Yes."

"Don't worry, sir, John is not the father of my children. I was a slave at Wisteria Hill, the plantation near Freedom. When John purchased it, we—that is my children, Rose, and I—became his property, though not for long. We were emancipated within the year. Your son is a good man, sir, an honorable man. If not for him, I would never have made it north, my children would have remained uneducated, not much better off than those in bondage, and life would hold little hope for them."

"And what of their father?"

Lily bowed her head, the lump in her throat making it difficult to speak. "Henry—my husband—remains a slave. He was sold south nearly five years ago. I will never see him again."

Frederic heard the despair in her voice and knew a greater dread. "You love your husband."

Lily's head lifted. "With all my heart."

"*All* your heart?"

"Yes," she averred.

A lengthy silence descended on the room. Frederic wondered where John fit into the picture. It was obvious this woman had feelings for his son. But were they deep? Or did John merely fill a void left in the wake of a family torn apart—the dismal abyss of loneliness? The possibility stirred a memory and thoughts of Hannah Fields clouded his musings. Hannah had not only filled a void; she had seen firsthand the atrocities of slavery, escaping to this very same city. *Did she and Nicholas still live here?*

"I know what troubles you, sir," Lily was saying.

Frederic was drawn back to the present. "Do you?"

"John was there when I needed him most," she answered slowly. "But I love John as surely as I love Henry. I will always love John."

Frederic scoffed at the assertion, and Lily raised an irate brow in return.

"I see you don't believe me."

"Pardon me, Mrs. Clayton, but you avow your love for your husband and, in the very next breath, proclaim your love for another."

"Is it so hard to believe a woman could love two men?" Lily's voice cracked, her tears accumulating. "I assure you, sir, it isn't. I know I have two hearts. One was broken five years ago. The other is breaking now."

Frederic was dumbfounded and profoundly moved. Without warning, he thought of Colette, and everything was clear, crystal clear. "John is married now," he pronounced solemnly, "with a son or daughter on the way."

Lily digested the information, and her sadness intensified. She collected her emotions and whispered, "Then I pray he will be happy. He deserves to be happy. But first, I pray he will recover."

Frederic nodded. Declining breakfast, he stood and retired.

The second day was as tranquil as the first. John remained unconscious, though he groaned now and then. His eyes would sometimes flutter open, and he'd mutter incoherently before they'd close again.

That evening, he showed signs of fever, shivering under the blankets as a sweat broke on his brow. Lily continuously applied a cool cloth to his forehead, but by morning, the fever was raging. He shuddered uncontrollably, and his teeth chattered violently. He bucked against the compresses and pulled at the bedcovers to get warm, even though Lily kept pulling them away. Frederic and Michael prepared an ice bath. They stripped off his nightclothes and submerged him in the frigid water. He cried out in agony, struggling against the arms that held him down, but the bath worked, and as they settled him back into the bed, he slept peacefully. Within hours, the fever rose again, and he began to hallucinate, uttering fragmented phrases, reliving the confrontation with Blackford and calling out for Charmaine. Michael and Frederic submerged him in the water again, and again they succeeded in bringing the fever down.

Saturday, December 8, 1838

Frederic stirred in the cramped chair next to John's bed, the glaring sunlight streaming through the window slats, shocking him awake. He looked at John, who lay deathly still. Jumping up, he grabbed his son's hand and gasped in relief. It was cool, but not cold. Still, John was unresponsive to anyone's voice or touch, his breathing shallow, his face colorless.

Lily ran for Dr. Hastings again. An hour later, he examined John, then stepped out of the room with a grim shake of the head. "I'm sorry . . . I wish I could do more."

Michael studied Frederic, whose eyes were dark with grief, and pitied him. So valiant an effort, and now this. Michael looked down at John, his good and generous friend. The face was ghostly white, a face the priest had seen too many times while presiding over a bedside, administering the Last Rites. It was the face of death. He thought of his daughter. She would not be here to say farewell to the husband she loved.

Michael's eyes filled with tears. Silently, he recited the prayers for the dying, finishing with: *Sacred Heart of Jesus, pray for us . . . St. Jude, helper of the hopeless, pray for us . . . Father in Heaven, restore him to us . . .*

Late Evening

Frederic sat beside his son's lifeless body. With head bent, he clutched one of John's hands between his own, and brought it to his mouth in a fervent prayer. "Dear Lord," he murmured, "don't take him from me—not now!" He squeezed the hand harder as if he could infuse it with his own vitality. "I promised Charmaine I would bring you home, but not this way, Dear God, not this way!" He buried his head in the bed clothing and wept.

John looked down upon the curious scene unfolding below. His father was praying over his body, but he didn't feel the man's pain, only serenity. *Am I dreaming?* Someone was calling his name—not from the room, but from above and behind him. He turned slowly, and the corner of the ceiling opened wide, bathing everything in splendor. Far off, a woman was walking toward him, silhouetted against the bright light, and he shielded his eyes to better see her. She called his name again, her voice unfamiliar. Her hair was golden brown, her eyes like honey. She was plain, yet beautiful in her placid mien, and something in the way she moved reminded him of Colette. He knew she was his mother.

"John," she breathed again. "I've longed to see you."

There was a great distance between them, but his heart swelled with her greeting as if she were only a breath away. He took one last look at his father and turned back to her.

Chapter 8

Charmantes

BENEATH a blackened sky and cold, steady rain, the sorrowful procession picked its way along the craggy path to the cemetery. They stood before an open grave, where Michael Andrews intoned the dirge: *Eternal rest give unto him, O Lord, and let perpetual light shine upon him.* The men lowered John's casket into the deep hole, and the first shovelfuls of dirt were thrown on it. Charmaine closed her eyes and wept pitifully into Frederic's shirtfront, his strong arms encircling her. The twins were wailing. Paul was at their side, his eyes stormy. Flanked by Rose and Mercedes, George's head bowed farther to hide his tears, though his shoulders shook with grief. Charmaine couldn't bear it. She was going to die, too . . . *Oh God, let me die, too!*

She awoke, her heart pounding and her body saturated in a cold sweat. She was staring at the ceiling. It had been a dream—just a dream, yet she knew John was dead. She struggled out of bed, rolling with her cumbersome belly, but as her feet touched the floor, she doubled over in pain. She was in labor.

Elizabeth smiled at John as he approached, but oddly, the distance between them remained constant. His eyes left her face for the small child she held by the hand. It was Pierre, smiling up at him.

John broke into a run and, after an eternity, reached them. He lifted Pierre and the boy flung his arms around his neck. "Papa," he said. "Where were you?"

"Right here, Pierre," John whispered. "I was right here."

"We missed you! Mama and I missed you!"

John turned to his mother, but Colette smiled up at him now. He reached for her, and she stepped into his embrace. "You did well, John," she murmured. "You righted the wrong, and now it is over."

"Colette," he breathed, "Colette." He hugged mother and son tightly to him and savored her sweet fragrance. He was at peace.

Charmaine groped through the darkness to Paul's room, hunched over with another contraction. She rapped on his door, pounding harder when he didn't answer.

"Charmaine?" he queried when he opened to find her there. "What is it?"

Then he knew: The baby was on the way, one month early. He lifted her into his arms and quickly carried her back to her room. "Stay here, I'll get Rose and Loretta and set out for Dr. Hastings."

"Paul!" she called as he reached the door. He turned to face her. "John is dead. Dear God—I know he's dead!"

He returned to the bed, grasping her hand and holding it tightly as another contraction seized her, waiting for the pain to subside. "You don't know that, Charmaine."

"I had a dream," she moaned, her breathing rapid, "but I know it was real! I've lost him!"

"You're in labor, Charmaine, and your mind is playing tricks on you. Now, try to relax, and I'll be back soon."

He left her again, beset with worry.

Marie Elizabeth Duvoisin was born not two hours later, a loud wail greeting the doctor, who arrived too late. It had been a surprisingly easy labor, especially for a first child, and Rose beamed at her prowess as midwife.

Dr. Hastings stayed until he was sure mother and child were fine. The babe was small, but quite healthy, he reassured. Her early delivery was induced by anxiety, he diagnosed, which he admonished Charmaine to subdue, lest she bring on complications. He spoke to Paul on his way out. "I hope your brother won't be disappointed with a daughter."

"No, Adam," Paul murmured, "John won't be disappointed."

Charmaine gazed down at her infant daughter, who was already searching for a nipple. She wept, her tears falling onto her daughter's head, a baptism of abounding love.

"Marie, my sweet little Marie, if only your father were here . . ."

Leaning over, Charmaine kissed her head, the fuzz of red-blond hair, soft as down. The baby looked like John, already she looked like John, save the blue eyes, the beautiful blue eyes that opened now and then. Her tiny fist clutched Charmaine's finger, and Charmaine brought it to her lips for another tender kiss.

Rose and Loretta bustled about the room, removing the soiled linens, shooing people away from the door. "Give Charmaine a moment's peace. She wants to have the babe all to herself for a spell." The twins had been awoken with all the commotion, and they were the most anxious to see the newest Duvoisin.

Marie began to fuss, letting out a fierce cry that turned rhythmic, the volume increasing. Rose quickly dropped what she was doing and came around the bed. "She wants to nurse," she stated mildly and proceeded to show Charmaine the proper way to offer the infant her breast. The tiny lips rooted around and latched firmly onto the proffered nipple. The suckling sensation was both uncomfortable and exquisite. Together they fed a burgeoning contentment, and Charmaine was blanketed in an unfathomable peace.

When Marie fell asleep, she made herself presentable, allowing her pillows to be fluffed before sitting back into them. Twice Loretta attempted to put Marie in the cradle, but Charmaine cuddled her daughter all the closer. "No, let me hold her. I need to hold her." Loretta nodded in understanding. Rose invited the family in for their first visit.

Yvette and Jeannette danced with delight as they beheld their niece.

"Wait until Johnny comes home," Yvette said.

"He will be so proud," Jeannette added.

Paul stood at the foot of the bed, admiring the tender vision. Charmaine looked radiant, bearing the twins' comments with quiet dignity, a faint smile on her lips. He wished she were cradling his child. He loved her, he suddenly realized. If John didn't return, he vowed to take care of her and perhaps, if she'd have him, marry her.

Sunday, December 16, 1838

Charmaine had enjoyed a wonderful birthday, as wonderful as it could be without John. Next year would be different, everyone reassured her. This year, the entire household had taken great pains to make it a happy occasion. She even felt better, nearly restored to the woman she'd been before her confinement.

Now, with Marie sound asleep in her cradle, she stroked the mane on the rocking horse. She turned to the other birthday gifts, most of them for her daughter. Charmaine didn't mind; she enjoyed looking at the pretty little dresses and stockings. She spent the next hour or so rearranging drawers to make room for Marie's layette. She decided to combine John's clothing into five drawers, as there was more room in his chiffonier than hers.

She was working on the second drawer when she found it—tucked between two shirts, neatly folded and worn. As if scorched, she dropped Colette's love letter, her shaking hands flying to her mouth, the sheets fluttering to the floor.

Charmaine composed herself. She didn't know it was a love letter. She had only read a small portion of it that day almost a year and a half ago.

The days, the weeks, the months fell away, and she was back in John's room, searching for the twins, rankled by the draft that had strewn so many papers on the floor. She was picking them up again, rearranging and reading them. It didn't seem possible it was John, *her John,* who had stormed into the room that morning—that such terrible rage and hatred had ever existed between them. And yet, she'd gladly go back, if only he could be with her now.

The letter remained on the floor, yet, like a magnet, tugged at her heart. Indecisive, she stepped back. She shouldn't read it. *But John may never come home, and he is your husband. You have a right to know! You have that right.* But did she want to know? *It's no longer private,* her mind screamed. *John has told you everything . . . But has he really? Isn't it better to know for sure?*

Swiftly, she snatched it up. The last page was on top, and she read the closing: *Until we meet again, Your loving Colette.* She closed her eyes and swallowed hard. Why was she putting herself through this? She folded the pages, angry she'd started at all. John had been furious when she had read his private correspondence before. She would not be guilty of doing so now. Besides, she didn't want to know Colette's innermost feelings for John, refused to give them power over her. Drawing a ragged breath, Charmaine quickly replaced the letter in the drawer.

Her terrible nightmare took hold, and a chill chased up her spine. If the dream were real, if John *had* died, he was with Colette. He had her all to himself now, for his father had remained behind with the living. This letter John cherished and cradled amidst his personal belongings was testimony to his desperate love for her, even unto death. No wonder he wasn't afraid of dying in pursuit of Robert Blackford. He knew Colette was waiting for him in the afterlife.

Charmaine thought of the single letter she had received from him over three months ago. *If Colette were alive today, I would still choose you.* But Colette wasn't alive. She was in paradise with Pierre at her side. John was with his family now. She knew it. Charmaine just knew it. She closed her eyes to the vivid vision of them embracing him, and she fought back tears. "Oh God!" she moaned and threw herself on the bed, sobbing bitterly.

Thursday, December 20, 1838

Paul was alarmed to find the *Heir* docked in the harbor. She had left Charmantes in late November and should have been well on her way to Europe by now. "Will!" Paul called as he climbed aboard, "what has happened?"

The captain frowned. "I'm afraid I have some disturbing news, Paul."

Will Jones recounted the *Heir*'s arrival in New York, and the events that followed. Paul rubbed the back of his neck, not knowing what to make of it, Charmaine's premonition taking root.

"Your father told me to weigh anchor on the ninth if they didn't appear, but I waited an extra day to be certain. I even sent a man in search of your brother. Apparently, the police were scouring his place. They came snooping around the harbor, too—on the docks and at the warehouse—but were tight-lipped, so I don't know what happened. I would have been here sooner, but the weather down the coast was rotten, blizzard conditions nearly half the way."

Will read the dread on Paul's face and added, "Perhaps your father and John knew about the police and laid low. I know your father was concerned about police involvement."

"Or," Paul countered aloud, "Blackford injured them, and the authorities were looking for someone to contact the family."

Will shrugged. "At this point, we don't know enough to assume the worst."

"True, but how do we find out?"

Paul spent the rest of the day working alongside the dockworkers and sailors. The grueling labor of reloading the ship helped clear his mind so he could think rationally. He toyed with the idea of setting sail for New York immediately, but ruled that out when he thought of Charmaine. He couldn't tell her what he'd learned. She'd be terribly upset, and if he left before Christmas, she'd *know* something was wrong. That would add up to two more weeks of worry. No, the answers would have to wait a bit longer—until Christmas was over.

With dusk on the harbor and the lading finished, Paul came to a decision. The *Tempest*, his newest ship, was due in port any day now. After the holiday, he'd take her on to New York himself.

Christmas Eve, 1838

Charmaine sat on the sofa in the drawing room, little Marie comfortably nestled in her arms, sound asleep. This dismal Christmas Eve mocked last year's sad holiday, for although the manor was serene, it was a shaky peace. They hadn't heard from either John or Frederic for three months now. Though Paul assured her no news was good news, Charmaine knew her premonition had signaled some dire event. As she adored her babe, she offered up another petition to the litany of those that had gone before.

Rose and the twins fastened the last of the festive decorations to the mantel, their stockings hanging from the fireplace in anticipation of St. Nicholas. The girls had even fashioned a stocking for Marie. When Charmaine warned them about expecting too much, Yvette had countered that St. Nicholas was bound to come this year, since there was no Agatha to frighten the merry old elf away. Charmaine looked at Paul, but he seemed unaffected, his eyes twinkling in knowing merriment.

Joshua and George were playing a game of chess (they got along famously) while Loretta and Mercedes leafed through a catalog of baby items. Mercedes was large with child, her own days of confinement nearing their end. Soon little Marie would have a playmate.

Paul stood at the fireplace, deep in contemplation, his eyes going frequently to Charmaine. His attentiveness was not lost on Loretta or Rose. Espoir had been all but forgotten, and though he was needed more desperately here, they knew Charmaine was the reason he stayed on Charmantes.

George was worried, too, but his concern centered on John and Frederic. Paul had told him about the *Heir*'s aborted mission, and although he'd advised Paul not to jump to conclusions, he'd conjured a few terrible scenarios himself. When Paul decided to head for New York, he was relieved. If Mercedes weren't so near her time, he would have volunteered to go. But he wouldn't ask his wife to endure what Charmaine was enduring.

Presently, he stood and conceded the game to Joshua. Helping Mercedes out of her seat, they bade everyone goodnight.

Charmaine looked to the yawning twins. "It's time you found your beds as well. You don't want St. Nicholas to pass you by. I hear he only visits the homes of sleeping children." They went off with Rose.

With an expansive stretch, Joshua said goodnight, and with some reservations, Loretta said the same. Paul walked over to Charmaine and sat beside her. He didn't say a word, but he studied her with a faint smile.

Despite her sadness, Charmaine treasured the happiness that Marie stirred in her heart. She looked at him and saw the laughter in his eyes. "What are you smiling at?" she asked.

He shook his head and gave a slight shrug as if to say "nothing." When he was certain no one would return, he reached behind the sofa and retrieved four packages. Though each one was small, they were wrapped, complete with ribbons.

"What is this?" she asked in surprise.

"St. Nicholas has arrived," he said, before walking to the hearth and depositing two gifts in each stocking.

"What are they?"

"A set of playing cards for Yvette and dice."

"You're joking!" Charmaine laughed.

"On the contrary," Paul replied.

"But your father will be furious!"

"If he comes home, I'll be happy to face his punishment."

The spontaneous comment annihilated the cheerful moment, and Charmaine bowed her head to a sudden surge of tears. "I'm a coward, Paul," she whispered, looking down at her daughter. "If I faced reality, maybe this emptiness in my heart would begin to heal."

Her declaration reverberated about the room. Hadn't he come to believe the worst himself—John and his father had attempted to apprehend Blackford on the sixth of December and something had gone terribly wrong? *Are they dead?* Paul clenched his fists angrily, a violent reaction he had been unable to quell since the day the *Heir* had docked on the island.

Charmaine distracted him from his murderous thoughts. "What are in the packages for Jeannette?"

"A locket and a miniature horse," Paul replied, forcing a smile.

"Would you hold Marie for me?" she asked, wondering whether he would be comfortable with the request. *Had he ever held a newborn?*

But the invitation pleased him, and he plucked the baby out of her arms, cradling her as if he had done so many times before. Charmaine realized he'd most likely held Pierre and the twins when they were infants.

"Where are you going?" he asked.

"You'll see," she answered, sweeping from the room.

She came back with her own gifts and stuffed them into the girls' stockings, which were now bulging with booty. Satisfied, she faced him. "Marie won't sleep much longer, so I had best get some rest."

He nodded, for he had often heard the baby's cries during the night, but when she reached for Marie, he shook his head. "I'll take her," he offered.

Nestling the infant in the crook of his arm, he stood, put his other arm around Charmaine's shoulders, and accompanied her upstairs. The lamps burned low in the sconces, the house ever so quiet. When they arrived at her door, Paul strode into the room and gently laid Marie in her cradle.

He turned back to Charmaine, considering her in the lamplight. "What would you like for Christmas, Charmaine?"

"John," she gushed without thought, her throat constricted, "only John."

Just the answer I want! "Well, Charmaine," he proceeded, "I've been giving that a great deal of thought—ever since the night Marie was born. The day after Christmas, I'm setting out in search of your errant husband and my father. It's about time we found out what has happened." Seeing her surprise, he continued. "One of my ships is in port and is scheduled to travel to New York and Boston. I'll be on board when she sets sail."

"Paul? You'd do that?" she asked, her heart leaping with hope.

"My Christmas present to you. However—" he hesitated, hoping to provide a beacon in the storm he feared she had yet to weather "—I want a promise from you."

"What is it?"

"If I come back with bad news—and I'm not saying I will—I want your promise that, after a reasonable time has passed, you will consider marrying me."

Charmaine lowered her gaze to the floor, bombarded by many emotions.

"Is marriage to me revolting?" he queried, misreading her.

"No, Paul—of course it's not," she choked out, her eyes meeting his.

Realizing she was about to cry, he enclosed her in his arms. She grabbed hold of him and wept softly. He stroked her hair and kissed the top of her head, his heart aching with the feel of her in his embrace. When she lifted her head, he could hold back no longer. He lowered his lips to hers and tenderly kissed her. She accepted his gentle overture, then stepped back. "I love you, Charmaine," he whispered hoarsely. "I want to take care of you and Marie."

She was astounded, and new tears filled her eyes; now she ached for him.

"I—I know you do, Paul," she murmured, wiping her cheeks dry. "And I thank you for being here for me. But I can't—"

"Very well, Charmaine, I won't press you. But I want you to know you need never be alone."

She inhaled raggedly, aware she would have to face reality sooner or later. "I will consider your offer," she said. "But only after I know what has happened, when all hope is lost."

Paul retreated to the door. "Goodnight," he murmured, then slowly retired to his lonely chambers.

For a moment, Charmaine considered running after him. She longed to sleep in someone's arms, not to make love with him, but to be held, to feel protected once again, to shake off this overwhelming despair.

Marie began to stir, and she knew she wasn't alone at all. She lifted her daughter and climbed into bed. Marie nuzzled close, eagerly accepting her breast. Soon they fell into a peaceful, symbiotic slumber.

Christmas Day, 1838

Rebecca Remmen placed the boiled potatoes on the table and settled into her chair, watching Wade carve thin slices of the ham he'd brought home for their Christmas dinner. With fresh bread and sweet green beans, it was their finest meal of the year. They'd have the ham for a few days, and Rebecca would coax a soup from the bone, stretching this rare indulgence into a week's worth of meals.

It was pleasant having Wade home for the day. Usually, she was alone, and more often than not, lonely. She'd just turned seventeen, and Wade would not allow her to work anywhere in town, fearful a young woman as lovely as she would get herself into more trouble than she could handle, especially with surly longshoremen coming and going daily. She could take care of herself, but she hadn't convinced Wade of that, so other than the weekends when they'd stroll into town together to shop for necessities and socialize, Rebecca scarcely went farther than their tiny yard. Paul Duvoisin's grand ball had been the single most enchanting event in her short, disenchanting life, an occasion she treasured.

Three years ago, she and her brother had reached Charmantes, and life had drastically improved. They had food on their table, clothes on their backs, and a roof over their heads. Rebecca wanted more: to write a letter, to read a good book, to cipher so *she* could pay Maddy Thompson for their purchases. She was tired of cleaning the spotless cottage, sick of weeding the flowerbeds, hated tending the vegetable garden. She'd darned enough socks and mended enough shirts to clothe an army. But if she must do it, she'd rather do it for a husband. When her chores for the day were done, she would step out of the cottage and sit under a palm tree in the backyard, waiting for Wade to come home. Each night as dusk fell, she fantasized about a life of adventure, but most of all, she dreamed about Paul.

Her life had changed forever on the day the captain of the *Black Star* had marched them in front of the man and declared them stowaways. Paul did not scoff at her brother's daring scheme to start over. He listened when Wade described the squalid slums of Richmond. He understood their unorthodox pilgrimage to the "promised land"—Les Charmantes—the fabled paradise island of the Duvoisin dynasty. He nodded when Wade insisted he was strong and willing to work, that given a chance, he would make the Duvoisin family proud.

Those first few days, Paul saw to it they were fed and clothed. He set them up in the neglected cottage where they now lived and put Wade to work. Part of her brother's wages would go toward the purchase of that property. Over time, Wade did prove himself, assuming greater responsibility, ignoring the grumbles of some of the older men. Now three years later, he was in charge of the mill and had the respect of many, all because of Paul. For this, Rebecca's innocent heart placed Paul on a pedestal. He was her hero.

Though he hardly knew she existed, she was thrilled when she and Wade were invited to his spectacular ball. But Wade didn't want to go, maintaining they'd be out of place. She disagreed, and for weeks she'd pestered, wheedled, and begged, until finally, he gave in. Unfortunately, he was right. She was unprepared for the disillusionment of stepping into that grand banquet hall and beholding the most elegant of women in their finest garb. Paul would never notice her in her plain dress, certainly wouldn't dream of asking her to dance.

On a whim, she sought him out. All she needed was a few moments of his time; he'd have to notice her then. She knew she was attractive. She'd heard the whistles and catcalls from the sailors when she and Wade passed by Dulcie's. But she had botched her opportunity in the Duvoisin kitchen, had acted like a ninny. She'd vowed to be truthful with him. Yet, where had it gotten her? In his eyes, she was little more than a silly, tongue-tied girl, blurting out her childish adulation. For months, she had fretted over her behavior that night.

Her brother's illness last September changed all that. Although Paul might not like her, at least now he knew she wasn't some simpering simpleton. She could stick up for herself *and* her brother. Like Wade, she had strength of character.

"Rebecca?" Wade interrupted her deep contemplation. "What's the matter with you?" he demanded. "Why are you always daydreaming?"

She smiled brightly at him. "I'm sorry. What were you saying?"

"I'm going to be extremely busy for the next few weeks."

"Why? Is Paul going to Espoir again?"

"Weren't you listening to anything I said?" he chided with a scowl. "He's leaving for New York tomorrow to track down his father and his brother. He'll be on the *Tempest* when she casts off at dawn."

"But why is he doing that?" she queried in alarm, remembering

Felicia's words of yesterday. *Charmaine has him wrapped around her little finger. Why, he's so blind he'll do anything for her.*

"He's worried," Wade explained. "He hasn't had word from them in over three months. He'll be gone for at least two weeks and he's putting me in *total* control of the sawmill. That means no George checking in."

Rebecca cared little about her brother's gratification. She was very upset and ate most of her meal in silence, her brother's comments doing cartwheels in her head. When he left the table to leaf through a newspaper, she slipped next door to wish the Flemmings a happy Christmas and speak privately to Felicia.

"Did you know Paul intended to follow his father and brother to New York?" she asked when she and Felicia stepped out the back door.

"I'm not surprised," the woman said flippantly. "Charmaine's probably cried on his shoulder, and now he wants to make her happy by bringin' John home."

"But if she's after Paul as you say, why would she do that?"

Felicia laughed. "She doesn't really want her husband back. She just wants Paul to think she does."

"Why would she want him to think that?" Rebecca pressed.

Irritated by the obtuse question, Felicia's face twisted in haughty contempt. "Agatha got rid of Pierre for the money, and Frederic and John are probably dead at her brother's hands. Charmaine will have it all if Dr. Blackford kills Paul, too—her baby the sole heir to the Duvoisin fortune."

"Do you really think Dr. Blackford has killed Frederic and John?"

"You figure it out! Why else haven't they sent word?"

Rebecca was truly worried. If Paul's brother and father *were* dead, then he was headed for the same trap.

Felicia babbled on. "I wouldn't be surprised if she's working *with* Blackford."

"Oh, Felicia, I can't believe that!" Rebecca objected.

"No? Well, you don't know the woman like I do. Everyone knows her father's a murderer. She's been sly from the start. I'd even lay money down her daughter isn't a Duvoisin. She married John in April, one week after he came home. Babies take nine months to arrive. Hers came in eight."

Rebecca could not sleep that night. She didn't believe everything Felicia had told her, but still, she was concerned. Lying there in the dark, in the dismal quiet that mimicked her life, she decided she was sick and tired of sitting back and doing nothing.

Rising, she tiptoed into her brother's room and groped furtively through his drawers, pulling out trousers and a shirt. She couldn't write, so she couldn't leave him a note, and she wasn't fool enough to wake him. If she told him where she was going, she wouldn't get out the door. No, let him think she'd gone off somewhere on the island to be alone. She dressed quickly, pulling a length of rope through the belt loops of the baggy trousers and knotting it at her waist. She grabbed his cap off the peg by the door and tucked her hair into it, then took a chunk of leftover bread from the cupboard and crept out of the slumbering cottage.

In no time, she was on the wharf, standing before a tall ship, majestic and still on the rippling water. Stealing a glance in both directions, she quickly scurried up the gangplank. A couple of sailors were asleep on the open deck, but she hastened past them with her head bowed. Nobody could see her face in the darkness.

Where to hide? When she and her brother had stowed away over three years ago, they had squeezed between the large casks in the hold, squatting there for nearly a day. She did not fancy doing that now, but it was the best way to lie low until the vessel was well into the Atlantic. Then the activity on the deck would die down, and she could meander up above. If she kept her head down, no one would take much notice. She'd wait for the right moment to slip into Paul's cabin and hide there. She hoped he would stay above deck until nightfall. By the time he found her, they'd have voyaged a fair distance, and she'd have time to reason with him.

Wednesday, December 26, 1838

Paul left the house while the stars still studded the sky, a gibbous moon bathing the front lawns in heavenly light. He had said his goodbyes the night before, savoring his last few minutes with Charmaine.

"Take good care of Marie while I'm gone."

"You don't know how much this means to me, Paul," she had whispered.

"I think I do."

By the time he boarded the *Tempest*, the first rays of sunlight streaked the eastern sky. The sailors were preparing for departure in the predawn light. Philip Conklin, the *Tempest*'s captain, greeted him. Philip knew this was not a typical voyage, although the tobacco in the hold would be sold at auction in New York. Paul assisted with the preparations, and in less than a half hour, the *Tempest* was pushed from the pier. The tide was going out and the wind took hold of the sails. The ship sped out of the harbor, through the cove, and onto the open sea.

Six days, Paul surmised, and he'd have some answers. What would they be? Was he prepared for them? Never had he known turmoil of this magnitude, and he prayed God would be merciful. Did he want his brother dead? Certainly not. He was glad John had found happiness, even at his own expense. John and Charmaine loved each other. For that reason alone, he wanted to bring John home alive. But if providence deemed otherwise, Paul was prepared to step in and cherish Charmaine as his brother had. *Don't think about it*, his reasonable mind cautioned, for he knew her pain would be devastating. *What is done is done. Very soon, you will know the truth.*

Rebecca paced the cramped cabin. Her plan had gone off without a hitch. Since early afternoon, she had sat quietly in the stuffy cubicle awaiting Paul. She was tired and ached all over from hours squashed between hogsheads in the hold. The small bed looked inviting, but they hadn't traveled far enough yet, and she had to be awake in case somebody ventured into the cabin before dark. If that happened, she would bow her head, mumble an excuse, and scurry away. Once darkness fell, she began to breathe easier. The first day was over.

The hour grew late. Six bells rang out, signaling the sixth half hour of the night watch—eleven o'clock—and still Paul did not come. She began to think she was in the wrong cabin, though this one was next to the captain's quarters and spacious in comparison to the first mate's cell. So much the better if he didn't bed down here. She'd wait an extra day before confronting him. There would be time enough to convince him not to do anything dangerous, especially for his scheming sister-in-law. She, Rebecca Remmen, loved him—was *free* to love him! Perhaps she wasn't as old and as sophisticated as Charmaine Duvoisin, but she had never belonged to another man, either. Closeted together for days on end, he would recognize her love and hopefully return it.

She espied a knapsack tossed beneath a small table and opened it. It was filled with essential, finely tailored clothing. This was definitely Paul's cabin. She concluded he had chosen to sleep above deck, under the starry sky. Rubbing her eyes, she realized her fatigue was rivaled only by her hunger. She ate the last of her dry bread and washed it down with fresh water from the bucket that sat in the corner, then stretched out on the small cot and turned toward the wall. The rocking ship lulled her to sleep.

Paul entered the cabin near midnight and groped his way to the desk where an anchored lamp sat. Blindly, he struck the flint and ignited the wick with a tiny spark, illuminating the room with a low, glowing light. He rubbed the back of his neck, sitting down on a stool to pull off his boots and shirt. He stood to unfasten his trousers when he noticed the bundle in the middle of his bunk. Frowning, he stepped closer, staring down in irritation at the young man with long hair sound asleep in his bed.

"What in hell?" He gave the lad a sharp nudge.

The boy groaned and turned over. His eyes fluttered open in

confusion, and he scrambled from the bed, brushing the hair from his face.

"Jesus!" Paul swore angrily. This was no lad at all, but one Rebecca Remmen. "What the hell are *you* doing here?" he roared.

"I—I stowed away," Rebecca muttered.

"How? When?"

"Last night," she said anxiously. "It was easy. Everyone was asleep."

Paul rolled his eyes in utter amazement. "Why?"

Rebecca took a deep breath and bit her bottom lip. "Because I was afraid for you. I don't want you to—to get hurt—to be murdered."

Paul drove both hands through his hair. "Don't you think I can take care of myself?"

"No—I mean—I don't know," she stammered. "I was just—" She threw her hands up in the air. "I love you—and I don't want to lose you."

Terrific! Paul thought, jaw clenched. *Just what I need! An imbecile chasing me up the North Atlantic coast!* "Are you mad or just stupid?" he expostulated.

Rebecca's eyes widened, momentarily hurt. She had bared her heart, and all he could do was call her names. "Go ahead and make fun of me!" she blazed. "But I'm the only one who cares what happens to you!"

"I don't need you to care. I don't want you to care! Now get out, I'm tired!" He thrust a finger toward the cabin door.

"What?" she asked, aghast.

"Get out," he reiterated indifferently. "Find somewhere else to sleep."

"But—I can't go above deck. When the men realize I'm a woman they'll—"

His derisive laugh struck her dumb. "*Woman?* You have nothing to fear, my dear," he countered, his eyes raking her from head to toe. "They'll see you're only a little girl. Or is it a boy?" He thought of

Charmaine, and added, "After all, no *woman* would ever do what you've done."

Her throat stung, yet she gritted her teeth. "I'm more woman than your precious Charmaine!" she hissed, as if reading his mind.

His nostrils flared. "What would you know of Charmaine?"

"More than you can guess," she answered, raising her chin a notch.

"Try me," he growled. This girl was more trouble than she was worth.

"I know she's using you to get what she wants!" Rebecca exclaimed callously. "She doesn't love you, but she knows *you* love *her!* She's certain you'll do anything for her if she just acts shy and occasionally looks your way. She throws crumbs at your feet, and you grovel for the few you can catch!" In her insane jealousy, Rebecca blathered on. "It's disgusting, really, and everyone on Charmantes is laughing at you!"

"Out—get out!" he bellowed. In two strides, he grabbed her by the arm and pushed her toward the door.

"No! You can't send me out there!" she shrieked, slapping him across the cheek with all her might. "Let go of me!"

He was astonished, and his eyes turned steely, infuriated by her smug face, her hand poised to strike again. "Oh no, you don't!" he snarled, catching her wrist and giving her one hard shake.

"Let—me—go!"

"I've had enough of you, Rebecca Remmen. It's high time somebody put you in your place."

He dragged her across the cabin and sat hard on the cot, pulling her across his lap. She didn't scream, but she fought like a wild animal, and he had all he could do to pin her flailing limbs with one hand while he wrenched the rope belt free with the other. He yanked the pants down, baring her firm bottom. His palm smarted with the first crack of his hand, but he was gratified when she cried out. She thrashed violently, nearly squirming free. He readjusted his grip until she lay taut across his thighs. This time, he spanked her harder.

She yelped, then sank her teeth into his forearm. He released her with a loud oath, the bite deep, blood trickling from his wrist. "You damn little wench!"

She clambered from his lap and tripped over the trousers bunched around her ankles, lying sprawled at his feet. He threw back his head and laughed, lunging forward and grabbing hold of the pants, pulling them free. She was up in a flash, streaking bare-bum to the door. But before she could throw it open, he was upon her again, yanking her around. His anger had evaporated, vanquished beneath a rush of passion, the animal instinct to dominate and conquer, and he relished the arousal her struggles had ignited.

"Now, where will you go without any pantaloons? Or aren't you afraid of those men anymore?" She pushed hard against him, but he didn't budge. "I know," he chuckled. "You aren't frightened. You're a strapping lad! Let me see your muscles."

Before she could react, he ripped the shirt open, revealing perfect little breasts, round and inviting. Aghast, she pummeled his hairy chest with both fists, but he ignored the admirable attack as he swept the tattered garment from her shoulders, leaving her naked before him. He pinned her to the door, grabbing her bottom with one hand and the hair at her nape with the other. He pulled her head back and kissed her passionately, forcing her lips apart and thrusting his tongue into her mouth. His hand traveled from her buttocks along the curve of her hip and up to her breast, which he cupped and kneaded.

The sensual assault left Rebecca reeling. She relinquished the battle with a feeble punch, prisoner to Paul's blistering kiss and her own smoldering passion. If he didn't release her mouth she would faint, and yet she hungrily kissed him back, quickly noting how it was done. Her mutinous hands grabbed hold of his corded arms and swept over his broad shoulders. She savored the feel of his skin under her palms, her breasts crushed against his rock-hard chest, and luxuriated in the arousing heat of his body.

He abruptly tore away, and she teetered on weak legs until he scooped her up and turned toward the bed. She didn't fight him when he put her there, observing him through hooded eyes as he ripped off his trousers and joined her.

"So you want to be a woman?" he queried, his voice husky.

"Your woman," she murmured, titillated by the unbridled lust in his eyes.

Her words were as intoxicating as her unadorned beauty, and his loins ached for her, the fire that burned there volcanic. His mouth possessed hers again, a consuming, breathless kiss. When he released her, she sighed, but his lips pursued their sensual assault, tracing a searing path along her jaw and down her throat. His coarse moustache raked her soft flesh, meeting the callused hand that fondled a firm, yet pliable breast, sampling the delectable orb, teasing the nipple with his tongue until it stood erect.

The familiar wanton desire that was triggered whenever she looked upon him was stoked to an unbearable degree, and she dug her fingers into his shoulders, joyous tears trickling into her hairline. His roving hands continued to explore the curve of her hips, her belly, the inside of her thighs. Upward he stroked, until his fingers found and probed that most delicate of spots, already moist in anticipation of his lovemaking, the center of all pleasure, craving him now in unchaste abandon. She groaned with expectancy and agony when he mounted her.

She was a virgin. In all his thirty years, he had had many women, but never a virgin. The thought that this young woman had never lain with another fanned his ardor. He would make certain she yearned for him when this was over, so he fought to subdue his soaring need and lay still until her pain ebbed, basking in the sweet sensations of rapacious lust, until he could stand it no longer, her supple body responding beneath him. Shifting on his elbows, he began to slowly move inside of her, each throbbing stroke exquisite.

Rebecca pressed her head back into the pillow and closed her eyes to ecstasy. He kissed her all over, his lips constantly coming back to hers, then roaming afield again. His rhythmic invasion evoked familiar, ravenous sensations in her loins. As he grabbed her buttocks, she wrapped her legs around his hips to receive more of him. He rode her harder, faster, plunging ever deeper, and her body answered with a will of its own, hips writhing, the sublime sensations indescribable—building—the summit nearly reached. Suddenly, he groaned and, with one final thrust, collapsed upon her, clutching her closely in resplendent gratification. Surprisingly, it was his stillness, the press of his body, that catapulted her into the realm of rapture, an upheaval of such enormous proportion she shuddered violently, the spasm sucking him into the very depths of her womanhood, leaving her tummy and pelvis quivering, surpassing any act she'd initiated in her lonely bedroom. She lay with her eyes closed, astounded, her heart pounding, her breathing as ragged as his. When he moved, she hugged him closer, reveling in the feel of his blanketing body.

Eventually, he rolled on his side, still very close in the cramped cot.

"That shouldn't have happened," he muttered, more to himself than her.

She frowned up at him. "I thought it was wonderful."

He smiled in spite of himself, a plaintive smile. She was lovely, and she was a woman. He'd just made her *his* woman. But he was already thinking about Charmaine and was ashamed. This was the second time he had proposed to her and the second time he had dishonored that proposal. *What is the matter with me?* He rose and began to dress.

"I love you," Rebecca whispered, desperate tears welling in her eyes. "You'll marry me now, won't you?"

Paul looked back at her and saw her anguish. "No, Rebecca, I won't marry you. Like I said, what happened between us—it shouldn't have happened."

"It's your precious Charmaine!" she lashed out. "*Fool!* You *think* you love her!"

"Don't!" he warned, angry with himself when she faced the

wall. She was crying, but he feared if he consoled her, he'd take her all over again. Unsettled by that thought, he grabbed the blanket that had fallen to the floor. As he shook it out to spread over her, he noticed a strange scar on her derrière, below the curve of her hip.

"What's this?" he growled, touching the mark, irritated by the imperfection.

She vaulted as if branded, then recoiled. "It's from my father," she ground out. "He was cruel, too!"

The declaration hit its mark, and Paul stepped back, duly chastised. He tossed the coverlet on the bed and deserted the cabin. He needed time to think.

The night sky was black. Dense clouds roiled above, blocking even the brightest stars, the deck illuminated only by a series of dimly lit lanterns. Paul picked his way around the sleeping sailors, who preferred the open air to the stuffy forecastle quarters below. He went to the railing and stared out into the dark void, breathing deeply of the salty air.

What have I done? Not so long ago, he would have already dismissed this romp. But then, this experience had been different from any other.

He remembered his first sexual encounter. He had turned fifteen, and John and George thought it was high time they pay his way at Dulcie's. John wagered George ten dollars he wouldn't get through it successfully, but John lost that bet. Of course, Paul never let John know he had left the brothel concerned. Even though the strumpet had had more men than she could count, he worried that he'd impregnated her; no child should ever endure what he had.

There was no turning back, however. He'd tasted the pleasures of the flesh, and it eclipsed his fear of fathering a child. And there was no more paying. Paul knew he had charisma, and many of the women he met at home and abroad were ready and willing. They were always older or experienced, and he let them know from the start they would not leave his bed carrying his babe in their bellies. There were ways around it. He learned how to elicit great pleasure and to withdraw before he ejaculated. If the woman was responsive, especially if she had shared his bed before, she might satisfy him in her own way. His love life was robust, yet he was confident he had never spawned a bastard.

Tonight with Rebecca, that nagging fear hadn't even crossed his mind. He had taken her fiercely, spilling every bit of his seed deep inside of her. *What are the odds she'll conceive from this one time? Slim, very slim.* His heart mocked his rational mind. *Not slim enough . . .* Their lovemaking had been dynamic—intoxicating. Who had dominated whom?

He had heard tell a virgin did not experience the full depth of her womanhood, but Paul knew Rebecca had been deeply satisfied; even now, he could feel her hips undulating, hear her moaning in ecstasy. Was it because she loved him? He inhaled deeply, reliving those intense moments of consuming pleasure. Was this love? It couldn't be. He hardly knew her.

He raked his hands through his hair and thought once again of Charmaine. He had wronged her. But he had wronged Rebecca as well . . . just like his father with his mother and Elizabeth. *Don't think about it! Don't be a fool. Watch and wait. That's all you need do.*

When he grew tired, he went back into the cabin. Rebecca hadn't moved, and he assumed she had cried herself to sleep. Fully clothed, he lay down next to her and quickly dozed off. Almost as quickly, he began to dream.

He rode up to the manor on Alabaster. Charmaine was sitting on the swing, and little Marie was crawling on a blanket next to her. She saw him and waved. As he dismounted, she picked up Marie and walked over to him. Together, they strolled into the house and climbed the staircase. She put Marie to sleep and opened his bedchamber door, sauntering in. He followed her, closing and locking it behind them. She undressed and stepped into his embrace. He kissed her and lifted her into his arms, carrying her to the bed. He made love to her, but when he was finished, she rolled away from him, tears in her eyes, leaving him empty.

Next, he was headed for a day's work, checking on the mill and nodding to Wade. He turned his horse toward town. Then, he was walking up to the Remmen house. No one answered when he knocked, so he pushed his way in. Rebecca was standing there, her eyes flashing. She knew he'd been with Charmaine, and she spurned him. But he was certain if he kissed her, she'd be a slave to her passion. She attempted to flee, but he crossed the room in two strides and pulled her into his arms. She ceased to struggle when his lips conquered hers. He kicked the bedroom door open and took her to the bed. He rode her hard until all his passion was spent, then cradled her in his arms, satiated, savoring his ebbing pleasure.

"Paul—what are you doing?"

John was standing in the doorway.

Paul's eyes flew open. His breathing was ragged, his pulse quick, and beads of perspiration dotted his brow. He stared up at the ceiling, slowly realizing where he was; it had only been a nightmare.

Rebecca had turned in her sleep and was now cuddled close to him, her head resting on his shoulder, an arm thrown across his chest. Despite his resolve, he pulled her closer. ". . . but I do love you," she murmured. Paul swallowed hard, befuddled, for he wanted to cry. He closed his eyes to the urge and, after a long while, succumbed to exhaustion.

Light pouring through the porthole awakened Rebecca. Her head hurt, her eyes burned, and her body ached all over, especially between her legs. She shifted and realized her cheek rested on Paul's chest. She rolled away, rousing him. As his eyes opened, she was filled with shame and tried to cover herself.

"Here," he gently offered, stripping off his shirt and draping it over her bare shoulders. She pulled it tightly around her, dropping her gaze to the bed. "I'm sorry about last night," he remarked.

"You said that already," she replied hotly.

"We need to talk," he pursued, aware of her anguish despite her ire. "You're very beautiful, Rebecca, and someday you will find someone who will make you happy. But that someone is not me."

Her eyes glistened with tears, and once again, she averted her face. But he cupped her chin and forced her to look at him. "Last night, you said I loved Charmaine. You are right, I do. I set out on this voyage to find my brother, but if I don't bring him home alive, I'm going to marry her. I promised her that before I left, before all of this happened. Do you understand?"

She refused to answer him and pulled away.

"Do you understand?"

"Oh, I understand, all right! She's sending you to your death, just like she did with her husband and your father!"

Unlike the night before, Paul didn't get angry, though his brow furrowed. "What are you talking about?"

"If your father and John are dead, and Dr. Blackford kills you, Charmaine's baby will inherit the entire Duvoisin fortune. Isn't that true?"

Paul put his head in his hands and let out an incredulous laugh.

"Isn't it true?" she pressed, offended by his sardonic bemusement.

"Yes, I suppose it's true," he conceded. "But Robert Blackford is not going to kill me."

"He might—if you chase after him!"

"I'm not chasing after him, Rebecca, and Charmaine didn't want *John* chasing after him, either. I'm going to New York to find out what happened to my brother and father—to bring them home, one way or another. Where did you get these ideas, anyway? Not from Wade, I hope."

"He doesn't know anything about this," she hastily replied. "It was Felicia, Felicia Flemmings."

Paul scowled. "Did Felicia tell you I fired her for spreading lies?"

"No," she whispered. "She said she quit because she couldn't tolerate . . ."

"Charmaine," he supplied.

"But not everything she said was a lie!" Rebecca rallied, unhappy he still revered his sister-in-law.

"Perhaps she told you she has lain with me—many times," he continued sharply. "That she hoped our romps would turn into something more. That she's jealous because Charmaine married into my family and she did not."

Rebecca's face bore her injured pride. "And now you think I'm trying to do the same thing," she murmured, casting her eyes to the floor.

"No, Rebecca," he replied softly. "I don't think that of you."

She heard none of it, rising from the bunk and retrieving her pants from the floor. She pulled them on through her tears. "Don't worry," she whimpered. "Once we get back to Charmantes, you'll never have to see me again."

"When we get to New York," he said, ignoring her desperate promise, "I'll buy you something more appropriate to wear. Then, if I do find my father and John, I'll tell them you stowed away, hoping to see the city sights. Is that acceptable?"

She didn't answer, and he was uncertain if anger or pain left her mute.

Thursday, December 27, 1838

Benito St. Giovanni took the intrusion of John Ryan in stride. Things could be worse: the tunnel he'd nearly completed could have been discovered, or his time could have run out. When Ryan came careening into his prison almost four weeks ago, Benito had cautiously observed him for a week.

"What's this about John Duvoisin's wife?" Ryan had demanded.

Benito did not immediately answer, his thoughts lingering on the new Mrs. Duvoisin. *So, this is her family background. How revolting!*

When Ryan pressed the issue of John's wife, Benito said, "Does the name Charmaine Ryan ring a bell?"

John Ryan eyed him speculatively. *How does this man know my daughter's name?* Enlightenment came slowly.

The priest smiled. "That's right, old man. Charmaine is John Duvoisin's wife. I'd say your daughter has done quite well for herself. You, on the other hand, have not." Giovanni allowed the words to sink in. "It's common knowledge Charmaine's father—that would be you—beat her mother to death. John will not be happy when he returns to find you here. He has quite a temper, if you didn't already know."

"Whaddaya mean, when he returns?" John Ryan sneered.

"He's abroad right now," the priest supplied, "chasing down another murderer. Then he'll be back for us—you and me."

John Ryan pulled two rumpled letters from his pocket. "So these must be from him," he mumbled.

"Where did you get those?" the priest asked, his interest instantly piqued. Charmaine's name was written across both envelopes.

"Aboard ship. I heard Simons talkin' to the captain, heard my daughter's name mentioned, and I saw him hand these here letters over with a whole pile of others. Later, I moseyed on over to where they was settin' and helped myself. I can't read none too good, but I know how my daughter's name is spelled."

Giovanni smirked. "Would you like to know what they say?" Clearly, Ryan wanted outside information, but when Giovanni motioned for the letters, the man refused to hand them over.

"What did *you* do?" Ryan asked.

"I'm not prepared to talk about that."

"Well, maybe you ain't interested in readin' these," Ryan responded in kind.

So . . . Benito thought, *you and I speak the same language.* "Blackmail," he finally answered, "only blackmail."

Satisfied, Ryan shoved the letters toward the priest. Giovanni quickly ripped into them, then smiled broadly. They had plenty of time. John and Frederic were still searching for Blackford in New York, working on the assumption he had changed his name. It could be months before they returned.

By the next day, Giovanni decided he had no choice but to include John Ryan in his escape. In fact, Ryan might prove useful along the way, and in the end, he'd rid himself of the degenerate. Benito smiled with the thought. Once they were on the open sea, that wouldn't be difficult at all.

During the second week of John Ryan's incarceration, he learned how to dig a tunnel with a spoon. By the end of his third week, they had broken through. In four months, Benito's only apprehensive moment was Buck Mathers's simple declaration, "Either I'm getting taller or this ceilin's getting lower."

As December came to a close, their plan came together. Buck informed them Paul had left in search of Frederic and John. The time was ripe. An hour after sunset on the twenty-seventh of December, Giovanni and Ryan crawled out of the meetinghouse cellar and escaped into the night.

Luck was with them. The brilliance of the nearly full moon muted the star-spangled sky and cast eerie gray shadows on either side of them. They trudged the seven miles to Benito's cabin, reaching it just before midnight. They had planned carefully in jail, so there was no need to speak, Giovanni demanding silence, alert to any unusual sound.

Taking a lantern from the cabin, John Ryan went into the pine forest behind the outhouse and searched until he found the skiff tucked in a dugout and covered with brush. Turning it over, he placed the oars, spar, and sail inside and dragged it along a path Giovanni had told him would take him to the shoreline. Dusting off his hands, he headed back toward the small abode. He'd let the priest set the sail.

Giovanni prayed that the four items he'd secreted away months ago were where he'd left them. He wasn't surprised to find his home ransacked. He shook his head. Did they really think he was stupid enough to hide his booty here? Or were they the stupid ones? They hadn't even uncovered the pistol hidden beneath a loose floorboard under his bed. He dropped a bullet into the chamber and pocketed the extra ammunition. He retrieved his compass hidden in a cup in the cupboard, and took a length of rope from the laundry spilled all over the floor. Lastly, he lifted a silver key off a hook concealed behind a painting of the Savior. It unlocked the gates to the Duvoisin compound. He possessed another key, one that had been hidden on his person since the morning of his arrest. It unlocked his future.

Ryan returned just as the priest stepped outside. They nodded to each other and Ryan fell in step behind Giovanni. Their next stop: the Duvoisin mansion.

Wade Remmen sat at the kitchen table, running his hands through his hair. Rebecca had been missing for two days now. He knew his sister had been unhappy. She'd complained often enough of her boredom in the tiny bungalow, but he had ignored her, and now, he was beside himself with worry. When he awoke the day after Christmas and found the house empty, he hadn't been too concerned. He didn't like her going off on her own, but, lately, she'd grown exceedingly headstrong. Real anxiety took hold yesterday when he'd returned home from work and she was still missing. Where had she gone?

Felicia Flemmings hadn't been any help. She seemed to think Rebecca's disappearance revolved around her "love" of Paul Duvoisin. Wade was cognizant of his sister's infatuation, but Paul was a mature gentleman and Rebecca an uneducated girl with silly romantic ideas. When Wade left Felicia, he was no closer to knowing where his sister might be. Paul had departed the island on the *Tempest*; Rebecca knew that. Had she gone off to moon over Paul until he returned? *No,* Wade reasoned, *she's probably annoyed with me.*

Tonight, he knew he was deceiving himself. Something terrible could have happened to her. He hadn't been able to look for her during the day; however, he wasn't needed at the mill until morning.

That gave him hours to search Charmantes. He stepped out into the night, a bright gibbous moon lighting his way. Why he headed toward the Duvoisin estate, he didn't know, other than it was Paul's home. Perhaps Rebecca was drawn there, even if he was away.

Jeannette couldn't sleep. It had been a long time since her French doors opened all by themselves. Ever since Pierre's death, the "ghost" had become a distant memory. Not so tonight. Tonight she heard the door unlatch and blow open, even though there wasn't a breeze in the air. Unlike before, she wasn't afraid, though she would have felt a lot safer if her father, Johnny, or Paul were home. She woke her sister.

"What's the matter?" Yvette asked, rubbing sleepy eyes.

"The doors," Jeannette whispered, "they opened by themselves again."

Unperturbed, Yvette jumped up and pulled them closed, slipping the latch in place. "Let's see what happens now," she said.

"Can I sleep with you?" Jeannette queried, not at all pleased her bed was closest to the glass panels.

Her sister smiled. "Sure."

They snuggled under the covers, staving off the chilly December air. Minutes later, the doors blew open again. The girls looked at each other. Yvette rose and approached them guardedly this time. Then, on impulse, she stepped outside, determined to confront the elusive specter. There was nothing there.

She turned back into her room when a noise from below drew her around. She peered over the balcony in time to see the outer door to the chapel close, a reverberating "thump" assuring her she wasn't imagining things; the manor had indeed been breached. She frowned. Who would be going into the chapel at this time of night?

Giovanni and Ryan walked purposefully up the short aisle of the sanctuary. Their escape had gone without incident. Before long, they'd be far out to sea, watching the sunrise. While Ryan held the lantern, Giovanni stepped up to the altar. The chalice and ciborium had been restored to the sacrificial table, but not returned to the tabernacle. A good sign—only he possessed the key. *Idiots, the lot of them, not to question me about it!* He inserted the key and opened the small ark. The coins and precious jewels he'd extorted from Agatha Duvoisin were still cached there. Weighing the heavy treasure in his hand, he tied the bag around his middle with the rope, then carefully concealed it under his shirt.

"Is that all?" John Ryan whispered, his eyes narrowed in displeasure.

"It's enough," the priest assured.

"Enough for you," Ryan muttered, scanning the stone enclosure until his gaze returned to the vestibule by which they had entered. He began to formulate his own, very different plan. "This is some grand house. There's got to be a lot more in there," he said, throwing a thumb toward the side portal that opened into the manor. "We got plenty of time before the sun comes up. Let's see what else we can find."

"No!" Giovanni ordered. "We've been over this before. It's too dangerous!"

"*You've* been over it before," Ryan growled. "Now it's my turn to make some of them decisions."

"Go in there, and I leave you to your own devices," the priest threatened. "There will be no boat when you reach the shore!"

"And what if I just rouse the family," John Ryan rejoined. "You wouldn't want me to do that, would ya?"

Giovanni hesitated. Ryan was shrewd. He should have shot the slovenly albatross back at his cabin where the report of the pistol would have been swallowed up by the forest. Now, he had no choice but to give in.

Gloating, John Ryan attempted to placate the priest. "With all the men gone, it should be easy to get some more loot. You know this place like the back of your hand. Where should we look first?"

Yes, Giovanni mused, *why not pillage the house? Ryan is anxious to carry any additional treasure to the boat, and I'll be that much richer when I shoot him later on.* "The master and mistress's chambers," he breathed, allowing the old man his momentary victory.

"Lead the way."

Yvette shrank into the shadows of the ballroom just in time. She hadn't expected the chapel door to suddenly swing open, and she gulped back a startled scream. Her eyes widened farther as Father Benito stepped through the doorway. She didn't have to be a genius to figure out who was with him. Charmaine would be very upset to know her father roamed the manor.

Wade stood outside the Duvoisin compound. The imposing mansion was bathed in moonlight, but every window in the house was dark. He leaned into the gates, surprised when they gave way. The stable hands usually secured them by ten o'clock each night, unlocking them at dawn. Strange—they weren't locked tonight. He pushed them open and walked up the drive.

Jeannette began to fret when her sister did not return. She went out on the balcony again and peered over the balustrade to the chapel doors below. They were still shut, and all was quiet, but as she straightened up, she nearly jumped out of her skin when she saw the figure of a man approaching the house. She quickly ducked back into her room. It was time to go and wake up Charmaine.

Yvette followed the two intruders, keeping a safe distance behind them. They slunk across the banquet hall and passed through the ballroom kitchens before entering the rear service stairwell. They were headed for her parents' chambers. For a moment, Yvette debated taking the main staircase back up, but she discounted that idea, deciding it was safer to keep the two men directly in front of her. She waited until she heard the upstairs door close before racing up the steps herself, clutching the railing in the blackness. Reaching the second floor, she put an ear to each door and listened. All was quiet. Not knowing which door they used, she chose her mother's, slowly pulling it open and peeking around it. Moonlight spilled into the room through the French doors. No one was there. She tiptoed forward, past her mother's bed to the sitting room door. She listened at the door again. Nothing. She waited unending minutes, her breathing thundering in her ears, fearful of where the two men might be—perhaps in her father's chambers. Biting her bottom lip, she turned the doorknob gingerly, cracking the door, her eye pressed to the small opening. No one was there either, and she sighed in relief. She would head for her father's quarters next.

She pushed through the door and stepped into the room. Without warning, she was grabbed from behind and lifted clear off the floor. A filthy hand clamped over her mouth, muffling a scream. A man growled near her ear as she resorted to kicking and punching. "You better stop your goddamn thrashin' if you know what's good for ya, girl!" She did not desist until Father Benito stepped out of the shadows, brandishing a pistol.

"You've spied once too often, Yvette," he whispered.

When she struggled anew, he cocked the trigger, and she immediately stopped. "I believe you lost a riding crop behind my outhouse a year ago." He shook his head and clicked his tongue. "To think your dear stepmother thought it was the wind that spilled those crates to the ground."

Her brow tipped upward, and the priest chuckled menacingly. "Yes, I thought so. And now you'll learn what happens to meddlesome children." He looked at his compatriot. "I do believe we have a hostage, Mr. Ryan."

Ryan's lips curled into a greedy grin, his covetous eyes upon the girl he held. Giovanni smiled as well. "Tell us, Yvette," he said, stepping over to the table and relighting his lantern, "where did your mother keep her most valuable jewels? In a whisper, please. I'd hate for something to happen to your sister or your governess's new baby."

* * *

Charmaine was sitting in the armchair nursing Marie when Jeannette came in. "What's the matter?" she asked, reading fear in the girl's eyes.

Jeannette quickly explained, but Charmaine was not alarmed. After all, the mysterious ghost had never materialized. This was just another of Yvette's escapades. As for the apparition on the front lawns, it was probably a stable hand stepping out of the carriage-house apartments to relieve himself. Still, she couldn't permit Yvette to wander about the mansion at two in the morning.

Handing the squirming Marie to Jeannette, Charmaine stood and tightened her robe about her waist. "Come," she said, taking the baby back from the girl. "We'd best find your sister."

Wade circled the entire house, but finding nothing out of the ordinary, he decided to head home. Why had he come here in the first place? Now he feared he would not find his sister until she decided to return home, if she were able.

Rounding the corner nearest the stables, he heard voices. It was one of the twins and John's wife. "I don't know where she could be," the girl was saying as the two peered out the chapel door. "She said she was coming down here."

She sounded worried, as worried as he, and Wade was compelled to step forward, his presence eliciting a shriek from the pair of them. "Sorry—I'm sorry!" he apologized. "I didn't mean to startle you. It's me—Wade Remmen."

Jeannette was happy, but Charmaine frowned deeply, annoyed her horrified reaction had frightened Marie, who let out one fitful cry that instantly turned into a rhythmic wail. "What are you doing here—creeping up on us like that?"

"I didn't mean to frighten you," Wade averred, "and I wasn't creeping. I was looking for my sister, Rebecca. She's been missing since yesterday morning."

"What would your sister be doing here, Mr. Remmen?" Charmaine probed suspiciously, not at all pacified by his excuse, shifting Marie to her shoulder and patting her back until she quieted.

"Don't be angry with him, Mademoiselle," Jeannette implored. "At least now we know who was walking up to the house." Her adoring eyes rested on Wade. "You haven't seen *my* sister, have you?"

"No, Jeannette, I haven't."

Yvette knew she'd get herself out of this scrape somehow, but she was terribly frightened for her sister and little Marie. Therefore, she did exactly as she was told. She showed the priest her mother's hand-carved jewelry chest, vexed to find it nearly empty. "All of Mama's best pieces are missing!" she objected loudly, her eyes leveled on Benito.

"Quiet!" he ordered, wagging the pistol at her. Evidently, Agatha had purloined Colette's valuables first. "There must be money—a safe in these chambers," he growled. "Where is it?"

Yvette took them into her father's rooms. She went to his desk and pointed out the dummy drawer that not only concealed important documents, but also a moneybag filled with gold coins and, surprisingly enough, her own gambling purse. She didn't mention the safe in the wall. Apparently, it was enough; there was an avaricious gleam in Benito's eyes as he set the lantern down and emptied one into the other, then weighed the bulging sack in his hand. "Any more than this and we wouldn't be able to carry it," he commented wryly. "You and I should be set for life, Mr. Ryan."

John Ryan was pleased as well, snatching the satchel from the priest and strapping it around his waist with his belt.

"Now will you let me go?" Yvette asked defiantly.

"All in good time, my dear, all in good time."

"But my sister will be worried if I don't return soon."

The priest chuckled. "If she's as stupid as you and comes looking for trouble, we'll give her some."

Yvette smarted with the insult, then realized it bolstered her indomitable spirit. She wasn't defeated yet, and if she kept a level head, she'd get through this calamity with no greater harm done than the loss of her father's money, money that could easily be replaced.

They marched her back down the stairwell, Benito lighting the way, John Ryan wrenching her arm behind her so she couldn't escape him. They scurried across the ballroom, coming up sharply when the chapel door swung open.

Charmaine jumped and stifled a scream when Father Benito pointed the pistol at her, but her horror climaxed as her eyes flew to Yvette and the man who restrained her. Then, she did scream, for here she was, face to face with her nightmare: John Ryan!

"What are *you* doing here?" she cried, recovering enough to speak, oblivious to her daughter's renewed wailing that echoed loudly off the walls of the empty banquet hall.

"Well, Haley Charmaine," her father snarled, "word got out that you came into a bit of money, and just like before, you've been leavin' your pappy out. I reckon it's high time you shared the wealth."

"But how—how did you get here?"

"I ask the questions," Benito declared, turning to his young hostage. "Your sister did come looking for you, Yvette. A shame she didn't have the good sense to stay in her room." He waved the gun at Charmaine, demanding she calm Marie.

"She's upset!" Charmaine objected. "There's nothing I can do!"

"She's gonna wake up the whole goddamn house!" John Ryan barked.

Giovanni grew more agitated and quickly discarded the lantern. "Come here!" he ordered, leveling the weapon on Jeannette. "Now!" he shouted, grabbing hold of her arm and viciously yanking her to his side.

Charmaine gasped as he pressed the muzzle to the girl's temple. "No—please!" she begged. "Please let her go!"

"Now," Benito instructed coolly, "you go quietly up to your bedroom and you nurse that baby back to sleep. Then get down on your knees and pray I am merciful enough to release the girls when

I've finished with them. However, if you alert even one person in this house as to what is happening, I guarantee you will never—*never*—see Yvette or Jeannette alive again."

Jeannette whimpered.

"Please!" Charmaine implored. "Please release them now, and I promise we won't say a word to anyone!"

The priest coughed sardonically. "I think not."

Charmaine turned beseeching eyes on her father. "You're my father! Don't do this! Just let the girls go!"

"*Your* father?" the man sneered. "You ain't my goddamn flesh and blood! Your mother was a whore from the day I met her 'til the day she died!"

Charmaine choked back a sob, her grip on Marie tightening with the perverted assertion.

Benito cocked the firearm. "We are wasting precious time here. On the count of ten, Madame. Must I count?"

"Dear God!" Charmaine moaned and, by dint of will alone, fled the ballroom as the countdown began.

Wade had reached the gates when he heard a scream inside the chapel, but he concluded Charmaine and Jeannette had come upon a surprised Yvette. He started home, heading south toward the beach. He'd walk back to his cottage along the coastline, hoping to uncover something along the way.

St. Giovanni and Ryan prodded the twins forward, Benito with a shove to Jeannette's back, and Ryan with a boot to Yvette's backside. The girl turned on him recalcitrantly. "No wonder Mademoiselle Charmaine hates you so much!"

"Silence!" the priest snarled. "No more talking—walk!"

"Where are we going?" she demanded, unintimidated.

"Silence or I'll blow a hole through your sister's head!" Benito threatened.

Yvette did not speak again, her mind feverishly working.

* * *

Charmaine was at George's bedchamber door in all of two minutes, banging on it frantically until it opened.

"What is it?" he asked, panic-stricken.

"Father Benito—my father," she gasped, shaking violently. "They were here! They've taken Yvette and Jeannette!"

"Where? When?"

"Just now! But I don't know where! They warned me not to tell anyone. Benito has a pistol! Oh God, George—what if he kills them?"

George dashed back into the room and swiftly pulled on his boots. "Show me where they were headed," he urged, grabbing his shirt.

Marie was still crying and Mercedes coaxed her from Charmaine's arms.

George took Charmaine by the arm and they ran down the hallway. "Mercedes," he called over his shoulder, "wake up Travis and Joshua!"

The front lawns were deserted. George swore under his breath. "Damn it! I'll kill John for this!"

Charmaine looked up at him in surprise. "John? What do you mean?"

"It was his idea to send your father here."

Belatedly, he realized he should have kept his mouth shut. He lengthened his stride toward the paddock.

"What do you mean *his* idea?" she pressed, rushing after him.

"I'll explain later!"

Though she badgered him, he refused to say more. "Right now, we have to find the girls."

The horses were swiftly saddled and rifles pulled from the stable. They would search the harbor and Benito's cabin first.

"You must be careful," Charmaine enjoined. "If they see you coming, they may very well shoot the girls. They warned me not to tell anyone!"

"We can't just sit here and wait, Charmaine," he stated.

He swung into the saddle and spurred his horse forward, taking the main road toward town. Gerald and three stable hands whipped their own mounts into motion and fell in after him. Minutes later, Joshua, Travis, and Joseph Thornfield reached the lawns and headed north on foot.

Charmaine paced, unable to quell the urge to do something herself. She ordered Bud, the only man who had remained behind, to saddle up Dapple.

"But, Madame," he implored, "you can't go out on your own." Then, realizing he could not dissuade her, Bud did as he was told.

She was soon guiding her horse toward the southern shoreline, the only direction not taken by the search party. Moments later, she heard the clopping of hooves behind her and Bud reached her astride Champion. "I couldn't live with myself if something happened to you, ma'am," he said when their eyes locked.

The unlikely foursome trudged through the underbrush toward the white beaches about three miles away. The strenuous walk became more exerting once their feet hit the sand, and Giovanni and Ryan were panting, laboring under the burden of their plunder. More than once John Ryan wanted to stop, but the priest, tired though he was, pressed on. Jeannette was glad they'd slowed down, hoping someone from the manor was in hot pursuit, but Yvette kept her strides brisk, determined to wear the men out. When Jeannette regarded her, Yvette said not a word, but yanked one braid. Jeannette nodded slightly, acknowledging the signal, then thought of Wade. He was out here somewhere. Perhaps he would come to their rescue before her sister did something rash.

Wade frowned down at the skiff, thinking it curious that any boat was sitting on this particular part of the beach miles from town. No one came this far north to fish, especially with the bondsmen's quarters so close. He walked around the dinghy, noting the footprints and a furrow in the sand that suggested it had recently been dragged from the edge of the forest. Scratching his head, he followed the tracks and discovered a path at the edge of the woods. He continued along, coming upon Father Benito's dormant cabin. Again he scratched his head, wondering if his sister had come here.

By the time Benito and Ryan reached the rowboat, they were perspiring profusely. John Ryan plopped down in the sand, winded. Benito remained vigilant, his pistol drawn, but he released Jeannette to check for his maps.

Coming away from the skiff satisfied, he faced the twins, who stood side-by-side, complacent and maddeningly identical in the moonlight. "Jeannette, come here," he commanded.

Both girls stepped forward, though one eyed the other with a tilt of the head, her baffled expression visible even in the dim light.

Benito chuckled sagaciously. "Do you take me for a fool?" he asked pointedly of the girl staring straight ahead. "Now, I'll ask one more time. Jeannette, come here."

There was a moment of indecisiveness, and finally his suspicions were confirmed. The "confused" twin took another step forward. "I'm Jeannette," she whimpered. "Sorry, Yvette," she added, looking back at her frowning sister.

The priest's smile turned wicked. "Get in," he growled, motioning toward the craft with the gun.

"But I'm afraid of the ocean!" she objected fiercely. "Especially at night!"

"Get in or I'll shoot your sister!"

She hurriedly complied. John Ryan jumped in, too.

"Not you!" Giovanni barked. "Help me get her into the water. We'll set the sail once we're beyond the breakers."

Grumbling, Ryan climbed out, and together, they pushed the skiff into the foaming surf.

"What about me?" Yvette queried anxiously from the shore.

"You'll behave better on the sand!" Benito shot over his shoulder, struggling for a firmer grip on the rowboat as they confronted the first white-capped wave. "Stay put if you want your sister to live!"

Yvette nodded, her worried eyes riveted on Jeannette.

"Sit down!" he ordered Jeannette. "Not there—in the center!"

Jeannette obeyed, eyeing the pistol, watching the priest fumble with the rim of the boat, the gun becoming a hindrance. As the water got deeper and the breakers exceedingly rougher, Benito deposited the firearm onto the first bench, shoving the vessel forward unimpeded now. "Push harder!" he snarled at John Ryan. "One more—" he heaved "—and we're home free!"

As the next wave broke, Jeannette shot to her feet. "Run, Jeannette! Run!" she screamed.

Predictably, Benito and Ryan looked back at the beach, confounded. The girl in the boat instantly snatched the pistol and leveled it on Benito. Though startled, the priest laughed. "So—we didn't take Jeannette, after all. You think you're very clever, don't you, *Yvette?* But now what are you going to do? Shoot me?"

Yvette's frown was met by the next wave, and the two men had all they could do to hold onto the boat. "There's only one bullet in the chamber," Benito growled. "Shoot me and Mr. Ryan will strangle you! Shoot him and I'll strangle you! Now put the pistol down, like a good little girl."

The firearm was heavy. Yvette used both hands to raise it over her head and pull the trigger. The recoil sent her tumbling backward. Swearing viciously, Giovanni pulled himself up and into the vessel. Too late! Yvette flung the gun with all her might out to sea. Seething, he grabbed her by her hair and slapped her hard across the face. Unshaken, she kicked out, catching him in the crotch. He doubled over in agony, a high-pitched yelp rending the air. She smiled triumphantly, grateful for all the refined things she had learned from Joseph.

"Forget about the girl!" Ryan shouted. "Let's get this goddamn boat beyond the breakers! Everyone on the island musta heard that shot!"

Catching his breath, Benito took heed and jumped from the dinghy. With a final heave, they thrust past the surf and climbed in. Giovanni tossed an oar to Ryan, then grabbed one for himself. "Sit!" he commanded Yvette when she made a move to stand, threatening her with his raised paddle.

Pretending contrition and fear, she hunched over and cast hooded eyes to the shore. Jeannette was standing there with her hands to her face, oblivious to the fact that someone was running full speed toward her from the woods, or that two figures on horseback were bearing down on her from the west. As Benito Giovanni and John Ryan sank their oars into the ocean, they saw them, too.

Wade had torn off his boots and stockings. He charged the water at breakneck speed, ripping off his shirt and diving headlong into the breakers.

The priest swore, pumping the oar harder. "Pull, damn it, pull!" he yelled to John Ryan, letting out a pent-up sigh when they reached deeper water.

Suddenly, Yvette stood up and began stripping down to her undergarments.

"Damn it girl!" Giovanni scolded. "Are you daft? Sit!"

"Why don't we throw her overboard?" Ryan demanded, aware the swimmer was closing in on them. "We're havin' to pull her weight, too."

"No—don't!" she cried, trembling. "I don't know how to swim!"

The two men exchanged smiles. Needing no further encouragement, John Ryan jumped up and reached for her. But the skiff dipped sharply to the left, and he quickly forgot her, his attention drawn to his feet, planting them far apart, alarmed when the craft continued to rock.

"Sit down, man!" Giovanni shouted, dropping his oar and splaying his arms wide, then clutching the sides of the careening boat. "Do you want *us* to end up in the water?"

"He's too stupid to figure that out!" Yvette baited.

Furious, Ryan advanced again. "No little girl's gonna sass me like that!"

This time, the boat lurched steeply to the right, its rim plunging under the water's surface for one paralyzing moment, taking on water as it righted itself.

Petrified, the priest screamed, "You'll kill us both! Sit down before we capsize!"

Seizing the moment, Yvette began to bounce from foot to foot, giggling hysterically. The skiff oscillated back and forth, the water within sloshing from side-to-side, the waxing momentum growing more and more precarious.

Benito held on for dear life. "Throw her overboard!" he finally bellowed.

She was ready for John Ryan. When he dove at her, Yvette threw all her weight in the same direction, and the small vessel rolled with them, spilling them into the sea.

Cold water engulfed her, and she held her breath for untold seconds. Finally, she surfaced, gulping in precious air, treading water to stay afloat. Then, she was yanked back under, her foot ensnared. She thrashed violently, but could not loosen the human manacle that dragged her deeper. She bent over, using her hands to pry back the fingers that dug into her flesh, certain her lungs were going to burst.

Suddenly, she was free! Cupping great handfuls of water, she kicked up and out of the tenebrous depths, sputtering and coughing as she surfaced again, her chest on fire. Another second longer, and she'd not have survived.

Wade was there, encouraging her to swim back to shore. She marshaled every aching muscle and swam as hard as John had taught her. But when she reached the breakers, she was too tired to propel herself any farther. The waves curled over her and carried her the rest of the way in, depositing her in ankle-deep water, battered and shivering. Bud and Charmaine rushed forward and helped her to dry ground, where they wrapped her tightly in Charmaine's robe. Wade was not far behind, crawling out on hands and knees.

Within minutes, George and the stable hands reached the shore, searching the sea for the fugitives. The capsized boat bobbed beyond the breakers, but there was no sign of Benito Giovanni or John Ryan.

"They stole gold and jewelry from the house," Yvette said through chattering teeth. "John Ryan tied a sack of coins around his waist. It must have weighed him down. And I don't think Father Benito knew how to swim. He was terrified out there!"

"I don't think my father did, either," Charmaine added, turning away from the horrific scene. "Let's get you home," she whispered, trembling from head to toe.

Jeannette was kneeling beside Wade, who had donned his dry shirt and now sat, heaving on the sand. "Thank you for saving my sister's life!"

The man smiled at her. "Any time."

"I thank you, too," Charmaine added. "If you hadn't been here tonight, I don't know what would have happened to Yvette."

"You should be thanking Johnny!" Yvette exclaimed. "He's the one who taught me how to swim."

"You weren't swimming anywhere with Benito's hands around your ankle," Wade responded.

Yvette cocked her head to one side, suddenly realizing it was Wade who had freed her from the ocean depths. "I'm sorry," she whispered. "Thank you for saving me."

By dawn, they were all sitting around the dining room table reliving the incredible events of that night. George explained John Ryan's arrival on Charmantes and his incarceration with Benito Giovanni. When all was told, Charmaine could not remain angry with her husband, remembering his words the day he had left in search of Blackford: *If you could find your father and make him pay for what he did to your mother, what would you do?* John had known her innermost fears, had understood her desperate desire for justice, and had cared enough to do something about it. Unlike the authorities, he had pursued John Ryan, had sent him to Charmantes to face retribution for his crime, jailing him in secret to spare her any alarm. Neither he nor Paul could have guessed what would happen in their absence.

The sun was rising when the company disbanded. Charmaine invited Wade to stay and wash up at the house, but he refused. He needed to go home in case his sister returned. George offered to help search the island for her, telling Wade to take the day off work. "I'll see to it," George reiterated as Wade departed atop Champion. "By tomorrow, I promise no stone will be left unturned."

According to Mercedes and Loretta, Marie had screamed herself to sleep. Charmaine took the slumbering infant from Loretta's comforting arms and retired. In her peaceful chambers, she knelt down and thanked God nobody in her family had been harmed.

Sunday, December 30, 1838

Rebecca refused to speak to Paul. When he ventured into the cabin, she would turn away. She didn't eat the food he brought her, either, and at night, he lay on the bunk alone, wondering in the morning where she had slept, or if she had slept at all. He decided if she wanted to sulk, that was fine by him. After all, he hadn't pursued her—she had pursued him. And he had given her ample opportunity to leave his cabin that night. Even so, he was angry he dwelled on her predicament—that she was ever in his thoughts.

On the last night of their voyage, he found her asleep when he entered the cubicle, concluding she slept during the day when he wasn't there. He put the tray of food he carried down on the table. Tonight, he would force-feed her if necessary. She hadn't touched a morsel in four days. If this continued, she would make herself ill.

"Rebecca," he called, nudging her awake.

She rubbed her eyes, befuddled at first as to where she was.

"I've brought you dinner," he said gently. "You need to eat."

She sat up, watching him warily. She swung her legs over the edge of the bunk, his shirt and her men's trousers still in place.

Paul made light conversation, hoping the sleep had improved her mood. "It's quite good, actually. About the best meal I've tasted aboard this ship." He'd been stirring some soup, which he now carried over to the bed.

When she realized he meant to feed her, she turned her head aside.

"Rebecca," he said sharply, "you must eat something! You can't go on like this." Her clenched jaw began to quiver. "Please try it," he insisted, no longer cross.

She jumped from the cot and retreated to a corner of the room, taking her misery with her. When he approached, her back stiffened. "Leave me alone!" she moaned. "Why won't you leave me alone?"

At his wit's end, he brusquely deposited the bowl on the table, the soup sloshing over the edges. "Suit yourself," he stated irascibly. "Starve and see if I care."

"I know you won't," she said, but he had already stormed from the cabin.

Hours later, the food remained as he'd left it. He shook his head. She was stubborn, he had to give her that, and determined to make him feel guilty.

Monday, December 31, 1838

New York City came into view with the dawning of the sixth day. The *Tempest* made port in four hours' time, the delay caused by an icy Hudson River and the tremendous snowstorm suffered by a vast stretch of the Atlantic seaboard three weeks earlier.

As she docked, Paul returned to the cabin one last time. He threw on his cape, for the air was frigid, much colder than it had been two years ago. He caught Rebecca's intense eyes upon him, but she swiftly looked away. He hesitated. Her manner hadn't changed, yet something about her disturbed him this morning, something he couldn't quite place.

"I'll return by dark," he said. "I don't want you leaving the cabin. Do you hear me?" Unlike the past five days, she acknowledged him with a slight nod. Suddenly, he knew.

He left the cubicle and closed the door behind him, retrieving the key hanging above the doorframe. He locked the portal, the "click" sounding within the cell. Rebecca flew to the door, yanking on the knob. She banged on it with both fists, her escape plan neatly foiled. "Let me out!" she screamed.

For the first time in nearly a week, Paul felt satisfied. "You stay put!" he shouted back. With a smug smile, he disembarked, his destination John's row house on Sixth Avenue, the address George had given him.

As he left the wharf, he marveled once again at the throngs of people, the endless buildings, the noise, the very magnitude of this booming city. In the two years since he'd commissioned the building of his ships, the city had grown. Tonight, it was blanketed in white, a light snow falling atop the mountainous heaps already obstructing the roadway.

He hailed a cab, calling the address up to the driver who sat shivering beneath a thin overcoat and frayed lap-blanket, collar drawn up and cap pulled down low, breathing heavily into the hands he occasionally rubbed together to keep warm. Paul, a mite more protected from the elements, settled back in the seat of the enclosed carriage, taking in the sights, the smells, and the sounds. Still, his mind was far away, wondering what he would find.

John's house was locked tight. It was New Year's Eve, and Paul found some Greenwich Village residents at home. However, all of John's immediate neighbors had little information to offer. They hardly knew John except to say a passing "good day" when he was in town. One woman told him about the unprecedented event in early December when the New York City police had breached and then searched John's residence, questioning neighbors for the next two days, tight-lipped the entire time, offering not one reason why they were there.

Although relieved, Paul was confused; most of their inquiries had involved John's possible whereabouts and any family he had residing in the city. He began to wonder if his brother and father were on the run.

When he left Sixth Avenue, he headed for the shipping offices at the busy seaport. He was back at the New York harbor by mid-afternoon. The warehouse ledgers carried the names of other prominent New York shippers, and he combed over them, hoping to find the name of someone who might have offered John a place to stay. The clerks were brusque and lent little aid. By late afternoon, he decided to call it a day. Perhaps he'd have better luck tomorrow and locate somebody who could help him.

He hailed another cab and asked to be taken to a fashionable shopping district. For Rebecca, he picked out a lovely dress in pale green—it would match her captivating eyes—as well as undergarments, a nightgown, and plush robe. For himself, he bought a heavy redingote, a hat, and gloves. He'd been freezing all day in the bone-chilling cold. At least he'd be warm when he began his hunt tomorrow.

Darkness had already fallen by the time he boarded the *Tempest*. Though his day had proven unsuccessful, his evening did not. He found Captain Conklin talking to one Roger Dewint, John's New York shipping agent. Roger hadn't recognized the *Tempest*, but he had noticed the Duvoisin standard flying high on her mast and stopped by to introduce himself. Dewint had no news about John or Frederic; he did have a list of men who worked for John when his ships laid anchor in New York. Most were freed slaves. He agreed to meet Paul on the merchantman early the next morning, and together, they would make the rounds, locating as many of these men as possible. Finally, Paul was getting somewhere.

It was quiet when he unlocked the cabin door. For a moment,

he held his breath, wondering if Rebecca had figured another way to escape. But she was there, sitting in the dark on the bunk, wrapped in a blanket. He closed the door, pocketing the key. He deposited his bundle on the stool and lit the lantern.

There was a knock on the door, and he stepped in front of Rebecca as the porter dragged in a large tub. "I'll be back with the water, sir," he said.

After he'd left, Paul turned the lamp down low, obscuring Rebecca in the shadows. She eyed him suspiciously, but held silent.

The porter returned numerous times, and slowly, the tub was filled with steaming water. He left soap, a cloth, and a towel before retreating altogether.

Paul faced her with arms crossed over his chest. "You're taking a bath. Now, you can either bathe yourself, or I will do it for you. You have a half hour to decide." She didn't move. "Very well," he said as he grabbed hold of the door, "but remember, when I return, the water will be cold. The clothes I promised you are in that package—" he indicated the bundle "—if you change your mind."

Certain he'd carry out his threat, Rebecca undressed and settled into the tub as soon as he left. The cubicle had been mercilessly cold all day, and she relished the piping-hot water, closing her eyes and resting her neck against the tub's rim. After a while, she washed clean all the reminders of the days gone by. When tears welled in her eyes, she dunked her head under and washed her hair.

In less than a half hour, she left the tub, shivering, wrapping the towel quickly around her. She fingered the package on the stool, and against her own will, opened it. Inside, she found a gorgeous dress, accompanied by various undergarments and stockings. There was also a nightgown and robe, which she chose to wear now.

When Paul returned, he found her garbed in the thick robe. She looked lovely, her damp hair framing her beautiful, yet drawn, face.

He carried a tray of food. "Will you eat something now?" he asked, surprised when she meekly nodded.

There was a knock on the door, and she melted into the shadows.

Paul told the porter he wasn't finished with the tub yet and would keep it until the morning. "I'd like to bathe, too," he explained when the door closed.

They sat at the table and ate quietly. Although she consumed only a small portion of the fare, at least it was something. Setting his knife and fork down, Paul studied her. "Why did you intend to run away today?"

She stopped chewing and stared down at her plate.

"Don't you realize how cruel a big city such as New York can be? Am I so horrible you won't let me take you back to Charmantes?"

She could scarcely swallow for the burning lump in her throat. When she looked at him, her green eyes sparkled. "I don't want to shame my brother," she whispered. "He will know what has happened when I return. Better he doesn't know. Better if I just disappear."

She blinked back tears, and Paul experienced her pain. Embarrassed, she left the table and turned her back to him. "I've grown up these past few days," she rasped, "and I don't think I like being a woman."

Paul fought the consuming desire to take her in his arms and kiss her, to carry her to the bunk and make tender love to her, to prove her wrong. But his mind screamed: *Charmaine—remember your pledge to Charmaine.*

He drew a deep breath to calm himself. "Rebecca, no one need ever know what happened between us," he said evenly. "If all goes well tomorrow, I may have my father and brother with me when I return. If so, this cabin will be yours alone. I will tell everyone I found you in the hold, that you wanted to see the New York City sights, but now I'm bringing you home to your brother. I'll spend the remainder of the trip in the common quarters with the crew, and no one will question me."

It was not what she longed to hear. He seemed certain he was going to find his brother alive. Charmaine would have her husband back, and he would no longer be bound by his promise. Still, he made no pledge to her, not a single word of encouragement. She meant nothing more to him than a tawdry encounter that had claimed her virginity. She was like Felicia: out of sight, out of mind. In fact, she meant less to him than Felicia, for Felicia had shared his bed many times, and she, only once. He showed no desire to make love to her again. He *did* think she was a little girl. She'd best accept that or her heart would break, and she would not allow him that final triumph.

He waited for her to face him again, surprised and relieved to see she was smiling. She appeared pleased with his plan, and he breathed a bit easier. Perhaps everything would work out for the best.

Later, while he bathed, Rebecca studied him surreptitiously from the shadows. Even though he'd rejected her, she yearned for him still and battled the urge to offer herself to him. She remembered his rough hands, his impassioned kisses, and her eyes stung with tears. She had all she could do to hold tight to her spot on the bunk. When he rose from the tub, she turned away. He was lost to her. She *was* a little girl—a foolish little girl, with big, foolish dreams.

New Year's Day, 1839

Early the next morning, Paul left the ship, telling Philip Conklin he'd been down in the hold and discovered a stowaway, a young girl charmed by the notion of living in the big city. "Her brother will be distressed," he explained, "so I've locked her in my cabin until we leave port."

The captain raised a dubious brow, but said not a word. The hold had been unloaded the day before, and none of his crew had spotted her.

Paul found Roger Dewint waiting for him on the quay. Together, they walked along the many piers in the harbor, stopping from time to time to engage somebody in conversation.

By noon, Paul got lucky. Samuel Waters worked for John, had in fact, arrived in New York aboard a Duvoisin vessel. He was a runaway slave. It took quite a bit of coaxing, but Samuel capitulated, telling Paul he knew a Rose Forrester, whose sister was a good friend of John's. He gave Paul their address.

Chapter 9

Sunday, January 13, 1839
Charmantes

CHARMAINE woke with a start. Had Marie cried out? The infant's tiniest squeak could bring her out of the deepest slumber. She rolled over and peered into the cradle. Marie was still sleeping.

Paul had been gone for nearly three weeks, and Charmaine had counted the days, his journey ever on her mind. She had traveled to town every morning for the past week. Today would be no different. As before, the girls and the Harringtons insisted on accompanying her.

She visited the chapel before departing. Without a priest, she hadn't attended Holy Mass for over four months, but she found solace in the serene sanctuary and petitioned the Almighty to bring her husband home to her. She had not missed a day in her novena, nor would she until her prayers were answered.

Just before ten, they were on their way. Because it was Sunday, nearly everyone was strolling along the main thoroughfare, greeting neighbors and enjoying the cool breezes that would not last much longer. They did a bit of shopping and went to Dulcie's for lunch, but Charmaine ate very little.

Loretta looked at the food on her plate. "Charmaine," she chided lightly, "you haven't touched your meal."

"I've no appetite," Charmaine replied.

"But you must eat," Loretta proceeded, "for your daughter's sake. Starving yourself with worry will never do."

Charmaine had heard the lecture before and was grateful when Yvette interrupted. "Can we go down to the wharf after this?"

Charmaine nodded. "I'd like that."

Marie, who'd been content for hours, began to fuss. "Please, finish eating," she said as she stood with her baby. "I'll be back once I've fed Marie."

Loretta nodded, and Charmaine left them in pursuit of the carriage that was parked in the livery. Once there, she rearranged the cushions within the brougham, drew the curtains, and began nursing her daughter.

Marie's mouth opened wide, and Charmaine smiled down at the infant, watching her pursed lips working the nipple, stopping only to swallow. The tiny eyes rolled heavenward, satiated, her delicate eyelids, already fringed with dark lashes, closing slowly. Charmaine basked in the moment, as she did each time the child suckled at her breast. "My little Marie Elizabeth," she breathed. "What will this month bring for us?"

Is John still alive? Or would she be forced to face Paul's marriage proposal? Charmaine struggled to suppress the thought. But today, it was so vivid she could not ignore it. Would she wed Paul? Probably. Not so much for herself, but for her daughter and for him. She knew he was suffering, realized now how poignantly he loved her. Yes, if she were forced to recover from another loss, she would consider marrying him.

She was still staring into the distance when the carriage door was yanked open. "What goes on in here?" A toothless man peered in, tobacco-tainted saliva drooling from the side of his mouth. He wiped it away with the back of his grimy hand.

Horrified, Charmaine quickly drew her bodice together. "Sir! This is my carriage!"

He squinted at her. "Are you the new Mrs. Duvoisin?"

"Yes, I am. Who are you?"

"Martin St. George," he replied, dark spittle spraying in all directions.

The name triggered an ancient memory. "Martin, the farrier?"

"That's me. And what are you doin' in this coach all the way back here?" Oblivious to the baby she held, his eyes darted about, as if he'd find her lover hidden in the corner.

Suddenly she was laughing, laughing as she hadn't laughed in a very long time, laughing so hard she shook. *I mistook John for this man the night we met. Impossible!*

Marie squeaked in her sleep, and Charmaine subdued her mirth.

"What's so funny?" the noisome hostler demanded.

Charmaine sighed, wiping away happy tears. "Nothing, nothing at all!"

He shook his head, spat into the hay, and walked away.

She giggled again and then, making herself presentable, climbed out of the carriage, the slumbering Marie clasped firmly to her breast.

Loretta and Joshua had just stepped out of Dulcie's with the girls when she returned. Together, they strolled toward the harbor.

A shout went up, and Charmaine's heart leapt into her throat, missing a beat when beyond the peninsula, on the open sea, she caught sight of a ship's sails, bellied out. Pray God it was a Duvoisin vessel! Pray God it was from New York! Pray God it was Paul bringing John home!

Pedestrians migrated to the wharf, and soon there was a throng of onlookers. They stepped aside when they saw Charmaine and the twins, sensing the importance of the merchantman wearing into the mouth of the cove. Joshua led them to an unobstructed spot, where they waited for what seemed an eternity. Eventually, the vessel entered the inlet, and someone shouted, "It's the *Tempest*!" as it closed the distance to the quay. Charmaine's trembling hand flew to her mouth. She'd have her answer today.

"Look, Mademoiselle," Jeannette exclaimed, "it's Wade!" The man had drawn up alongside them, but Charmaine's eyes never wavered from the ship.

"May I hold Marie?" Jeannette asked, wanting to show off the babe.

Charmaine surrendered her daughter without a thought, and Jeannette giggled when Marie objected with a squeak and a squirm.

The *Tempest* grew in size and majesty, sailors now visible fore and aft, making ready to moor the one-hundred-fifty-foot vessel, some high on the forecastle deck, others on the quarterdeck, many climbing the ratlines to reef the sails, all immensely busy. When Yvette made a move to run ahead, Joshua grasped her shoulder, urging her to stay put. Charmaine didn't recognize anyone on board, and she brought folded hands to her lips, uttering a swift Hail Mary.

Loretta patted her arm. "God's will be done, Charmaine."

Charmaine inhaled, praying she could accept her cross and go on.

A scrape of wood on wood, a great groan, and the ship settled into place. Ropes were thrown overboard, and the longshoremen scrambled to loop and tie them to the pilings. Finally, the gangplank was lowered, and in consternation, Charmaine recognized Father Michael Andrews, lending an arm to Frederic as they stepped forward to disembark.

"Papa!" Jeannette cried exuberantly and hurried to him with Marie in her arms, welcoming his embrace as he stepped onto the stable quay.

Charmaine's eyes flew back to the deck above, but there was no sign of John or Paul. She looked at Frederic again and read sorrow in his eyes, even though he smiled her way. Her heart froze. *He hasn't come back with John! He's come back with a priest—my family's priest!* She had her answer. *He's brought Father Michael here to comfort me.*

Gulping back a violent sob, she turned away and buried her face in Joshua's shirtfront. As his arm encircled her, she caved in to her grief.

Yvette's squeal sliced through the hum of the crowd. "Johnny! It's Johnny!"

Charmaine pivoted around, the name reverberating, sundering her every emotion. Miraculously, she beheld her husband hobbling down the gangplank, supported by Paul, who clutched his arm. He was there—thin, his face pale and drawn—but really there! Although his expression was pained, his eyes lit up when he saw her. Incredulous, she stood rooted to the spot, the entire boardwalk strangely hushed. Behind her she heard Loretta ask, "Is that John?" When he reached the pier, he smiled his familiar, crooked smile. "Will you have this prodigal husband back, my Charm?"

All her anxiety evaporated, and she ran to him. He pulled free of Paul and stepped forward. She fell into his open arms, his name on her lips. Tears of joy replaced those still moist on her cheeks, and she felt his arms quicken, his face buried in her hair, his embrace so fierce she could scarcely breathe. Then his head lifted, and his hand spanned her face, thumbs stroking her cheeks to wipe her tears away, his fingers cupping her head. He leaned forward to kiss her, and she wrapped her arms around his neck, meeting his lips in impassioned fervor. There they stood in broad daylight, unconcerned about friends and family, the ship's crew, or the multitude watching them.

Frederic's heart swelled, Michael's throat contracted, and Loretta and Joshua hugged each other, each in exaltation. Charmaine uttered John's name over and over again as she caressed his face and ran her fingers through his hair, categorizing his every feature, as if to confirm she was not dreaming.

John held her at arm's length, perusing her from head to toe. "Well?" he queried. "Where is she?"

Although Charmaine frowned, Jeannette stepped forward, offering up the small bundle she lovingly held. "Here she is, Johnny. Here's little Marie."

John tenderly took his daughter into his arms, looking down at her in awe, chuckling softly when she wiggled, yawned, and cooed in contentment. "She's beautiful," he whispered hoarsely, his gaze meeting Charmaine's. "You did an exceptional job, my Charm."

"We both did," she replied.

She was suddenly aware of the many onlookers around her. John's regard shifted to Michael, and Charmaine wondered why he was there. She noted the significant look that passed between them, and her eyes narrowed.

John smiled innocently. "What?" he asked.

"I know something is brewing," Charmaine supplied. When John shrugged sheepishly, she said, "Are you going to tell me what it is?"

His crooked smile deepened, dimples visible now. "What do you mean?"

"Never mind," she said, dismissing him with a wave of the hand. She'd find out sooner or later. She found Michael Andrews studying her intently. She couldn't begin to guess what he was thinking.

Mostly, he was pleased to know his daughter could read her husband so well. The couple obviously liked each other as much as they loved each other. God had smiled down upon their union.

"So, Father Michael," she said, stepping over to him and clasping his hand, "what has brought you all the way to Charmantes?"

"John, actually," he answered simply. "I've known him for five years. He's a close friend."

Charmaine's astonishment made John laugh. "You see, Charmaine," he said, "I'm not in league with the devil as you once believed."

She rolled her eyes and turned back to the priest.

"John has been a generous benefactor to the St. Jude Refuge," Michael expounded.

Charmaine's expression grew incredulous. "My husband? The man who doesn't believe in God?"

"But I do believe in good people and good causes, my Charm."

Frederic interrupted the exchange. "Come, John," he prodded

with concern, "you've been on your feet long enough. It is time we get you home."

Charmaine was amazed by the man's display of affection.

"He was gravely ill, Charmaine," he explained, "and is still recovering from a serious injury. He's been advised not to exert himself."

"I'm fine, Charmaine," John reassured, seeing the worry on her face. "The worst is over, but Father is right. I would like to sit down."

She nodded and took Marie from his arms. The babe slept on.

"Did you get him, Johnny?" Yvette asked. "Did you kill Dr. Blackford?"

The wharf fell silent until Frederic spoke. "He's dead, Yvette." Deciding it was best to get the story out and over with, he added, "When he attacked your brother with a knife, I shot and killed him. He's no longer a threat to our family."

"Good!" Yvette exclaimed.

Paul offered to arrange transportation from the livery, but as he turned to leave, Charmaine grabbed his arm, holding him there a moment longer. A hint of a smile reached his eyes, and she could see he was happy for her.

"Thank you," she whispered hoarsely, "for everything."

His smile grew dynamic. "You're welcome. Now—no more tears!"

Rebecca tore her burning eyes from Paul and Charmaine, hurried down the gangplank, and headed home. Since the afternoon John and Frederic had boarded the ship, Paul hadn't said two words to her. Now she knew why. It didn't matter if John was dead or alive. He would always love Charmaine. She must forget him.

The Duvoisins ambled down the pier toward the road. Charmaine had completely forgotten about Loretta and Joshua, but found them smiling at her. She went to them with John's arm looped through hers and Michael Andrews flanking him on the right.

"John, this is Loretta and Joshua Harrington," she stated proudly, "Mr. and Mrs. Harrington, this is my husband."

"Ah, yes," John grinned devilishly, "Joshua—the Prophet. I'm sorry I didn't remember you in Richmond, but you weren't wearing your robes—"

"John!" Charmaine admonished, her eyes shooting from Joshua to Father Michael, who was snickering behind a raised hand. "I've told the Harringtons you're not as incorrigible as they've heard. Must you prove me wrong?"

"Actually, I'm worse," John replied. Catching her frown, he turned serious. "No, my Charm, I'd never do that." He took Joshua's hand. "Thank you for bringing your wife to Charmantes and looking after Charmaine in my absence." He turned to Loretta and gave her his most charming smile. "Mrs. Harrington."

"Pleased to meet you," Loretta nodded dubiously before speaking to Charmaine. "Let me take Marie so you can help your husband to the carriage."

The twins accompanied their father, bantering effervescently. "Papa," Jeannette exclaimed, "you don't have your cane!"

"I lost it somewhere along the way," he commented, his arms encircling their shoulders. "But I don't think I need it any longer. Not with the two of you to lean on and all the excitement behind us."

"You and Johnny are not the only ones with exciting news!" Yvette cut in. "Wait until you hear what happened to us!"

"Let me help John into the carriage. After that, you'll have my ear all the way home."

The brougham came to a standstill at the end of the wharf. John waved off the hands that offered help and, with some difficulty, pulled himself up and in. He exhaled with a grimace, which he tried to conceal by asking to hold Marie. Charmaine obliged. Then she and Michael climbed aboard, she settling next to John and Michael sitting opposite them.

As the coach pulled away, she grabbed hold of John's arm and hugged it, her eyes devouring every line of his face. He was studying his sleeping daughter again, marveling over her delicate features.

Michael's heart once again expanded with gladness as he watched them, the interior of the vehicle bathed in a very tangible love.

"I'm dreaming," she whispered, drawing John's eyes from Marie. "I know I'm dreaming."

"No, my Charm," he smiled, "I'm really here."

"But I had a premonition—the night Marie was born—that you had died!"

He put his arm around her and pulled her close. "I did die," he whispered. "But your mother sent me back to you."

She gaped at him. *"My mother?"*

"Yes." John nodded, regarding his slumbering daughter again. "Your mother, Marie . . . She was my savior long before I met you, my Charm. Only I didn't learn she was your mother until last August. *She* was the one who helped me through that terrible time before and after Pierre's birth, and *she* introduced me to Michael."

"Sweet Lord!" Charmaine gasped, goose bumps rising on her flesh.

"What is it?"

"It was *you*," she whispered. "My mother once told me, 'the greater the wealth, the deeper the pain.' I didn't understand what she meant, had no idea of whom she was speaking. But after Pierre's death, her presence was so strong. I felt her there beside me in the chapel. And then the next day, during the funeral, those words kept coming back to me. For days they went through my mind. Now I'm certain she was talking about you, John—you and your pain!"

John remembered telling Marie his father's fortune had ruined his life, firmly believing Colette had forfeited their love for it. He looked from his wife to Michael. "It appears she brought us together, Charmaine." He shook his head with the weight of it. "If I had known of your mother's life with John Ryan, I swear I would have put a stop to it. But she never burdened me with her troubles. She was only concerned for mine. I didn't even know her surname or that she had died. I was in New York when it happened. And I certainly didn't make the connection between you, John Ryan, or her." When he spoke again, there was anger in his voice. "I promise you now, Charmaine, he will be punished."

She took a deep breath. "You don't have to worry about that."

The remark shook him. He knew from Paul that Ryan had been incarcerated on Charmantes in early December. "What has happened?" he asked in dismay.

She related the story of Benito St. Giovanni and John Ryan's escape. More than once, John swore under his breath, his scowl deepening as he contemplated the danger in which Charmaine, his daughter, and the twins had been placed. But the finale brought a twinkle to his eye, and he couldn't resist saying, "Good thing I taught Yvette how to swim."

"That's exactly what Yvette said," Charmaine replied, "but my father could have killed her." She bowed her head. "The Good Lord's mercy spared her."

"He wasn't your father, Charmaine," he said, perceiving her guilt and knowing it was time to bury the lie. "You mustn't blame yourself."

She looked up in surprise. "How do you know that?"

John was equally astonished. Obviously, she knew a portion of the truth. *But how?*

"Charmaine," Michael whispered softly, cautiously, "I'm your father."

Charmaine's expression bordered on the mortified, but John squeezed her hand, encouraging her to listen compassionately.

"I loved your mother deeply," Michael affirmed, clearing his throat. "I didn't know she was carrying my child, Charmaine. I didn't know the truth about you until nine months ago."

His confession came hard.

"She just left one day. When she returned to St. Jude, you were already a little girl. I thought you were John Ryan's little girl." He pulled a letter from his pocket and offered it to her. "It's from your mother."

Charmaine took it, studied the neat, familiar handwriting on the envelope.

"Marie gave it to John years before she died," Michael continued.

"She asked me to pass it on to Michael should anything happen to her," John interjected. "But I didn't learn about her death until this past spring."

"Even then," the priest continued, "John didn't make the connection between you and Marie because I never mentioned your name. I went to the Harringtons the week of Paul's celebration. That is when I found out where you were—when I realized John must know you. But it wasn't until he came to me for information on your island priest that all the pieces of the puzzle fell into place."

There was a long silence, Charmaine speechless, John and Michael giving her time to absorb the incredible story.

"I loved her, Charmaine," he reverently proclaimed, "and I would have left the priesthood if I had known she was with child. But she didn't want me to do that, and she guarded her secret until she wrote that." He nodded toward the letter Charmaine still held in her hands. "She sacrificed her own happiness for me . . ."

Michael lowered his head, and Charmaine knew he was fighting back tears. She reached across the carriage and took his hand. "All these years, I believed my mother never knew a moment of happiness. I'm glad to discover I was wrong—you loved her dearly. I know she loved you."

He looked up, his eyes sparkling, and no further words were necessary. Hands clasped, they basked in the miraculous revelation they were family.

The baby stirred and John gazed down at the wriggling infant. "Would you like to hold your granddaughter?" he asked.

When Michael nodded, Charmaine scooped Marie from John's lap and passed the little bundle to him. He snuggled her in the crook of his arm and his tears fell freely. Charmaine grasped John's arm with both hands and laid her head against his shoulder. She closed her eyes in a prayer of thanksgiving, certain she would be weeping tears of joy for many days to come.

They were nearly home when Marie began to cry, refusing even the comfort of her mother's arms. "She's hungry," Charmaine explained, and then more softly for John's ears, "She fell asleep before she had her fill and needs to be nursed."

He tilted his head and whispered, "Can I watch?"

She blushed scarlet, her eyes flying to her father, hoping he had not heard. He was only smiling tenderly at her, and she turned to John, pleased to find that wonderful, familiar deviltry dancing in his eyes.

"If you'd like," she answered sweetly, that lopsided smile now dominating his handsome face, his brow raised in astonishment over her bold response.

As the carriage rolled through the front gates, Michael sat in awe of the majestic mansion and its grounds. The coach drew up to the portico steps. Charmaine placed the fidgeting Marie in John's arms and alighted, holding up a hand to wave off any assistance. Marie started wailing immediately, but Charmaine was there to take her back.

George emerged from the house, laughing heartily when he caught sight of John climbing from the carriage. "How are you, weary traveler?" he called, rushing forward and eyeing Michael who had also alighted.

"A bit frayed around the edges," John chuckled, "but no worse for wear." He introduced George to Michael.

"Did you get the bastard?"

"My father did," John answered somberly.

The other coaches had also arrived, and their passengers spilled out, flooding the cobblestone drive, a clamoring crowd of family and friends.

Charmaine's voice rose above the others as she issued a spate of orders to the servants who appeared at the doorway. "Travis, please take Father Michael's luggage up to one of the guest rooms. Joseph, could you summon Dr. Hastings? Tell him I'd like him to check on John. Millie, would you take Marie and change her, then bring her to my bedroom. Cookie, could you brew a pot of coffee and prepare us a nice spread of food? Mrs. Faraday . . ."

A great hush blanketed the terrace, save Charmaine's authoritative voice.

"I told you," Paul said to Frederic and John, "she's in charge now."

Charmaine swung round to face them. "And you—" she pointed to John "—up to bed!"

"I'm ready whenever you are, my Charm."

George chortled, but Charmaine shook her head, choosing to ignore the ribald comment. "George, Father Michael, would you help him manage the stairs?"

In no time, John was in his room. She pulled down the coverlet of their bed. John winced as he sat and slowly drew his legs up and onto it. Suddenly, she was aware of the great effort he had exerted at the quay, remembering the pained expression he'd attempted to camouflage when he'd climbed into the carriage. "Now will you tell me what happened?"

"Blackford stabbed me in the side," he grunted, releasing the breath of air he'd held. "My father got there just in time to keep him from doing worse."

"I knew it!" she said, concern giving way to anger. "You *were* in danger!"

"It's over now, Charmaine. Don't be angry with me."

"Why didn't you write?"

"I *did* write—at least three or four letters."

"I only received one—from Richmond!"

"I wrote twice from New York."

His face contorted as he readjusted himself on the pillows, and her ire flagged. “Lie still,” she admonished, brushing the hair from his forehead and dabbing away beads of perspiration.

When she’d finished, he grasped her hand and drew it to his mouth, kissing it tenderly. “I missed you, Charmaine. I promise I’ll never leave you again.”

“You’d best remember that,” she warned, “because I intend to hold you to it.”

With a soft rap on the open door, Millie brought in the wailing Marie. “Thank you, Millie,” Charmaine said. “Please, close the door on your way out.”

John looked on in amusement as his wife reclined alongside him and unbuttoned her blouse, offering the greedy infant a large pink nipple. He drew an uneven breath, the quickening in his loins oblivious to his injury. His hungry eyes consumed every inch of her. “It might be a while before I can make love to you, my Charm,” he whispered, “but I long to do so right now.”

“I yearn for you, too,” she murmured, leaning over her daughter to steal a kiss from him. His hand cupped the back of her head, and he held her lips to his for a few moments longer.

When Marie was asleep and swaddled comfortably in her cradle, Charmaine turned back to the bed. John had fallen asleep as well, and she shook her head, alarmed by his weakened constitution. Rest was what he needed.

She closed the door quietly behind her, wondering if Joseph had returned with the doctor yet. Voices drew her to the dining room. She found all of her loved ones at the table: Joshua and Loretta, George and Mercedes, Rose, Yvette, and Jeannette, Michael, Paul, and Frederic. Her eyes met Frederic’s. He rose, and she went to him, wrapping her arms around him, laying her cheek against his chest.

“Thank you for bringing him home to me—alive.”

Frederic closed his eyes. “We have God to thank,” he murmured, “and the people who love my son. I didn’t realize how many they were.”

* * *

Marie was wailing, waking John with a start. He sat up in bed and looked into the bassinet. The babe was squirming, her face beet-red. He lifted her to his shoulder and rocked her gently, to no avail. His eyes traveled to the door, wondering why Charmaine hadn't yet appeared.

Loretta heard Marie crying from the staircase. She'd left the large company in the drawing room, where Charmaine was entertaining the family. When the pulsating protests did not abate, she quickly went to the bedchamber and knocked. There was no answer, so she opened the door and stepped in to pacify the babe before she woke her convalescing father.

She found John sitting at the edge of the bed with Marie in his arms. He turned at the sound of her entrance, and his face dropped. "Not the milkmaid yet, Marie," he soothed.

Loretta smiled and went to him. Marie was wriggling fiercely, working her way down his chest in search of a nipple.

"She was on my shoulder a moment ago," he commented helplessly.

"She's looking for her mama's bosom," Loretta supplied delicately.

"Well, she's at the wrong address."

Loretta chuckled. "Here, let me take her. She could be wet or soiled." She lifted Marie from his arms, put a nose to her bottom, and sniffed.

John frowned. "Any other way to check?"

Loretta smiled again as she hastened toward the changing table in the adjoining chamber. "She needs her nappy changed."

John followed her. Loretta laid the babe on the soft table. Marie immediately stopped crying. "She knows where she is," John mused.

"They learn quickly," Loretta replied, as she worked at the diaper pins.

Loretta changed Marie adeptly. Lifting her off the table, she offered her, clean and happy, to John. He took her into his arms. "You're quite good at that," he said.

"I've had a lot of experience—five boys."

"How long do babies stay in those?" he asked, nodding toward the diapers.

"About two years, or a bit longer. It depends on the child."

"You know, we don't have any plans for that room you're staying in. Are you sure you want to leave? Free room and board for two years, or a bit longer, depending . . ."

"I would love to stay, but Joshua is anxious to get back to Virginia, and I miss my sons and grandchildren." She eyed John pensively. "I trust you are back for good, Mr. Duvoisin?"

"Yes, I am, Mrs. Harrington. I had a score that needed to be settled. It has been, and I'm not going anywhere now."

Somewhat satisfied, Loretta pressed on. "Charmaine is the daughter I never had, Mr. Duvoisin. I want her to be happy. I love her, you know."

"Not as much as I do, Mrs. Harrington."

Loretta nodded, reassured by the declaration and his apparent sincerity.

"If Charmaine is your daughter, that makes me your son-in-law," John continued. "So why don't you call me John? That is, if your husband will have it. I believe he has some other names for me."

Loretta laughed heartily; this man was quick and quite irreverent. No wonder her mild-mannered husband didn't like him. "Very well. As long as you call me Loretta."

Rebecca closed the door to the cottage and leaned back into it. She was home, but it offered no security. She closed her eyes for a moment, hoping the spinning room would settle, certain the floorboards below her feet rocked like the ship. When the wave of nausea ebbed, she headed listlessly toward her bedroom. She would remove her beautiful dress and never wear it again.

The door banged open behind her, causing her to jump, and Wade strode into the room, eyes furious, jaw set. He slammed the door behind him, and Rebecca flinched. "Where the hell have you been?" he growled.

There was no point in lying. "On board the *Tempest*," she whispered.

He swore under his breath, eyes raking her from head to toe. "You little slut!" he blazed, satisfied by the pain he read on her face. But she raised her chin a notch, and he struck out again. "Are you his mistress now?" When she frowned in confusion, he pressed on in disgust. "Those fine clothes must have bought a great deal."

She looked down at the lovely gown, blinking back tears. Without a word, she walked toward her bedroom.

Wade charged across the kitchen and blocked her path, swatting away her hand as she reached for the doorknob. "Damn it, Rebecca! Answer me! How could you have done this to me—to yourself? That's what we ran from—why we stowed away! We've built a new life here. How will we face our friends now? Doesn't that matter to you?" When still she refused to respond, he ran his hands through his hair. "It matters to me!"

"I'm glad they're more important to you than I am!" she sobbed. Unable to bear his abuse any longer, she shoved him out of her way and pushed into her room. Slamming the door shut, she fell facedown on her bed and wept.

Paul entered his bedchamber and breathed a sigh of relief. It had been an exhausting three weeks, and he was glad to be back home, in his own room and in his own bed. But as he sat down to pull off his boots and unbutton his shirt, he felt forlorn, the empty room, desolate. Tired as he was, he pushed off the bed and walked out onto the balcony.

Rebecca Remmen, what are you doing tonight?

He hadn't seen her slip off the *Tempest*. Then again, he'd been preoccupied with helping his brother and making the arrangements to get everyone home. During the nine-day voyage from New York to Charmantes he had guarded his silence, speaking very little to her to bolster his stowaway story and protect her honor, even though he had tarnished it. Everyone on the ship had accepted his explanation, seemed to believe him, though John had raised a dubious brow.

Paul wondered over his own deception. When he feared his brother was dead, he'd had a reason to pretend disinterest in Rebecca, but now he was free to court her. So why hadn't he done so? There was nothing stopping him from bringing her home to his bed tonight. His heart thundered in his ears as he relived the heady memory of her naked in his arms, inexperienced, yet meeting his ardor with uninhibited carnal zeal.

But Rebecca wanted more than his bed. She wanted to be his wife, wanted his love. Was marriage to her so intolerable? No, he realized without trepidation. He would savor making love to her each night, would be content to claim that right. He had thought of little else the last eighteen days—since the night of their unbridled union. Never had a woman obsessed him so, not even Charmaine. Even if Rebecca ignored him, he would enjoy having her here if only to look at her. He admired her stubbornness, and he burned to tame her. But mostly, he longed to hold her, to comfort her, to make her happy.

Tomorrow, he would visit her, just to see her again, to be intoxicated. Finally, he was able to settle into bed, and after a while, sleep.

Diabolical dreams beset him, fragmented visions of Rebecca running frantically through a sinister forest with hooded fiends close on her heels, dogs barking and tracking her down. She was crying, calling for him, and his heart raced. He awoke in a cold sweat and jumped up.

The consuming need to know she was all right spurred him to action. In less than ten minutes, he was dressed and in the stable saddling a confused Alabaster. He thanked the gods the night sky was clear and the moon bright. It was nearly one o'clock in the morning when he rode down the deserted dirt road and stopped in front of the Remmen cottage. A soft glow spilled out of the kitchen window. Someone was still awake. He tied Alabaster to the picket fence, strode up to the small porch, and rapped on the door.

Wade was drunk and scowled darkly at him. "What the hell do you want?"

"May I come in?"

"No," he growled, his words slurred, "you may not come in!"

"I would like to see Rebecca," Paul pressed.

Wade's wicked laugh ended in a hiccup. "Of course you would," he sneered sarcastically, astounded by the man's imperious gall. "She's only seventeen years old! If you think I'm going to stand back while you satisfy your lust on her, you'd better think twice! You just try to step into this house—you just try to touch her—and I swear I'll break your goddamn neck!"

"You're drunk," Paul said softly, disheartened Rebecca had told her brother about them.

"You're damned right I'm drunk!" he cried. "How do you think I felt this afternoon when my sister stepped off that ship, dressed in the most elegant gown a rich man's money could buy? What do you think everyone else was thinking? She disappeared for three weeks, and suddenly, she's back? They all know she's a whore now—*your whore!*"

Paul's blood boiled, but he knew Wade was right. Many were at the landing stage today; surely they had come to the same conclusion. And the dress! Paul had only longed to make her happy. Now he realized he'd unconsciously wanted everyone to know she belonged to him, the gown an emblem of his desire. But in so doing, he had exposed her to public censure, Wade a harbinger of the castigation yet to come. Fleetingly, he thought of Yvette and Jeannette, and what his reaction would be under similar circumstances. *I'd throttle the bastard!*

"I want to speak with Rebecca," he insisted.

"And I told you to go to hell!" Wade snarled.

Paul's mind was made up, and he easily pushed his way into the cottage.

Wade went after him with a vengeance, and before Paul knew what had hit him, they lay sprawled on the floor. Then the shock was gone, and Paul grabbed Wade's shirtfront, rolling over and pinning him down. "Now, listen to me," he growled. "I *will* speak with your sister. Whatever you think about her, you're wrong, and I'll hear no more of it, do you understand? I love her, and I'm going to marry her. *That's* why I'm here."

Paul pushed up and off the floor, then extended a hand to Wade, whose anger had turned to confusion. "Marriage . . . ?" he murmured, making no move to rise. "But you can't—I mean, you don't—"

The strange response ended there, as apparently he fought off the effects of his inebriation. He grabbed hold of Paul's proffered hand and stood. "I'll get Rebecca," he said soberly.

Paul's relief was momentary, for the bedroom was empty, the green dress spread reverently across her bed. He drove a hand through his hair, gripped with worry. To where had she flown now? Her grief had been great, and certainly, Wade had made it worse. *I don't want to shame my brother. Better I just disappear.* Well, Paul wouldn't let her disappear. He'd find her—tonight!

"Do you have any idea where she might have gone?" he asked.

"No," Wade whispered, suddenly ashamed, cringing with the memory of how he had treated her. "I said some rotten things this afternoon."

"We have to find her."

"Felicia!" Wade suggested. "Next-door. She might know."

Paul hastened to the house, rousing all within with a heavy fist on the door. Felicia's gruff father opened it, capitulating grudgingly when it was clear Paul would not leave without speaking to his daughter. Felicia was standing before them moments later.

"Where is Rebecca?" Paul demanded.

Her sleepy eyes turned shrewd, and suddenly, she was smiling. "I saw that beautiful gown," she replied sweetly. "But Rebecca said she wasn't going to be bought and paid for—even by you."

"What else did she say?" he pressed through clenched teeth.

"Just that she's moving on—to a new life," Felicia answered smugly. "I tried to warn her about you, but she wouldn't listen. She kept saying she was going to marry you. Some girls have to learn the hard way. Anyway, now she knows better."

"Really?" Paul scoffed. "Well, Felicia, if you happen to see Rebecca, tell her I intend to marry her."

He didn't wait for a reaction, but clamped an arm around Wade's shoulders and led him back to his cottage. "I know where to look. Stay here and sleep it off. Meet me at the mansion first thing in the morning. I'll be there—with Rebecca."

Wade began to object, but Paul countered with: "I need to speak to Rebecca—alone. Now, please, go to bed." Without further ado, he headed toward the *Tempest* and the cabin they had shared.

Moonlight spilled through the porthole, illuminating the cubicle. Rebecca was sound asleep in the bunk, her raven-black hair fanned across the pillow. An ineffable happiness seized him. If he hadn't come tonight, she would have been gone in the morning, lost to him, perhaps forever. Why had he been so foolish? Why hadn't he wed her on the ship? There had been a priest at his disposal to see the vows exchanged and the union blessed. He had vacillated again, but no more. This might be the worst mistake of his life—or the very best beginning. For Rebecca, he was willing to take that chance.

Sitting gently on the edge of the bed, he took her hand in his, and brushed the hair from her face. She stirred, and her eyes fluttered open. She stared up at him for a moment, dazed. He smiled down at her and could tell she thought she was dreaming.

"I've come to take you home," he said softly. "To *my* home."

She pulled her hand away and rubbed her eyes. Her brow gathered and she pushed herself onto her elbows. "What are you doing here?"

"I couldn't sleep, Rebecca. I was worried about you, so I went to your house. Your brother did not put me at ease."

"He hates me now," she murmured, her head bobbing forward. "I knew he would."

"He doesn't hate you."

"He's ashamed of me. He has a right to be ashamed."

"No, Rebecca," Paul refuted, gently gripping her chin and persuading her to look at him, "he doesn't have that right. And after tomorrow, no one will dare insult you. If they do, they will have to answer to me."

She was bewildered, but he stood and extended a hand to her, inviting her up and out of the cot. "Come," he said. "Let's get you home."

"No!" she said. "I want to go far away from this place."

"Come," he insisted. "This is your home—here, on Charmantes, with me."

"I won't be your mistress!"

"I'm not asking you to be my mistress, Rebecca," he declared. "I'm asking you to be my wife."

Her green eyes swiftly filled with tears, but then she was shaking her head "no." "I don't want to marry you now."

Nonplussed, he felt as if the air had been knocked out of him. "Why?" he managed to utter. "Why not?"

She gulped back her agony. "I want you to love *me*. I couldn't live knowing you wished I were Charmaine. You've only come because she's lost to you."

"No, Rebecca, that's not true. I swear it is not true."

"Isn't it?"

"Rebecca, since I made love to you, I haven't been able to think straight. At first, I was confused. I was worried over my brother and Charmaine. What happened between us was so exquisite it frightened me. Even after I knew John was alive, it frightened me. But tonight, when I was alone in my bed, I realized how unhappy I was. Not because I had lost Charmaine, but because I had lost you—*you*, Rebecca. You're the one I want."

He bent forward and kissed her, a slow, tender kiss that deepened in intensity. Her hands found their way to his shoulders, and she pulled herself up and into his embrace. Abruptly, he drew back. "Now, will you marry me?"

"Yes, oh yes!" she sobbed, pulling him close and kissing him ardently.

His resolve to wait until they were back at the mansion crumbled, and in seconds, they were stripping off their clothes and making fierce love. When they had finished, he enfolded her in his arms. She nuzzled against him and sighed in quintessential happiness. He could feel the moisture of her tears on his chest, and he relished an unprecedented sense of contentment.

Monday, January 14, 1839

They woke to the caterwaul of seagulls and the sun's light.

"We'd better get up," he urged, "or Captain Conklin will be setting sail again with us aboard."

Rebecca smiled up at him. "What made you change your mind about me?"

"I never changed my mind," he said honestly. "I think I loved you from that very first night."

"But you called me a little girl then."

"You're not a little girl, Rebecca. You're all woman—my woman." He kissed her passionately, then sighed. "I've had many women, but not one has ever made me feel the way you have, and no woman has ever loved me the way you do. I'd be a fool to throw that away, wouldn't I?"

Her arms encircled his waist, and she rested her cheek against his chest. "I've loved you—for such a very long time."

He kissed the top of her head, squeezed her tightly, and then stood to dress. She followed suit, pulling on her breeches and shirt. Paul chuckled.

"I told Wade to meet me at the manor this morning," he said. "We'd best hurry if we're to get there ahead of him."

Rebecca puzzled over the remark, but didn't question him about it.

They left the ship to find an agitated Alabaster waiting for them, hooves pawing the dirt at the end of the pier, ears flicked back. Paul quickly untied the stallion and patted his neck in apology. He mounted, reaching down for her. Rebecca hesitated, but he grabbed her arm.

"Everyone will be looking at us!" she objected, holding back.

"Let them look!" He laughed.

His words touched her heart. She pulled up behind him, wrapped her arms around his waist, and pressed her cheek against his back, certain she would awaken at any moment.

John and George stepped off the last stair of the landing when Paul and Rebecca walked through the doors. One look at their disheveled appearance, Rebecca's outlandish garb, and John chuckled knowingly. "What have the two of you been enjoying—a nature walk?"

Rebecca bowed her head, but Paul put an arm around her shoulders and pulled her close. "Where is Michael?"

John's grin grew wider. "Has my brother come to his senses?"

"Steady, John!" George warned, despite Paul's confident smile.

"That's right, John, I have. Rebecca and I are going to be married—this morning, if possible."

"Well, then, Paulie, congratulations are in order." John extended his hand in a gesture of genuine goodwill, even as he was thinking: *You should have married her on the ship last week, you horny bastard!*

The morning was spent making all the arrangements. Rebecca was closeted in one of the guestrooms, where Millie helped her bathe and dress in the wedding gown Mercedes had kindly offered. Though the fit wasn't perfect, a few hasty alterations made the garment more than acceptable. Paul also bathed, donning the suit he had worn for the ball. Father Michael prepared the chapel for its first Mass in nearly five months.

At precisely noon, Rebecca Remmen grasped her brother's arm and walked down the short aisle of the chapel. Jeannette blushed as they passed by her pew and Wade smiled down at her. She looked up at her father, hugged his arm, and giggled softly when he winked at her. Paul stood tall at the altar, ready to receive his bride. Wade handed her over, and the couple stepped before Michael.

Frederic looked on with pride, thankful Rebecca had become Paul's obsession. During the voyage home, it had been obvious Paul was smitten with the girl, keeping her at arm's length, as if she'd swallow him whole if he came too close. Though everyone wondered what had happened between them, Frederic didn't have to guess. He read the hunger in his son's eyes, knew the feeling all too well, even the circumstances. Paul's desire for Rebecca mirrored his fierce love for Elizabeth. God had been very good to his family.

After the ceremony, Paul led his beautiful wife to the archway, where they received heartfelt congratulations. Wade was the last to embrace his sister. Paul noted the guilt in his eyes. Or was it something more? Apprehension? But Rebecca hugged him close, too happy to hold a grudge. When he smiled shamefaced at Paul, Paul clapped him on the back, letting bygones be bygones.

Michael rearranged the altar, placing the chalice and ciborium off to one side in preparation for the other two marriage ceremonies he would perform later that day. It could be months before they ascertained the legitimacy of Benito St. Giovanni's priesthood, and Michael planned on returning to Richmond very soon. He'd been away from the refuge and church far too long already. John and Charmaine, as well as George and Mercedes wanted to be certain God sanctified their unions, so Michael gladly accepted their invitation to preside over the reaffirming nuptials.

Fatima Henderson whipped up an afternoon fete, and family and friends gathered on the porch and lawn to celebrate Paul and

Rebecca's wedding in the mild, winter breezes. Overseeing all the details, Charmaine eventually headed to her chambers to nurse Marie and check on John. As she reached the portico, she espied Paul and Rebecca alone for the first time that day and changed direction.

"Congratulations," she said when she reached them. Looking pointedly at Rebecca, she added, "welcome to our family. You've made Paul and the entire family very happy today."

Rebecca was amazed by Charmaine's genuine warmth, and she nodded slightly.

"I'm glad you made the voyage in search of John," Charmaine said to Paul. "We both benefited from it."

Paul responded with a dashing smile, pleased she had attempted to put Rebecca at ease. "Thank you, Charmaine," he said simply, though Charmaine read much more in the depths of his green eyes. They had journeyed a long way together, and she treasured the unique bond they would always share.

Wade joined them, followed immediately by Frederic. "Mr. Remmen," Frederic declared, "my daughter insists I thank you for saving her sister's life."

Wade coughed uncomfortably. "It was nothing, sir."

Frederic refuted the modest denial. "Charmaine has confirmed the entire story. I am forever in your debt."

Wade rubbed the back of his neck self-consciously, and Rebecca smiled, intensely proud of her brother. "Wade is bashful about compliments, sir."

"Be that as it may," Frederic continued, "I am grateful and will, from this day forward, consider Wade a member of this family."

"Thank you, sir," Wade replied, taking Frederic's hand and shaking it heartily, a smile breaking across his face.

Charmaine shooed John into the dressing room so she could complete her toilette alone. "It's my wedding day, and you mustn't see the bride until she enters the church."

"All right, all right," he laughed as she gave him a final shove through the doorway. "I know when I'm not wanted."

An hour later, she descended the great staircase, wearing the gown she'd donned the evening of Paul's ball, her hair cascading down her back. Today, as she walked down the aisle on Joshua's arm, she looked more spectacular than on that wondrous night nine months ago. Motherhood agreed with her, her figure curvaceous to a fault, her ample bosom straining against the décolletage of her bodice. She was radiant and took John's breath away. When she reached him, she gave him a brilliant smile before turning her eyes to her father, whose happiness mirrored her own.

Family and friends looked on, overjoyed to share in their second, more profound wedding ceremony. The chapel echoed with sniffles and sighs, and to the congregation's amusement, Marie shrieked now and then, adding her own two cents to the proceedings.

As the Mass neared a close, Michael asked for the rings. Charmaine watched quizzically as John searched his pockets for the simple wedding band he'd shown her earlier in the day. It had belonged to his mother. When her smile turned to a frown, he whispered, "Not to worry, my Charm, I know it's here somewhere." He finally dug it out of his waistcoat pocket and presented it to her—the largest, most brilliant diamond ring she had ever beheld. Her eyes grew nearly as wide as the stone itself, and out of the corner of her eye, she could see her father smiling broadly at her. A murmur shook the chapel as John lifted her left hand and slipped the beautiful stone on her finger.

"With this ring, I thee wed," he pronounced solemnly.

She stared at the fiery diamond a moment longer, felt the weight of it. She looked up into John's happy eyes, the delight born of her astonishment sparkling there.

It was her turn. She slipped off the plain, loose band she'd worn around her index finger and reached for his hand. "With this ring, I thee wed," she choked out, as she pushed the ring over his finger, tears evident in her voice.

When she was composed, Michael proclaimed, "You may kiss the bride!"

John pulled her into his arms and brushed his lips across hers. Then he buried his face in her wild locks and savored the fresh scent of her.

She hugged him close. "I can't wear this ring, John Duvoisin!" she murmured heatedly near his ear. "It is huge and very heavy!"

"Then I will have to find another young lady who will," he whispered back, squeezing her the harder. "I love you, Mrs. Duvoisin. That ring is only a small token of my love and affection."

"I love you, too!" she averred.

Someone coughed, and Charmaine realized they had prolonged their embrace beyond the realm of decorum. She broke away, but John kept a possessive arm around her shoulder, and together they received the congratulations of all those in the chapel.

She was conscious of the ring all day, its size alone making it impossible to ignore, and her fingers rotated it continuously. At dinner, John caught her studying it, her fingers splayed upon the linen tablecloth. "Do you like it?" he asked.

"No," she breathed, looking at him beseechingly, "I love it. But it wasn't necessary, John. All I'll ever want is you. You know that, don't you?"

"Yes, I know that, my Charm." He nodded toward it. "Read the inscription."

She hadn't thought to look inside the band. She removed it and read the writing there. Once again, her eyes filled with tears. "I'll always be your charm, as long as you'll have me."

"Forever," he whispered. "I'll have you forever."

He grasped her hand and brought it to his mouth, his titillating kiss sending wisps of pleasure up her arm. He read the look of longing in her eyes. "Later, my Charm," he promised, setting her heart to a rapid beat. "Later . . ."

* * *

Having cleared the altar of the final wedding feast, Michael headed to the dining room for dinner, crossing through the ballroom and into the foyer. For the first time since his arrival yesterday, all was quiet there, and he stopped for a moment to study the portrait of Colette Duvoisin, the painting that had given him pause the moment he had first stepped into the mansion yesterday.

So this was the woman who had started it all, her pulchritude unrivaled, precisely as John had told him. He was so deep in thought he didn't hear Frederic's approach until the older man was standing beside him.

"She was very beautiful," Michael said.

"Yes," Frederic replied. "In a few more years, my daughters will look exactly like her, especially Yvette."

This surprised Michael. Frederic smiled now. "Personality plays a great part in one's looks. Yvette is more like her mother than her sister will ever be. Colette was full of fire and very vocal about her beliefs and crusades. She would have approved of your work, Michael."

Before Michael could ask him what he meant, footfalls echoed from the hallway. Frederic turned slightly to regard John.

Michael considered both men. The mending kinship was fragile and, he feared, easily broken.

Frederic's eyes returned to the magnificent portrait. "I think I shall have the canvas taken down," he commented.

"No, Father," John breathed, "don't remove it. I feel secure knowing Colette is watching over us."

The remarkable declaration intensified in the sudden silence. Frederic broke the aura. "I'm afraid I've forgotten something in the chapel," he murmured and walked away.

John watched his father disappear through the archway, staring after him pensively.

Michael permitted John his faraway thoughts. "Shall we go in to dinner?" he finally asked.

"You go ahead," John replied, never looking at him. "I'll be there in a minute."

The light of the joyous day was waning, and in the chapel, the shadows lengthened. The stone enclosure was cool, and Frederic lit the candles on the altar. He edged into the front pew and knelt. Burying his face in his hands, he offered a prayer of thanksgiving. His prayers had been answered. When his Maker called him home now, he could go to Him in peace—clear of conscience. He had done everything within his mortal power to atone for his many mistakes and sins.

He lost himself in the quiet sanctuary, the consuming peace here, and opened his heart and soul, inviting Elizabeth's and Colette's guiding presence.

A hand came down on his shoulder, and his eyes lifted to John, standing behind him. He watched in surprise as his son settled next to him. They sat for many minutes without speaking.

"Thank you," John murmured, fighting the moment's reticence.

Frederic turned to find his son's earnest eyes locked on him.

"I would be dead if you hadn't been there for me." John sighed deeply. "When you had the seizure, I left you for dead. I didn't care if you lived or died. I *wanted* you to die. After everything I did to you, you could have—*should have*—left me for dead, too. I didn't deserve to have you stay by my side."

Frederic looked back at the altar, struggling for words. "Thirty years ago, I abandoned you, John. Even though you were innocent and vulnerable, I abandoned you." He swallowed hard. "I was there in New York because I love you, John. No matter what you had done to me, I wasn't about to abandon you again."

Another lengthy silence took hold.

"I saw Pierre that night, Father," John whispered. "I saw my mother, and I saw Colette. I was with them." He looked at Frederic again. "They are in a peaceful place. Mother wants you to know she loves you still. And Colette . . . she loves you, too."

Frederic turned tear-filled eyes to the altar. "I loved her, John," he rasped.

"I know you did, Father. I know you did."

Frederic could say no more.

John rose and placed a comforting hand on his shoulder, held it there for a moment, then turned and left.

The dinner table was voluble and animated, filled to capacity. Only the head and foot of the table remained vacant. John eventually joined them, followed a few minutes later by Frederic. Each in his turn smiled at Charmaine, and she wondered where they had been. Now all twelve chairs were occupied. John and Frederic were quickly drawn into various conversations, often talking across the great expanse to each other. Charmaine sat back, overwhelmed by the wholesome banter of a loving family.

How many dinners she had passed in her parents' home on tenterhooks, fearing her father? Even when she lived with the Harringtons, she had always yearned for a family of her own. Here it was before her now: a boundless feast. Her mother's presence was strong, and she bowed her head in renewed thanksgiving. At long last, peace and love reigned under this roof.

When the table was cleared, everyone migrated to the drawing room. Even John, who had rested again after their wedding ceremony, insisted on joining them. As additional chairs were pulled from the study, Michael sat on the piano bench near John.

"This pianoforte is similar to the one you have in New York," the priest commented.

"It's identical," John said. "I purchased both from the Bridgeland and Jardine Company when they were first introduced five years ago. Perhaps you've heard of them?"

When Michael shook his head "no," John continued. "The sound of this particular piano is powerful and brilliant. The manner in which it is strung heightens that quality, making it a far superior instrument to the pianofortes manufactured a decade ago. I was quite taken by the demonstration they gave and, once I'd played it myself, immediately ordered four."

"Four?" Michael queried. "You purchased *four*?"

John chuckled. "One for New York, one for Richmond, the other for the plantation, and the fourth for here. It was quite a feat to secure it on the ship. But it did make for an interesting welcome when I arrived here. I thought my sisters would enjoy learning to play, and thanks to Charmaine, they have."

Frederic joined the conversation. "John is quite an accomplished pianist himself. It was the one thing at which he excelled when I sent him to university."

"I've heard him play," Michael remarked, unmindful of John's snicker. "Unfortunately, I've always interrupted him."

"Well, then," Frederic said, "perhaps he'll perform something for all of us now. That is, if you feel well enough?" He regarded his son, his eyes filled with pride.

Yvette and Jeannette moved closer and took up the petition, "Yes, Johnny, please! You used to play for us all the time. We'd love to hear something now."

"What would you have me play?"

"Anything!"

"Something special!"

"Why not play the piece you composed?" Frederic suggested.

John's eyes turned turbulent, and he looked to Charmaine. She was chatting with the Harringtons.

"I . . . I don't think I could," he hesitated.

Frederic read his misgivings. "It would please me to hear it, John."

John scratched the back of his neck, then acquiesced. Frederic and Michael found vacant chairs. Yvette sat in her father's lap. Jeannette grabbed Paul and Rebecca's hands and pulled them into the gathering, then settled next to Frederic, who patted her head as John began to play.

The opening chord echoed, and all banter ceased, eyes turning to the man at the piano. His fingers traveled the familiar path across the keys, resurrecting the melancholy rhapsody. Pouring out his life and soul, John played, arpeggios rising in a frenzied fugue, turbulent and discontent, effete and hopeless, surrendering at last to a tender, tumbling cadence of bittersweet yearning. Then a sweet, new melody rose from the despair, a delicate strain that wed the somber with the bright, the harmonious threads amplifying in a reverberating crescendo. Then it ended: a triumphant, solitary chord.

Someone started clapping. John raised his head and turned slowly around. His eyes traveled to Charmaine, who sat spellbound. He winked at her. It had been accomplished; he'd found the resolution to his composition.

"Johnny," Yvette broke in, "I didn't know you wrote that!"

Charmaine was astounded. *John . . . of course, John had composed the piece!* Why hadn't she guessed it? But more important, when was she going to realize he would never cease to amaze her?

"You didn't know your brother was so talented, did you?" Frederic asked his daughter.

"Yes, I did!" Yvette countered, eliciting everyone's laughter.

The merriment died down, but Frederic remained pensive. He hugged Yvette and Jeannette close, giving each a tender kiss atop their heads. He could feel Colette's presence close by and savored the poignant moment.

John stood and crossed the room, drawing Charmaine out of her chair. She, too, was thinking about Colette. *I hope you were listening, my dear friend.* A distant memory answered: *Perhaps your touch is exactly what the piece needs . . . bend the masterpiece . . . possess it, as it has possessed you . . . then, when your love is the music, the harmony will be perfect.* Colette had been speaking of John. Colette knew; somehow, she knew!

Looping her arm through John's, Charmaine allowed him to lead her from the room. They strolled along the front terrace, where it was cool and quiet. When they were opposite the ballroom, they stopped, and John leaned back against the balustrade. Charmaine stepped into his embrace.

"That was beautiful," she murmured.

"You've made it so, my Charm," he answered, studying every inch of her face, stroking her cheek with his hand. He pulled her against him and kissed her tenderly. "I love you, Charmaine, more than you'll ever know."

Rebecca trembled as Paul led her into his suite of rooms, closing the door quietly behind them. The day had been overwhelming. Now here she was with him, on her wedding night. She felt giddy and intoxicated, but mostly frightened. The grandeur and sophistication she'd experienced today were a world apart from her servile background, all of it quite intimidating. As the day had progressed, she began to question her foolhardy belief that she could ever live up to the role she had coveted for the past three years. She turned to face her husband, anxiety written on her face.

"What is this?" Paul queried with a chuckle. "You're not suddenly afraid of me? This isn't the wench who scarred me for life, is it?" He rolled up his shirtsleeve, extending his wrist toward her so she might see the bite mark she'd left there three weeks ago.

"I could never be afraid of you. But this house—" she indicated the lavish room "—and your family—who they are—all the things they know and own and can do! I was stupid to think I could fit in—that I was old enough to fit in. I don't even know how to read and write!"

She began to cry and Paul felt a painful twinge in his breast, his love for her fierce and daunting. He went to her and pulled her into his embrace. "Rebecca . . . Rebecca . . ." he murmured into her hair. "You have made me so happy! You're honest and strong and proud. You're not afraid to stand up for yourself."

Her cheek was pressed to his chest, and as he chuckled again, she found comfort in the deep rumble beneath her ear.

"You've plagued me, Mrs. Duvoisin: my thoughts by day and my dreams at night! Now, don't tell me you don't belong here with me. You're as much a Duvoisin as anyone else in this family."

"But we hardly know each other. There are things—"

"No buts."

He held her at arm's length, studying her intently. "You want to learn to read and write? Then you'll learn. Anything you want to do—just tell me, and it will be done. Do you understand?"

"Yes. I think so."

"Good," he said, and his smile turned wicked. "Now, I don't want to hear any more of this nonsense or I'll be forced to put you across my knee and give you something to cry about!"

"You wouldn't dare!" she taunted, her heart suddenly pounding, her cheeks flushed in anticipation of his lovemaking.

Paul savored undressing her, and she, him. He carried her into his bedchamber and set her down on the mattress, making love to her throughout the night. By dawn, they were spent.

"You will soon be carrying my child, Rebecca, if every night is like this," he said huskily.

She smiled down at her flat belly and stroked it. "I think I already am," she murmured shyly, grateful he had pursued her last night, his resolution that they wed putting to rest her brother's volcanic protestations.

Paul's hand quickly covered hers, his dark fingers spreading across her tawny flesh. "I thought as much," he replied, his ardor inflamed with the knowledge their first passionate encounter had made them a part of each other. His hand moved down from her tummy and stroked between her legs. When a guttural groan escaped her lips, he rolled on top of her and took her again.

John lay with Charmaine asleep in his arms, pondering the miracle that had brought him home. He remembered and relived that surreal place—that place in the light where his mother, Pierre, and Colette had embraced him. In his mind's eye, he was there once again in paradise, holding his lost family in his arms—his son and the woman who should have been his wife.

Death . . . So simple a solution.

"John," Colette breathed when he relaxed his embrace. "How is your father?"

The peace that enveloped him was shaken. "My father?"

"He is crying. He is praying for you. He doesn't want you to die."

"Why do we have to talk about him, when *I'm* here with you? Now I can take care of you."

"You did take care of me," she whispered. "Agatha and Robert—they have chosen to go to that other place . . ."

"And we can finally be together," John stated vehemently, "with our son."

"We are not meant to be together," she dolefully replied. "That is not our destiny. Frederic is part of me, John. I belong to him, and he belongs to me." She brought his hand to her lips and kissed it tenderly, tempering the blow. "You must go back and reconcile with him."

"I don't understand . . . ?"

"He never meant to hurt you, John. He loves you. Don't you hear how he weeps for you?" Her melancholy eyes bore into him, and he could hear his father crying. "Charmaine has abundant love to give—to my children—to you. She needs you as much as your father needs me. You've known that for a long time, haven't you?"

The blues and blonds melted into mellow browns, and his mother was smiling up at him once again. Pierre was no longer in his arms, but nestled at her side. Behind him, John heard a baby cry. "You don't belong here, John," she affirmed. "Go back. Go back to your father and tell him I love him. Tell him *you* love him. Go back to your beautiful new daughter, and go back to Charmaine. She loves you so . . ."

The baby cried again. His father was talking to him, begging God's mercy, and John could feel the man's deep sorrow, his Gethsemane. He yearned to comfort him, take away the agony. His breast ached, and he drew a deep breath to ease the pain. He longed to hold Charmaine. If he could just get back to his father, he knew he would hold her again.

John turned away from the light. Then he was back on the ceiling of the room. His father was still there, bent over the bed. A priest was mumbling prayers; it was Michael. John looked back at the light, but it was quickly fading away. His gaze shifted, and he saw a woman at the foot of his bed. She looked so much like Charmaine. It was Marie, and she was smiling and beckoning to him. John reached for her. He had too much to live for. He'd fight to live.

He was no longer on the ceiling. He was sleeping, and for a few moments longer, he reveled in oblivion, at peace knowing his son was safe and happy in his mother's care. When his eyes fluttered open, he saw relief and joy wash over his father's face. Frederic grasped his hand even tighter, and John was comforted by the contact. "Father," he groaned before closing his eyes again, content he'd chosen life over death . . .

Thinking back on that incredible experience now, with his beautiful wife asleep in his embrace and his newborn daughter slumbering in the cradle beside their bed, John realized a miracle *had* brought him home. Elizabeth, Colette, and even Marie had sent him back to Charmaine. But he couldn't tell her that. Not that she wouldn't believe him, but she didn't want to hear about Colette. He would never allow Colette to come between them again. Colette said she belonged to his father, and he was willing to accept that. It didn't matter anymore; it was over; it was finally over. With a sigh, John hugged Charmaine tightly and closed his eyes. A resplendent serenity settled over him, bathing him in hopefulness.

Epilogue

Friday, March 8, 1839
Accomplished

THE day dawned bright and glorious, but today they would be leaving, leaving Charmantes to travel to Richmond and on to New York City. Charmaine attempted to combat another onslaught of sentimentality. John came up behind her, reading her thoughts as she took the last of the clothing from her dresser drawers. "Don't be sad, my Charm. We won't stay away forever." She turned in his arms and kissed him. When he had gone, she finished packing.

Colette's letter was not where she had left it, though John's shirts were still there, and she wondered if he now carried it with him. Did he realize it had been moved, possibly read? She was going to ask him about it, tell him she had found it, almost read it. Someday, she decided, but not today. Today was sad enough.

He had been home almost two months now and, by all signs, fully recovered. The mild weather of March was upon them and, over the last few weeks, they had spent many happy moments together. Her father and the Harringtons had returned to Virginia in late January, and she was looking forward to seeing them soon. Why then was she downtrodden? Charmantes. *This* was her home, would always be her home.

She no longer wore the fiery diamond on her finger, choosing

Elizabeth's wedding band instead. The spectacular ring was suspended on a long gold chain Frederic had presented to her as a wedding gift and rested under her clothing, near her heart. "I'll wear it on my finger for special occasions," she had promised John. "But for now, I feel it's safer here," and her hand had gone to her breast.

"I'm certain it is," he had responded devilishly. "However, that diamond will be on your finger when we arrive in Richmond. I want those gossipmongers to *really* have something to wag their tongues about!"

"John!"

"You can't tell me you're not looking forward to seeing them turn green with envy when you flash that ring their way . . . Admit it, Charmaine!"

Unable to deny it, she had blushed, making John chuckle.

At breakfast, Frederic's countenance was melancholy. Mercedes was also pensive, cradling her newborn son in her lap. George ate heartily, but said little. Sniffles carried from behind the kitchen door. Only the girls were bubbly, excited to be traveling abroad with their brother, out into that other world they'd heard so much about. Charmaine was certain if they were not coming along, the room would erupt into tears.

Marie began to fidget, but before Charmaine could get up, Frederic went to the bassinet. With her nod, he returned to the table with his granddaughter, holding her on his lap. "You're to bring her back," he enjoined.

"I will," Charmaine vowed, but Frederic's eyes were fixed on John.

"Don't worry, Father," John appeased. "Charmaine won't allow us to stay away for very long. We'll return by fall."

"The fall?" Yvette protested. "We want to go to New York and see snow! Why would we want to come back here in the fall when it's usually rainy anyway?"

John gave her a lopsided smile. "It doesn't normally snow until

January or February in New York, Yvette. We can always venture there in winter. And perhaps Father will come with us then."

"No," the man stated. "I've had enough of New York to last me a lifetime."

"And we can't be away when Rebecca's baby arrives," Jeannette interjected.

"Rebecca's baby, huh!" Yvette reproved. "Wade is the only reason you want to come back. You are hoping to see more of him once the baby is born." Jeannette smiled with the thought of it, but Yvette bristled in disgust. "I think New York and snow are far more interesting than him!"

Rose shook her wizened head. "We won't be seeing much of anybody if Rebecca and Paul decide to make a home of Espoir, and I am getting too old to travel all the way there and wait on that little bundle's arrival."

John nodded. "To think, in a few more years, there will be a new generation running around Charmantes, instigating mischief and mayhem."

"I don't know, John," George countered. "You have a daughter, not a son. It won't be the same as the three of us."

"Thank heavens!" Rose replied.

"You never know," John said devilishly. "Marie could grow as unruly as Yvette. Everyone knows she's worse than the three of us combined!"

The room roared with laughter, and though Yvette objected, her eyes twinkled loftily.

Shortly afterward, they departed in three carriages filled to capacity, waving goodbye to Mercedes and Rose, who stayed behind.

The town was busy, with two ships moored in the harbor. Paul descended the gangplank of the smaller vessel. "I arrived in time," he said, taking in the entire company as they alighted from the carriages. "I wanted to say goodbye."

With immense pride, Frederic watched his two sons exchange

handshakes. "Take care of yourself, John. And don't stay away too long."

"I won't be allowed to," John replied. "And don't you work too hard, either, Paulie. Save some energy for that lovely wife of yours."

"I get more rest when I go to work," Paul rejoined rakishly.

He turned to Charmaine in time to note the blush that spread across her cheeks. His eyes fell to her slumbering baby, cradled in her arms. "By the time you get back, we might have one of our own to show off," he said affectionately.

"We hope to return before your baby arrives," she replied, smiling up at him.

He stepped closer and embraced her, placing a gentle kiss on her cheek. "Take care, Charmaine. We'll miss you."

"Come on, come on!" Yvette insisted. "You act as if you'll never see each other again. I want to get going!"

"Just a moment longer, Yvette," John cajoled. "Why don't you and your sister scoot up the gangplank and find your cabin?"

Yvette scrambled away, but Jeannette turned to her father with tears in her eyes. She hugged him tightly and whispered, "I'm going to miss you, Papa."

"And I, you, princess," he answered hoarsely. "But you will have a wonderful time and come back to Charmantes with many stories to tell me."

Before her tears spilled over, she turned to Paul and gave him a quick kiss, too. Then she hurriedly boarded the ship in pursuit of her sister.

John watched his father, realizing just how empty the manor would be with almost everyone away. "So, Paul," he said, hoping to dispel what could quickly turn into a maudlin farewell, "you came to see us off, did you?"

"Actually, no," Paul chuckled. "Rebecca is still in the cabin. We've decided to move back here, at least until the baby is born. None of the servants want to stay in the house, anyway. They maintain it is haunted."

"And what do you say?" John asked, piqued by his brother's uncomfortable laugh.

"I'm more comfortable at home. No one cooks like Fatima, not even Rebecca. And she is lonely there. Her friends are on Charmantes, and Mercedes is at the house."

George agreed, knowing his wife missed Rebecca and would grow lonely with Charmaine away. Rebecca and Mercedes had struck up a friendship, and Mercedes had begun to teach Rebecca how to read and write.

"Well, then," John breathed, "I guess it's time we were on our way." He looked to his father and extended his hand.

Frederic seized it and pulled John into his embrace. "I'll miss you, son. Don't stay away for too long."

"I won't, Father," John answered, grabbing hold of his father before stepping back. "Don't let the tobacco wilt while I'm gone."

Inhaling deeply, Frederic chuckled and nodded.

With a happy heart, Charmaine embraced the man next. "Thank you—for everything," she whispered, but Frederic held her at arm's length and looked at her quizzically as if to say he should be thanking her.

"Take care of my granddaughter."

"I secured the cradle to the cabin floor," George told John, "so Marie should be comfortable during the voyage."

John clapped his friend on the back, put his arm around his wife, and together, they embarked. When the last of the luggage had been loaded, the girls joined them at the rail, waving goodbye. The gangplank was raised, and the ship pushed from the pier. The first sails were released and instantly snapped in the wind, the lofty gales taking hold and pulling each canvas taut. The girls scampered off again, but Charmaine and John remained starboard side, watching as Frederic, Paul, and George turned away, heading for a typical day of grueling labor. Additional sails were unfurled, and the packet began to pick up speed, easily propelled through the inlet.

Charmaine looked up at John, who'd turned Marie in his arms

so she could see everything around her, her back propped against his chest. She could hold her head up now and was alert, her large brown eyes riveted first on the gulls that squawked and darted in and out of the rigging, then on the aquamarine water.

Charmaine hugged John's arm and sighed. He had convalesced quickly, strong once again, thanks to rejuvenating rest and Fatima's good cooking.

"Don't be unhappy," he coaxed.

"I'm not," she said. "Now that the departure is behind me, I'm looking forward to seeing your homes in Virginia and New York.

"*Our* homes," he corrected.

As they forged into the open sea, the winds increased, the sails billowing like giant pillows on towering spars high above them. Those on the deck were buffeted by gales that caught in their hair and whipped at their clothing. Jeannette and Yvette squealed in delight, sidestepping sailors who tried to concentrate on their work. Soon, there was nothing to see but ocean, and Marie began to fuss.

"She needs to nurse," Charmaine remarked. John smiled down at the protesting babe, then escorted his wife and daughter to their cabin one deck below.

When Paul returned to the other ship, Frederic spoke to George. "I've a favor to ask of you. I'd like you to make a trip to North Carolina and a plantation known as Silver Maple, west of Durham and south of Burlington."

George's interest was piqued as Frederic produced a paper from his pocket and handed it him. "Maximilian Sledge owns the Silver Maple plantation and a slave named Henry Clayton. I want to purchase that slave. Actually, I want you to purchase him under your name. I don't want the Duvoisin name mentioned in any of the negotiations."

"Why?" George asked, further intrigued.

"Mr. Clayton has a beautiful wife, who is free and lives in New

York City with their three children," Frederic explained. "Lily Clayton helped save John's life, and I would like to repay her." The memory of Nicholas Fairfield and Hannah Fields was potent, a driving force. They were of another time, and yet so much a part of everything that had happened. That realization allowed him a glimpse of Colette's smiling face, and he knew that, wherever she was, she greatly approved. He relished the vision a moment longer, then turned back to George, who remained attentive. "It is the least I can do for her and her children."

George nodded, having met Lily two years ago when he had gone in search of John, bearing Colette's letter. "But why me?" he queried.

"Because, according to Michael Andrews, Maximilian Sledge would not sell Henry to a Northern sympathizer like John. His Southern loyalty runs as deep as John's abolitionist views, and Mr. Sledge was not about to sell a slave who would ultimately be freed. Therefore, he must never know your intentions concerning Henry Clayton. He must believe you are purchasing him to work on another plantation. To that end, you are to tell Mr. Sledge you've purchased a plantation and are interested in buying three strong men. Henry mustn't be singled out, or Sledge will grow suspicious."

"And what if Henry is no longer at Silver Maple?" George queried.

"According to what I've heard, he was too powerful a man to lose, lighter skinned and very big. However, if he has been sold south, do whatever it takes to find him and spend whatever amount to purchase him."

"And after I've done that?"

"That second address is Lily's home in New York," Frederic said, nodding at the paper George now held in his hands. "Once you've secured the purchase, sign the documents entitling him to his liberty and transport him there."

"And the other two men?"

"I'm certain John can find them work in New York."

George nodded, but Frederic could read hesitation in his eyes.

"If you're concerned about leaving your wife behind, why not take her along on an extended holiday?" The younger man's reservation disappeared, and Frederic produced a sizable purse. "If you need more than this, there are signed notes within. They can be redeemed in the States through the Bank of Richmond."

"Well, then," George said. "I guess it's a matter of asking Mercedes."

They turned together to begin the day's labor. When Frederic reached the end of the boardwalk, he looked up at the meetinghouse, remembering his precious Colette. *For you,* ma fuyarde, *for you . . .*

It was dark when John left the cabin. The twins were finally asleep, giggling for the longest time before succumbing to the lull of the rocking ship. Marie had been fussing since they left port, but she eventually accepted the nipple Charmaine had been offering all afternoon. She'd sleep soundly once she had nursed her fill.

John strode to the railing and contemplated the ocean, the choppy water that no longer mirrored his life. Contented, he breathed deeply of the salty night air. After a while, he reached into his shirt pocket and withdrew Colette's letter. He unfolded it, and his eyes roamed over the delicate script. It was impossible to read her words in the poor light, for there was only a crescent moon, and the lamps on deck burned low. It didn't matter. He had memorized every line. He brought the stationery to his lips and savored the delicate scent of lily that still clung to the pages. Slowly, he allowed the sheets to slip from his fingers. The ocean breezes caught them, catapulting them high into the air, tossing them about like the seabirds that had careened around the ship that afternoon. The leaflets were carried off, three white specters flying effortlessly in the freedom of openness, luminescent against the inky night. They relinquished the buffeting updrafts and fluttered to the water, settling on the swells and floating serenely away.

Charmaine grasped his hand.

Startled, he turned a guilty face to her. But she said nothing; rather she squeezed his fingers and looked out at the vast emptiness.

"Charmaine—" he began.

"I found the letter," she whispered before he could say more. "I didn't read it. I was *afraid* to read it."

"It's over, Charmaine," he promised. "It doesn't matter now."

"But you kept her letter—*all this time*."

He heard the despair in her voice, wanted to put it to rest forever. "And you should know why. You should know what it said," he murmured, beckoning her to step into his embrace as he leaned back against the railing. With his arms around her waist and chin atop her head, he recited:

My dearest John,

I cannot know your present state of mind. It is not my intention to cause you greater pain. I pray you receive this letter. I have every faith in George to deliver it into your hands.

I know I have few days left in this life. If I am to go to the afterlife clear of conscience, I must do what I can now to end the terrible hatred between you and your father. I desire eternal serenity, but without your help, this is impossible. Your father is in a miserable state, consumed with jealousy, anger, and sadness. If he leaves this life this way, then I will be responsible, because I am the one who came between you. I do not want to die knowing he will shortly follow me in such a state of mind. The ferocity of his rage belies the depth of his love, but he needs somebody to show him the way. I was unable to do so, but I know you are. If you have ever truly loved me, please take my dying prayer to heart, return home, and make amends with your father.

I also beg your forgiveness. I am sorry for turning to you in my loneliness and selfishly taking your love, only to aban-

don you to suffer all on your own. I think of you every day, wonder how you are, and pray you will be happy again. I long to see you just one more time before I leave this earth. If I could only behold your smiling face before I close my eyes, I wouldn't be so frightened of going into that dark, endless night.

Our son is a beautiful child, John. I beg you to come home to see him. I want Pierre to experience the excitement for life that only you can show him, and I want you to know his innocent love. He has so much of it to give, and you need that love desperately.

I beg you to look after Yvette and Jeannette's happiness, too. If your father cannot put his bitterness behind him, the only love my children will have when I am gone is that of their young governess and Nana Rose. It is important they know the love of family, so please, please take care of them for me. Show them how to run and play, how to laugh and sing.

I love you, John. I love you for the comfort and happiness you brought to me, not once, but twice. I love you for showing my daughters how to seize the day during that miraculous time when we were all together. I love you for your courage in letting go, for sacrificing your own desires in the noble interest of doing what was best for everyone. Live and love again, John. There is somebody in this world who deserves the privilege of sharing your unique zest for life and your beautiful, intense love.

Even though I know I am dying, I have hope for the future and for my children—hope that their lives will be happy and that some day, a true family will surround and embrace them. I have hope you will find contentment in this life and a loving wife and children you can call your own. And lastly, I have hope you will find empathy in your heart for your father. Forgive him, John, so we can be forgiven. If God is so good as to take me into his perpetual light, I will watch over and pray for you and all of my loved ones here on earth.

Until we meet again,
Your loving Colette

Charmaine was weeping by the time he had finished, her arms wrapped tightly around him. On a ragged breath, he finally spoke. "Yes, I came home, but selfishly, it wasn't to answer Colette's prayer."

"And yet," Charmaine said in amazement, "her prayer *was* answered all the same." Suddenly, the tears she shed were bittersweet and joyous. "You saw her, didn't you?"

"Yes, Charmaine, I saw her."

"But you came back to me," she choked out, lifting her eyes to his. "Why?"

"I had a choice," he rasped. "And I chose you."

He pulled her farther into his embrace, buried his head in her hair, and held her more fiercely than ever before. He was weeping, and she could feel his tears trickling down her neck, uniting with her own. "She never belonged to me, Charmaine," he breathed. "But you do. You're all mine."

"Always," she promised, "and forever."

A+

AUTHOR INSIGHTS, EXTRAS & MORE...

FROM

DEVA GANTT

AND

AVON A

TOPICS FOR DISCUSSION AND AUTHOR INSIGHTS FOR *FOREVER WAITING*

1. Three compelling themes drive the Colette Trilogy and are identifiable once *Forever Waiting* comes to a close. Discuss:

HOPE AMIDST HOPELESSNESS

An evening mist settled over the moss-scarred walls of the stone church, shrouding it in hopelessness . . . A resplendent serenity settled over him, bathing him in hopefulness.

The opening and closing lines of the Colette Trilogy are the very heart of the Duvoisin story. *A Silent Ocean Away* opens with a solitary man, John Duvoisin, praying for the death of his father, Frederic. In his despair, he contemplates the most wretched of solutions. At the close of *Forever Waiting*, John recites a very different prayer—Colette's prayer. To understand the paramount message of the Colette Trilogy, the reader should compare and contrast John's self-serving prayer in the prologue with Colette's prayer in the epilogue. What deeper understanding about life's tribulations had Colette achieved in her journey that John and Frederic had yet to learn? Think again about author insights at the end of *A Silent Ocean Away*. To what extent did Colette yield herself to death in the interest of restoring the Duvoisin family and achieving God's greater good? Thus, the driving theme: Even in the most egregious of situations, there is always hope, and happiness is *forever waiting*, especially for those whose hearts are not hardened.

WHOLESOME LOVE VERSUS DESTRUCTIVE LOVE

Love—in all its forms—is explored in the Colette Trilogy: first love, passionate love, maternal love, fraternal love, selfish love, guilt-ridden love, deadly love, and ultimately, paternal love. Each one impacts the Duvoisins, bringing *Forever Waiting* to its sublime conclusion.

Conversely, several characters are beset by heartache yet choose to meet it in opposing ways. Identify the parallelism between the following characters:

- Agatha and John
- Agatha and Marie
- Father Michael and Father Benito
- Paul and John
- Paul and Frederic
- John and Pierre

AUTHOR INSIGHT:

AGATHA AND JOHN . . .

Frederic breaks his betrothal to Agatha, just as Colette does with John. Both Agatha and John are embittered; both eventually resume a love affair with their intended spouse. Despite his anguish, John takes the high road and bows out of Colette's life. In contrast, Agatha chooses to nurture her hatred and, no matter the cost, claim what she desires.

AGATHA AND MARIE . . .

Marie finds herself alone and pregnant, as does Agatha. Where Marie sacrifices her own happiness for the welfare of her unborn child and the child's father, Agatha clings to her anger and invests all her energy into planning retribution.

FATHER MICHAEL AND FATHER BENITO . . .

Both priests are disillusioned with their ministry. Michael stays the course, whereas Benito turns his back on all that is holy.

PAUL AND JOHN, PAUL AND FREDERIC . . .

Paul loses Charmaine to John much as John lost Colette to Frederic. Paul also loses his status of favored son. Though Paul's "moral compass" is dubious in books 1 and 2, he epitomizes the man who learns from others' mistakes and, faced with the same dilemmas as John and Frederic, chooses the noble path: He sets aside his enmity and brings the truth about Agatha, his mother, to John. Though he could exploit the opportunity to seduce Charmaine after John leaves in pursuit of Robert Blackford, he eschews this and sets out to bring John home instead. Likewise, he does not abandon Rebecca as Frederic did Agatha.

PIERRE AND JOHN . . .

Pierre and John are more than parallel characters; to Frederic and Colette, Pierre symbolizes John. Look back to Colette's death in *A Silent Ocean Away* and discuss her enjoining words to Charmaine: *"But him!" Colette struggled anew, as if Charmaine hadn't understood. Frantically, she grasped at Pierre in an attempt to reach his governess. "He needs you the most . . . because he's the most vulnerable . . . and I wasn't able to give him . . . what he—"* Of whom is Colette really speaking? Similarly, Frederic showers the love upon Pierre that he had never shown John, and at times speaks to John through Pierre: *"I love you, son," Frederic murmured heavily. The words were sincere, and though they were spoken to Pierre, Frederic's eyes were on John, leaving Charmaine to wonder for whom they were meant.* (page 190, *Decision and Destiny*). Lastly, Frederic keeps vigil at John's sickbed in *Forever Waiting*, though in deference to John, he keeps away from Pierre's deathbed in *Decision and Destiny*.

FORGIVENESS, TRANSFORMATION, AND REDEMPTION

Many readers have commented on the agonizing silence in book 1, thus the title *A Silent Ocean Away*. The first step toward forgiveness and redemption cannot be taken until key characters begin talking to one another and decide to behave constructively. Charmaine lays the groundwork for this in *A Silent Ocean Away* when she asks Yvette to apologize to her father. In *Forever Waiting*, Yvette and Jeannette follow Charmaine's simple example by suggesting that Frederic write to John and apologize.

"Then why don't you apologize?" Yvette offered. "That's what Mademoiselle Charmaine tells us to do when we've made a mistake."

"I'm afraid it is not that easy," Frederic faltered.

"Yes, it is!" Jeannette chimed in. "I have an idea, Papa. You can write him a letter and tell him you're sorry. We can help you write it, can't we, Yvette?"

Though the seeds of transformation are planted in *A Silent Ocean Away* and begin to germinate in *Decision and Destiny*, they do not bear fruit until *Forever Waiting*. Discuss how John, Frederic, and Paul decide to behave differently—*constructively*—and are therefore transformed.

AUTHOR INSIGHT:

JOHN . . .

At the close of *Decision and Destiny*, John leaves Charmantes. This "stepping back" is a constructive decision not to manipulate circumstances as he had in the past. On their journey in pursuit of Blackford in *Forever Waiting*, John allows himself to understand his father's actions and upon their return home, finally forgive him.

FREDERIC . . .

At the close of *Decision and Destiny*, Frederic abandons his self-imposed exile, retakes the helm of the Duvoisin empire, and begins to nurture a relationship with his daughters. In addition, he vows never to hurt John again, and though he falters on occasion, does his utmost to uphold this vow. In so doing, he discovers it is never too late to apologize, to ask for forgiveness, to abandon a destructive path and chart a new course. Even so, redemption comes at a high price. Frederic must experience John's pain to receive absolution. Like John:

- He endures a three-year exile of isolation in his own home
- He loses those whom he loves dearly: Colette and Pierre
- He suffers an agonizing deathbed vigil

Finally, Frederic rectifies his transgressions against John by rescuing and comforting him when Blackford is finally apprehended. The Duvoisin family is restored when Frederic and John share a mutual quest to avenge Colette's and Pierre's murders.

PAUL . . .

Paul redeems his family's passive indifference to John's original exile from Charmantes. This indifference was the crux of John's anger with Paul: *"Hurt him? What about me? There was a time you were sympathetic to me."* (page 66, *Decision and Destiny*) and *"All these years—and that's what you think happened? No wonder you sided with Father"* (page 265, *Decision and Destiny*). Only after Paul experiences his own heartache can he finally empathize with John. Thus, he confides in John when confronted with the truth about his mother. Conclusively, Paul makes reparation for all the evil leveled upon John. He does this by forsaking self-interest and setting out to bring John home at the end of *Forever Waiting.*

Readers should further note the transformation that occurs with John's three returns to Charmantes: Initially, he is met with—and harbors—disdain (*A Silent Ocean Away*, chapter 9) then uncertain hopefulness (*Forever Waiting*, chapter 2) and finally, sheer joy (*Forever Waiting,* chapter 9).

Readers should also discuss Charmaine's influence on each of these men. Through her words, insights, and actions, she plays an integral role in all three transformations.

2. Symbolism and foreshadow are effectively employed throughout the trilogy, but not fully grasped until the close of *Forever Waiting*. Discuss the significance of the following objects:

- Pierre's lamb
- Frederic's cane
- John's cap

AUTHOR INSIGHT:

PIERRE'S LAMB . . .

Pierre's lamb symbolizes Pierre. Pierre is the sacrificial lamb that redeems his family. The evil that Agatha and Blackford set out to commit—annihilation of the Duvoisin family—is thwarted and, in fact, turned to good.

FREDERIC'S CANE . . .

Frederic's cane symbolizes Frederic's spiritual malady: his soul is crippled more so than his body. Though his physical impairment seems improved at the beginning of *Forever Waiting*, it is not until he rescues John that he is healed emotionally. Ironically, he throws down the cane to help John to his feet and never picks it up again.

JOHN'S CAP . . .

John wears two caps throughout the trilogy. The first symbolizes his cynicism. Just as he places it on each of the children's heads to shield them from cruel reality, he, too, uses it as a shield. Thus, the first cap embodies John's life until the climax of the story. That cap is lost, but Charmaine—his salvation—purchases a new one. The second cap signifies the new and happy direction his life will take, even through immeasurable heartache: assuming his rightful place as a beloved member of the Duvoisin family.

3. Discuss the relevance of:

- The lightning and thunderstorm the night John first arrives home
- Colette's horses: Charity and Chastity
- Colette's portrait
- The three hairbrushes

AUTHOR INSIGHT:

THE THUNDER AND LIGHTNING

The thunder and lightning symbolize John and Paul; the storm, their rivalry, as well as the story itself. *But the worst did not come . . . Though it rumbled, it did not roar, as if is were purposefully holding back, circling them, waiting for the kill* (page 287, *A Silent Ocean Away*). Charmaine equates the storm with Colette's death, and during this storm, the French doors in the children's bedchamber open for the first time, signifying Colette's presence as a herald of John's return.

COLETTE'S HORSES: CHARITY AND CHASTITY

Charity and Chastity signify Colette's dual personalities. Much like her twin daughters' dramatically different personalities, Colette has two sides, as John suggests to Charmaine in *Decision and Destiny* (page 71): *"Miss Ryan," he snarled, "the mistress Colette was a very different woman than the one you have painted . . ."* Charity—the spirited and pert personality—is the Colette Frederic knows. Ironically, Chastity—the subdued and mothering personality—is the Colette John knows. Readers should examine John's story about the two horses in *Decision and Destiny* (page 116) and identify the foreshadow in this passage.

COLETTE'S PORTRAIT

Colette's portrait demurely oversees all that transpires in the Duvoisin manor. It is the focal point of three powerful scenes: The painting is a poignant reminder of Colette's loss in *Decision and Destiny* (page 196): *"That's my mama . . . Isn't she boo-ti-ful? . . . She's not alive no more."* The portrait becomes Agatha's undoing and triggers the first sign of her insanity in *Forever Waiting* (page 183): *Agatha confronted her adversary—the woman who taunted her even in death . . . The blue eyes stared back, so lifelike, they condemned her from the lofty perch upon the wall . . . Like the wife, it was time for the painting to go.* Most important, it sends John into the chapel to forgive his father at the close of *Forever Waiting* (page 415), fulfilling Colette's prayer: *"No, Father," John breathed, "don't remove it. I feel secure knowing Colette is watching over us."*

THE THREE HAIRBRUSHES

Each of the three hairbrushes is symbolic. On the night of John's return in *A Silent Ocean Away*, he steps on and breaks the hairbrush Charmaine had tossed across the room. It is John's first step toward breaking with his past. In *Decision and Destiny* Agatha uses her hairbrush to ruthlessly spank Pierre, and John wrenches it from her, throwing it across her boudoir. At this moment, John glimpses Charmaine's integrity and valor, marking the turning point in their relationship. Lastly, John's Christmas gift to Charmaine in *Forever Waiting* is an ivory hairbrush. It embodies their untainted relationship, which stands in stark contrast to the one he shared with Colette.

4. The supernatural seems to play an integral part in the conclusion of *Forever Waiting*. Consider the following:

- Did Colette's ghost coax Agatha into the waters off Espoir?
- Who induced the dream shared by both Frederic and John?

- Did John experience an out-of-body experience where Colette, Elizabeth, and Marie sent him back to the realm of the living?

AUTHOR INSIGHT:

For the nonbeliever, each question can be logically explained: First, Agatha was insane. Second, John and Frederic's shared dream was a coincidence fed by mutual guilt and obscure memories. Third, John's out-of-body experience was a hallucination, nurtured by subconscious images and a grave illness. However, it is far more interesting to entertain the idea: What if . . . ?

5. The Colette Trilogy has multiple triads. The following are the more significant sets of three. Discuss their importance, then see how many others you can identify:

THREE PRAYERS

The prologue of *A Silent Ocean Away* opens with John's prayer of death. After Pierre's death in *Decision and Destiny,* John offers his prayer of grief. At the close of *Forever Waiting*, he recites a prayer of absolution and redemption.

THREE CHAPEL/CHURCH SCENES

The prologue of *A Silent Ocean Away*, opens with John praying in the St. Jude Refuge church. At the close of *Decision and Destiny*, Charmaine and John grieve Pierre's death in the Duvoisin chapel. At the end of *Forever Waiting*, John forgives Frederic in the same chapel.

THREE PIANO SCENES

In *A Silent Ocean Away*, Colette finds Charmaine at the piano, playing John's unfinished composition. Through Charmaine's eyes, this encounter evokes melancholy and yearning. In *Decision and*

Destiny, Charmaine finds John at the piano, playing the very same piece. Through her eyes, this encounter offers wonder and possibilities. In *Forever Waiting*, Charmaine beholds John's resolution to his poignant composition—symbolic of his life; yet unlike the first two encounters, this one is surrounded by family and love. It heralds happiness and promise.

THREE BOYHOOD RECOLLECTIONS

George's recollection in *A Silent Ocean Away* is brimming with humor and camaraderie, John's in *Decision and Destiny* with mischief and daring, Paul's in *Forever Waiting* with imagination and adventure. All three allude to deep boyhood bonds and a simpler time, in sharp contrast to their present lives.

THREE IMPORTANT LETTERS

Colette's letter to John, Marie's letter to Michael, Frederic's letter to John—each pivotal to the plot.

THREE RETURNS AND THREE DEPARTURES

John departs Charmantes three times and returns three times. The reader should consider character evolution with each return. Upon his first return, John is hate-filled and Frederic is hesitant; upon the second, John is hesitant and Frederic is hopeful; upon the third, Frederic and John are both joyous.

ADDITIONAL TRIADS:

Charmaine comes across Colette's letter three times.
Chapter 7 of each book contains a dramatic death.
Charmaine and John share three kisses before their marriage; each one highlighting Charmaine's maturation: She's indignant with the first kiss, submissive with the second, and willing with the third.

Charmaine receives three gifts from John: the horse, the hairbrush, and the diamond ring.

6. Agatha, Robert, and Benito are the primary villains of the story. Discuss whom you consider the most nefarious and why.

AUTHOR INSIGHT:

Though abhorring Agatha, one reader expressed sympathy for her, citing that Agatha never knew the predominant part Robert played in scripting her life and pushing Elizabeth into Frederic's arms. As for who is the most evil, we leave the reader to decide.

7. Pierre's death is more painful than Colette's. Discuss the necessity of his death in driving the story to its dramatic conclusion.

AUTHOR INSIGHT:

Like his lamb, Pierre is the sacrifice that opens the door to healing. The loss of Pierre is the turning point of the entire story. The death of an innocent demands that key characters take responsibility for their behavior and decide to change. The reader should contemplate if this is true to life: Does a family tragedy move people to change?

8. Contemplate Charmaine's journey through the trilogy and her growth from innocent young woman to mistress of the Duvoisin manor.

AUTHOR INSIGHT:

Charmaine's interaction with Paul and John contributes to her maturation as a woman. Although she evolves from naïve admirer to intelligent pragmatist, her inner innocence and integrity remain steadfast. These qualities have a subtle yet tremendous influence on those around her, including her coworkers (Mrs. Faraday) and her employer and father-in-law (Frederic Duvoisin). Ultimately, the dream for which Charmaine is *forever waiting* is fulfilled. The reader should compare the Duvoisin family table at the close of *Forever Waiting* with the wretched Ryan table at the trilogy's opening in *A Silent Ocean Away.*

9. In twenty years, the States will be marching toward a Civil War, and the Duvoisins will find themselves embroiled in it. With John and Paul holding opposing convictions concerning slavery, predict what will happen to the family as the conflict escalates.

DeVa Gantt

Authors' photo by Deborah Michaels

The workday is over, the dishes put away, and the children are tucked into bed. That's when **DeVa GANTT** settles down for an evening with the family. The other family, that is: the Duvoisins.

DeVa Gantt is a pseudonym for Debra and Valerie Gantt: sisters, career women, mothers, homemakers, and now, authors. The Colette Trilogy, commencing with ***A Silent Ocean Away,*** continuing with ***Decision and Destiny,*** and culminating with ***Forever Waiting,*** is the product of years of unwavering dedication to a dream.

The women began writing thirty years ago. Deb was in college, Val a new teacher. Avid readers of historical fiction, the idea of authoring their own story blossomed from a conversation driving home one night. "We could write our own book. I can envision the main character." Within a day, an early plot had been hatched and the first scenes committed to paper. Three years later, the would-be authors had half of an elaborate novel written, numerous hand-drafted scenes, five hundred typed pages, and no idea how to tie up the complicated story threads. The book languished, life intervened, and the work was put on the back burner for two decades.

Both women assert the rejuvenating spark was peculiarly coincidental. Though Val and Deb live thirty miles apart, on Thanksgiving weekend 2002, unbeknownst to each other, they spontaneously picked up the unfinished manuscript and began to read. The following week, Deb e-mailed Val to tell her she'd been reading "the book." It was a wonderful work begging to be finished, and Deb had some fresh ideas. By January, the women's creative energies were flowing again.

Unlike twenty years earlier, Deb and Val had computer technology on their side, but there were different challenges. Their literary pursuit had to be worked into real life responsibilities: children, marriages, households, and jobs. The women stole every spare moment, working late at night, in the wee hours of morning, and on weekends. The dictionary, thesaurus, and grammar books became their close companions. Snow days were a gift. No school, no work. Deb could pack up overnight bags, and head to Val's house with her two children. The cousins played while the writers collaborated.

Wherever the women went, they brought the Duvoisins along. From sports and dance practices to doctors' offices, from business trips to vacations, an opportunity to work on their "masterpiece" was rarely wasted. One Fourth of July, Val and Deb edited away on their laptops on blankets in the middle of a New Hampshire baseball field while their families waited for night to fall and the fireworks to begin.

Both women agree the experience has been rewarding and unexpectedly broad in scope. Writing a story was only the beginning of a long endeavor that included extensive research, arduous editing, and painstaking proofreading. Next came the query letters sent to agents and publishers, each meeting a dead end. Self-publishing was the only option—a stepping-stone that would enable them to compile a portfolio of reviews and positive feedback. Thus they became adept at marketing their work, all in the pursuit of reaching a traditional publisher. Within two years an agent had stepped in and HarperCollins agreed to publish the work as a trilogy.

Today, the women look back at their accomplishment. The benefits have been immeasurable. Perhaps the dearest is the bond of sisterhood that deepened: they have shared a unique journey unknown to most sisters. Their greatest satisfaction, however, has been seeing their unfinished work come to fruition: the Duvoisin story has finally been told.

Visit Deb and Val at:
http://web.mac.com/devagantt

WITHDRAWN

HICKMANS

WITHDRAWN
Brunswick County Library
109 W. Moore Street
Southport NC 28461